P9-CEN-084

BY ROBERT OLEN BUTLER

The Alleys of Eden

Sun Dogs

Countrymen of Bones

On Distant Ground

Wabash

The Deuce

*A Good Scent from
a Strange Mountain* (stories)

They Whisper

THE DEUCE

◇

A NOVEL BY

Robert Olen Butler

Henry Holt and Company
New York

For my wife, Maureen,
and for the Children of Dust

Henry Holt and Company, Inc.
Publishers since 1866
115 West 18th Street
New York, New York 10011

Henry Holt® is a registered trademark
of Henry Holt and Company, Inc.

Published in Canada by Fitzhenry & Whiteside Ltd.,
195 Allstate Parkway, Markham, Ontario L3R 4T8.
Originally published in hardcover in 1989 by Simon and Schuster.
Reissued in cloth and paper in 1994 by Henry Holt and Company.

Portions of this novel have appeared in
different form in Fame *and* Genre.

Library of Congress Cataloging-in-Publication Data
Butler, Robert Olen.—1st Owl book ed.
The deuce / Robert Olen Butler.
p.   cm.
I. Title.
[PS3552.U8278D48 1993]   *93-6303*
813'.54—dc20   *CIP*

ISBN 0-8050-3197-9
ISBN 0-8050-3139-1 (An Owl Book: pbk.)

Henry Holt books are available for special promotions
and premiums. For details contact:
Director, Special Markets.

Printed in the United States of America
All first editions are printed on acid-free paper.∞

1   3   5   7   9   10   8   6   4   2
1   3   5   7   9   10   8   6   4   2
pbk.

THE DEUCE

ONE

⬦

I wish it was simple just to say who I am, just to say my name is so-and-so and that makes you think of a certain kind of person and that would be me. I think of other names and there's no doubt about there being faces with them, clear faces, even if I didn't already know who I was talking about: Kenneth (you can watch a Kenneth from the back row of a courtroom, and he's damn good); Norma (and you'd never get the soft scoop of a Norma confused with a Nicole, who'd probably have hair in her armpits and think it's sexy; that would really piss off the Norma I've got in mind because when she looks in the mirror, she tries to see a Nicole). I think of the name Nghi and I see a face (maybe you can't, but I can, and she's in the dark with shouting in the street and heat lightning out the window); even Joey, poor Joey, has a name that lets you see a part of him that maybe's not there on the surface but is there just the same. He was more of a kid than me in some ways. Innocent under a stupid I-always-know-what-I'm- doing surface, like a Joey.

But me, I've got three names. And so I've got to go through all this bullshit just to start talking. I'm Anthony James Hatcher, Tony. I'm Võ Đình Thanh. And I'm The Deuce. Don't ask me which one I use. It's too early for that. I've got to tell you some things first.

The me that's Tony Hatcher is from the Jersey Shore, just outside of Point Pleasant, which is about the most pansy-assed name for a place you could think up. The Deuce is from Forty-second Street, New York City, the street that gave me the name, since that's what it's called by the people who make their lives there. And Võ Đình Thanh is from Saigon, Republic of Vietnam, now known as Hồ Chí Minh City, named after a man who had the stupidest-looking beard in history. It's hard to think that a man with a beard like that could've caused as much trouble as this guy. And if he'd shown that beard on the Deuce he would've been rolled and his throat cut by the first mope who saw him.

But that's where I was born, in Saigon. You ask almost anybody hanging around the Port Authority or out on the Deuce where they were born and they give you a who-gives-a-shit shrug, but when I say I was born in Saigon, it's not just that you can look at my face and see that I'm not any all-American, it's also that I can sit back in my head and I can be in Saigon as clear as any damn place in New Jersey. Even as clear as New York, even the East Village or the bus terminal or Forty-second Street itself. I was there, in Saigon, till I was six, nearly seven.

It's easy to hear the snap of the scissors out the window that said that the nougat seller was coming and my mouth would start watering and I'd jump up on the bed under the window and I'd look down past the roof of the bar next door where you'd see rats sometimes as big as any Point Pleasant backyard squirrel. But squirrels are rodents that you can take to, right? Cute things, but it's just because of their tails being bushy, and these rats on the roof next door had these tails that looked like somebody'd scraped all the fur off them with a dull knife and the fucking rats liked it. Anyway, I'd be up on my tiptoes and looking on down into the street where the old woman had her pot of nougats and I'd want one of those things so bad my teeth would ache.

Not that the goddam candy was so important to me or that it means a goddam thing in what I'm trying to tell you. It's just that it's my earliest memory of Saigon, and I wasn't even two, I bet. Funny how that works, how some of the stupidest things are clear in the memory but some important things are gone altogether. A kid maybe is going to find little things as interesting as big things because he's never been anywhere yet and not been through any real heavy shit yet and he doesn't have sense enough to know what's important and what isn't. All the damn peddlers are there in my head still selling away. Like the old woman clacking her bamboo sticks in front of her pot of soup, and only now when I remember it does it sound like bones snapping.

Gunshots in the night, out in the street in front of the bar, and it didn't scare me at all. I'd be curled on a mat on the floor and all I could see out the window was the night sky, and if Momma was alone that night and it was just her and me, the shots only told me how safe I was, only meant that what was out there in the street had nothing to do with me.

And my mother was alone a lot of nights. I can see her sitting in the dark, maybe smoking—she didn't smoke much, but once in a while, after we were quiet in the dark and I guess she thought I was asleep, she'd sit by the window and sometimes she'd smoke and the little red spot would flare before her face and then dart off and the smoke would plume away and I'd wonder what she was thinking about. But I wouldn't say a thing, I'd just watch her.

I'm sure she helped me remember so much about Saigon. We had a little game that we'd sometimes play. We'd remember things together. We'd sit and she'd say, What's the nicest thing you remember about yesterday? And I'd tell her. And then she'd ask the same question about last week, and I'd tell her whatever it was—maybe running out in the alley with a bunch of straw that we'd lit, some of the other kids and me—and even if what was nice for me was something that scared her, like us playing with fire, she'd still say, That's good. That's very good. If it's nice, you remember that. If you like it, then you remember that. And then she'd always end up talking about her own memories. She had memories, too. There had to be something good in her past, because she would talk about it. I wish I could remember more of the things that were good for her, but there's only a few.

Like when she was a girl, a young woman, maybe even the same age—I never thought of it this way till now—the same as when I took off from New Jersey. She might've been sixteen just like I was. But she was still in some village down in Vĩnh Bình province and she had a boyfriend who shit on her. He was running around with some other girl, so my mother went to a sorcerer, some old hag who lived out in the forest or wherever, and my mother got a paper amulet and in it she wrote the name of this boy and his date of birth. Then she went to the Mekong and caught a fish and before the fish could die she stuffed the amulet into his belly and threw him back in the river.

What was supposed to happen, according to my mother, is that the boy would turn crazy and, just like the fish swimming along in the river, he would wander out of town and drift all over the countryside till he died of exhaustion. My momma laughed when she told this—I can hear her laugh like a splash of water that makes you blink and shake your head. She said she really looked forward to going out just before he died and she'd find him thrashing around on the ground, his mouth frantic, like a fish sucking at air, and she'd whisper her name in his ear.

But instead, the boy got two other girls pregnant at the same time and ran off with a third and my mother said it was just her luck to have stuck that amulet in a fish that was ready to drop his seed in some damn spawning ground. She laughed again at that and said she came to Saigon soon after.

This was all Vietnamese voodoo and I don't think my mother ever quit believing that shit. She'd always laugh a little when she started talking about it, but she never did do anything important without going down in the alley and crouching with some old lady with red teeth who was an astrologer. Her teeth were red from betel nuts, which can give you some kind of high, so it's not surprising that this old hag thought she could tell the future. But my mother believed all that with a clear head. She probably even tried that fish trick again on some of the Americans who came and went and who she always cried over, every fucking one of them no matter how quick they were gone. So there was probably a bunch of fish swimming around in the Saigon River with GIs' names in their bellies and my mother sitting in her room at night smoking and waiting for these sons of bitches to wander off and die. Maybe too much fucking can make you a little crazy like that. I don't know.

Then it was all over, all that. At least for me. One of those short-time boys, see, decided to return. It was 1974 and my momma was with a guy named Claude. He'd been more or less living with us—he would come maybe three or four times a week and stay all night and there'd be no quiet smoke for my momma that night and they'd send me out to play early in the evening. I knew not to come back for a couple of hours. I'd hang around with a bunch of kids—a lot of them older kids, former Saigon cowboys, but they didn't give me any trouble. They liked me. So I'd stay out and let old Claude do his thing, and even when I'd get back to my momma's place and it was time to sleep, the two of them would start going at it with me curled right there on my mat. Not that I wasn't used to it. I don't remember the first time I was aware of the noises and the men. It's one of those memories that somehow isn't there, even though the sound of the nougat lady is. I must've thought my momma was dying, the first time I heard the sounds of fucking. I must've figured that she couldn't catch her breath, that maybe she had a fish bone stuck in her throat or something, but I just can't remember it.

Anyway, it was 1974 and it was probably March or April, because it was that terrible time of year when it's not the dry season anymore but it isn't the rainy season either. It never quite rains, but the air gets thick and wet like it would feel if one of the Tự Do Street lepers died and got reincarnated as the air. Claude was still around in 1974 because he had an embassy job, I think. Or maybe he was C.I.A. All I really remember about him clearly was he had enormous feet. He'd sit on my mother's bed and pick at his toes and these feet were as big as river bass.

It was late afternoon and my mother and I were crouched near the hot plate she kept over in the corner near her little Buddhist ancestor shrine. She was waiting for Claude to arrive at any minute and she was kind of hurrying me along with my rice. I was taking it slow. I figured old Claude could sit and pick at his feet and just wait for whatever it was my momma gave. Waiting wouldn't hurt him.

"Hurry up, child," Momma said, and she brushed at my face in a vague kind of way, like she had to do something motherly but she didn't quite know what it was. She'd been having trouble focusing her mind for a while. For maybe a year or so she'd been really strung out, real nervous and jumpy. I figured it was the American GIs going home. I've got no memories that would prove anything else, but now I can see, I guess, that she was on something.

So after telling me to hurry, she got up and took her empty rice bowl into the bathroom and I heard the water running. I chased a grain of rice around the rim of my own bowl with my chopsticks. That's when there was a knock at the door.

Momma came out of the bathroom quick with that look on her face—the oh-sweet-strong-man-I'm-aquiver-from-waiting look—but I knew it wasn't Claude. Claude still knocked, for some reason. He was from Georgia and I guess he was polite. But this wasn't his knock. I knew that right off. Claude's knock sounded kind of unsure of itself, like every time he came over, it was the first time he expected to ask her for her pussy and he wasn't sure what she'd say. But this knock was sure of itself. Rap rap rap. Three times and then a patient wait.

I was watching her as she opened the door, but I couldn't see outside from where I was sitting. I heard her gasp. Her first words right after the gasp were in Vietnamese, so I figured it was a Vietnamese outside. She used the phrase "Trời ơi." I still use the phrase once in a while myself. It's the only Vietnamese I've really kept, after all that. It sort of means "oh God." "Trời" is god. But trời also means heaven or the sky or the air or the weather. And "ơi" can have a hey-you kind of meaning, like if you say it, you've got a rightful claim to make. So the phrase has you covered no matter what kind of mood you're in or what you happen to believe about God and that stuff.

My momma said it this time with real shock, and she took a step back and her hands dropped to her sides and for a moment I got scared. Maybe it was Thiệu's police or somebody. But then in steps this American.

Right away there's something familiar about him. I figure he's one of the men that have burrowed their way in and out of here since I was old enough to remember. I check this guy out: he's pretty tall and he stands real straight, stiff even; his hair is dark but his skin is very pale, like he's stayed out of the sun all his life; and his face has the same upright feeling and you wonder why that's so till you realize that he's kind of stretched out between his brow and his chin, a long face. Real familiar. He looks over at me and there's sort of a stopping in him. Then he shoots me this little smile like he thinks I should know him and he turns to my mother.

I stop watching for a moment and chase that grain of rice some more while I'm still trying to place him. But I let that go when they start talking.

"Kenneth," my mother says, and her hands go up and start pushing at stray strands of hair, fixing the hair, smoothing at it when it's really her face I bet she wanted to fix, since she was gaunt and frazzled-looking, like I said.

"Nghi," he says, "we've got to talk."

My mother opens her mouth, but nothing much comes out. She turns away a little and I don't know if I heard anything out of her but I knew she was starting to cry.

"This is the boy?" this guy Kenneth says, and he comes over to me and crouches down.

From across the room I hear my mother say, "Yes," in almost a whisper. Meanwhile the man is looking at me real close. He's right there with his mouthwash breath in my face, but he doesn't touch me, he just looks. "Chào em," he says, and he does pretty good with the pronunciation, getting the falling tone on the "hello" part. Usually an American will mess up the tone and say real clearly "Rinse you."

But still he doesn't touch me, and standing behind him now is my mother, and she says in her worst pidgin, "He talk talk English good." Kenneth gives her a slow, hard look over his shoulder and at the time I figured he was disgusted by her English, but I see now that he was thinking about how it was that I got exposed to so much good English.

So I say, "Hey, how you hanging, GI. Fuck you and the horse you rode in on." Not that that was my best English. As a matter of fact, I really did speak the language pretty good, even then. I just wanted to test this guy out and he jumps up real quick and turns to Nghi.

It was the wrong thing to say because it just made Kenneth more single-minded about all this and that meant I was to be put safely out of earshot. But he was real concerned about my welfare outside the front door and Momma says to me in English, "You go Auntie Noi's. Go chop chop."

Chop chop. Can you believe that shit? If she'd tried as hard as me to learn English, maybe things would've turned out differently that day. Who can love a woman who talks like that? So she starts kind of fluttering her eyes at me, a signal, I figure, not to say anything about there being no Auntie Noi. I don't think she even knew anybody named Noi, and that was quite a clever lie under the circumstances. She didn't want this guy to know how I hung around the streets on my own at six years old.

So I take my time, and Kenneth is looking at me while I'm licking off my chopsticks and putting down the bowl very carefully on the floor and arranging the chopsticks on it parallel, just so. Finally I get up and head for the door and as I pass Kenneth, he gives me a little pat on the shoulder. I think of a couple of things to say at that, but I choose "Keep your hands to yourself, you goddam fairy," just to make sure their conversation will be loud enough for me to hear crouched outside near the door, which is old Auntie Noi's as far as I'm concerned.

I go out and I just barely pull the door to behind me. Nobody seems to notice and I can now give it a tiny little push and it cracks open a couple of inches. I press against the wall and wait. At first there's no voices at all, but there's a muffled sound, and I figure they're kissing or something. It's dark in the hallway, even in the day, and it smells of piss and of the people from the street who come in to sleep at the bottom of the stairwell. If this Kenneth guy is kissing my mother, I can be a little bolder, so I stoop and put my eye to the keyhole. All I see is the far wall.

Then my mother drifts into view. Her head's bowed and I can see that she's crying. That was the muffled sound. She drifts on and all I see is the wall again. The man could be anywhere, so I ease back and wait for them to start talking.

Finally Kenneth says, "Do you know why I'm here?"

"No," my mother says, and her voice is a little blurry.

There's a long pause, and then he says, "Look at yourself."

I know now what he was talking about, but my momma played dumb. "Nghi very poor," she says. "No money buy clothes, fix up pretty."

There's a sound of movement and I wonder what's happening. I return to the keyhole and look and I can't see. I push the door just a little to get a different view, and Kenneth's got his back to me. He was probably checking out my mother's eyes—dilated, drugged. And he was looking at her arms for tracks or up her nose for signs of what he knew she was making of her life. Gathering evidence, like a good district attorney.

There's a sudden flash of movement beyond him—Nghi pulling away, and then he jerks out of view and I push a little farther to follow all this. By now I've got both feet in the room and the damn door is almost halfway open and just about the time I realize this, the door is suddenly swinging away and there's Kenneth towering over me like a P.A. cop over a sleeping wino with that look of pity for a hopeless fuck-up.

Kenneth crouches down and says, "Aren't you supposed to be at Auntie Noi's?"

"Auntie Noi is sick," I say, and I glance over to my mother, but she's got her back to this whole scene.

"Sick?" Kenneth says, smiling like I'm cute. That's the look that really bothered me at the time, and I began to think of something to say to wipe that look away. But before I could speak he says, "What's your name?"

I don't come up with anything quick as a phony name, which seems funny to me now. That's the easiest thing in the world to do, for a smart-ass kid like I was. Maybe there was suddenly something in his voice that told me I better play it straight for a while, that this guy wasn't just one more American in for the short-time action. I say, "Võ Ðình Thanh."

"Is that your only name?" he says.

That struck me as odd, which shows you how young I was. "Yes."

"Hasn't anybody ever given you an American name?"

"No," I say, but this interview has gone on long enough so that whatever I sensed about this guy is fading away and my basic instincts are coming back. I stick my finger in my mouth and throw my gaze to the ceiling like I'm in serious thought. "Well," I say, "one GI called me 'Little Asshole.' Is that an American name?"

This time the only reaction I get out of Kenneth is a throbbing at his temples, and my mother turns her face to me with a sad look. At least I'm smart enough to know when I'm heading in the wrong direction, and I say, "But that was a bad guy who my mother didn't even like. She kicked him out in no time." This doesn't seem to help. Kenneth's throb continues and my mother looks sadder than ever. I don't like all this anymore and I wish I had gone on downstairs like they'd wanted and just waited for this all to blow over.

Then Kenneth's hands suddenly come out and bracket my shoulders and he says, "Do you know who your father is?"

I'd heard this before from others and this wasn't my favorite question. There wasn't ever anything smart-ass to say and no way to hide the little rush of tears, which I was waiting to grow out of since very few of my friends had a father and they didn't seem to give a damn. And I didn't have much real information on this because my mother wasn't talking and I had learned not to ask. So all I knew to say to Kenneth was "No. He was some American and he's gone."

Kenneth takes a deep breath at this, but he doesn't say anything. He keep his hands on my shoulders and he looks at me and I'm getting really pissed off at these tears that I've got in my eyes and I say, "He was a little asshole."

This time Kenneth gives me a half smile, like he has a twinge of pain and he wants to be cool about it. "Little?" he says.

I like the question "A *big* asshole," I say.

Kenneth stands up. "Maybe Auntie Noi can use some help, if she's sick."

"Okay," I say and I beat it out of there real fast, closing the door with a bang behind me. I go down the stairwell and stop in the alley near the downstairs door. I rub my eyes hard with my forearm and I don't feel like going any farther right now. I don't know how long I stand there, but what snaps me out of it is the sight of Claude coming up the alley. There's a couple of kids running alongside trying to get money out of him and he's trying to brush them off the best he can with these little shrugs and his head ducked down, and I can't imagine how he ever had the balls to ask my mother to fuck him.

But I suddenly realize what's about to happen, and I've got to figure out what part I'm going to play. I could send old Claude upstairs right away, Momma needs you quick, and then follow him and watch the fireworks. Claude sees me now and he looks down at these kids dogging him like I put them up to it or something. It's then that I figure this new guy couldn't be any worse than Claude and his damn toes, so when Claude arrives, I say, "Momma told me to wait here and tell you she went to get her hair cut so she'll look real pretty for her sweet Claudey. She wants you to meet her on the veranda of the Continental Palace Hotel real soon. Chop chop."

Claude shuffles his feet and lights out just like he's never heard me lie before. Somebody that goddam stupid didn't deserve to get into my mother's pants.

I didn't hang around either after that. I'd done my mother a favor, I figured, and I sure didn't want any more questions, so I took off for a couple of hours. When I got back, Kenneth was gone and my mother had nothing to say. Even later on, when Claude showed up again and it was clear I'd lied, Claude whined at her and glared at me, but he was always a Georgia gentleman and he didn't hit me or anything. Momma just looked tired, and she gave me a nod toward the door and out I went again.

There was no more about this man Kenneth for a few months. But looking back, I guess something had already been decided. I should have known when I saw myself in a mirror a couple of days after he'd gone. It was a tall mirror outside a Hong Kong tailor on Lê Lợi. I looked and all of a sudden I saw how my face was stretched out between my brow and my chin. And I noticed how my eyes were smoother, I could see the lids, more American. It flashed in me that maybe there was a connection between this face in the mirror and that guy with his hands on my shoulders staring at me with my mother looking the other way and crying. But he hadn't been around since, and I didn't let myself think any farther. I figured if nobody was talking, I shouldn't open my own mouth.

And the days went on and my mother stayed quiet. Not just about the visit from this man, but about everything. We didn't even play the memory game. She sent me out more often, and she grew thinner and more strung-out-looking. Claude hung around for a few weeks longer. It's interesting to think now that Claude must have been part of the drug stuff. He just didn't look the part, but I guess you never can tell. When he left, I kept expecting still another man to come along. But there were fewer Americans around, and among the Vietnamese only the big-shot politicians had any money for what my momma was selling. She started working in the bar again, hustling Saigon Teas, though business was bad there too. It was just her and me and this silence.

Then things changed all of a sudden. It was on Wandering Souls' Day, which is another bit of Vietnamese voodoo. It's this big day for the Buddhists, and my mother was a Buddhist. She wasn't real religious but like those little New Jersey Christian ladies at the terminal who read their Daily Word and doll up Sundays for some mild hymn-singing. Not that my mother was even that regular about the outside rituals, but she had her little shrine to her mom and dad, who were both dead, and she said her prayers there almost every day and she burned incense.

Any smell of incense makes me think of her. Some big black guy in a robe and rope sandals and a hat that looked like the top of an aspirin bottle used to sell incense out the Eighth Avenue entrance to the terminal, and whenever I'd walk past him—this guy who was maybe the most exact opposite human being from my mother on the whole face of the earth—I'd think of her. Sometimes—especially right after I'd arrived in New York and hadn't got as far as I thought I would and I was trying to figure all this out for the first time—I'd even have to go walk around the block real fast to work off the tears. The tears used to be over a faceless, nameless father, but I did outgrow that, and then they were over this woman who sat there on her knees, her bare toes all lined up behind her, waving the incense before that little shrine in our room in Saigon. I'm not ashamed now to admit I could cry. But I didn't like doing it, so I walked around the block and came in over on Ninth Avenue whenever that black guy had his incense burning. He wasn't even any on-the-level religious guy. He was just trying to rip off the bleeding-heart whites who figured, I guess, he'd be their spirit friend or something when they were about to be mugged by some bad-dude black guy.

But see how my mind can wander when I think of the incense? Just like that wispy little snake of smoke climbing off my mother's finger-tips. I was saying about Wandering Souls' Day, it's real important for the Buddhists. Once a year there's a holiday in the Kingdom of the Dead. Whoever's died and not gone to the Buddhist heaven—like people who get offed suddenly without getting a chance to review their sins—they get to take a breather from their everlasting torment. And if their loved ones pray for them real hard on that day, maybe God hears it and says to the guy being prayed for, Hey fuck-up, come on over and have a drink with me. Then he gives the sinner a celestial drink called cam lộ which is like the bottle of Ripple a wino once in a while gets that makes him all teary-eyed with regret over his life. The dead guy drinks his cam lộ and remembers his sins and is so sorry that God decides to forgive him. That's how it's supposed to go, but it doesn't often happen like that (which doesn't surprise me), and it can never happen at all without the prayers of the Buddhists left behind.

So on this day my eyes are watering from all the incense in our place and my mother is praying nonstop all morning. I lie on my mat and keep my eyes shut because lately I haven't been feeling good. I just don't seem to want to go out much. Maybe I'm waiting for my mother to start talking again and I don't want to be gone when she does. I peek at her doing these endless prayers and I feel a little jealous of all those words going up with the smoke to a bunch of dead people.

Then finally she stops and gets up and I hear her washing herself in the bathroom. I think of getting up and sneaking over and taking a peek, but this time I don't. I like to watch her bathe. She's smooth and she seems—I don't know what—innocent maybe. Anyway, this day I wait for her to come out, which she does, and she tells me to go with her to the bar.

The place was a couple of doors down the street. This was a far-flung strip of bars, a mile from the real hot spot along Tự Do. This strip started because nearby there were some old French hotels where they housed GIs. But in 1974 the hotels were only half full of journalists and low-level embassy people and most of the bars were closed. The name of the place where my mother worked was Texas Girls, and before the American pullout most of the girls wore cowboy hats. I can see sweet Nghi, fastest pussy east of the Pecos, with her Hong Kong Stetson pulled down over her ears and some big guy with his fatigues tucked into lizard boots lifting her up and swinging her around in the center of the bar and yelling wahoo or some shit. Nghi held on to her hat and she saw me at the door and she didn't know what else to do, I guess, so she lifted the hat, tipped her cowboy hat to me.

But on this Wandering Souls' Day we went down and the Texas Girls Bar had its tables pulled together in the center of the room and there was a whole lot of food—boiled chickens, sticky rice cakes, roast pork, fertilized chicken eggs cut in halves with their tasty little red spots showing. This was part of the whole ceremony. The dead souls were crowding into the room, was how it went, and they were hungry as hell from burning for a year with nothing to eat.

There were no clients when we came in, just the bartender, who called himself Jake in keeping with the theme of the bar but whose real name was Minh. He was fat enough to look like a politician, but he never said much and my mother figured he was a VC in disguise. At the back of the bar were the other three girls (there'd been a dozen a few years earlier). They were all praying at a little shrine back there with photos of the previous two owners of the bar and five of the girls who used to work here, all of them dead suddenly from one thing or another and probably wandering out there in the fire. I checked out the room to see if I could see any of the spirits, and I thought I saw a suspicious thickening of the air behind the bar where the Texan hats were piled and gathering dust.

My mother deposited me in one of the booths, under a neon Budweiser sign that made my skin red, just like I'd look if I died suddenly, I thought. She went on back to the shrine and knelt with the others and started praying for these girls—a couple of them had been her friends, one had died from a Swiss Army knife out in the alley near our downstairs door. Some GI probably got that knife as a going-away present from his mom before he went over to Vietnam. It had a blade for opening cans that was nicked up from use. I know this because the knife was taken out of the girl before the police came and it ended up in the general possession of the kids of our alley, passing from hand to hand like it was magic or something. I thought of that years later with a bunch of other alley types in the Lower East Side. But I want to get to this event. Kenneth is outside the bar waiting to come in and I keep getting sidetracked, like I'm not ready to leave Saigon.

Okay, so there he is in the door and I see his stretched-out face like it's my name written on a hit list. He scans the room and he doesn't like what he sees and all of a sudden I'm feeling like it was his fault that my mother had stopped talking. He did something to her the last time. Whatever it is that bothers me about her—her silence, her men, the noises with the men while I'm lying there in the dark, the wasted look in her face that just gets worse and worse—all these things are gone in a flash, in a turn of this guy's head. He sees me and smiles, but it's a grim smile.

He steps in, and Jake says, "Hello, pardner," and starts wiping the bar in big circles, the same routine he's always used on a customer stepping into the place when it's empty.

It's like Kenneth doesn't even hear him. He comes over to my booth and I pull back. "Hello, Thanh," he says.

I don't say anything. I've got this knot in the center of my chest and it's cinching tighter and tighter. I look toward the back of the bar to see if my mother knows what's happening. She's on the floor with the other girls. Four long drapes of straight black hair. I glance back to Kenneth and his eyes have followed mine. He straightens up and I feel like I've betrayed my mother, giving away her hiding place. I stand up on the seat of the booth and say, real loud, "Don't go near her."

Kenneth's face swings back to me and it yanks my breath away, like I'm looking in that mirror on Lê Lợi. He must know what I'm thinking because he squares around and says, "Thanh, do you know who I am?"

You'd think with all those tears I never could control over this whole subject that if I didn't exactly like this guy who suddenly shows up and decides he's got this big claim on me, at least I'd be intrigued or something. I'd held off thinking about this particular connection till this moment and there was a lot of reason to stick around, if not to learn some things about this guy and why he decided to come back, then at least to see what it was that he and my mother were going to decide to do. But as soon as he asks me this question and I can't avoid the answer, I leap over the back of the booth seat and make a dash for the door.

"Wait!" Kenneth yells, but I don't. I'm out the door and I turn left toward Trần Hưng Đạo and run as hard as I can till I'm at the corner under the marquee of the movie house where they play all the Chinese kung fu movies. I stand there gasping, but not so much from being out of breath as from this bucketful of cockroaches running around on my skin. That's all the feeling was, just that. Nothing about mothers and fathers and love and hate or shit like that, just this scrabbling little feeling all over my body like little cockroach feet.

Then I look back down the street and I see Kenneth and he's running this way. He sees me look and he raises his hand to tell me to wait and I say to myself, All right, you son of a bitch, you want me, you gotta catch me.

I go out on Trần Hưng Đạo and run across the near lane just in front of a big old Citroen truck and pull up to wait for a little cluster of motorized xích-lôs to whiz past with grins from the drivers. Then I'm across Trần Hưng Đạo and I look back and Kenneth is following, but he's held up by the traffic. I beat it east past a low building with cave-mouth storefronts, some of the big metal doors only half rolled up. A few more stores and just beyond a florist is a little gap between buildings and I'm into it. It smells of rotted flowers and it's wide enough for Kenneth, but it won't be easy for him, and I'm out the other end in an alley and a couple of chickens thrash out of my way clucking.

Right or left: I go right, doubling back, really, not the obvious choice, and I run hard with my head down till I count ten, thinking he can't possibly be through the little passageway yet. I look up to see what I can do next. The alley ends on the street up ahead and to the left is a big stucco wall. On the right going by are a few doorways into apartments and coming up is a stairway to a balcony along the back of the building with the storefronts. Apartments up there too. I can't go over the stucco wall and so the question is, do I take the chase back to the open streets.

I slow up and then duck into the stairwell and climb as fast as I can without making a clatter on the metal steps. At the top, the balcony is solid and I crouch down where I can't be seen. I wait. Soon I hear the scuffle of feet a little way up the alley. Kenneth emerging from the passage. I expect him to go to his left, but instead I hear steady footsteps coming down this end of the alley. Slow, like he knows what I did. Then he says, "Thanh?"

I look around. There are three doors off the balcony and I choose the second one because it isn't the closest, which would be an obvious choice, and it isn't the farthest, also an obvious choice. I creep silently on my hands and knees to the door and try it very gently. It gives and I slip into a dim room. There's a big straw mat under me and I push the door silently shut, hoping like hell that there's nobody home. I hear Kenneth call my name again—muffled, distant—and I try to stop the heaving in my chest.

After a few moments I look around and my body jerks up even before my mind realizes that somebody's here. On a pallet at the far wall of this little cement room a woman is sleeping. She's on her side, facing me, with her head tucked on her lower shoulder and her upper arm bent so that it looks like she has just finished sucking her thumb. The hand is there just below her mouth and the thumb is extended and I can imagine her sucking her thumb even though she's about my mother's age.

She sleeps on and I watch her, waiting for the thumb to go back into her mouth, and I think she is very beautiful lying there, I want to lie down beside her. I hear Kenneth's cry one more time, very distant now, and I look at my own hands. I sit down and lean against the door and I watch this woman for a long time, even after Kenneth is obviously gone. I watch her for as long as I dare, thinking even to wait for her to awake and find me. She does not move in her sleep. She is very still and her hand stays curled there by her face. There's a stillness in me, too, but finally I figure I'll only scare her when she wakes. So I go out as quietly as I came in.

I didn't return to the apartment for many hours. I don't know if I really figured I'd beat this thing, but when I opened our door I knew he was there even before I saw him, and I knew there was nothing I could do. He was on the bed, though he had his clothes on and Nghi wasn't with him. I smelled the incense. I turned and there she was at her prayers. But the stick of incense was burned down low in its holder on the shrine and her hands were lying on her knees, very still, and her bowed head looked more sad than prayerful.

"Please don't run, Thanh," the man said.

I didn't look at him. I kept looking at my mother and I didn't hear any movement from the bed. He was playing it more carefully this time, thinking that if I ran again, he could never catch me, I could always give him the slip. I waited to see what my mother would do, but she just kept her head bowed. She didn't even look up at me. That puzzled me at first. But then I got the drift. She was part of this whole thing.

So I turned my face straight ahead. I just looked at neither of them. I looked straight ahead and it was like I was alone in the room. They didn't mean a thing, the two of them. They weren't even there. It was just me in the room, and things were simpler then. I only had one name, after all. Võ Đình Thanh. There was no Tony yet, no Deuce. No Kenneth James Hatcher either, not even a Võ Xuân Nghi anymore. I was alone and that was okay with me. But I didn't realize the kind of trouble I was in when I looked for words to run through my head to keep me calm and I couldn't decide between trời ơi and fuck you all and I started to cry instead.

TWO

✦

Who do I seem like to you? I listen to myself talk sometimes and I say, Who is this kid? I don't sound Vietnamese. I learned English early. Maybe my mother knew it would happen all along, that somebody would come for me and I'd end up in America with a TV and a backyard and a good pair of sneakers. She was the one who pushed me to learn English. She made her men teach me. I had me a whole goddam faculty of nameless language teachers, these guys sitting on my mother's bed in their underwear saying, Okay, kid, what's this? An apple, right? Say apple. From the mess hall. Say mess hall. What's this? Say pocketknife. What's this? Say greenback. And I was good at it. That's an apple. Mess hall. Yes I want to eat the apple. Pocketknife. Greenback. And what's that, GI? Is that your cock poking out of your underwear? Yeah, kid. That's what I use to make your momma very very happy.

Well, shit. I wanted my momma to be very very happy. And I guess she wanted me to be happy, too. So she made me learn English to get ready, and then there I was on a jet plane with this guy Kenneth. She must've known all along. But didn't she figure whoever it was would come back for her too? Did she dream that dream only for me? She didn't learn much English. But maybe that was just because it was a little late for that. A kid can learn better.

2 5

Do you take me for that? A Vietnamese kid who's an American now? The newspapers and magazines love us American-Asian kids. We're smart as hell. You can see us on the cover of Time. Look at these kids. They don't really look like Americans, do they? But surprise. They are. And because they don't look American, they don't look all that smart either, right? Surprise again. That's why they're such a big deal on the cover of this magazine. And I *am* smart, like it says right here.

But there's something a little different about me. Those are good, obvious Asian faces on the magazine cover. You look at me and there's something a little odd. Unless you see me next to Kenneth James Hatcher of the district attorney's office. Then to some people —and I always hated their guts—it was cute. They'd say, Oh yes, I can see it. No doubt about it. If you just ignore those odd things about him—the untamed spray of black hair; the insistent roundness of that face, in spite of how the features are stretched out just like yours; the remaining hint of an Asian hood to his eyes—if you ignore those things, what we have is an authentic replica of you, Kenneth, in all your manifest Americanness, coming through in this kid's face.

Manifest. No GI in his underwear taught me that one. Hey, kid, my cock sticking out of my shorts makes your mother's profession manifest. Can you say manifest? No, that was from Kenneth. After all, I was brought up for ten years by a guy from the district attorney's office, a guy with a big future, maybe even in Trenton and beyond. I grew up in the streets and then I returned to them, but those middle ten years had to give me something, a smart Asian kid like me.

It took a while, though. It was very tough at first. My first few nights in that big house were terrible. The silence was terrible. There were a few other big houses around and a whole shitload of trees. I liked trees okay—there were some really fine trees in Saigon —but in Saigon I wasn't living in the middle of their goddam den and there wasn't that awful silence so that all you could hear were the trees. With the constant roar of Saigon, I never knew that trees could make sounds, but they sure do. I'd lie in bed—which was too damn soft, by the way, like I was being sucked into a pit—and it would sound outside like these trees were all bending down to grab me or something. They'd moan and creak and their shadows would flash around through the crack in the blind.

It was bad until finally I heard a sound that I knew. A really fine sound, a lucky sound. It was the song of a cicada, somewhere out there in the dark. This was a solitary voice instead of a whole bunch of them, but it let me hear in my head all the cicadas singing in Saigon. Lousy reedy voices, like the girls at the bar singing with the jukebox, but that was just fine with me. It was lucky to catch a cicada and make that song private for you. The cicadas were called ve sầu, the sorrowful insect. I guess that was because they spent seventeen years waiting underground and then they just had a week or so to mate before they died. That's why their voices were so harsh. They didn't have any time and they were scared and they had to make a connection right away or there'd be nothing to show for their short, sorrowful lives.

In Saigon we'd find an old shoe and make glue by dissolving some of the rubber crepe with a little gasoline. Then we'd take a pot of that glue and a bamboo pole and go out in one of the neighborhoods that had the big tamarind trees, or we'd go over to the Botanical Garden. This is when we were after the mature insects, not the nymphs. We'd see one up on the trunk of the tree and we'd dip the tip of the pole in the glue pot and lift it real slow till the final push. The cicada doesn't know what the shit's going on except this sure as hell isn't the female cicada he's been calling for.

He's got two red eyes, like two little drops of blood squeezed up and ready to run, and these big papery wings that you can see through. You can see all the veins in them. He puts up a loud ruckus coming down on the end of the pole, but when he's in your hand, he shuts up. Smart. He can't run away, so he just clams up and waits to see what's next.

I took my cicada back home, the one year I did all this. I was five, I think. Momma was still pretty calm and she let me keep him. She knew it was good luck. She believed in it. So we kept that cicada on the wall, and after a day or so he began to sing. My mother and I would lie awake—I knew she was awake because she'd say, "Oh listen, Thanh, we have luck now"—and we'd listen there in the dark. You couldn't much sleep anyway because that cicada sang very loud. He sang for a week and then he stopped and we knew he was dead. He still clung to the wall, but he was dead and we didn't touch him for days. It never occurred to me at the time, but that cicada had to pay a big price for whatever luck he brought us. He never did get his mate, see. That was out of the question there on our wall.

So when there was the sound of a cicada outside Kenneth's house, I knew I had to catch one. This was the first cicada I'd heard, which meant they were just coming out. I'd never caught one of the nymphs at night, but I knew how.

It was still pretty early in the evening. Nobody was in bed but me. Kenneth had these ideas, which he explained to me in detail, about six-year-olds needing sleep and how this was going to be a much better life than Saigon. I still wouldn't talk to him and I didn't even look at him much. The six-year-olds-need-sleep stuff was bullshit to me, but I was in no position to argue and I was glad to at least get away by myself in the dark.

So I waited. I lay awake for a long time—a few hours, I'm sure, because when I finally got up and crept out of my room, the house was dark. Catching a nymph is easier than catching a mature cicada. All you need is a flashlight. I remembered one from a few nights before, when I'd come out of my room to find the toilet. I'd forgotten which way to turn in the hallway—too many goddam rooms in this place—and after a moment Kenneth emerged from his bedroom and he had a flashlight. "This way," he'd said, like it was easy to read my mind, and he'd flipped the beam toward the bathroom.

Anyway, I knew where I had to go if I wanted to get what I needed to catch my American luck out there on the tree. I slipped down to his bedroom door and it was open about six inches. So he could listen for me, I guess. He'd heard me come out the other night when I was looking for the toilet, but I felt certain that that was earlier in the evening. I put my ear into the open space and I heard real steady breathing. After a moment more of waiting and sort of just appreciating what I was up to—sneaking into this guy's room to steal something from under his nose—I pushed the door open enough so that I could squeeze in.

There was a faint light in the room, coming from a crack in a door in the far wall. I'd caught a glimpse of that little inner room on my first day—it was still another bathroom, and it made me wonder at how much shit these Americans must produce to need all these bathrooms. I waited a moment to let my eyes adjust to the bit of light, and then I crept over to the bed.

Kenneth had his face turned to me and his mouth was moving a little, a kind of munching motion. As I watched, he seemed to grow restless. He turned on his back and I held my breath, expecting him to wake up. But then his mouth opened and he started to snore. Beyond him was his wife.

At this point I'd not had very much to do with her. She was a figure in the background. This get-a-Vietnamese-kid thing seemed to be Kenneth's show. She'd smiled at me when we first laid eyes on each other and she'd bent over and given me a hug. She smelled like one of the girls in the bar, the one who always painted her lips a little bigger than her real ones. It was a flowery smell like that passageway I'd led Kenneth through in our little race.

I watched her sleeping. In fact, I went around to her side of the bed for a moment because I still hadn't gotten a chance to have a good look at her. She didn't smell here in the bed, except maybe a little sour. Her hair was scattered all over the pillow and her mouth, which was pretty small, a pinched little mouth, had a kind of pout on it. I watched her for a while, but there was nothing to it, really. It was like watching a crack in the wall or a snag in the mat or a scab on your knuckle when you're feeling sort of bored and empty.

I went back to Kenneth's side of the bed and he was still snoring. I figured the flashlight would be close at hand and I eased open a drawer in the nightstand and there it was. I took the flashlight and closed the drawer and went back out, pulling the door to behind me so that it was just like I found it.

As soon as I stepped outside the house, I stopped. It was a warm night, windy, like I said, with the trees hissing around above me. It was very dark, the darkest place I'd ever been out of doors. The yard was big and now I was very aware of the silence behind the trees. My shoulders felt real heavy all of a sudden and my hand went down and I almost dropped the flashlight. I lifted the thing, but it took all of my strength. There was something in my eyes, warm. Tears. I discovered the tears in my eyes like they were somebody else's, and that was really scary. I knew I was feeling alone, but that was like I wasn't even with myself anymore.

Then I heard the cicada again. His voice rose and died away, like he suddenly realized there was nobody to hear him. He was singing alone because he'd come out too soon. I followed the pointed silence after his song and then he sang again as I neared his tree. Not that I was after him. It was a nymph I'd catch with my flashlight, but I wanted to be near this guy who was singing. He could bring me luck by my just being under his tree, I figured.

Overhead was his silence. What the fuck gives, he was thinking. Where is everybody? I flipped on the light and crouched down on the big roots. I was feeling more myself again. This was a special kind of luck, to catch a nymph. Not only would it eventually sing for me, I'd get to watch it change into the big guy with the red eyes. And even as I was thinking about how I was doing okay, the light fell on a nymph in the dirt near the root and he wasn't even all the way out of the ground yet.

He kind of hesitated in my light, but then he squeezed out of his burrow and I bent down and let him walk up into my palm. I gently closed my hand around him. He was brittle, crusty, but he was trembling. When I felt that, I didn't say anything to him, like you might expect from a little kid. I knew enough not to talk to an insect. But sure I felt bad. Insects can get scared. And that's when I thought about how the cicada in our apartment in Saigon never did get to mate. I almost put the nymph back when I thought of that, but I sure as hell didn't want to return to that house without the luck I came for, so I figured maybe I didn't have to keep him singing for me till he died. A few nights' worth would be all the luck I needed. Then I could put him back on the tree.

I switched off the light and headed toward the house. When I got to the door I looked at the flashlight and thought of just pitching it into the trees. Let old Kenneth suddenly realize that something happened in his house that he didn't have any control of. But then I decided that it wasn't worth making that point yet. I was still sizing up the whole thing.

So I crept upstairs and into their bedroom. Kenneth was still snoring with his mouth open and his wife still pouting and I put the flashlight into the drawer. I knew they wouldn't wake up with that cicada in my hand and I went back to my room.

This room I was living in astonished me, really. First of all, it was just mine. I was the only kid. I figured at the time that Kenneth's wife just took care of things, like the girls at the bar. I knew how it was done and all, having a baby, and a couple of the girls had kids, like Nghi had me. But I also knew that when they started to gripe around that there was a baby on the way, there was something they knew to do to take care of things. I didn't really know exactly what it was. They had to disappear for a little while, but it all seemed pretty routine, and that's how I figured I happened to be the only kid in this big house and how I happened to have this room of my own, which wasn't much smaller than our apartment in Saigon.

The other astonishing thing about the room was that it was full of stuff. Furniture, toys, a record player, a tape machine, a TV, and it all seemed to be mine. Things I'd always figured someday I'd be able to steal for myself were suddenly given to me and I didn't exactly feel bad about that, but it sure did puzzle the hell out of me for a while. It was certainly something to be said in favor of this otherwise terrifying turn of events, but even as all that helped keep away my tears now and then, it also kept me quiet.

Still, the only things in the room that *really* seemed to be mine were the pair of Saigon sandals under the bed and the cicada in my hand. I switched on a small light over the desk and looked around. The shade on the lamp by the bed was rough, like burlap, and I went to it and opened my hand and held the nymph gently between my fingers. His legs started working and I let him feel the shade and he grabbed on at once. He turned a little this way and that and finally seemed satisfied. I lay down on the bed and propped up some pillows to wait for him to change.

I fell asleep almost at once, but somehow I knew when it was time. I woke up very casually. I just opened my eyes and I was looking at the nymph and I could see the crack beginning along his back. I didn't move. I lay there and watched as the crack grew, and inside was a dark shape. I don't know how long the whole thing lasted. It seemed like a minute and it seemed like all night. But finally the cicada rose up from his skin and he was black and wet and he dragged himself free and moved away from the empty shell. He sat and stretched his wings and his darkness began to change. One moment he seemed black and the next moment he was a predawn gray and then he was dark green. I drew near him and he folded his wings. He seemed at home. His eyes were as red as two drops of blood, just like I remembered. Then I went to sleep.

In my dreams I heard my cicada singing. I felt calm and I was lying on the grass under a tree and the song was very loud. *Very* loud. I woke up and I realized that the cicada who sang in my dreams was singing even now on the lampshade beside my bed. There was a dim light in the room—the dawn seeping in from the window—and I only had time to smile and prop myself up on an elbow before the door to my room flew open.

It was Mrs. Kenneth and she was in her nightgown and her hair was wild and she seemed full of some real strong feeling. I figured that was some sexy dude of a cicada—look at the mate he called in no time at all. I sat up laughing at this idea and I said, "He's ready for you." I think I said it in Vietnamese, but the laughing alone was probably enough to piss her off, if the cicada itself hadn't already done the job.

She flipped on the overhead light and shot me a real tough glance. It was funny, but at first I was glad to get some clear feeling out of her. I kind of liked her for that brief moment, though that was soon done with forever. She lunged across the room and when she saw the cicada, she said something loud and glanced at me hard again, though this time I wished she'd just return to the way she was, a figure in the background with no feelings at all.

She began looking around the room and she found one of my slippers under the bed and she picked it up and then I knew what she was going to do. Kenneth was in the doorway by now and I cried out for him to stop her, but he didn't move and I leaped out of the bed and fell against her, clutching for her arm but instead getting two handfuls of her nightgown. I dragged on them but she only leaned a bit and she swung my sandal—my own sandal, which made it all worse—and there was a nasty little crunching sound.

I cried hard for a long time. I rolled up into a ball in the bed with my face to the wall and I would not say a word to either of them and I cried. Even after the tears were gone I cried, a reedy rise and fall, and I imagined a crack suddenly appearing along my spine and it widened and inside was a dark form and the crack grew and this body I was in fell away. But when I tried to imagine what it was that emerged from the crack, I couldn't. I'd start with the eyes. Two eyes the color of blood. But it was no good. I didn't know what kind of creature I was inside.

THREE

⧫

She didn't last, Kenneth's wife. Two years more, maybe. I think I was eight going on nine when she left. By then she and I had a kind of working arrangement. She wouldn't hassle me, I wouldn't hassle her. With Kenneth she was giving and receiving enough shit to fill her life just fine.

We wouldn't talk much, Kenneth's wife and me. But once in a while when we were all at the dinner table in a funky deep silence and I knew they'd been at each other, she'd give me a look. A real funny look for me to figure out, because I knew what a lot of their arguing was about.

Once, right near the end, I was upstairs doing some homework. I was good at homework and it was safe inside those books. Doing math problems or reading some of those history chapters—I liked the Wild West a lot, and the Paul Bunyan stuff, Casey Jones, these guys had Vietnamese faces in my head, they had a real familiar feel to them—but doing all that stuff, the math problems and writing out the answers to the questions at the end of the chapters in the history book, it was like I was having a conversation with somebody. There'd be things to figure out together and we'd find a conclusion and we'd think how it was that we did all that together.

Anyway, this one night when I was working I heard loud voices from downstairs. I'd heard this kind of thing often, ever since I arrived. But it had been getting worse lately. I knew that. "He's my child." Those words in Kenneth's hoarse, hollering voice rushed up the steps and made me put my pen down. One, the conversation was about me. Not for the first time, but here it was right now. Two, this was a declaration from Kenneth that was never really made directly to me and when I heard it—even secondhand—it still stopped me. It made me look around that room full of all that stuff, stuff I'd lived with for two years, and it suddenly all looked a little funny, like I'd snuck into the Saigon Museum after the curator had gone home and it was mine but it wasn't. Funny that Kenneth saying he was my father should make me feel less like his son, but I guess that's because the way I'd come to accept where I was didn't have anything to do with accepting him as my father.

But those words stood me up and pulled me out the door and brought me on my hands and knees and then on my chest in a quiet crawl to the top of the stairs. I peeked over the edge and I could see the foyer and the arch into the living room. That's where the voices were coming from.

"*I'm* the alien," the wife said, and her voice was fat with tears. "And it didn't just start when he came."

"Ignorant jealousy," Kenneth shouted, but his voice was under control now. I wondered if he still had one of those three-piece suits on that he wore to work. If he did, I could imagine him with his thumbs stuck in the vest pockets like he always did to get control of his voice.

"There may be some jealousy in it," the wife cried. "But it's not ignorant. I'm alone here. All alone. And don't use that Mr. D.A. pose with me. Get those goddam thumbs out of your vest pockets." See, the wife knew all about him too. "Your only real wife is your own goddam future. And that bitch is out there in the courts and she's fucking her way down to Trenton."

I had a twist of regret there. I wished I'd talked more with this woman. I should've made her madder. I should've gotten her attention. I liked this woman. She would've made a good bargirl, I figured. One of the lively ones. One of the ones that always made me laugh.

Then she said—more like hissed—"And what have I got? This house and some other woman's child."

I even forgave her that. She was upset and I hadn't done anything to make her like me, that was for damn sure.

Kenneth had an answer for that one, though. He said, "What options do you have but other women's children? That doesn't have anything to do with me. It's you."

"I can't help my body," she said, and then she began to cry real hard.

What she said impressed me at the time by showing that she could be sad and she could be hurt, things that I hadn't realized about her. But years later the words themselves came back, several times. When I would somehow become aware of what I looked like, this mix of American and Vietnamese, once in a while I'd think of Kenneth's wife saying she couldn't help her body. Not that the words ever helped me. If anything, they just made me sad. Missed chances, I guess. Not that she would really have understood what I was going through. Her own problems were too strong for that, and she always figured I was part of them.

I remember so much. That was a gift from my mother, and a curse, too, like some Vietnamese voodoo curse. Like Nghi wrote my name and birth date on a piece of paper and stuffed it into the belly of some goddam elephant or something. Some damn thing.

But I remember that look Kenneth's wife would give me sometimes at the dinner table. Once it was particularly strong. Just after the argument that I listened to from the top of the stairs—maybe it was the next day, or even that night—I was sitting there using the tip of my spoon to pop bubbles in my soup and I looked up and she was staring at me. It wasn't the hard look, the you-little-fuck-up-of-an-alien look that she used on me when she was mad. It wasn't the pitying look either, when she seemed to be thinking that I was only a little pathetic bastard of an alien. This one still had some of the sadness and hurt in it that I'd heard in her voice during the big argument. Was she trying to share that hurt with me somehow? Was she seeing the connection that I saw years later? At the time it just puzzled me, because I knew it wasn't the couple of moods I'd learned to recognize in her, but I didn't know what else it could be.

Anyway, it doesn't make a goddam bit of difference, really. She was gone soon after that. Not that I missed her. Things were simpler without her. I'd been talking with Kenneth for some time, or he'd been talking to me, and I'd listened to him quite a bit. He was trying real hard, I guess. And the fewer overheated adults in my life the better, was the way I figured it. Kenneth's wife gave me a hug before she left and she still smelled like a bargirl. She was getting weepy like a bargirl, too, but I knew this was best all around.

That same night Kenneth came up to my room to talk to me, the way he'd been doing for some time. He sat down on the edge of the bed. I faked a yawn to try to keep him from going on too long, though this was from habit. On that night I was quite a bit more interested in what he had to say. I propped up a pillow and I lay back to listen and to watch his face change.

He had a way of starting out a long explanation of something—why people talked to each other the way they did; why I had to do things a certain way; why *he* had to do things a certain way, like punishing me. He didn't hit me very often, and then only on the butt, and then only after a lot of words. Anyway, about his face. When he started out on an explanation, his scalp and his forehead would be stretched back real tight. Like this night when his wife left him.

"Tony," he said, "when a man and a woman get married, they have things in mind for their life together, like having children and working, doing something that they're good at, and making money so that they can have the things they need, like enough food and a nice house, a nice place for their children. Sometimes, though, the plans that the man and wife make get changed. Certain things become more important than they realized at first, and other things become less important. But the husband and wife might not change in the same way, and there might be a big difference between them as time goes on, a *big* difference. And if there is a big difference and that difference makes them fight all the time and they make each other miserable . . ."

Now, all of this was said with his face stretched tight. This was the setup, and in just about all of his talks, when he had a point to make, it went like this. The setup turned on the little question that was coming up. And it was now that something always happened to his face. His ears would drop. He'd let go of the stretch in his face and his ears would drop down, and as they did, he'd say, "Is it right...?" like in this case he said, "...is it right for those two people to stay together?" And as soon as his ears dropped, you knew that hell no it wasn't right. Whatever it was, when the ears went down, the answer was no, it wasn't right.

On the night when Kenneth's wife left him, he waited for me to answer that question. Most of the time I didn't have to say anything at all. He and I both knew what the answer was supposed to be. Once in a while I may have mumbled no, it's not right, just to be done with it and maybe help cut the conversation short. But this time he stopped and he was waiting for an answer, and when I realized this, I looked at him closely and I could see that there were tears in his eyes. Now, that threw me off. I don't have to tell you that I'd never seen tears in Kenneth Hatcher's eyes before.

When I saw them, I figured I better give him the answer he wanted, but it also made me actually consider the question. So somebody had changed and that meant it was time to split. I suddenly thought of Nghi wobbling around the apartment in Saigon with druggie eyes, wide open but not seeing, and I was supposed to tell Kenneth no, it's not right, but I didn't feel good and I felt tears in my own eyes.

So Kenneth suddenly reaches his hands out and holds my shoulders, like he did in Saigon. "I'm sorry," he says, and his voice is gravelly and soft. "I know how important it is to you to have a stable family. I'm sorry I messed this up, Tony. I have this job, see. And I think it's important." He hesitates, and it's clear to me that he's trying to control his voice, though this time the problem isn't yelling, and instead of digging for his vest pockets (he's wearing a Rutgers sweatshirt anyway), he seems to be arranging his face. Around his eyes and mouth and at the temples are all these little twitches, and he drags the back of his hand over his forehead. When he finally starts another explanation to me, his face isn't stretched at all. His ears are already down and the face is very calm, though his eyes are still full of tears.

"My job," he says, "tries to make things right for people who are hurt by others. People can be bad to each other. God knows in Vietnam there was enough of that. It was something poisonous that got in the air over there and everybody breathed it, everybody. If you drew a breath you did something wrong, simple as that. Only the dead could be innocent over there."

Kenneth stops for a moment and he looks off toward the window. To tell the truth, at the time I didn't really know what the hell he was talking about, but he was lecturing again and he was sounding down-right gentle—I'd not picked up on anything in him that seemed what you'd call gentle before, and, well, that was a lot for me to take in. Especially with the bad thoughts of my mother in my head, how toward the end there'd been times when she had trouble even standing up. I wouldn't let myself have any specific memories of that, but even just knowing it made things very strange. And now Kenneth is sitting here and I suddenly understand that he can be sad and he can be hurt just like the wife who's gone, the one who looked at me with eyes full of all that, and frankly this is all pretty scary. I tell myself, Shit, I'm stronger than the whole bunch of them. Everything's okay, I tell myself.

Kenneth turns his face back to me and says, "It still goes on, the bad stuff. It's human. But people have to pay when they hurt others. That's what my job is about. To make them pay. Not to get revenge. To do it without anger, even. But to do it. To make sure that if people make others suffer, there has to be a price for that." He reaches out now and covers one of my hands with his. This is some-thing new. He says, "That's my job, and for me to do it right, it takes a lot out of me."

He seems to want to say more, but he's not looking at me. His face is sort of lowered and I figure he's missing his wife and feeling guilty about it. His hand feels cold and his face is as slack as sleep. He doesn't ask the usual question, but I figure he could use an answer anyway. I try to think how he would ask it, but I'm still not real sure about all the issues here. I've been following his feelings more than his argument and I can't think what to say "No, it's not right" to.

Then he squeezes my hand and I just say, "It's okay. Really. It's okay."

If old Kenneth had a wife leave him every week, maybe we would've gotten on better. That real tender moment there, was that all bullshit just because I went on and on after that, for years, through a whole goddam childhood and fucking puberty and all that, and it didn't happen again? Or is the bullshit the feeling that it never really happened at all, even once, could never happen, that kind of thing? Me telling him everything is okay while he sits there without any of the Mr. D.A. crap, with fucking tears in his eyes, even. Sure it happened.

And I stuck it out. For ten years. Why was that? Beyond the fact that I was trapped, a little kid half a planet away from his mother and from all he knew. As I said, at first things were pretty terrible. But there was the letter from Nghi.

One evening, not too long after the thing about the cicada, Kenneth came up to my room. There was still a faint stain on the lampshade and I would lie in my bed for probably hours, my face to the wall, and I'd think about Saigon and my mother and my friends from the alleys. Pretty pathetic. This one night I was there on my bed and I'd reached the point I often reached where I was weary of thinking about what I'd lost, it wasn't doing anything but making me feel bad, and with the tip of my finger I was tracing a path through the maze of little stipples of plaster on the wall.

Suddenly Kenneth walked in and he sat down on the bed. I kept moving my finger on the wall, and he said, kind of low, "There's a letter from your mother."

I sat up quick and I grabbed it out of his hand. I was six, remember. I was smart and my mother made sure I learned things, but I hadn't learned to read very much. Still, I looked at her tiny, loopy handwriting and I felt a flash of connection to her, like I'd just touched her hand.

This lasted about a second, is all. The words at the top of the page weren't even Vietnamese. I recognized my name, but the letter was in English. I guess that was so Kenneth could read it, since I couldn't read very much myself. I looked at him.

"I'll read it to you," he said, and he took the letter. He cleared his throat and began. "Dear Thanh, Now you Tony, no Thanh. You dad Kenneth. He come take you, you go America, stay America, good for you. Later maybe I come America. Sick now. Later. You stay

America father. He good man. Good for Thanh."

Kenneth read the words just like she put them down. He didn't fix a sentence, not even a word. I heard my mother's voice at her worst—speaking that damn pidgin English—and it was coming through the mouth of this man, and I nearly snatched the letter from his hand and ripped it to bits. I was about to, in fact. But he said, "There's a little more here written in Vietnamese. Can you read it?"

I didn't say anything, but I took the letter from him and looked at it. I knew a little bit of the Vietnamese alphabet, but I couldn't put together words. Except I could read the word for love, and it was here in her letter to me, twice. I'd learned that word when she'd traced it in the sweat on the mirror in our bathroom. One night I'd been watching her through a crack in the door and I must've made a sound or something and she realized I was there. Her hair was wet. She was standing at the basin and her hair hung down her bare back in slick black coils and I wanted to touch them, I wanted to grasp those wet ropes of hair and climb up her. But I just held my breath and watched her, and she leaned forward and with the tip of her finger she traced the word "yêu." Then she spoke it. "Yêu." It's two syllables, both vowels. Eee-ooo, like a little cry of pleasure. She turned her face toward the door and she smiled and said, "Cô yêu em," I love you, and she used for herself the word for a young un-married woman. She turned back to the word on the mirror. "This is love." And as she said it, showing how the sound moved through those letters, the word faded and was gone. I went into the bathroom and she kneeled to me and I hugged her and she smelled like soap and rain and I plunged my hands into the heavy wetness of her hair.

I looked at the word in her letter, love, and I folded the letter and put it into the pocket of my pajama top. "What did she have to say?" Kenneth asked, and you could hear him trying to be casual about it.

"She said she loves me."

Kenneth nodded at this and he got up real slow, as if I was lying there asleep and he didn't want to disturb me, and he left the room. When he was gone, I took the letter out and I carefully ripped it along the space separating the part she'd written in English from the part she'd written in Vietnamese. I crumpled her English words into a tight little ball and I threw them into the wastebasket. I put her Vietnamese words at the bottom of a drawer in the desk, and it wasn't until just a couple of years ago that I was ready to go back to it and try to read it.

The Vietnamese have an alphabet, but the letters have different pronunciations and there are important marks over the letters that show you the tones and these tones make a big difference in the words, so just learning to read English letters wasn't enough. As the years went on, I sort of lost my command of the spoken Vietnamese language because I never used it. That made it tougher to try to translate the note. And I finally understood that the early promises that Nghi would someday come to the States were lies. So for a long time I didn't want to know what my mother had written because I knew that even the Vietnamese words would be lies.

But finally, at a point when I felt that I really didn't give a shit anymore, I went to a library and found a Vietnamese dictionary and I translated the message. "When you someday can read this," she wrote, "I don't know where I'll be. But pray for me on Wandering Souls' Day and try to love your father. I love you and I'm sorry."

Vietnamese is a simple language, and if there's sometimes a doubt about what somebody's saying, exactly, in English, you can bet you've got the same problem in Vietnamese. I guess if you stop and think about it, it should be pretty clear that when Nghi said "I love you and I'm sorry," she wasn't saying that she was sorry that she loved me. She was probably sorry for being a fuck-up and needing to worry about prayers on Wandering Souls' Day. But as I sat there at the library table in Point Pleasant, New Jersey, I sure as hell was sorry that I loved her. She knew from the start that she wasn't going to see me again. She'd set it all up. And as far as I was concerned, she could wander around in the fire for fucking forever.

FOUR

◆

How long can you feel like that about a woman who's your mother, like you don't even give a shit if she's off in some supernatural world having her ass fried? When I was on the Deuce and I'd traded that too-soft bed in New Jersey for a piss-stained mattress in a squatter building in the East Village and Joey was about to get fucked, it felt sometimes like forever, you could feel that forever. But it's like a junkie thinking a high is gonna last forever this time, like there's no seconds ticking by at all and the feeling's gonna go on and on. Even if he's crashed a zillion times before. There'd been periods all along when I did care, when I'd go a little crazy over the memory of her.

When I was fifteen, it came on me suddenly. It was a night in early summer and I had my window open. The wind in the trees outside sounded like the sea. I'd gotten used to the trees. They didn't scare me any longer, they were the best part of Point Fucking Pleasant. They were pleasant, the trees, even when down the hall some woman was moaning and calling out the prosecutor's name, oh Kenny oh.

This night there was some of that. Kenneth never did find himself another woman for very long. This one's name was Tracy, which later struck me as funny because that was the favorite phony name for the ladies on the Deuce to feed their johns. This Point Pleasant Tracy had been around, in and out, for about three weeks. But it's not her, really, that's important in all this. It's the trees.

They made me think suddenly of the South China Sea. That's how it came on me, this thing about my mother. I'd not thought much about her, really, since I'd translated her note. But it was the South China Sea that came out of the roar of those trees beyond my window, and I lay in my bed and listened to that roar and I could see a sail on the sea. I was in the back of a big black car and the windows were tinted and I knew it was sunny but the sea before me was easy on my eyes, blue and full of sunlight, and I could watch it without even squinting, like it wanted me to watch, like I was peeking at it through the bathroom door and it was naked and it liked me to watch.

The sail was on a sampan, some ragged-ass fisherman out there, but it was a big thing to me. I was maybe five, maybe not even quite that. My mother had herself a man, and it seemed real strange to me, because he was Vietnamese. I'd gotten so used to her being with Americans that this guy was a real surprise. He was some government official. He had this car and a driver and he was taking my mother and me to a government resort compound in Vũng Tàu, the swanky Vietnamese seaside resort down in Phước Tuy Province that the French had called Cap St. Jacques.

My mother was sitting next to me in the car, and while I watched the sea I was aware of her, all along my right leg and up my right arm I was pressed against her. I could have it both ways, my eyes free out there over the sea, dipping with the sampan and running along the shore, while I was calm and still and attached to my mother. I felt small beside her and that was comforting. It's funny about that. Even now that I'm nearly eighteen and I'm big—I've been pretty big for my age ever since I hit my teens, especially for somebody with Asian blood in them; that's something that Kenneth gave me, I guess—but even now, when I'd tower over my mother, I can't think of her as anything but bigger than me. It's all I ever knew of her, and even when I can see her very clearly in a way I never could before all the things that happened in New York City, even seeing her as a woman, I can't shake this sense of my being a child with her. Not that there's any comfort about the feeling. It's something a lot different from that. But she just doesn't get any smaller, that's all.

I looked away from the South China Sea and up at Nghi. She had sunglasses on and her head was tilted back a little, though she didn't seem to be asleep. Beyond her was the government guy, jabbering away. He was really odd-looking to me because he was fat. Vietnamese don't get real fat, and so this guy was just sort of chubby by American standards, where even the poor can look fat. But in Vietnam, he was obviously getting too much to eat and that was a kind of guy that I'd not seen a lot of. Some of the old ladies in the alley were a little heavy, I guess from having children, but a fat man was somebody to watch out for, a guy who could do things to people.

So my mother had her head thrown back and she was listening to the man and I looked at the long curve of her throat. She wasn't caring about a thing. This guy couldn't scare her. She was soft and I was pressed against her and she belonged to me, really. This guy wanted in, but I just knew she was sitting there thinking about me.

I looked back outside and the seacoast road took a curve and up ahead I could see the hills of Vũng Tàu. There was a wooden lighthouse on one, a radar antenna on another, houses scattered on the hillsides, and at the foot of a hill coming up was a big white Buddha looking out to sea.

"Momma," I said, "it's him." I touched her wrist and nodded toward the jabbering man on her other side and then at the statue. I knew it wasn't really him, but the Buddha was as fat as a government official and I imagined this man sitting cross-legged beneath the hill, both his hands raised with the thumbs and forefingers delicately joined, like he'd just pulled the wings off two flies at once.

First my mother and then the man looked back to the passing statue and my mother ripped off her sunglasses, narrowed her eyes at me, and gave me a sharp little pinch on the leg. I guess she thought I was being disrespectful to Buddha or something. But the man turned to me and laughed. He lifted his head and laughed real hard and he reached across Nghi and patted me on the same leg that was stinging from the pinch.

Meanwhile, down the hall old Tracy was feeling real good and making a racket about it. I was lying in bed and I turned my face to the wall. The memory had taken a turn away from Nghi, but the thing that started it, the sound of the trees and the memory of the sea, wouldn't let me feel bad about her, even if she got a little pissed off with me about my remark. In fact, as soon as the government guy laughed so hard and obviously seemed to like me for what I'd said, my mother rubbed the spot she'd pinched like she wished she hadn't done it. She put her arm around me and she whispered something I didn't catch. Maybe she said she was sorry. Maybe she said she loved me. Maybe she just cooed at me a little bit like she wished she was spending the weekend in the apartment in Saigon with just me instead of having to go to bed with the guy who was still laughing about being compared to Buddha. I don't know. But she was holding me and she was warm and she had a smell about her that was like a Thai papaya, just cut open and red and full of juice.

I kept looking out to sea for that long weekend in Vũng Tàu. I can see now how stupid the compound was. Up on the coast highway there was a big metal gate with guards. Inside was a villa and a courtyard and banana trees. But at the back the whole place opened onto a white sand beach and there were no gates, no walls, just the open sea, like the VC would never figure to go around to the back.

But I'd go out there onto the sand and sit and watch the sea—the sampans nodding by, the gulls swooping around, and that far horizon, a long, clean razor-cut at first glance, but if you kept staring at it, you could see it wrinkling just a little, all along its length. The whole horizon had this raggedy edge and it seemed to me that there was a lot more going on out there than met the eye. It scared me a little bit, but I wanted to stare at it all the time.

Except when my mother came down to lie in the sun or giggle around in the breakers. Then I'd watch her, though I'd quick glance out to the horizon again if she looked at me or if her government man in his goofy swimming trunks looked at me (his trunks were square and baggy in the butt, like they were full of shit).

She was beautiful, my mother, though I guess that wasn't the big thing that kept me fixed on her at the time. I can see now—I could see on that night in Point Pleasant—that she was beautiful, but when I was four or five I'm sure I didn't know what the hell all that kind of stuff was about, really, in spite of all that went on in our apartment. At least, I didn't know what it was to *feel* a woman is beautiful.

But she was beautiful, my mother. She was smooth and she was slender and in her bikini her skin was dazzling to me, as dazzling as the flash of the sun on the South China Sea. And she didn't seem to mind being out in the sun. The other beautiful women of Saigon spent a lot of their energy outside trying to shield their skin from the sun. I guess they didn't want to look like the peasant girls, with sun-darkened skin. A beautiful Saigon girl was working all the time to have pale skin. Which is just the kind of thing that can make a person crazy, real crazy. Because their skin was kind of dark to start with. Vietnamese skin has something to it that makes it a little dark, not like the skin of what you think of as an American girl, but I guess the American girls are just what they wanted to be like. Goddam fucked-up Vietnamese girls. Most of them were something they should've appreciated. They were clearly one thing or another. You have to be pretty fucked up if you can't appreciate that, if you're one thing and you spend all your time worrying about trying to look like the other thing.

But my mother never seemed to care about that. She was pure Vietnamese and she'd come from a southern province and she never did quite get into the habit of trying to look like something she wasn't. Her eyes and her skin and her hair and her slick little cat's body were pure Vietnamese, no doubt about it.

And she really cared about how beautiful her feet were. I don't mind that. There's nothing about a woman making her feet beautiful that denies being Vietnamese. But it was another one of those big deals for the pretty girls of Saigon, and I guess it was partly for the same reason as keeping pale—they didn't want to look like a peasant girl. A peasant girl's feet are rough, made for walking around the countryside and wading out in the rice paddies. My mother would sit on her bed and put cream on her feet and carefully trim and paint her toenails, and her feet were beautiful, slim and smooth, and each nail was a perfect oval.

When she lay down beside me on the beach at Vũng Tàu and she was on her stomach, her head on her arm and turned away, I liked to watch her feet. I liked when their bottoms were turned up. I liked the little ripple of her instep, like the horizon out there on the sea, and sometimes her feet would move, they'd angle in toward each other for a moment and then straighten, or her toes would flare or curl, like her feet were taking part in some dream she was having, the same way that other people's faces or hands twitch in their sleep, but my mother's feet would always move gracefully, like her dreams were always beautiful.

These are things that when you're fifteen and you remember them when you're lying in bed and it's hot and the wind is blowing outside and some woman is moaning down the hall because she's getting balled, it makes you a little squirmy. It makes you goddam squirmy. Now don't get any half-asssed psycho-shit ideas. How the fuck is a kid going to be having the Oedipus crap about his mother when he hadn't laid eyes on her since he was six years old? She was just fucking beautiful, is all. And she made me think of women in a general way. Shit, if the hard-on I had was really for her, it would've been easy to do something about that. But I'd be damned if I was gonna jack off thinking about my mother. The idea never even entered my mind.

Besides, there was a shitload of static in my head about this real clear fact of her being pure Vietnamese. When I was fifteen, that whole problem caused me as much squirming as being horny. I couldn't even just sit there in my head and simply watch my mother on the beach without all that other crap coming up.

Like when her government john came up and sat on my other side. I had to figure out if I was going to get up and get away from him or just play it cool and put my mind out there on the horizon and to hell with him. But before I could figure out what to do, he said to me, "Thanh, you're a good boy."

I shot him a glance. He was turned around facing me and it didn't seem to be just an offhand remark. This seemed like the start of something bigger, and I was real suspicious of him, needless to say. It may have been the only time anybody other than my mother had said I was a good boy, and she only did it when she was in such a sloppy emotional mood that it always made me feel uncomfortable. I stayed where I was, but I didn't look at him. I studied the sea and waited to see what this guy was up to.

"Your mother has made some mistakes," he said. "But she's got a good young son."

It was a funny way to talk—it took me a moment to realize he'd just referred to me. I glanced over at him and he was looking at me very carefully. He was making me nervous, and I thought again about jumping up and getting away from him.

He smiled. "Do I scare you?" he said.

"Sort of," I said.

"I'm not scary. The world's scary, but I'm not."

"You talk funny," I said.

"I guess I do," he said. "But I know some things, Thanh. Do you believe that?"

"Sure. Why not."

"Can I tell you something, and when I do, will you try to remember it?"

This was starting to bore me and I just shrugged.

"Okay," he said, and he paused like something real important was on its way. But all he said was "You're Vietnamese."

"Of course I am."

He smiled again. Then he spoke in a very quiet voice, very gentle, like he was talking to a very good boy. "Just remember it. Someday people may look at you and say that you're this or that, but you remember that you're Vietnamese. You could not be living on earth except for a hundred generations of mothers and fathers who were all Vietnamese. They're watching you and their blood is inside you and nothing at all can change that. Will you remember what I'm saying to you?"

I shrugged again, kept up the casual pose, but inside, my boredom was definitely gone. I was thinking about the blood of a hundred mothers and fathers being inside my body. This was a serious wrinkle on the horizon and I stared hard at this man who'd showed it to me.

He said, "Tell me you'll remember what I've said. Things are going to be hard for you and your mother sometime. For all of us. But this is what it's all been for. That we're Vietnamese." His hand rose and drew near my face, but he did not touch me. His voice grew softer still, hardly loud enough to be hard over the breakers. "We're all Vietnamese, no matter what your mother did in order to make a fine young son." His eyes moved beyond me and I followed them to my mother. She was lying very still. Her skin was dark and her feet were side by side, the insteps joined like a cupping of hands to hold a drink of water.

I rose up from my bed in Point Pleasant, New Jersey, and it was quiet down the hall and I stalked around the room in a sweat but without any clear idea about what I was feeling. All I knew was I didn't feel good about anything, not this heat, not this room, not the trees outside, not my fucking memories, not Kenneth Hatcher, not me—especially not me, I realized, and that was a little bit of a shock because I'd always figured fuck everybody else, at least I was okay. But I didn't feel good at all about me.

I had to piss and that made me mad and I yanked open the door and stormed down the hall. The bathroom door was closed. There was a noise inside and then the door suddenly opened and there was Point Pleasant Tracy. She reared back and gasped, and I liked scaring her. She had a bath towel wrapped around her, and her tits, which were very large, were bulged up on either side of the knot on the towel. She started babbling about oh it's just you, you scared me to death, and she was juking around a little like she was real anxious to get by. I didn't do anything to help her. In fact, I put out my hand and leaned on the doorjamb and deliberately blocked her way. She clutched at the knot on the towel and gave me a stupid little smile, and I looked her up and down real slow, not because I was so interested in her, but because I wanted to make her sweat a little.

She had a splash of freckles right below her throat that dribbled down into her cleavage and out of sight behind her fist. I could see that fist tighten on the knot as my eyes stopped there. The towel was black and it made her look like she had no blood in her at all, she was so white. I looked down at her legs—she had skinny ankles and I didn't know how they could ever balance all that tit up above—and then I looked at her feet.

The toes were chubby and square at the tips and the nails were ragged, like she tore them when they got too long. Her feet made me angry. They were ugly and they made her ugly, even if she did have big tits, and I looked her in the eye real steady and said, "You were making a lot of noise tonight."

She kind of giggled, and for a moment I thought of Mrs. Kenneth, what she would have done if I'd confronted her like this. Slapped the shit out of me, maybe, at least told me to mind my own fucking business. But this Tracy just giggled and fidgeted with the knot.

"Look," I said. "Do you know the truth about him?"

This made the giggling stop. She narrowed her eyes at me and said, "Who?" though she knew damn well.

"Kenneth," I said. "The guy you were making all that noise with. Why do you think I live here? Look at my face. You can see what kind of girls he really likes. He likes the Asians. You know how fat you're getting. He likes the slim little Asian girls. He talks about that all the time. He's got a Vietnamese girl who he's planning right now to bring over here to live with him. He won't tell you about it and he'll lie when you ask him, but he's pulling strings in Trenton and in Washington to bring this girl he really loves over here. For him, fucking you is just slumming. Look at the face in front of you and you'll know what I'm saying is true. Look at my goddamn face. You're just the worm in the tequila, bitch."

Well, a lot of the words that came out took me by surprise too. But it was nothing to the shock on the face of Point Pleasant Tracy. She shoved past me and she felt soft for that flash of a moment and she smelled like soap, a nice smell, but I didn't care, it only meant it would be easy for her to find somebody else that would make her moan around in the night. I still thought she was ugly, in spite of that soft rush past me and the smell. I thought of the jagged nails on her square-tipped toes and I stepped into the bathroom and pissed and then went back to my room to wait for the fallout.

There were voices down the hall, but I couldn't make out any words, didn't care to, either. I suddenly didn't give a damn about Kenneth and whoever his woman was this month. I lay on the bed and curled up before the wall and my face burned with the thought of that stupid and really unexpected lie about Kenneth bringing some Vietnamese woman to America. Did I have Nghi in mind when I'd said that? It was all that childhood memory crap just before going to take a piss. Nghi was still there in my head, is all. I didn't really care anymore. "Fuck no," I said aloud to the wall. And anyway, it was a good lie to tell Point Pleasant Tracy. I could hear her crying now. Kenneth's ears were probably about to fall. Is it right for you to believe a half-breed punk kid instead of me?

I thought of the face I kept forcing Tracy to look at. My face. The hooded eyes, the roundness of the Far East, a foreigner here on the Jersey Shore. And the pudgy government man's hand rose in my mind and his face drew near, round as the sun over the South China Sea, and he said, You're Vietnamese, and we both looked at my mother and she was beautiful. She turned her face to us and smiled, a wide, brilliant smile. Vietnamese have good teeth.

It was a long while before my door opened. The voices had stopped maybe an hour ago. I hadn't been able to hear if somebody left the house. Not that I tried, really. I think I even dozed off. I was exhausted. But finally my door opened and I stayed where I was, facing the wall, and then the edge of the bed sagged. Kenneth had sat down. He waited in silence, and already I was a little surprised. I guess I expected him to charge in and give me a long speech leading up to some kind of physical punishment. I figured if anything was worth some whacks on the butt from Kenneth, scaring off his big-titted bimbo with lies would be. Even if I was getting pretty old for that kind of thing.

But Kenneth had crept into the room very quietly and now he was sitting there and not saying a word. I didn't make a sound either. There was nothing to say. I hoped Tracy was gone, but I couldn't figure out why I should give a damn about that. Tracy or somebody else. Somebody or nobody. Why should I care? Let Kenneth fuck around the way he wanted to.

I realized that my hand was moving. I was tracing a path with my fingertip through the stipples of plaster. At the moment I realized this, Kenneth spoke. "She's gone," he said.

I didn't say anything. I just drew my hand back from the wall real slow and laid it on the bed.

"I don't think she'll be back," Kenneth said.

I listened real hard to hear some kind of anger or disgust in his voice, but I found none of that. I didn't know what was there, and so when he spoke he caught me way off guard. He said, "Sometimes I must seem as bad as your mother." Then the son of a bitch actually apologized to me and crept back out of the room.

Kenneth could surprise you now and then. I guess that's another thing there should be some question about. How long can you hang around with your father—your real jump-in-her-hole-and-make-this-thing father—and keep on wanting him to step in dog shit or fall down a flight of concrete steps or at least just get the fuck out of your life? After all, he could surprise you now and then. Like when he apologized because he figured he was acting like a whore. Or when he took me down to the beach at Coney Island one day.

We tried everything, once. I guess he really wanted to find something we could do together that would make us feel like we had a normal little American father-and-son thing. We had one trip to the Bronx Zoo, one trip on the Staten Island ferry and then to the Statue of Liberty, one baseball game in Yankee Stadium, one hike in the woods in some mountains upstate somewhere in New York. Stuff like that. I guess if I'd come back from any of that and said, Wow that was fun, Dad, let's do it again, we would've done it over and over and Kenneth would've been a happy man, he would've gotten his money's worth out of his trip back to Vietnam. He would've gotten the son he wanted. And I would've gotten the father that I was supposed to want. Every kid wants a father. Right? But I just couldn't get up for all that. I think I tried. Every once in a while I think I wanted to just put a smile on this face of mine and say Wow Dad or some such shit, but all these little trips depressed me too much to fake anything. Maybe if you took a kid who spent his first six years hiking in the woods or riding ferry boats or going to baseball games or whatever and then dropped him into an alley in Saigon with people up on their back balconies cooking bún bò and with a big old scrounged ammunition crate sitting over next to the stairwell by a motorcycle everybody knew was stolen and with half a dozen other kids hanging around waiting to take off with you and there's nobody in all the dark twists of the alleys or out in the bustle of the streets who can tell you what to do, if you put one of your Point Pleasant kids in that kind of place and expected him to feel good there, expected him to feel like a kid, you know, like the world fit into him somehow and he could have some fun with it, then you'd get the same reaction that I was giving old Kenneth.

Anyway, he took me to Coney Island once. I was maybe nine or so. I must've been nine, because the wife had been gone for a while but Kenneth was still just getting into the swing of things with the girls. I remember sitting on the beach and behind me was the boardwalk and all the rides, the voices over loudspeakers saying to step right up and all that shit. One or two of the rides were good, but I was in some weird sort of mood that day, I guess. I was always in a weird mood when we made these little formal attempts to be something to each other.

I sat on the sand and it was a gray day. The sky was gray, the water was gray, the sand was gray. It had all turned gray soon after we arrived and I figured Kenneth would silently blame me and my mood for it. I sat on the damn sand and there were all these bodies around me. It was gray, but it was real hot and the beach was packed with people that I didn't want to even look at. And out on the water was a big old oil tanker, some jagged oil smear of a boat moving out there right at the edge of the horizon. An asshole art teacher once told me not to draw my boat at the top of the water, that the boat was nearer than the horizon and it was wrong to put it there. But that's how the thing looked from where I was sitting on the beach. Just the straight line of the horizon and the boat sitting right there on top. An ugly fucking boat. I guess I was thinking about the white sands of Vũng Tàu and the flash of sun on the water and the sampans out there with their crescent sails and my mother lying very still, almost near enough for me to smell the salt water and the sun-tan lotion on her, and Coney Island was a shit-hole compared to that. Then right in front of me some fat woman was dragging a little kid past and I looked away. Kenneth was sitting beside me. I'd almost forgotten him. He'd been real quiet for a while. He hadn't started bringing dates with him on our little trips yet, so it was just him and me and a beach full of strangers. He seemed to be looking right through the fat lady going past. I kept staring at him, at the gray smear of the late afternoon beard on his cheeks, and there didn't seem to be anything in particular in my head. Not that I was aware of. I just stared at this man who was my father and finally, as if he knew I'd been doing this all along, he turns his face to me, real slow. I don't look away. I just wait and he looks at me and his eyes don't have any pull in them at all. They're sort of flat. No demands, no accusations, no expectations, just sort of flat and maybe a little sad. Not that I have any feeling about that. I just look at him and he looks at me.

Then he says, "How you doin', pal?"

This was nothing real new. He'd always used little names for me. He tried a lot of them, like trying new places to take me, I guess. I didn't feel like his pal and he couldn't have felt like mine, since that kind of thing has to go both ways. But this time when he called me pal I thought I heard something in his voice that wasn't just an effort to say the thing that would make all this whole father-and-son stuff turn out the way he thought it should. He sounded like he was wishing for something. He needed a pal and he wished I really was it. I'd heard that sound in kids, already. Some of the kids that were real bad-off in the alleys, some of the lepers or a Cambodian kid I knew once who had real dark skin and who the other kids called người đen, the black one. You always knew when a leper kid or this Cambodian talked to you and called you some familiar name that he was trying out a wish with that name. And that's what this white American adult with some big fucking important job and a big house and car sounded like to me, and needless to say I was a little surprised.

And once in a while with the kids, if you were in a mean mood and because you knew what was behind their words, when one of them called you something like pal, you might say something casual back to him and call *him* pal. I'm not proud of this kind of thing, you understand. People can be real bad to each other, even kids, even me. I'm no fucking angel. And the leper kid or whoever would always react so that you knew for sure about all the longing in his calling you pal in the first place. Anyway, I try it on Kenneth, just to see if I'm hearing right. I say, "I'm doin' fine, pal," and I'm right. His eyes get real big and he squares around to me and it's like he's about to grab me up in his arms with the next thing he says, no matter how trivial it is. And that's just how those certain kids in the alleys acted. And what was next for me was to just coldly back off. Because you're not really feeling anything anyway, see. So there's nowhere for this to go. And it was the same with Kenneth. I was real interested to see him acting like this, but there wasn't a goddam thing I was feeling about it except that. Just some goddam curiosity. Sure I wish there'd been some other feeling right then. Things would've been a lot easier for me as well as him. But there was nothing. Kenneth had surprised me. That's all it was.

And you understand, it happened more than twice. But it would always happen when things had gotten so lonely or so boring or so—I don't know what to call it—*foreign*, maybe, that when the surprise came, all I could do was see it and say to myself, What a fucking surprise, and then it would all get heavy again with the boredom and the loneliness and I'd just get angry at the son of a bitch, even more angry at him than if he'd been one clear thing, one stupid American in a big house who figured he could own anything he wanted, instead of this guy who could seem so meek sometimes, so goddam vulnerable. It wasn't easy, all this, and finally I'd had enough.

About a year after I'd had my little scene with Point Pleasant Tracy things got real bad. Not only at home but at school too. I haven't mentioned school much because it doesn't amount to more than a few rat turds anyway. Well, that's my first reaction when I think of school, but I guess it helped keep me from going crazy and one day just running into the breakers on the Jersey Shore and disappearing. Not school itself, but the work, learning. I was a real good student, like I said before. But I kept that to myself. Though I couldn't keep it from my teachers.

They'd call me in after class, or the counselor would sit me down in his glass cage next to the principal's office, and his leatherette picture frames would be all over his desk and the bookcase behind him, and his all-American family was smiling away, throwing bone-eating radiation all over the office with those smiles.

You could always see through the counselor or whatever teacher was talking to me privately. They'd start off making their eyes slide around the room as they harumphed and squirmed and doled out all those supportive things about how outstanding my work was, but when they got around to the concerns they had about my emotional well-being, about the kind of kids I chose to hang around with, kids who weren't on my level at all, then you could see how their eyes snuck back to my face, and once they got there, they stayed, fixed on this face that must have seemed so strange to them.

I read that in Vietnam we're called children of dust. That's how the teacher's fixed gaze was. Like this kid sat down in front of you that wasn't skin and bones and blood but dust, something scraped up from the ground and shaped wondrously into this creature that looked at first glance like a human being, but my god it's made of dust. Now dust isn't slime or shit or something like that. A child of dust won't usually get looks like you're something disgusting. Maybe in Hô Chí Minh City, but not usually here. There's even a kind of wonder about the look you get. How did such a thing as dust, which is so light and apt to blow away and scatter invisibly into the wind, how did it take this shape, just like a person, though it's real clear just by looking that there's something different here. That's what was in the eyes of these people who were so worried about my emotional well-being.

Now when I say that I don't usually get looks of disgust, I'm talking about from the people who are supposed to be running the show, the teachers and counselors and all of them. The asshole all-American teenagers are another thing altogether. They're able to find just about anybody disgusting. If you're half American and half

Vietnamese, that's a pretty good invitation for their contempt. Not that it was constant. The ones who make a life out of hassling somebody usually go after the ugly ones (I'm odd, but not ugly; Norma the would-be Nicole thought I was pretty good-looking and I'm not gonna argue with her, since she finally got her a real wide sample to compare me with). The ugly ones they go after, and the smart ones (they got me there, too, though they never did dream just how smart I was) and the nerdy ones (even if the nerdy ones aren't smart and if you look at them close you can see that they're not even close to ugly). But I did get my share of shit. I'm just glad a word like "manifest" never popped out of my mouth or I never would've gotten off the hook.

But I'm talking too much about something that isn't important. I seem to drift when it's time to get to the tough changes. Like when I was plucked out of Vietnam. Or like this change I'm talking about now, when I was about to run off. It did start at school, though. In the strangest way, if you stop and think about it. I got really really pissed off at somebody, and I guess even now I don't know if I understand it.

I was late getting into one of my classes. American history, I think it was. I'd been caught smoking in the john with Sanchez. Sanchez was a little guy I'd been hanging around with since eighth grade or so. He was the guy who told me about margaritas and the worms in tequila. But that was in the lunchroom where he told me that. We made some small talk in the lunchroom, but mostly we'd just smoke together, after school out under a big oak tree just off campus or in the john just about anytime during the day. When we smoked together we'd never say much, but he'd pace around and shake his head yes a lot, like we were saying things that he really agreed with.

I don't want to make him sound crazy or anything. Out on the Deuce he'd look crazy, I guess. But between us, it was all right. He didn't do that with anybody else, I think. I never saw him do it except when we were smoking in the john. I didn't know what to talk about with him and he didn't seem to need much. He'd look at me— maybe it was that face of mine that made him think things that made sense to him. I don't know. But it was like we said a lot, and it was funny, but I kind of felt it too. He was much smaller than me, a real little guy, and he was very dark and his skin was bad, pocked from something that had come and gone long ago. He looked a lot older, even though he was sixteen like me. And when he paced around shaking his head yes, I felt like I was agreeing with him about some damn thing. Maybe how it felt to be us.

But Sanchez was just the reason I was late getting into class that day. I came in and I gave my late slip to Mr. Brandt, an I'm-just-one-of-the-guys shoulder-thumper about Kenneth's age who kept bringing up Vietnam in his history lessons and shooting me significant glances. Brandt just sighed whenever I played the fuck-up, and he nodded me over to my desk.

That's when I saw the new girl. She was in the desk next to me. Already some of the all-American types were winking at me and you could hear their shitty little minds whirring away trying to think of things to do to me and this girl. She was Oriental. I figured Chinese, at first glance. And there was no confusion in this one. There was nobody's blood in this girl other than the generations of her Chinese ancestors. She had her face just slightly lowered, but as I approached, she glanced up at me and this was the round, flat face of a pure Chinese. Do you understand the Orientals' eyes don't really slant? It's an extra flap of skin called the epicanthic fold that makes you think that. You can see it in me a little bit, but this girl had the classic epicanthic fold. See, her ancestors originally evolved in a real cold part of the world and their eyes needed extra protection. But everybody on earth had that same fold on their eyes in the womb. Every last one of those purebred whites sitting in that classroom leering at this girl and me had eyes just like that when their mommas were still deciding whether or not to go after them with the end of a coat hanger.

I'm not really telling you what I felt about this girl, though. Her snow-bred face was just goddam gorgeous, it seemed to me. You try to figure out exactly what makes a feeling like that and you run into trouble. You think of these goddam labels, like smooth. Yes, her face was smooth, but it was so smooth it felt like I was looking at some really private part of her, like her face was something she had to close the curtains to expose, her face was something I could only peek at in secret through a crack in a bathroom door. So smooth that my fingertips itched to touch it, I wanted to run my forefinger along the sharp parting of her straight black hair and down her forehead and onto her nose and my finger would make a faint whistling sound, like I was running it down the surface of a mirror. And the more I realized how completely without compromise her face was, how clearly Chinese it was, the more I liked it.

I sat down and tried to play it cool, but I wanted to look at her so bad I couldn't sit still. Finally I opened my notebook on my desk and turned my face to the left-hand page but strained my eyes farther to the left, across the aisle to the girl in the desk. My eyes followed the long drape of her black hair as it fell over her shoulder and down her chest, and then I just stared at this perfect face. I watched her like that for a long time and she never glanced my way, which made me think she knew I was looking, and Mr. Brandt never called on me, though he must have realized I wasn't listening to him.

When the bell rang, I made sure I filed out of the classroom behind this girl. I didn't give a shit about the all-Americans and what they'd say, I had to talk with her. She turned to the right and though my own class was to the left, I followed her, catching up in a couple of steps and then coming alongside.

"Hi," I said. "You're new."

She glanced at me with her face still lowered a little bit and then she looked away. It wasn't like she was putting me off. It was just shy. Oriental girls are supposed to have this shyness thing bred into them, aren't they? It didn't bother me. I liked it. Besides, she spoke right away, so I wouldn't misinterpret the look. "Yes, I am," she said. It wasn't just a nod or even a simple "yes." I got a full "yes, I am." I have to say all this to make it clear that what started happening in me didn't have anything to do with being rejected or shit like that. It didn't even occur to me at the time that she might see me the same way the other kids did. She was coming from a different direction on that whole thing, but my face would've been just as strange to this girl who was pure yellow as it was to a kid who was pure white. But this only came to me much later. It didn't have anything to do with what happened next.

"What's your name?" I asked.

"Nancy," she said, and I fell back a step and inside I started to seethe.

"Nancy?" I said, and I could hear the shock in my own voice. It turned her face to me and I stepped up beside her again and I felt as if the biggest fucking skin-tailed rat in Saigon was trying to eat its way out of the center of my chest. *"Nancy?"*

You could see that she was getting a little concerned. She was looking at me closely now, and she said, "Yes. Nancy Lee."

"Lee," I said. "Right. Sure. Nancy." I knew now that it was anger driving the rat in the center of my chest. That motherfucking rat was pissed as hell. Here was this beautiful Chinese face watching me and she said her name was fucking Nancy, like she had long golden locks and lids on her eyes as round as knuckles. "How the hell did you get a name like Nancy?" I said.

"What's the matter with you?" she said, and her eyes were darting all around, like she was looking for an alley to duck down.

"What's the matter with *you?*" I demanded. "You're Chinese, aren't you? So why do you have a name like Nancy? Look at your face. You've got a great face. A perfect face. So why the fuck do you have to be Nancy?"

By now we've both stopped in the middle of the hallway and I'm shouting. But it's starting to dawn on me that I'm acting real crazy. The rat's gone now and the nesting hole he's eaten in the center of my chest is empty and threatening to collapse.

The girl has squared around to confront me and she says, "Who do you think you are? I like my name. My mother and father gave me that name. And I'm not Chinese. I was born in Hackensack."

With that, she turns as if she's going to walk away, but she's a smart girl, because before she goes she confronts me again. "So what's *your* name?" she says.

If I weren't so conscious at that moment of how really off-the-wall I'd been acting, I might have said it. As it was, the answer actually shaped itself in my mouth and when I realized it, it scared the shit out of me. Tony, I was going to say, which is just what this Nancy from Hackensack expected. I was ready to say my name was Tony.

So if saying it seemed real wrong to me, what the hell was I doing living it? That's what I was thinking when I walked into the house that evening. I'd stayed out till after dark, which was pretty late, since it was getting on in the spring and the days were longer. I didn't hang around with Sanchez or any of the other guys. I got out of the school building quick, before anybody could say anything to me about the scene in the hall, and I beat it down to a rusty old jetty on the beach. I walked along the shore and found a spot in the woods at the beach side of some big old house that had been empty for a couple of years.

I don't know if I was thinking anything out, exactly. I sure wasn't *planning* anything, like running away. I seemed mostly distracted by little things, like stripping the bark off twigs or throwing rocks into the surf, shit like that, little things that I guess just took up my head while something I wasn't real conscious of was going on in that rat's nest. I may have cussed out the horizon a couple of times when Hackensack Nancy got too close to the surface of whatever was going on, but mostly I was just waiting for something to happen. So when I walked into the house, I was starting to ask myself that question: what was I doing, living the life of Tony Hatcher?

Kenneth came to me in the foyer like he'd been worried. I'd been out this late a lot of times before. Half the time he wasn't even home by now himself. But tonight he met me in the foyer and he asked how I was. I figured somebody had called from school to worry at him over my crazy behavior. But I was wrong. He was kind of sheepish, and then who should appear at the door to the living room but Point Pleasant Tracy.

"Hi, Tony," she said, and she was sheepish too. She hadn't been in the house since my run-in with her a year earlier, and I suddenly realized why she and Kenneth were fidgeting and sneaking little glances at each other and generally acting like they were the ones who were sixteen and had just walked into the house after dark and after the dinner was probably cold. This made me smile, though I'm sure it wasn't a reassuring smile for these two. It was more like a sneer, I guess, because I knew they'd been seeing each other secretly since the little run-in. Trying not to upset me. Trying to make it look like Kenneth wasn't as bad as Nghi.

I sure wasn't in a mood to hang around the two of them, so I ignored Tracy, told Kenneth I'd make a sandwich later, and I went up the steps two at a time and I slammed the door behind me and stood in the center of my room. I didn't turn on the light. I stood there panting in the dark. I realized I was having a little trouble breathing. Maybe the run up the stairs, I thought. But I knew that wasn't it. It was some damn emotional shit. Fuck this, I thought.

Then there was a knock on my door. "Can I come in?" Kenneth said.

I wanted to say no. But I didn't want to just stand there hyperventilating in the dark either. I suddenly was real tired and the darkness on my eyes felt like it was made of sand, so I groped my way to the chair at my desk and sat down. I turned on the light.

"Tony?" Kenneth said.

"Yeah," I said. "All right."

So in he creeps, looking guilty as hell, and he eases himself down onto the edge of the bed like he's got the worst case of piles anybody's ever had. I decide I'll take him off the hook right away, because this whole display seems pretty stupid to me. "Look," I say, "I can figure this out. You and Tracy have been hanging around on the sly. I don't give a shit. You can screw who you want."

Looking back I can see how he misread me at that point. The tone of my voice was saying, This whole thing really bores me, I don't fucking care about you and your life, you don't mean a thing to me and your guilt over this is ridiculous. But that's not what Kenneth was hearing. He was listening to the same tone in my voice and hearing, You've really let me down, I depend on you for stability and a clear sense of right and wrong and here you are screwing around like my mother and maybe you're going to abandon me the way she did. That's what Kenneth was hearing, and that's the impossible thing about people trying to talk to each other, because if you imagine yourself inside Kenneth's head, knowing as little as he knew about me and never figuring out how to go to the source for the truth, then you can see how logical it all seemed to him.

He says, "Please hear me out, Tony. I know I've told you bits and pieces of this, but I want to say it all at once so you can understand real clearly why you're here. I feel very stupid sometimes because I just took for granted that you could be plucked out of your home and family, such as it was, and taken to the other side of the world by a stranger who says he's your father, and you'd naturally understand why he did that."

At this point Kenneth stands up, pulls a chair from the corner of the room, and sits down right in front of me. No more piles. No more meekness or guilt. He's working himself up for this, his D.A. thumbs twitching for vest pockets but having to settle for his belt loops. The man seems like pure bullshit to me now, and he says, "You understand, don't you, that I love you?"

His hooked thumbs make this declaration even more bizarre than it would be on its own, which still would be plenty bizarre. These aren't words that Kenneth is used to speaking. Sometimes, though, he's sharp. Just like he knows what I'm thinking, he explains, "Tracy said I should be sure and tell you that. Not that she had to convince me about the feeling. I always have the feeling. But she says I should come out and tell you. She's a sensitive woman, Tony. She really is." For this his thumbs unhook and he leans forward.

"You see," he says, "I've always thought it was clear to you that I love you. I figured I'd proved that already. I did it by going back to Vietnam to get you. Vietnam was a terrible place for me, Tony. It was for a lot of Americans. But I knew you were there. My son. My own flesh and blood. It was real easy for so many men just to ignore something like that. They had children in Vietnam, but it was easy to forget. That was over and done with for them, even if there was a life on the other side of the world that existed because of what they did, that carried a part of them with it. It's hard to explain. But I came back for you even though I hated that country and feared it. That's a powerful proof of love."

He pauses, but it clearly isn't for himself. He's watching me real close, waiting for all this to sink in, I guess. All that stuff about fatherhood should have impressed me. He was probably right about how easy it was for most of those Americans to just walk away. But the only thing that jumps out of what he's said is that he hates Vietnam. I feel the same crazy rush of anger that I felt with Nancy earlier in the day. The rat is back, but this time I don't want to lose control.

So I hold real still, keep my face calm. I'm not going to say a thing. Kenneth keeps waiting and watching me, and then he looks a little closer and you can see his mind whirring away in there and I know he's way off the track. But what the hell can I say to set him straight?

Then he says, "But I know a child needs a mother, too. I'm sure you've wondered many times why your mother never came to America. It's not a pleasant subject, Tony. I hoped it would just go away, but I guess that was wishful thinking on my part. I didn't know how to explain all this to you when you were younger. But you're old enough now, and you're wise beyond your years, I think. So I'm going to tell you straight. Your mother was . . ." Kenneth starts groping for a word and even the rat in my chest stops scrabbling around and rears up on his back feet, nose twitching, waiting for something juicy.

But Kenneth turns gutless for a moment. He says, "Well, she wasn't really interested in coming to the U.S. She wouldn't have fit in here at all. That was clear to me, and it was clear to her too. She was . . . Listen, Tony, you were just a little kid. There were things that you wouldn't pick up on. Your mother had a drug problem."

If anything showed on my face at that moment, it was, You asshole, what six-year-old on the streets of Saigon wouldn't know if his mother was on drugs. But the asshole read it wrong again.

"It's true, Tony. And I don't think she really wanted to do anything to try to get clean. Do you understand? And it's worse than that. You've got to understand why I would come and get you and not try to keep her with you. Your mother . . . It's hard for me to say this, but you're going to have to know this and get through it so you can have peace of mind. Your mother was a . . . prostitute."

The word came out soft, flat, he seemed to have no feeling about it at all, and I sounded that word out in my head and it was a pansy-ass word, it made me mad. If the son of a bitch banged up a whore and hated her for it, he should at least have the balls to call her a whore and do it with feeling. "Prostitute?" I say.

"Yes," he says, and he kind of ducks his head like he's embarrassed.

"You mean a bargirl?" I say. "Did you meet her in a bar?"

"Yes. In a bar. She was a bargirl. That's where I met her."

"A whore, you mean. A bargirl's a whore."

"Well," he says, and I can see he's starting to breathe a little faster, "not all bargirls are whores."

"Sure they are, for a price."

"I don't know about that."

"But my mother was. You said she was a prostitute."

By now Kenneth's got some color in his damn face and his hands are twitching and he says, "Yes, she was a prostitute."

"A whore."

"Yes. She was a whore," and now he's found a word that's got some feeling in it and I'm getting pumped up too.

"A whore and a druggie," I say.

"She was a whore and a druggie," he says.

This comes out of Kenneth's mouth like spit, and the more Kenneth hates my mother, the more I hate him, and the more I hate him, the more I want to hate him, and I say, "You couldn't live with a whore and a druggie."

"No man could," Kenneth says and he jumps to his feet.

"You hated her."

"Can you see why I couldn't bring her back here, Tony? Can you imagine how much I loved you to go back to a woman like that to get you? And she took money for you. All I did was tell her what she was and offer her money and she took it. She sold you to me, Tony. Sure I hated her. You would've come to hate her too."

At this I jump up and it's like I'm in slow motion, my chair falling back and my chest filling up like I've been pumped full of hot sticky air, and before the chair can hit the floor behind me my hand is rising and doubling into a fist and I shift a little, square around in front of this long face, and I want to brace myself, to get a good solid place beneath me so I can hurt this man, but my fist is way ahead of me and it's already leaping for this man's face and it's weak, too weak, I want to hurt him bad, but I can't make the fist move fast enough. The blow glances off the side of his head and then Kenneth's arms are around me.

I don't remember all the stupid scuffling and shouting that followed, but I was finally left on my bed, curled up and facing the wall. Kenneth had been real gentle and he'd talked real softly and he'd said he was sorry, that it would be all right, that I'd needed to do this and he was happy that I had. Shit like that. I was facing the wall and I thought to trace the path in the plaster, but I didn't have the strength to lift my arm. I just lay there and I probably already knew what I was going to do.

I must have, because when Kenneth comes back into the room later and says, "Are you okay?" I answer, "Yes."

He says, "I'm sorry for losing my temper about your mother. It was my fault, what happened."

I don't say anything about this. Kenneth already seems a long way away.

"I've got very good news," he says, and the bed sags. "I hope you'll think it's good news. I'm sure you will in time, because what we went through an hour ago just shows me very clearly what it is that you need."

I knew it before he even said it, and it was all I could do to keep from laughing. He said, "Tracy and I are going to get married."

I just curled tighter and put my hand over my mouth to keep any sounds from coming out. I was already packing in my head and figuring out how to put my hands on the cash that Kenneth kept stashed around the house, and finally he patted me on the shoulder and left.

Tracy at least gave me a theme for the good-bye note. I wrote, "So long, Kenneth. Thanks for the education. Since by the time you read this I'm long gone and for good, you won't have to marry fat Tracy so I can have a mother. It wouldn't have worked anyway. I'm Vietnamese."

FIVE

◆
◆

This wasn't the first time I'd run away. I'd done it once before in Saigon. I guess it wasn't too long before Kenneth showed up, because my mother was already strung out pretty bad. I think I said before that I didn't know at the time what her problem was, but come to think of it, I had to. I knew damn good and well what was going on when I took off one day with about a thousand piastres I got from her purse and some almond cookies and an extra pair of underpants and a Pepsodent toothbrush all folded into a big handkerchief. I knew she was a goddam druggie. I'd seen enough of it around the streets and the kids talked about it a lot and once I'd even had a drag on a joint of what I was told was real good GI pot. And that made it seem even more ridiculous to me, because I hated the feeling I had with the drug floating around inside me, hated losing my head, hated having my insides change. If something that wasn't part of you—smoke or pill or powder or whatever—could change what's inside you, then that's it, man, you might as well be dead. It wasn't *me*, those drugs. It wasn't me, and if it wasn't me, then fuck it. My insides were my own.

That's probably why I was trying to run away in Saigon. Nghi was getting pretty weird and she was getting inside of me. I was sad all the time. I ran one afternoon after she said she was going out and she gave me some piastres for soup for supper from the lady at the corner. I got the thousand piastres from her when she was taking a piss. I was digging my hands around in her purse and listening to the spiky hard stream of her piss and I could imagine her on the pot having trouble sitting up straight. A thousand piastres isn't very much, mind you. Just a few bucks. But it was all she had, and it wasn't like I'd thought this out real clear. I just wanted to take what I could and get the hell out.

So I took off after she left. I even stopped at the mouth of our alley and watched her up the street getting into a xích-lô, and I wondered how she was going to pay. The driver looked to be about a hundred years old and I figured she didn't have anything he could use and there'd be a big fight. When he pulled away, blue smoke from the two-stroke engine filled the air and it looked like the driver had been some little old wizard who'd just made my mother disappear in a cloud of smoke. He'd taken her off to her terrible fate in the land of the dead. I even stood and watched for a moment till the xích-lô was visible again and the old man was just the driver, bent over his handlebars.

My mother was headed to the center of town and so I took off in the other direction, which shows how little I'd thought this thing out, because in that direction was Cholon. That was the Chinese part of the city, and the Vietnamese never could quite get used to the Chinese, seeing as we had a couple of thousand years of history of being conquered by them and then throwing them out only to be conquered again. And there were the kids' stories about the Chinese catching stray Vietnamese children and putting them into a real special dish that all the Americans were crazy about but didn't know what it was they were eating. Or maybe they did. Some of the tales said that the high-ranking Americans—the generals and the embassy people—all were in on the secret ingredient, and they loved that soup. One of the little girls around the alley didn't have a left arm and she almost never came out of her apartment and the word was that she'd lost that arm in Cholon and it ended up in a bowl of soup fed to the U.S. Ambassador himself and it was so good he had a special detachment of C.I.A. agents out looking all the time for this girl so he could eat some more of her.

I don't know how much of that I believed, but when I realized I was heading for Cholon, I turned down a side street and headed for the river. I guess I already knew this wasn't going to work out. Even at six I couldn't kid myself for long. But I went down to the river and sat on the bank and ate the almond cookies and watched the gunboats go by, and none of the sailors waved at me from the boats. It was just the Vietnamese fighting at that point and they all looked real nervous.

I sat by the river for a long time, knowing I'd be going back home. I tried to decide if I should spend any of the thousand piastres and finally figured that she owed me at least that. So I took a long stroll along Chương Dương, which followed the river, till I found a nougat seller, and I ate nougats till my head was spinning and my mouth was puckering. Then, when it was real dark and real late, I zigzagged my way back home along the most indirect route I could figure out. She was asleep, though at least she was alone.

The next day she didn't say a word but bumped around the room like she was blind, and she kept smacking her lips and going into the bathroom and cupping her hands under the running water and sucking it up with a sound that I hated even more than the sex sounds. Still, she never let on that I'd done anything unusual. So for a week I pestered her to play the memory game. She kept waving away the suggestion, putting me off, but I kept it up and finally she must've figured she'd never get any peace until she did this thing.

So she asked me in a thin little voice, What's the nicest thing you remember about yesterday? And I said, Last week, ask me about last week. She kind of shrugged and she went through the motions. What's the nicest thing you remember about last week? she said. And I said, It was when I stole a thousand piastres from you and ran away to Cholon and snuck into a Chinese restaurant in some stinking little street and I hid and watched them carving up a little girl and throwing chunks of her into a big kettle and then they saw me and I had to run like hell to get away and the only reason I came back here was because I had to hide out or I'd end up in a fucking Chinese soup.

She didn't believe me. That was pretty clear. She kind of smiled, and I could've kicked myself for laying it on too thick. Of course she didn't believe the soup part, but that way she didn't have to believe any of it.

"It's true," I said. "Not the soup part, but I did run away from you and I did steal from you. Didn't you miss the thousand piastres?"

"That was okay," she said, and the little smile was still there, just at the corners of her mouth. Her lipstick was uneven. One side of her mouth looked a little larger than the other. "Did you get some nougats with the money?" she asked, like she hoped I did.

"Yes," I said, and I was feeling real sorry for her all of a sudden. So I said, "And you, Momma, what's the nicest thing you remember from yesterday?" The little smile vanished and there was only her uneven mouth and I knew right away that there was nothing, and I said, "Last week. Anytime last week. What's the nicest thing?"

She turned her face away, though I didn't get the feeling she was doing any thinking. It was funny, but it made me remember the little girl with one arm. I was prowling along the backstairs balcony of her building one day not even thinking of her, I was just prowling. But I passed the door of her apartment and I looked in and I stopped. She was standing in the room and she didn't have a shirt on. She wasn't much older than me, so she didn't have any tits yet or anything, but there was her stump, naked and smooth as a teacup, and I stopped and stared and she turned her face away just like my mother turned her face when I asked her to remember. I stood there staring at the little girl and she never said a word and my mother didn't either.

And that was that. And what's important right now is that I had a couple of hundred dollars in my pocket and a duffel bag with more than just almond cookies and a toothbrush. I'd thought this one out a little better. When I left Kenneth's house in the middle of the afternoon following the announcement of his engagement, I knew enough to avoid any public transportation till I got far away from Point Pleasant. I had it in my mind to go to Montreal. I figured since I wasn't American, there was no sense in staying in America. I'd read that there were a lot of Vietnamese in Montreal. That's what I was, after all. And it even amused me to think that I'd be running to the same place where a whole bunch of American draft dodgers ran in order to avoid ending up in Vietnam. I was going to go to Montreal, find the Vietnamese community, blend in, get a job, and on and on like that.

I wonder how it would've turned out if I'd actually gotten across the border. Could I have convinced the Vietnamese that I was one of them? They had eyes to see. Fucking blend in. I doubt it. It would've been fuck vous, child of the dust, and the bus you rode in on. But I didn't consider any of that in my flight from Point Pleasant. I just walked briskly on, snapping twigs under my feet and scattering squirrels all along the way, the little fuckers running halfway up their trees and twitching their fuzzy tails at me.

I had a bus in mind, but it was in New York City. There were buses to Canada out of the Port Authority Bus Terminal, I knew, and as I thought about hitching a ride into New York, I realized that I was kind of a spectacle striding down the streets of Point Pleasant with my duffel bag over my shoulder. I tried to stay on the deserted streets and I cut down some alleys and across a park and through some commercial lots, and finally I ended up on a strip of State Highway 35. I tried for about an hour to hitch a ride, hanging back and turning away when Jersey plates went by and thumbing like crazy when I spotted an out-of-state license approaching.

Finally a guy in a van with Virginia plates stopped. He was pretty young, with bad teeth and a soft Virginia accent ("I aboot went past you," he said). I made it a point not to say anything about myself, sticking to vague grunts when he asked me questions, and he soon just drove in silence. But the first thing he asked me was my name, and I said, "Thanh."

I thought maybe this would all go pretty quickly. After a drop-off at an office building up the highway—he worked for a computer software firm—the driver got onto the Garden State Parkway. I watched out the window as I raced away from the past ten years and I was thinking about how this state was some fucking garden, full of oil tanks and refinery smoke and witch grass growing out of Mafia carcasses.

But it turned out the Virginian wasn't actually going into the city.

He stopped in Hoboken and then was heading upstate. By the time I got somebody to tell me where to catch a bus across the Hudson and I stood around in front of some gas station in Hoboken for an hour counting the damn ding-dings behind me as the cars came and gassed up and went, it was getting to be early evening. Eventually I found out I was on the wrong corner, and at last I caught a bus that fumed its way in the dying light through some ragged-ass streets and then into the Lincoln Tunnel.

There was one nice moment, though, coming up over a viaduct just before the tunnel. I pressed my nose to the window and took in a long swoop of a view of New York spiking up across the river and starting to light up. I thought: Kiss my ass, you whore; you look good from here, but I'm getting the hell out of this country. It was a nice little nasty feeling and it was nicer and nastier because it came from some part of me that really loved the look of that ragged skyline going black against the sky. Then we were in the tunnel and it was full of this yellow light that made me look like I had a bad liver, and the tunnel was real tight, a fucking gun barrel, and I kind of slumped into the seat and closed my eyes.

I looked again when the lights inside the bus came on and we were out of the tunnel and corkscrewing up a ramp into the Port Authority terminal. The darkness looked greasy out there and down on the street I saw a flash of red neon saying Budweiser, like in the Texas Girls Bar, and the bus kept spiraling and the street disappeared and with just the darkness of the ramp outside I noticed the face-oil imprint of my nose on the window. I touched it with my forefinger and rubbed it out. Not a trace, I said to myself, though it instantly seemed silly. I imagined Kenneth dusting every bus in New York for noseprints to try to find me. I smiled at that, but the thought turned into a real question about how much Kenneth would do to try to keep what he figured was his. I decided I'd done pretty well so far covering my trail. I felt as safe from him as I did from the guys in the metal and glass enclosures that were passing now outside the bus window. These guys were all in suits and their shoulders were slumping and some of them were reading newspapers that they'd folded into tight little rectangles no bigger than the pictures of their wives and kids on their desks. I guess they didn't want to stick out of their own little spaces. They were safe with their elbows tucked into their sides. Nobody like that could touch me. If Kenneth commuted on a bus, I knew he'd fold his newspaper just like that.

Then the bus wheezes to a stop and I grab my duffel bag and get out quick, stepping into the hum of bus engines and the smell of exhaust. I follow the line of passengers down some steps under the belly of this big fat snake of a duct and everybody's moving like they know just where they're going, but that's okay because so do I. We make a hairpin turn and the snake can't turn as fast as me and he runs into the wall and I float on down the steps with some white girl on a poster at the bottom lifting her glass of iced tea to toast me on my way and I give her round eyes a sneer as I pass.

And I'm taking everything in. Ever since I saw New York just before going into the tunnel I've been taking everything in, every little thing, and I feel a kind of racing in my chest, like I'm running real fast, though I'm not, I'm walking slow and it feels good to walk slow right now, like it's my own pace and I've got all the time I need to do whatever I want.

Then I'm in this concourse and I stop altogether. There's people rushing past, heading for the buses. It's maybe six-thirty now and it's still the end of the rush hour and these guys have their ties loosened and they're sweating as they jog past. Some goddam dentist-office music is coming out of the walls, but even that doesn't really bother me. I take it in and watch the loose ties flapping past and I'm in no hurry.

I don't even care which way I go for now and I stroll off and soon I'm at a turning and there's a bar here and some woman is laughing inside. Bargirl, I think, but the laugh is low-pitched and phlegmy. American. I imagine an American bargirl with curly phony blond hair and ugly feet and she's maybe six feet tall and she doesn't even think about her ancestors, doesn't even have a picture of her parents, doesn't even remember what their birth dates are, much less pray for them so they can go to heaven.

I can think like that without feeling I'm some hypocrite, because in my duffel bag I've got a picture of my mother. I never did quite go so far as to throw out the last picture. It's not a fancy portrait or anything. It's only a snapshot of her, taken by one of her men, I guess. She's in the left foreground, just her face and shoulders, and she's standing on the fourth-floor balcony of our apartment building, but you can't see the railing. You can just see her face and her bare shoulders, and beyond her is the jumble of low, corrugated Saigon rooftops and farther out some higher, flat-roofed apartment buildings, and squeezed between a couple of tin houses you can even see a tree, one little puff of green in all of that, and Saigon just floats there behind my mother's face like it's coming out of her, like what you see is just her mind projected behind her. And her face is beautiful.

I want to find a place now, out of earshot of this goddam bar, and look at her face. So I take this turning in the concourse and I pass a bowling alley—a fucking bowling alley, of all things, where I can imagine the guys sweating in their business suits and bowling shoes, their loosened ties flapping over their shoulders as they run at the pins. Ahead, the concourse ends and there are suits and briefcases guttering into doorways leading to gates. But off to the right is a little empty stretch of wall and these people rushing past aren't seeing a thing and I go to a spot against the wall and I put down my bag and crouch beside it. My mother's in the pages of a book, "Madame Bovary"—I said I was smart, but it's not in French, it's some other guy's words, really.

I didn't look at her when I decided to run away. I just took her out of the bottom of a drawer and put her in a book without even glancing at her. I wasn't sure—here in the station I'm still not—what she had to do with all this. But here's her face and it's beautiful. This was when things were good with her, before the Americans had left, probably. Her eyes are clear, though I can see now that they're maybe a little troubled. She's beautiful here, but her face is mostly in shadow and there's no smile—not a trace of a smile. Her lips are full and barely reddened—she seems more schoolgirl than bargirl. I bring my face close to the picture, close to her face, and her hair is scattered softly on her shoulders and it seems more than ever that what is behind her—the clutter of Saigon—is something that has just sprung from her mind, because that's what's on her face. Her face says, You see what's really inside me; I'm not ashamed of it; I don't particularly like it, but there it is; I'm a lot more complicated than you ever dreamed. That's why her face is at once so beautiful and so empty of any smile, any attempt to charm the camera. She is what she is, and there is no apology and no shame and no self-pity and no regret. She is just this beautiful Vietnamese girl with the city that owns her spewing out of her head and she knows what she is and it's okay.

I stared at her face in the bus terminal for a long time, and then I put the photo back into the book and buried it in my duffel bag. It was time to move on. Time to go to Montreal. So I retraced my steps, went back past the stairwell with the girl and her iced tea, and up ahead was a sign that said Ticketing and I went on and found a deep well of space—the escalators down to the main concourse—and I didn't even stop at the balcony overlooking the concourse to do one of those power trips, standing and looking down on all the suits dashing around and the ladies with their Bloomie's shopping bags and me feeling superior. None of them talk about it, but that's something a lot of the guys who hang around the bus terminal like to do. Sooner or later all the toughs find their little perch up there and they kind of moon around telling themselves at least they're better than all those fools running around down there below them. But this was no pose for me. I just wanted to get the hell out. So I hit the escalators fast and went down them walking, making the steps even as they moved. It only took me a couple of seconds to decide to head toward the Eighth Avenue end, and it turned out that I'd guessed right because almost immediately I found the long-haul ticket windows.

No one was rushing around over here. There were Greyhound and Trailways windows and people were sitting on luggage and leaning against the walls and shifting slowly from foot to foot in the lines to buy their tickets. I didn't look too close at any of the faces because I didn't want anyone to look too close at me. And I sure as hell didn't feel in a small-talk mood. So I just got in the back of one of the Greyhound lines and I kept my face down and I moved when the people in front of me moved.

I did look out at the concourse once and see a Port Authority cop strolling by, and even though I was in the best possible place to throw off any suspicion, I did have a little flinch of concern about some cop seeing me and taking me for a runaway and collaring me till they could find out who I was. But I was a pretty big kid, as I said. I'd always be smaller than Kenneth, but hey, I was big for an Oriental and I could be taken for twenty, easy. And I was in this line that meant I had clear business at the bus station. I turned my back to the passing cop, faced the ticket window. There were only a couple of customers ahead of me now.

I thought about my money and dug it out of my jeans pocket. It was a wad of bills I'd collected from a metal box in Kenneth's desk and a false-spine book in his library and it wasn't until I had the money in my hand that I realized I was acting like some goddam hick showing his money in public. I'd already started this, so I pulled the wad to my chest and kind of bent over and took out five twenties. There was another hundred or so in smaller bills and these I stuffed back into my pocket. I folded the twenties and held them tight in my palm and then I sort of looked around to see who was watching, and I felt like an even bigger fool. A lot of fucking good it does to look around after flashing your money. Everything I learned in Saigon was about getting the stuff, not having it, so I was a little street-stupid about protecting money.

But still I looked around, and everybody I could see just seemed bored. The woman behind me in the line was reading a Daily Word. Over at the wall was a stack of bags and a guy with a tie but no coat and with an eagle tattoo on his forearm and his wife in curlers collaring a little kid who was straining to run out into the concourse. Down the wall from them was a girl with hacked hair and cutoff jeans sitting on a suitcase, her legs spread in what looked like weariness, and a couple of guys nearby—they were white, young, maybe twenty, heavy-lidded—were shooting her thighs little glances. I turned in the other direction and the Trailways line was full of blank faces looking every way but at me, and a bum was working his way up the line trying to get some money.

He was pretty bad off, this bum. His shoes were split open and there were skin sores running on his feet and his coat was spattered with pigeon shit and his fingers were swollen so that it looked like he couldn't move them. The hands just went out, palm up, but the fingers never moved, even when somebody put a coin in the palm. And he was telling everybody that he wanted the money so he could come up with a cure for cancer. That was his story. He was real close, he said. And nobody laughed at him or even told him to fuck off, they just ignored him, except for one woman with a black bun of hair and a mustache that I could see even from where I was standing, and she put the coin in his palm without a word. And I thought, Maybe she knows somebody who's dying of cancer and she's this real smart woman who can see past the man's face and hands and clothes and she knows he's telling the truth, knows that the way he looks is a lie, that in some flophouse just off Forty-second Street a cure for cancer is just a few quarters short of being completed.

He came to me and I gave him a quarter and, of course, he was exactly what he looked like, a bum, and his eyes were flat black, the color of the Thị Nghe River on the edge of Saigon near the Phan Thanh Giản Bridge, where a thousand families live along a thousand meters of riverbank. When I gave him the quarter he squinted hard at me, trying, I guess, to figure out what this face before him was, odder in this place even than his. I turned away from him and the line moved and soon I had a ticket to Montreal and some change from the hundred dollars and about three hours to wait for a bus.

I stepped out into the concourse and the rushing businessmen seemed to have thinned out a little bit and there was a man in a tuxedo and a woman with a corsage walking this way and another well-dressed couple not far behind them, and drifting across the space between them was a grimy old woman scratching her crotch furiously. She was doing this as she walked, and it looked like she was operating some kind of lever that was the thing that made her move. She was a skell, like the man begging quarters at the ticket line. It's a cop term, I think, but everybody around the Port Authority calls them that. Like a mope. A mope is a criminal. The mope's crime can be anything, just so it's done around the terminal or out on the Deuce. But a mope can be real well dressed. A skell is a bum or a bag lady, a grimed-up mope, though the skell's crime might just be the fact that he's a bum or a bag lady, somebody who gets in the way, dirties up the world, smells bad, looks bad. Not that I knew any of this as I was walking along that first night on my own in the city. I was just struck by the fancy couple and the old woman pulling her lever and how they were so close, moving along in the same place at the same time. I guess the rich in Saigon had always kept themselves apart more clearly. You'd see the Americans in among the poor sometimes, but they were there with some kind of purpose and they were always above it, somehow; but this was democracy in action that I was seeing in the Port Authority Bus Terminal, and both the couple and the skell were very natural about it. It was like I was seeing all this for the first time. I'd been in New York before. Kenneth had brought me in a few times to see the sights or whatever, but I hadn't seen a thing, really. On my own now, with a ticket to Montreal in my pocket, it was different.

That's how it all seemed to me. I was feeling really good for a few minutes. The world was new, or some such shit. But I wanted to find a locker to put my bag in for the next couple of hours. Maybe I could find a little food. I'd portion out the money carefully, but I could afford something to eat. And then I could maybe go out and walk around New York a little bit.

I moved on past the escalators that I'd come down earlier and I started looking for lockers. I had time and I was feeling loose and good and so I just sort of wandered around a bit, not even thinking about where I was going, my head full, I guess, of all that crap about finding a job in Montreal and turning into this Vietnamese guy among a whole colony of Vietnamese in a new land. Eventually I went down to a lower level and out a door and entered a taxi roadway that passed through the station. The place was full of car fumes and lounging cabbies and honking from Forty-first Street at the far end. I crossed the roadway and the sliding doors opened for me and inside was an old woman with a shopping cart stuffed with newspapers and plastic bags and old shoes and she said, "Get your fucking eyes out of there, half-breed."

I went on past her, just kept walking. I guess I should have known that she was too far gone to instantly find the right label for me even if she did read my face that fast, In fact, a long time later I saw this same woman at a newsstand on the suburban concourse chewing out a blind guy who worked there, a guy who you knew to look at was southern or maybe eastern European and as soon as he said a word you knew was Italian. The first thing she called him was "half-breed." Half Italian and half blind, I guess. But on that first night I just knew that she'd seen me for the fraud I was. And if the bag ladies of New York understood what I was, then the Vietnamese in Montreal would. There was nowhere to go and I was suddenly breathless and walking slower and slower.

This end of the corridor was quiet. There were no lockers, just a narrow passage in scab-red brick and nobody was around and I'm thinking that maybe there are no lockers at all. Now I'm passing a package express office but it's all closed up and dark, and ahead are some doors out to Ninth Avenue and I can hear traffic out there but it just makes this corridor seem even emptier and quieter. I get a grinding feeling in my groin and I'm moving real slow when my head says I should be getting my ass out of this place. Then behind me the old woman is cursing again and that makes me think everything's all right and back to normal and I even stop altogether to show myself what a baby I'm being.

Except I should've realized that the old woman was cursing because somebody else was passing her and heading this way and I should've realized that I couldn't show my money like I'd done and get away with it and as a truck passes up ahead there's an arm on my throat and the doors at Ninth Avenue plunge out of sight and the shadows of the ceiling flash past and I'm off my feet and falling backward and there's a pain rushing up from my throat like vomit and I'm twisted onto my belly and there's a splash of fire on my head and my eyes fill with gnats and then darkness.

SIX

⁚

You talk about your life and sometimes you get into a bind like this. You come up to a real big moment and you don't know what to say next. There's just too much. I could talk about what I'd be right now if I'd been a little smarter that night or a little lucky and I'd been able to get on that bus to Montreal with a few bucks in my pocket, like I planned. But you might be interested to know that whenever a thought like that has presented itself to me, my reaction has always been the same: Fuck that. That's no fucking way to live, thinking about what might've been. Things just *are*, that's all. You do what you can for yourself, but you don't have to believe in wandering souls and celestial drinks and incense for your dead kin to realize that somebody else is running this fucking show. Even that night, right after the mugging, I didn't waste more than a few seconds thinking about my goddam stupidity. It was done.

So I won't talk about that. I guess I could just take it one moment at a time as I woke up on the floor with my head full of studded snow tires on dry pavement. But fuck that. It hurt like hell and I finally got into a sitting position. Big fucking deal. I went through a quick check of losses and my pockets were pulled out and all the money was gone and the bus ticket too. I turned and after the corridor stopped spinning around I saw my duffel bag dumped out nearby. I moved over there and my head seemed to be calming down a little bit. Maybe it was the bump and the fact that it'd been on my mind not long before the mugging, but I went for "Madame Bovary" first. I guess I figured if they actually took time to steal the picture of this sexy Oriental girl it would be in order to whack off with it in some john stall somewhere and that would really piss me off bad, old Nghi giving that kind of something to one more asshole in this fucking world.

But she was still there. And suddenly that look on her face—the clear, vaguely troubled eyes, the unsmiling mouth soft with *knowing* —it was obvious to me. She saw all this coming. She was troubled for *me*. She was looking me in the eyes right then and there in the Port Authority Bus Terminal and she was saying, You poor baby, it had to be like this. And this isn't just something I'm thinking up now, more than a year later. I saw that in her face with my head throbbing and the corridor tilting, and I returned her look and I whispered to her, "Fuck you. If you knew, why the fuck did you let me go?"

I could've thrown her across the floor, made sure she landed face-up and let the janitor have her, still another guy to look into those exotic eyes and think about putting his hands on her. But instead I slipped her back into the book. And I put the rest of the stuff back into the duffel bag. There'd been nothing in there to steal. They'd even left a little radio that was beat up enough to make it worthless to them.

I cinched the bag shut and waited till the corridor was level, and then I got to my feet. I expected to fall back down, but after leaning against the wall for a few moments I actually got my head cleared. I could feel my heart in my temple and every beat was a flash of pain, but I knew I was okay. I stepped to the window of the package express office and looked at myself in the glass. I could see the swelling on my head—the knot wasn't as big as it felt—and I realized that there was blood. I didn't think it was flowing and I had sense enough not to touch it. I'd go to the rest room and try to wash it a little bit and I figured I better avoid the police or there'd be questions and I'd be collared as a runaway and that would be that.

It was now that I realized I'd already made a decision. I had no money and nowhere to sleep and no food and my head had settled into a skin-level sizzle and a deep pulse of pain, but I would not go back to Point Pleasant. If New York was the end of the line, then that's just the way it was. I'd been stripped down to just me, and my face was hazy in the glass, the eyes and the mouth and all could've been anybody's, and that was okay. I figured I was rid of all that. I slung the duffel bag over my shoulder and stepped out of the corridor into the little foyer at Ninth Avenue. I needed the washbasin and I turned and moved to the escalator and I rose and there was a fucking police station at the top.

But I didn't panic. I was conscious of my face and I knew it didn't change, even the blinking of my eyes. I was cool. Fuck Montreal. I knew I could do this thing, even in New York. I even paused at the top of the escalator and faced the glass facade of the police office and I was a little disappointed that there were no cops in view. The door was around a corner and these windows were covered with posters. Through half-opened venetian blinds I could see shadows moving, but there was no one to see me, and when a suit pushed past from the escalator, I even walked over to the window and stood there and would have peeked in through the blinds except I was caught by the posters instead.

There was a whole gallery of full-face-and-profiles of murderers and thieves, the usual mean motherfuckers of the world with the faces that even if they were tough-looking never got anywhere near to showing in some wild twist of the mouth or a stunning glint of the eyes the kind of shit they were capable of doing. Who could read even the meanest of these faces and find a hatchet going chunk chunk and some woman's arms falling off or shit like that?

And right in the middle of the gallery were some posters with only full-face photos, grainy from copying. And these said RUNAWAY, and the faces were just as tough to read and they said OUR DAUGHTER or OUR SON and instead of the stiff little WANTED BY DETECTIVES, BOROUGH OF MANHATTAN there was PLEASE HELP US FIND OUR CHILD or even WE LOVE YOU, DEBBIE ANN, AND WE WANT YOU HOME. And I just couldn't look at the birthday-party smile of this white girl and read these pleas and find the kind of family scene to split them up like this, with the girl probably already strung out on drugs and fucking herself to death on Forty-second Street and the parents ripping at each other because their daughter is gone forever. I found myself getting pissed off at all of them, all these goddam faces. Everybody's got some problem. Fuck that. I just didn't want to hear about it. Me, I had to find a basin and wash the blood off my face and figure out what I was going to do next.

So I moved on, and I passed a lingerie shop and a beauty parlor and a barbershop and they pissed me off too—because of all the fucking meaningless primping in the world, I guess—and then there was an island shop selling nuts and chocolate and now the smell of chocolate pissed me off, and so did some guy behind the counter craning his neck looking at me as I went by. I turned my face away from him so he couldn't see my blood and then I found a sign to the rest rooms and I kept my face down till I got there.

Enough about my wound already. It keeps coming up. But I washed it off pretty good and I just gave it one quick glance in the mirror without even looking at the rest of my face. I just wanted to get out of the place fast. People were hanging around in there and there were sinuses working away in some stall and I didn't have much patience left. So I went out and I followed the subway signs, which took me back past the main escalators and the Greyhound ticket windows, and you'd think that I would've started wishing I could turn it all back to when I first stepped into the line, but I just looked away from the goddam place. It didn't mean anything to me now. I was already thinking about the subways. I could maybe get myself onto a subway and keep riding for a while.

The steps to the subway were beyond Greyhound and I went down into the smell of doughnuts and piss and the air was thick and I could feel the trains rumbling under my feet. I followed a ramp down deeper and then I had to make a decision on which way to go, Downtown and Brooklyn to the right or 42nd Street and 8th Avenue to the left. "Downtown" sounded farther away, so that's the way I turned. And it was a good thing. There are a few places underground where it's real easy to sneak into the subway. Since I didn't have a penny, I was lucky now to find one of those places, with the token booth about twenty yards up ahead, the clerk facing away at a right angle selling tokens to a little line of people, and immediately beside me the yellow exit doors, which can be easily opened from either side. One of them was even stuck open already and I flashed through it and went down more steps and found myself on a platform with my shoulders jiggling up and down in a fuck-you kind of joy that was about as sharp as I could imagine it being if I'd just punched out my mugger and got my ticket back. Funny thing. I guess I really felt on my own in that moment, felt like I had some skills that would get me by. It seems a little stupid to me now. It was such a simple little thing I'd done, but I was feeling real good.

Then this dank wind starts blowing and the people along the platform begin to pull back even before there's a train to be seen. Then there are lights down the track and a big blue "A" is rushing this way. A for America, and I think fuck that. Then it's A for Anthony and I think fuck that too. I can't think of anything else and my little jiggle of good feeling stops.

It only took something that idiotic to do it, which shows you how much I had to learn about being on my own, and when the train stopped, I hesitated. But just before the doors closed, I wised up enough at least to curse myself and step into the car. Then I thought A for Asian, not that I was going to let that stupid little game get to me anymore. But sure, A for Asian.

It was a newer car and cold air was blowing around me and that made my head feel a little better, and I sat down in one of the nursery-yellow molded seats that faced sideways. Across the aisle from me were three empty seats, but at the next stop, Thirty-fourth Street, a little rush of passengers came on. I watched some woman with a shimmery, silk-looking dress and some Macy's bags as she went on up the aisle, and when the doors ding-donged shut, there were two guys in the seats across from me and they were Asians. Chinese probably. I figured from this I was on the right train. They were maybe in their twenties and good Chinese sons, I bet, with their neat sport shirts and quiet talk, their heads alternately bending near each other's mouth to hear without anyone shouting. I watched their faces and I was conscious of my own face, in some odd way, like I'd just rubbed it with a loofah sponge. I ran my hand through my hair. I don't know what was in my head exactly, except that I felt kind of contented there watching these two guys talk to each other.

I felt like it was just the three of us riding this A train, just these two Asians and me, and I wasn't so different from them, not different at all. I looked at their mouths as they spoke, to see if they were speaking Chinese. Thousands of Vietnamese words are Chinese and in the most important part—in the tones, the music—the two languages are very much the same, and I wanted to lean nearer and listen and I imagined them looking up at me and recognizing that I was some sort of kinsman. A cousin. Their being Chinese made me Vietnamese. But the train stopped only once before they stood up and moved near the door and grabbed on to the silver bar in the center of the aisle and waited to disappear.

I got up, too. I hefted my duffel bag and drew near them and I put my hand on the silver bar just above theirs. We rushed into the station and they said no more. They just watched out the window as the train came to a stop, and then the doors were open and they stepped through and I followed them. They went downstairs, even deeper into the ground, and I was right behind them. When we were on the lower-level platform I realized that I was much taller, that walking as close as I was, when I held my gaze straight out I could clearly see over their heads. I slowed a bit to fall farther behind and I felt like ducking my head, like I was a freak walking into a room full of people and I was scraping the ceiling.

They got on a downtown F train, F for fuck all this shit, but I got on, too, right behind them. Then one of them said to the other, "Over here," and when they turned to the left, I went to the right. I did sit immediately, facing the center aisle, and they were still visible a few rows down.

I was feeling bad again and I thought about getting off the train at the next stop. They'd never see me as kin. I would look really strange to them, these two prissy little Chinese boys. Their fathers probably owned a restaurant in Chinatown and they caught Vietnamese refugee children and put them in the soup. Fuck them, they didn't even speak Chinese and I looked more American than they did. Besides, I was Vietnamese and the Vietnamese hated the Chinese, have hated them for two thousand years.

I looked everywhere in the car but at them, and the walls and the windows and the seats on this car were filled with graffiti and they were dazzling, all these scrolls and stars and splashes of color, and I realized something about the words spray-painted in the car. There wasn't a single Fuck You or Kiss My Ass or anything like that. It was all names and streets. Fox 138, Snake 127, Cool Dude, Rapzapper, on and on, just these guys saying, This is me. This is my name and that's me and if you sit in this subway car you have to come to terms with me because I sat here too, and I am somebody. And by the time I'd figured all this out, it was East Broadway and the two Chinese guys were up again and ready to get off the train, and I thought how far they were from putting a name on the wall here—there were no Chans of Mulberry Street sprayed in red across the ceiling, nothing even like it, but it made me think that I didn't have a name either, there were no Tonys of Point Pleasant or Thanhs either. Thanh of Trần Hưng Đạo: that was gone forever. The doors closed and the train started up and I realized that Thanh of Trần Hưng Đạo was a six-year-old kid who was dead long ago and Tony of Point Pleasant was worse than that, and what did that mean for me? Who was it sitting there on the fucking F train with his head throbbing and a duffel bag at his feet? And the train was running fast and the sound of it was like knives scraping outside, like knives rubbing and sharpening each other and at the end of the line they'd be ready to carve up anybody who didn't have a name for the walls.

I suddenly felt very tired and I closed my eyes and laid my head back for a while and when I woke, I could see bright words floating against a night sky and this place was so familiar that I thought I was still asleep and dreaming. In yellow: Cyclone. And farther down, in red: Wonder Wheel. And between them were clusters and swirls of colored lights and I looked back to the names all around me in the subway car, but we took the turn and the subway lights flickered out and the names grew dim and all the colors outside finally registered in me.

We were at Coney Island. The train pulled into a station and I was facing the running and spiraling lights, but I kept my eyes lowered, I saw only the blurred reflections of the neon on the floor. The train moved and I didn't know what I wanted to do. I figured the next stop was the last and I looked around and the half-dozen remaining passengers were all getting to their feet. I could just walk across the platform and get on the next train back to the city and keep riding, but I'd had trouble sitting still even to get this far. So I got up.

As soon as I stepped off the train I was glad to be in the air and moving around and I could smell the water even through the piss and brick smells of the platform. I followed the crowd down a long ramp and I lagged behind and by the time I hit the little stands selling beach balls and straw hats and stuffed animals with sticks up their asses, I was alone again and glad about that. I hurried by the hot dog stand because I was getting real hungry, and then I got lucky again because at the mouth of the station was a trash can and I beat all the bums to a half-eaten hot dog that was still sitting in its cardboard cradle and even had a little sauerkraut left on it. I put down my duffel bag and ate the hot dog with both hands.

When I was done, I picked up my bag and I felt pretty good. I looked off to the left and down the street I saw the Cyclone again, the big Coney Island roller coaster, and the little rush of good feeling I had from the hot dog faded and I crossed the street with my mind pinched shut. I had to figure out a way to deal with all this now-you're-feeling-good-then-zap-you're-feeling-bad crap. So there was something about Kenneth and that roller coaster, so fucking what? I walked past bumper cars and a water pistol shooting gallery and at the first street leading toward the boardwalk I smelled the salt water real strong again and because of the South China Sea this smell was mine, just mine. So I turned down the street and lowered my face and cut off the sounds and I walked until I was going up a ramp of wooden planks, and then I was on the boardwalk.

The smell was good and I was glad to find that the ocean had disappeared into the dark. It didn't look at all like the place where Kenneth had brought me and drawn me into being a little shit to him. The beach was dim, but I could see it running out to where the darkness took over and you could hear the waves, and there were some figures moving around, no two of them together. I thought maybe this was a mistake, coming here, because suddenly I couldn't even hold my bag, it sagged and rested beside my feet and I couldn't imagine finding the strength to pick it up again. At first I took this to be sadness, and maybe it was. But I told myself I was just tired and that the tiredness was making me depressed, like when I'd wake up in the middle of the night and the trees weren't even making any sounds outside and still I was sweating in fear and I couldn't make it go away except to step back from myself and see how crazy it was. That's what I did now, stepped back. It was just tiredness and it was looking at the beach that made me feel bad, but it didn't mean the beach couldn't give me a place to sleep and I figured a sleep would make me feel good.

Still, I couldn't bring myself to plunge right down there, so I turned to my left and looked off along the boardwalk, which was strung with yellow lights as far as you could see. This was just the fringe for all the lights of the park and I found myself drawn, not into all that but at least along it for a ways. So I slung the bag over my shoulder and strolled on down the boardwalk and I passed the kiddie rides—all the ladybugs and caterpillars and fish with long-curled eyelashes going around in circles—and I passed the gunfire from the arcades. And then I stopped because I saw the Cyclone again, and it was as white as the stars in the sky over Point Pleasant and it was big-shouldered, its tracks mounting at both ends, and the lights strung all along its run were steady, not flashing, not moving, just steady there in the open space while between the Cyclone and me was all this crap, whirling wheels and spinning buckets and neon chasing up and down poles and shit like that. Kenneth took me on the Cyclone that day at Coney Island and the memory wanted to play itself in my head but I cut it off, and it wasn't that I was scared of it, I knew that much. It was something I didn't try to explain to myself. I just did it. I just turned around and I walked off.

I quickly passed beyond the park and the boardwalk stretched on far away and soon I was beside another park and it came on me with a little shock because I didn't see it coming. I was aware of the darkness to the right, the inland side of the boardwalk, but then in the dark was a shape, vast, filling my sight with its suddenness, sitting in this large ragged field: another roller coaster. I stopped and leaned against the rail and tried to make it out. Turned from the strings of lights, my eyes adjusted and I could see this coaster as it was, a dark brother to the Cyclone, every bit as large and similar, too, in sitting with its broad shoulders squared away at a right angle to the sea. With my eyes I followed the highest track at the near end and I slid down the boardwalk railing so I could see the track plunge down, disappearing behind some trees, as if it had dropped into the earth. But there was only silence here, silence and this field full of chest-high weeds and a darkness like a Saigon alley, thick and still. And the coaster was dead. Long ago, it seemed. There was a little house at its near base and the windows gaped darkly into the ragged field like everyone who could care about this place was dead or had left home long ago. I felt my own mood slipping quickly down, like it would drop behind some trees and into the ground, and I turned away.

I found the next set of steps and went down to the beach and it was hard walking, digging my feet out of the sand and staggering now under the duffel bag, and I made for a pier down the way where none of the light from the boardwalk could reach. My weariness came on me suddenly, like the dark coaster, and my head was hurting, but as I drew near the pier I could see a figure underneath and then another, and when I passed into the shadows there was the smell of bums and I turned around again. Not that I had anything against these guys who lived in the streets and all. I'd always known people like that back in Saigon. But I just didn't want to be around anybody right then and I moved back the way I came, thinking I'd find a place out in the open to sleep. The sand was fine-grained, soft, and I could sleep anywhere.

But there was a danger in that, being visible. A passing cop with nothing better to do could see me and then there'd be trouble. And yet, even as I thought about the dangers, I stopped. I could see the lights of the park in the distance. I could even see, far away, the white end-curve of the Cyclone, like the prow of a ship. I felt very weak and I set my duffel in the sand and sank down beside it. Just to rest a moment. Just to think. Just to figure out what was next for me.

But as I sat on the sand, the skeletal white ship of the Cyclone sailed into the center of my mind and I remembered the day here on the beach with Kenneth. He'd already called me pal and I'd toyed with him and let him down and it was later in the day and he wanted to go on rides. To me it seemed like a bad idea. I was a kid all right, but this kind of thing just wasn't my idea of a good time. Like baseball and all the rest of it, I guess. Most of the rides seemed stupid. But I'm not going to bullshit about this. The Cyclone scared me. Look, other kids might get scared by dark alleys or lepers or rockets falling in your neighborhood or some drunk foreign soldier shooting off a pistol outside your window or rats as long as your whole fucking arm from wrist to shoulder., But that was nothing to me. So it wasn't like I was a scared little kid when I was nine. I've told enough of my life so far for that to be clear, if nothing else is. I was just scared of this one thing, this big fucking thing that was taller than the tallest oak trees in our yard in Point Pleasant and with these tiny little open cars that they put you in to fall off the top.

But I think I was feeling a little guilty about how bad I'd suckered Kenneth in and then stuck him again with my coldness. So I let him drag me into the park and I rode a couple of the fucking kiddie rides with him and he kept talking about how the *real* ride was the Cyclone. He was saying things like how Charles Lindbergh—and he stopped, even, and explained Lindbergh to me—how Lindbergh said it was better than flying in an airplane, and when I finally figured out how long ago that was when this guy must've said that about the Cyclone, it made things even worse. The fucking roller coaster must be so old it's ready to fall down, I figured.

But of course I didn't let on to Kenneth about my being scared. And a few times he looked at me closely and he must've known what was going on in me, but he never accused me once of being scared. He just kept talking about how much fun it was, how his own father had taken him on it when he was even younger than me. Kenneth never mentioned his own father much. His father had been dead a long time. I never knew him. And I could see how this Cyclone was a real important place to Kenneth, like in trying to feel he was a father to me he had to go do what made his own father feel like a father to him. Something like that. Well, finally he said, "Just look at it. Just look at it and give it a chance to soak in."

So I gave it a chance. We walked down the little street beside the coaster and there was nothing happening. Things were very quiet, but the web of white wood mounting above me was enormous, *much* taller than our trees, and there was this scrabbly feeling in my chest and when Kenneth picked up one of my hands from my side, I yanked it away from him. But we kept walking down the street till we were at the ticket booth and I knew how clear it was that I was scared shitless and I didn't want to be proven both a mean little bastard and a coward on the same day, so I said yes.

"Great," Kenneth says, and he lunges to the booth.

There aren't a lot of people riding the thing. Even Kenneth notices it and says we're lucky, we caught it in a slack time, but I figure people know something Kenneth doesn't and they're staying away. But I follow him through a maze of little metal fences and we go up a wooden ramp. Just swinging out of the station, rolling right past us, is a three-car train and I count the people real fast so I can check out if there are any losses when it returns. I notice the riders are mostly grab-ass American teenage boys, just the kind of kids I feel a real sharp Vietnamese nine-year-old contempt for, and that makes me fight hard against the churning in my stomach. I'm getting to be pretty angry at myself, but frankly it doesn't stop the fear, especially when I hear a distant rushing sound and screams.

Kenneth puts us at the edge of the platform right at the front, where the first car stops, and I look across the track to the operators, two guys in T-shirts slouching by this big lever, and they have enormous arms and one of them has a long, twisted mustache stiff with wax and they've got a radio playing an opera, people singing loud in a foreign language, and the guy with the mustache who looks like he could break Kenneth in two over his knee is trying to sing along, is half closing his eyes and throwing his head back and singing and he looks like the happiest guy in the world and there is a great rushing sound behind me and wild screams. I jerk around and see the train flash behind the station and climb sharply and turn to plunge again.

Kenneth puts his hand on my shoulder and I face around and the guy across the track is still singing and still looking very happy.

The screams keep circling out there somewhere and finally they approach and burst from the mouth of a tunnel beyond the far end of the platform and the train screeches to a stop long before it reaches us. I instantly know why—to keep people from counting. I watch the riders standing up and staggering out and my own legs grow weak and I am having trouble focusing my mind on the count and I lose track twice as they're disappearing down an exit ramp, but I can swear that there's one missing. And I imagine him—a little kid— crumpled on the ground beneath the highest hill, and there are other bodies, from past rides, lying all around.

Now, the thing about it is that through all this, it's like Kenneth isn't even there. The train slides quietly in front of me, like a snake slithering through the grass, and I'm so scared I expect to fall down, but I don't even give Kenneth a glance. I don't want him to see me like this, of course, but there's more to it. It's like I'm going through all this alone, like it doesn't have anything at all to do with Kenneth. It's not even him anymore who's put me up to this. It's a rocket hitting just across the street and another whistling in. It's a GI drunk in front of the bar whose pistol shots are coming through our window now, tearing chunks out of our wall. Whatever. It's something like I've already had to deal with. It's a night alone in a bed in Point Pleasant, New Jersey, with the smell of my mother still on my skin.

I step into the fucking train and Kenneth is jabbering away and a bar comes down across my lap and locks and I grip it hard and some woman is singing on the radio, her voice rising higher than you can ever expect it to, like she sees some terrible thing in a dream and what she sees is the train rolling. And I'm on it. And the track turns to the right and dips gently and then we face a great hill. The train jerks. I'm sitting in the front seat of the front car and I can see this thick chain clanking up this hill and it feels like I've been turned on my back, no hill can be this steep and hold anything on its slope and yet we keep going up, very slowly, and all I can see is the sky. "Hold on," Kenneth says, and the words are so ridiculous I can't even force out a laugh, though I'd like to, just to show that all this is like nothing to me. I've been through worse. I've been through a fucking war. But I feel like a fucking baby because I can't breathe now, I can't even draw a breath.

Then the train comes up over the top of the hill and for one long moment it's level and I can see the ocean before me and it's the biggest single thing I've ever seen and I figure that means I'm dead, this is how dead people see things. Then the front of the car begins to dip down, slowly at first, it keeps dipping, dipping, and we're facing straight down, the track is straight up and down and I wait to fall and then the air begins to rush, faster, we plunge and the rush clots in my chest and I'm punched back into the seat, my scream is pressed back into my throat, and then I'm crushed straight down and the thought flashes that we're at the bottom and then we curve up and my head snaps back and we run up a hill and at the top I float up, I'm out of my fucking seat and I'm sure this is the moment, I'm weightless and I'm flying up and the train will pass away beneath me and I will fall.

But the car turns and I drop and the track hooks around the opposite way and I'm looking down another hill, just as steep as the first. At the bottom are beams crossing the track and I know that one of them is going to take my head off, but as we plummet I realize that Kenneth is even taller than me, he'll get it first, and I look over to see if this is going to happen and the beams flash overhead and I hear Kenneth say, "Wow," and as we rise again I watch him and I know he's smiling, his eyes are squinty with delight, and he's smiling with his mouth open, like he's trying to shout the smile, and I think that I've never seen him look happy before, and now he's wildly happy, happier than the man with the mustache singing opera, and beyond his head huge letters run by—CYCLONE—and we've crested a hill and then we're falling again and Kenneth darts his eyes to me a little bit and he shouts, "Don't you love it?"

And for a crazy moment it's me who feels like the father and this man beside me who feels like the little boy. For more than a moment, I guess. I look away from him and the rest of the ride doesn't scare me anymore. I'm used to it now. I just watch my hands squeezing at the bar in my lap and I can't shake the feeling about Kenneth. I'm real tuned in to all the little oh-boys and wows he's doing beside me and I worry once when out of the corner of my eye I see him take his hands off the bar and raise them over his head.

So we went around a couple more times, up and down, shit like that, and then we were through the tunnel and it was over. But what the fuck was I supposed to do with a feeling like that? I failed this guy as a pal, how the fuck was I supposed to act if I felt like the district attorney's father? That's what I wanted to know sitting there on the sand in the dark starting to drift into sleep with my head on my duffel bag. I forced myself awake. I couldn't sleep on the beach without risking a run-in with the cops. And then I'd end up back in New Jersey and I'd have the same problems all over again. Like, who the fuck was I supposed to be with the man?

I stood up and hefted the duffel bag and I staggered across the sand and up onto the boardwalk. No one was in sight and without even thinking about it I just moved off a ways and went to the railing and threw my duffel down into the weeds. Then I swung my legs over the rail and dangled with my hands from the edge of the board-walk and dropped down and I landed square and I felt the jolt in my head, but the rest of me was fine. I picked up my bag and moved through the weeds and there was a smell of rotting flowers, not a bad smell really, and I didn't look up until I was right under the coaster. Above me its frame was just a burrowing of the dark, like the paths of moles in black earth, and I could smell the rotted wood. I saw a thickening of shadow up ahead and I went there and it was the trees where the first hill dropped out of sight and I found a space there in the soft, rotted leaves and I lay down and slept.

SEVEN

◆

The next morning I was sure I'd fallen from the coaster: Kenneth was speeding on away from me and I could hear his scream, though I couldn't decide if it was from the thrill of the next hill or from anguish at my death, because I knew I was dead, I was looking up from the ground where I'd fallen and been broken, and through the ragged limbs of a tree I could see the track of the coaster. But the struts and braces and railings were black. This wasn't the Cyclone. I was puzzled. The Cyclone was white. My head was throbbing and I listened hard for Kenneth but his screams were gone and I was awake. I looked up through the trees at the track and it was just like in my dream. But I knew where I was now, and I wondered briefly how Kenneth was taking my disappearance back in New Jersey. It was just a thought. I didn't let myself picture him or anything.

I sat up. The pain in my head beat down into my eye and I was stiff and my mouth felt like I'd been chewing the bark off the tree all night. But I got up and I thought of the old xích-lô drivers in Saigon, the real old guys who couldn't afford motors and who spent all day pedaling people around Saigon. They always amazed me, and I thought of them and how they must have felt getting up every fucking day. Just like this. But I forced myself to get going. I found a break in the fence and opened it far enough to drag myself and my duffel through. At the park rest room I washed up the best I could with cold water and no soap and then I went out on the boardwalk to beg some money. Right away some guy bought me a couple of hot dogs. I got him to do it because I told him about the mugging and he looked real close at the bump on my head and it was clear that he was impressed with it. After I'd eaten and gotten a few bucks to boot from this guy who couldn't take his eye off my wound, I remembered where I got the beggar instincts. A leper in Saigon I used to talk to now and then told me once with a real matter-of-fact tone that his business had gotten a whole lot better after his nose fell off.

But after I'd freed myself from the coaster yard and gotten some food, I sat in the sand and watched the water and my head just filled with chickenshit little things. I scratched my heel for probably twenty minutes and I was focused just on that. And I watched some gull swooping around. I watched him for a long time, followed every move, every little strut on the beach or float on the sea or circle in the sky. It was cloudy, but it never rained. The gull hung around for a long time till he finally took off to the west and went beyond the pier and vanished. Maybe he came back later. I couldn't tell. It was all right being a gull, I figured. No one could tell one from another. It was easy to avoid standing out. Not bad.

And the day went on and on like that. Only a few little unpleasant memories that flickered in and I blinked them away. Once, I dug the money I'd been given out of my pocket and counted it—a little over three dollars in change—and instead of the leper, this time my mind found its way to the time I did a little begging in Saigon. Oh, we always asked any GI we saw for money. That was usual. We'd get it sometimes too. But once, near the end, Nghi asked me to go down and hang around the bars or go down to one of the hotels and see if I could get some money. Times were a little tough, she said. And you could tell it hurt her to be asking me to do this. She started crying and her hands shook when she put them to her face. She'd never asked me to beg and she'd even said now and then how things weren't so bad, we never had to beg. So I went out and hung around the bars and I guess I got a few piastres after a while. I don't remember exactly. It was no big deal. I never blamed her for that. Maybe I should have. But it just meant that she wasn't sleeping with enough men or selling them enough Saigon Teas in the bar with their hands up her dress and trying to put the moves on her. I could've done with a lot less of that, and if that meant more begging, it would've been okay by me.

But in the sand there on Coney Island I didn't want to run all that over and over, so I just put it out of my mind and I dozed and watched the water and this lasted most of the day, I guess. I kept waiting for some feeling to come to me. I was empty there. Even sitting on a cloudy day on the beach where Kenneth had brought me didn't provoke anything. I just sat and kept scratching at my heel and I was at least glad I could control what I thought about. But a heaviness had settled inside me, like I'd been slowly filling with the sand from the beach, and toward sunset it began to scare me a little bit. I didn't give a shit about anything. A cop even walked by and I looked him square in the eye and the defiance of it wasn't even fun, the risk of it wasn't exciting or scary, it was just nothing. I didn't give a shit anymore.

So I decided to get back on the train, just to change the scene, just to ride. I quizzed my stomach very seriously and decided I could wait a little longer. That was the new rule. If you can possibly wait, then don't eat. So I went straight to the station and when I was on the train I sat in a sideways seat with my back to the window. There was nothing out there I wanted to see. But after a while, I looked up at the string of advertisements running above the windows. One was in Spanish and I think the company wanted to train hundreds of cash register operators and send them out into a world in desperate need of them. There were lots of exclamation marks and a picture of a woman with a tremendous mane of black hair smiling out over her cash register, and you could see in her face how this whole thing had transformed her life. I was surprised to feel a sneaky little envy of her. Maybe it was the clubbiness of it all. The sign knew what language this woman spoke, it spoke to her and gave her what she wanted, and all the women like her would see her and know it was for them, too.

The next sign was a travel poster to some exotic place, I didn't even notice where; the picture was full of jungle growth and there was sand and a vivid blue sky and a woman with long legs. I went on past it and saw the word "Abortion," an ad for an abortion clinic, and I dropped my gaze straight down to the floor. I grew aware of the pulse in my throat. They say that the heart starts beating in the womb real early. At just a few weeks. I could see my mother crossing the sand, her legs smooth and long, and I forced my way out between them and it would have been easy for her to have stopped that. She wasn't ready for a kid. The girls around the bar knew what to do. Did she think about it? My heart was beating even then. At ten weeks, eleven weeks; Kenneth was still hanging around. Maybe she didn't even know for sure yet and already my heart was beating just like it is now, an unbroken chain of sound, it's beating now and there was a link of beats backward all the way to Nghi's womb. So inside her some other things of mine weren't formed yet, like lungs or street smarts or the guts to run away or whatever, so what? I was on this coaster car already, I was going up the chain lift and surely you can't get off unless somebody lifts up the bar and picks you up and throws you out. And she didn't do it. I never asked her about it, but when I figured out they could do something about being pregnant, I wondered why Nghi went through with it. But for whatever reason, she didn't abort me. And in my throat now I felt my heart racing. And my eyes filled with tears that were too complicated for me to even try to think about. But I did think, Look at this. The sand in my veins is gone. I've left fucking Coney Island, at least.

And I rode the train, and with my return to life after the beach I was getting restless. I started thinking about getting off the subway, getting into the streets, but it was night and I didn't know the neighborhoods. Then we came to Forty-second Street and it was something familiar to me. I leaped up and got off like it was the place I'd been waiting for all along, and I went upstairs and into the night.

The F train had brought me to Sixth Avenue. I was facing a bunch of dark trees across the street in the park next to the library, and rising over them was the top of the Empire State Building, its spire sprayed with white light. There were cars flowing past in the street but the sidewalks were almost deserted and I thought about the night and I considered the trees, but I'd slept under trees already and I didn't like it. You couldn't trust the parks anyway and I looked to my right, west on Forty-second, and there were lights that way. They drew me now because you could see they weren't anything like the lights of Coney Island. These were city street lights and I knew city streets. That was what I was born to.

I heard a siren up ahead and I began to walk. Between Sixth and Broadway was a run of storefronts locked up tight with metal doors and I just watched the lights up ahead sharpening from a blur of neon into specific things—theatre marquees, car headlights, taillights, the blue strobe of a police car, a running of words on a building. I could hear car horns and a kind of distant hum and getting nearer I could see guys hanging out of packed cars as they turned west into Forty-second and the lights promised Sexxational Triple Bills and Live Nudes and Pizza and Souvlaki and Cameras and Videos and I was on the corner of Broadway and Forty-second, Times Square, and drumbeats floated through the crowd and voices pushed past me, Cocaine, Smoke, Watches, Fuck you man, Hey Jack where's it at, honking horns, a siren way off, the sound of steel drums which reminded me of cold water and above my head in running lights The President Says and Israel Says and the world is talking and I get a familiar feeling I can't place right away because on the surface there's this scrabbling around, this messy energy, and it's a city, it's city streets, and I think it's no different from Saigon, the rush around me was like the rush of motorcycles and xích-lôs and the press of beggars and the girls from the bars and GIs and it was still the welter of people and sex and drugs and electronics and drinks and food and me invisible, me slipping through the cracks and watching it all without getting sucked in and me finding what I need and doing what I want.

So I slide up Broadway a ways and on a concrete island between Broadway and Seventh Avenue, which cross here, there's a big stand selling Christmas trees and there's snow, even though it's almost summer, and I look closer and the snow is a whole shitload of cotton or something and there's these two tall thin women throwing their heads back and there's blond hair flowing out behind them and these women are wearing mink coats and carrying Christmas packages and they are arm in arm and they take two steps forward in the path between all the Christmas trees and then they stop and back up and take the two steps again, and they do this over and over. There's some guy I can hear now saying, And step; Good chickies; And step; Good, good; And step. And he's got a big camera on a tripod strung to him by a cord and these two gorgeous women are two-stepping up and going back and striding again and throwing their hair and lifting their heads in big Christmas smiles and I turn and on sheets on the sidewalk are leather belts and books and records and a guy with incense and I'm pitched up real high right now and it's Nghi all right curling up into my nose but this time all it does is make the link stronger between one city street and another.

I go back to Forty-second and head on west and guys slide by me and say to me, What's up, my man? What's up? Man, it's time for the world to change, do it for yourself. And I know what they're selling but since I'm not buying I can still suck off their nerves and their slyness and I move on down the street and naked women with stars in their crotches puff kisses at me from posters and some guy is selling flowers, little red bouquets, and two guys in a niche in a building front, one of them sitting on a standpipe with a guitar and the other at his elbow, are singing over and over, We love you Jesus, we love you Lord, and they both have their eyes closed and I slow down and watch them all the while I'm passing and they never open their eyes even for a second. And there are bright gaping doorways and inside are walls full of bodies and people on the street drift in little groups with the drug sellers slower, alone, stopping, watching, and all the couples here clutch each other close but their smiles are going outward, to the building fronts, and their eyes narrow and their heads cock toward the ones who lounge against the bricks be-tween doorways. And the cars roll by and heads come out of the windows, torsos, and there is shouting and cursing and whistling and I'm sliding along, Not now man, Nothing right now man, and I feel like I'm invisible, like nobody can touch me, not even the cops who are on the corner up ahead in a circle, six of them, shooting little glances over their shoulders and talking to each other and pounding their nightsticks on their palms and fidgeting and I pass them right by.

I stop on the corner and I'm facing west, looking across Eighth Avenue, and ahead the lights, the hustle, are gone. I look on the south side of Forty-second, and up at the second-story level is a long row of X's, like a cordon of policemen. A bus moves behind them. This is the Port Authority Bus Terminal again, but there's no thought at all of going home. The terminal holds me only as a place maybe to rest, even to sleep. I've got the bag. It could look like I'm traveling. But the place is just too public for now. The back of my neck is conscious of the circle of policemen behind me. I can feel their attention turning to me. Fuck them. I could walk right past them, I could go up Forty-second Street the way I've just come. The energy of the street felt good and I almost do it, almost turn. But it's getting late and there's nowhere to go that way, except the subway again. No more underground for me. Not tonight. Still, the darker street ahead depresses me and I realize that my hunger isn't going to wait much longer. To my right, up Eighth Avenue, there's more life, people and lights. That's the way I head.

I don't get fifty yards before I hear the snap of scissors. I stop because it's a Saigon sound and at first it seems natural here. But as I turn to look, it's not like I'm expecting to find a nougat seller here or anything. The scissors snap again and I'm in front of a little food store with fresh flowers in big vases all around and a long chest of ice with bottles of juice and watermelons and cantaloupes. Sitting on a little stool with a pot between his legs is an Oriental man and it's this guy who's got the scissors. But right away I know he's not Vietnamese. He's a thick-chested little man with a face that's severely square and his eyes seem to have no lids at all. I know right away he's Korean. I've seen Koreans in Saigon, soldiers from the Tiger Divisions fighting there, and you can always tell a Korean. This one is clipping the ends off green beans and his scissors go snap and his eyes come up from his work idly and he watches figures moving by. I follow his gaze and see a woman who is all pale bare leg gliding past on red stiletto heels and she has a black leather skirt as high up her thighs as a pair of shorts and with her is a black guy with a Barcelona hat the color of a peeled banana, and his coat and pants are the same. I look back to the Korean and his face shows nothing. He watches the couple pass and then he lowers his eyes and snips off the end of a bean, delicately, like it has to be real precise or the bean is ruined.

He looks up at me and something flickers in his face. I'm not sure what part of his face moved, exactly. Maybe it was an overall softening at the sight of me, in spite of his tough squareness, like he recognized something. Anyway, he finally gives me a little nodding smile and I nod back and when he returns to his beans, I look into his shop. A big sign on the window by the door says Moonies Not Welcome. Down the center of the store I can see a long salad bar—with meticulously cut green beans somewhere on it, I figure—and I also figure they must sell sandwiches and stuff like that, something better than a hot dog. I take a step inside and turn away from the square-faced woman behind the cash register and I count my change. About two bucks.

I stuff the money back in my pocket and stroll around and find a cold case full of sandwiches. None of the stuff is marked, though. I pull out a tuna salad sandwich and take it to the register and the woman—probably the guy's wife, though she could be his twin sister for all I can tell—grabs the sandwich and snaps open a paper bag. "How much," I say just before she rings it up. At this she glances over my shoulder.

I turn and follow her gaze and the man who was cutting beans is standing at the door. He's still looking at me like there's something between us. "Fifty cents," he says, and I look back to the woman who nods me a smile and I find myself with a sharp little clash of feelings. I can't help but believe that what they see in me is the very thing that made me do what I've done for the past thirty-six hours. They see me as some kind of Oriental cousin. I'm not an American to them. I'm something else, something closer to what they obviously are. But I'm also starting to get that pissed-off feeling again. This sandwich is no fifty cents. This is a handout of the worst kind, the kind you don't ask for, with the superior little smiles to go along with it. Maybe I'm not Vietnamese to these two, I'm just a fucking kid.

The hope that my face can inspire an Asian kinship and the fear that they just think me a kid—these two feelings kind of tussle around in me for a moment till the practical part of me overcomes my pride and makes one more request. I'm thirsty too, so I ask for a Coke and they give me that for a quarter and now I just want to get the hell out of there. The Vietnamese never liked the Koreans much either, to tell the truth.

So out I go into the street and I guess I'm ready to be quiet for a while because all the noise and the crowd just make me itchy up and down my arms. My city in Vietnam always had the alleys to go to after the streets and I liked the dark, liked to crouch alone there and just listen in from a distance to the singing and arguing and crying and murmuring coming from the balconies all around me and no one could see me in the dark. Nothing can be as dark as a Saigon alley. So that was my mood now in New York. There are no alleys around, but I think of the darker, quieter stretch of Forty-second. I go back to the corner and cross and the sidewalk slopes a little downhill and I begin to walk west.

The first shop down the street is called Survival and in the window is a mannequin wearing steel helmet and gas mask and flak jacket and olive drab shirt and pants and camouflage combat boots. I kind of snort at him as I pass, meaning, Maybe that's what *you* need, but I can survive with just what I've got. But I'm not kidding myself, and I'm not really trying to. The sidewalk stretches on and not much of anybody is up ahead, just the street and the sodium vapor lamps and some cars and I guess the river is somewhere out there, and my stomach is churning even though I've had something to eat and I'm a little breathless even though I'm walking downhill. The problem now is to sleep somewhere.

On I go and I watch the shops pass for a while—a deli, souvenirs, a Greek restaurant, art supplies, a red brick church with a black iron fence, each post topped with a little iron flower, a hotel with piss stains along its front wall and a guy with his sleeves rolled up standing in the doorway and behind him, leaning against the front desk, some woman running a finger up and down inside the strap of her tank top. Then I just stop watching things and walk with my head down, crossing some avenues, my legs moving like they have a will of their own because I don't know where the fuck I'm heading and I can only hope they do. Once I look up when I pass the clean, wet smell of lumber, a smell I never knew in Saigon, but the place is shut up tight and I can't see the white stacks of wood like all the stacks in a shop in Jersey where Kenneth took me once. He talked too much, as I recall, when I just wanted to walk around in the middle of all this naked wood stacked way over my head and sniff it in silence.

Not long after passing the lumber company I find a stoop and sit on it. My shoulder is aching from carrying the duffel bag and my knees are tight and my feet hurt and I just have to stop. The stoop has a little iron banister and I lean against it and it feels real good. So I sit there for a long time, ready to sleep but afraid to. Every couple of minutes my head slides down the iron pole and drops off and I jerk awake. I can't sleep in plain sight. It would invite a cop. I figure I probably can't even just sit here too long without running a risk. But I do sit on the stoop for quite a while, fighting off sleep and gathering up, bit by bit, a real serious little panic about what to do next.

Then my head jumps up and there's a face before me. I'm not sure I'm really awake because the face isn't clear, though it's just a few feet away. The face is dark, but not in its skin exactly, it's dark like the night is dark, like it's only a reshaping of the night air. Then I understand. I'm looking into the face of a bum. A grimy, thin old man with a wide mouth that looks like somebody tried to cut his throat from ear to ear but cut too high. I expect the guy to ask me for something, but he just stands there, his body facing west on Forty-second and his face turned sharply to the side to look at me, and he says nothing at all until finally he looks back the way his body is heading and he says to no one particular, "It ain't easy." Then he moves off.

I figure the guy is probably crazy and he was probably talking about something that happened to him twenty years ago, but I can't shake a feeling that this old man has been around and knows how to survive in the streets and his words are full of some special wisdom. It's late now and I wonder where this guy is going. So I get up and hoist my duffel and the old man is standing up on the corner, waiting for the light to change, though there are no cars passing in front of him. I stay where I am until the walk sign appears, and when the old man starts off west again, I follow.

He's wearing a shaggy old suit coat and he walks with a kind of roll of the shoulders, like his feet hurt and he's trying to put as little weight on them as possible. But he keeps up a pretty good pace and he seems to know where he's going and I figure he may not even be drunk. We head on west for a while and then up ahead I can see the wide run of Twelfth Avenue and beyond it is the river, I know. There's a gap out there in the dark and I can see a far ridge of lights which must be the bluffs in New Jersey. The old man turns uptown on Twelfth and disappears. I try to hurry these last few steps to the corner but my legs don't seem to be able to work any faster. Finally I'm at Twelfth Avenue. The old man up the way is standing on the curb waiting to cross. He's looking back in this direction, watching for traffic, and I'm sure he sees me. I think I even see him nod at me, but I can't be sure and immediately he's crossing the street.

I try to figure where he's going and I look beyond him and I'm startled to see the cut-off end of an elevated highway that thrusts this way from uptown. The highway just stops up there. It runs to a metal guardrail and it stops, and behind the rail is a cyclone fence where the fender of a gutted car is twisted up like a cop raising his hand to warn traffic away. The supports and the cradle of the road-way pull off a little of the light from the street below, but mostly it's dark up there, the highway has no light of its own. Beyond it, though, there's a great brightness and I'm startled again, this time by long strings of yellow light tracking out into the river on what looks like—and then I realize really is—an aircraft carrier. The lights run from the bow up to the conning tower and down to the stern like the span of a bridge and at the near end, on the bow, is a jet plane posed in a leap from the deck and lit in white from beneath. For a second I think that this is where the old man is going. That he's the ghost of some pilot lost in the jungles of Vietnam and he's finally found his way back to his ship and it sure as hell wasn't easy. Then I figure I'm getting a little crazy from tiredness and this is just a bum, but I hope he's a bum with a good idea of where to go. He's walking along a guardrail now in the center of Twelfth, right beneath the elevated highway, and he seems very far away and moving faster.

I take a quick look at the traffic and hustle across the street. I put my head down and concentrate on catching up. Faded hazard stripes pass beneath me and there are hubcaps and broken bottles and bits of shapeless cloth and ground glass and grit and then I sense a barrier, a shape looming ahead, and I look up and lift to a stop. The old man is facing me and I'm close enough to see that his eyes are as clear and intent as a jet pilot's. He steps nearer to me and I can smell liquor on him now and my chest heaves once and I realize I'm disappointed in him, and that makes me feel real stupid. What the fuck did I expect? Then he says to me, "You don't have a place to sleep," and the voice sounds steady enough and he's right about why I was following him and I'm glad to feel once again that he might be okay, at least for a bum.

I don't know whether he expects me to tell him he's right. But before I can get any words out, he says, "Stay behind me," and he turns and walks on. So I do what he says. We follow the median guardrail up Twelfth Avenue for a few more blocks—real short blocks, since they're going uptown—and when we about pull even with the aircraft carrier, I see that he's heading for a ramp that climbs into the center of the overhead highway. We pass a weather-beaten police sawhorse barricade and a sign saying the West Forty-sixth Street ramp is closed, and the ramp is a long upward slope. I see the open sky ahead of me and I stumble on something soft and lumpy and I don't look back at it, I just keep my eyes on the old man's back and trust him to know the path through whatever is asleep or drugged or dead along here.

All around me is a darkness like the split second before passing out and we climb the ramp and a woman's voice slithers out from the shadows: "Want a date, honey?" I hadn't been on my own in New York for even two days, so I didn't know all the different ways a hooker could approach a guy. This is a very common one, I later found out, the standard approach for the prosperous Times Square whores. But on my second night, in the dark there, as I climb through things soft and dead to this highway of ghosts on the rim of the city, the idea of this woman's voice asking to go on a date makes me flinch in astonishment and then even scares me. It makes me feel a little crazy. Where the fuck am I going? A harsh, heavy whisper almost at my elbow, "Johnny," and the voice is sexless in its whisper, I can see in my mind a hairless face, rubbery, neither man nor woman, or the corpse of a cat speaking, and far off to my left a tinny TV voice winds up and spins out, "Here's Johnny," and there's laughter ahead in the dark and behind in the dark and the first voice, the woman, calls again, "Come on, honey, how about a date?" None of this stops the old man who leads me on and I follow, but I'm starting to stagger, my legs feel like they are only stacked at the knees, the bones are about to slide off and fall and shatter. I'm climbing into madness here. This is where the faces from the posters on the Port Authority police window have all disappeared. That was Debbie Ann, loved by the parents she couldn't stand, who I'd tripped on back there, soft and not moving. And all the runaways had been led here by this old man who only needed to remind them that it ain't easy and they knew he was right and they followed him.

And I follow him. I keep on, and up ahead he reaches the top of the ramp and I draw near even though the blood is pounding in my head so bad I feel faint. "Stay close," he says, which isn't the advice I want to hear at that moment. But I do what he says. I get close enough to smell the liquor on him again, and for a moment that's reassuring, he's just a bum. Then I realize the smell could be some goddam spiritual drink like cam lộ that God gives to his special demons so they can go out and gather up all the kids he wants to dump on.

I peek around me a little bit and there's a faint orange light at the edges of this place up here, spilling from the lamps on Twelfth Avenue. It's a highway, all right, but full of cracks with weeds biting through, and we're walking down the center. To my right, on the city side of the highway, is an iron ledge and I can see bodies strung out all along there, tucked under the ledge. Sleeping, I tell myself. Sleeping. And off to the left, on the river side, is a high cyclone fence and the weeds are thick and there are more sleepers, but they are harder to make out, they're just a lumping up of the shadows. Beyond them, beyond the fence, sits an enormous cruise ship with fat-faced decks and the thing is lit up like Broadway and all in white and you can read on its bow that it is the Queen of some fucking Caribbean island or other and there's too much crazy shit going on and I wish I could just lie down in the weeds under the cyclone fence or over there under the iron ledge and sleep and I wouldn't even care if there were dead bodies around me or not.

But on we walk, the cruise ship is gone and the darkness up here deepens and at my left hand a stone median starts up and underfoot we crunch glass ground to bits long ago and suddenly the old man stops and whirls around to face me and he says, "If I didn't stop you now, you would've died." I drop my duffel and I'm ready to do something, run or fight or some goddam thing, and then the old man shrugs and says, "At least you would've broke both your legs."

"What the fuck are you talking about?" I say.

"Move up right beside me, but don't go a step farther," he says.

I hesitate, as you might imagine. But now he's letting on that whatever danger I was in wasn't from him and I sure can't think of a good way to back out of this whole thing now. I could pick up my duffel and say fuck you and turn around and get the hell out of there, but I don't want to face that ramp again, not in the dark, not alone. So I find my hands clenched and up about waist high and I lower them. Then I step up right next to the old man.

This is a real dark stretch of the highway and at first it's hard to see what he's talking about. But then I can make out an even darker space on the roadway right at my feet. I look to the left and it edges up to the concrete median. I look to the right and it cuts across just about this whole lane of the road, a deep, dark gash in the highway, a chasm. I look up the lane and it's maybe six or eight feet to leap the hole. Now it's easy to understand what the old man was talking about. Walking along here at night you'd never see the thing coming and you'd be in it without knowing what happened.

The old man says, "You don't walk in your sleep, do you?"

"No," I say.

"Good thing for you," he says and he leads me along the edge of the hole and around it, in the second uptown lane, and then back along its other edge. "This is a good place to bed down," he says and he strips off his coat and rolls it and he curls up right at the edge of the chasm with the coat under his head. Instantly his body is still. It all happens so fast that I grow conscious of how I'm standing—my weight on one foot, my duffel hanging half down my arm, my head angled just so, all these things are exactly the same as when he spoke. And now he seems to be asleep, and it seems, too, that all he has to do is roll a little bit in his sleep, shift only slightly, and he would disappear into the hole.

I retreat from the edge a few feet and I look around, but I don't really concentrate on the shapes or bits of light in the night. My body is shredding with weariness and I put my duffel at my feet and I lie down with my head on the bag and I can see the high fence that keeps out the cruise liners and jet planes and I feel my mind fading, and off somewhere the way I came, far off, I can hear the sobbing of a woman.

EIGHT

⧫

Where do I sleep, how do I wake. When I took off from Point
Pleasant I didn't expect that to be a big deal in talking about
my life. The sun was high when I woke after my second night alone.
I sat up and the old man was gone, of course, and the chasm seemed
even bigger and uglier—its edges were jagged—though I didn't look
down in it yet. I had to piss bad and my clothes felt like they were
made out of grease and I was starting to stink and I was hungry and
every goddam muscle was sore. Big fucking deal. Even now, talking
about all this, I get so goddam caught up in all these details that only
I could care about and it feels like me and my own goddam body are
the whole fucking world. They aren't now, they weren't then. All
those drunks and whores and lunatics were dropping into holes all
night, suffering and dying and shit like that and I was dreaming
about clean underwear or whatever. Or wishing my eyes were
shaped different. It pisses me off. Some fucking woman sobbing out
there in the night. But it was morning and things were quiet. I stood
up and stretched out the kinks in my neck and legs and I just glanced
at the hole and it was dark and you could see steel rods sticking out
of the broken concrete. Fuck that.

There weren't so many bodies around now. They'd all gone off to
drink or fuck or talk to themselves in the street, I guessed. Com-

muted off to their day of work in the big city. There were a couple of sleepers still, or corpses, along the fence. I heard some voices and turned uptown and saw where one of the lanes of the highway dead-ended at a concrete barrier and beyond the barrier it went on another fifty yards to a chain fence. In the fifty yards were some shanties made out of rusted iron planks and scrounged wood and tar paper roofs and there were a couple of stuffed shopping carts parked nearby and a big pile of garbage all along the railing opposite the shacks. Two women were standing in front of the nearest shanty. One of the women was white, one was black, both were dressed in the short skirts and cutaway tops of whores, but the clothes on these two looked grimy and ragged even from where I was standing, maybe fifty yards away. The women were very thin, their legs were spindly and splotched, and they had their backs to me but I knew they were either old or ugly or both. It was some old shell of a whore like this who must've spoken to me coming up the ramp, and as I said, I didn't know enough then to hear how pathetic it really was, the woman still using that roundabout little approach—asking to go on a date—even though there were no appearances to keep up there in the dark with her body stinking and aching and her underwear dirty. And still she did it how she was taught, the classy way, I guess, Do you want a date? But I did know enough to figure how desperate these two I was looking at must be, and there was a real bad little moment then because you don't look at scrounged-up shacks without thinking of Saigon and you don't look at whores without thinking of your mother and the two of them together made me imagine her in the doorway of a shanty on stilts out over the Thị Nghe River and nobody stopping in to fuck her because there was garbage running in the river under her bed. I tried, but I couldn't see her as old or ugly, and for a moment I even got mad at the idiots passing her by.

Then the white whore moved off, crossed the barrier, and went over to a patch of weeds near the big cyclone fence. She put her back to me, though I don't think she even knew I was there, and facing the fence, she stripped down her pants and crouched and pissed in the weeds. It struck me that whatever modesty the woman had was directed at the bums and the other whores living up here on the abandoned highway; the exposure of her front was to the world beyond the fence. I thought of the captain and crew of the Queen of Wherever standing with binoculars on the bridge and watching her and she didn't give a fuck about that, it was us she kept her back to. She remained crouched there, her cheeks spread like a gull's wing, and I turned away.

I had to piss, too, and I stepped closer to the big hole. The steel reinforcing rods fanged out of both edges of the broken roadway, but the gape between didn't open to Twelfth Avenue as I expected. In fact it was pretty shallow, maybe four feet deep, dropping to a closed floor of some kind, which was full of trash. The old man was right the second time—maybe you'd break both legs, though the steel rods would give you a nasty jab if you were coming along here too fast. Anyway, I was glad to see this thing for what it was, since it had made me so nervous in the night. I looked around and on this side of the highway there was only one sleeper under the iron railing. I knelt by the hole so that I was sheltered by the concrete median and couldn't be seen even by the two whores, and I pissed into the hole and it felt real good.

I did get an idea, though, and made sure to piss into a far, dark space because the hole was going to make the day a lot easier for me. I cleared a place to sit against the median—there was a lot of broken glass, big shards of liquor bottles mostly, scattered along here. Then I sat and changed my clothes. I didn't want to spend the day carrying my duffel bag around again, so I figured I could put the clean clothes on, hide the bag down in the hole—it was worth the risk of losing it if I didn't have to lug the goddam thing around—and then I could wash up at the bus terminal later on. My head where I'd been hit only stung some on the surface and it felt scabby, and actually, moving around like this after sleeping till practically noon, I was feeling pretty good.

When I'd finished dressing and hiding the bag, I stood by the hole and I was bouncing a little, jiggling around. I was ready for the city. So I followed the highway back past the ships and I looked ahead and with a little flutter in my chest I saw the ramp approaching. But

I didn't break my stride and when all of a sudden I could see down the slope to Twelfth Avenue, there was only one old man sitting at a railing holding a Styrofoam coffee cup in one hand and licking a piece of waxed doughnut paper in the other. I walked down the ramp and I let myself peek at its surface, though I don't know what I was nervous about seeing, bloodstains maybe. But of course there was nothing except grit and ground glass and shit like that, and at one spot there was a clotted mass of old clothes, but that was over against the railing and not out in a place where I might have stepped on it last night. So I just didn't think about that anymore. That's the way it was now. If it had been a bum's old clothes or if it had been a dead cat or if it had been Debbie Ann, who somebody missed real bad, the thing was that the ramp was empty now.

So then I was in the street and walking along the median under the abandoned highway till I crossed Twelfth Avenue and turned east on Forty-second. When I got near Ninth Avenue, I saw the dark-rose-colored bus terminal up ahead and for a little way there were trees growing up out of the sidewalk, skinny little trees on both sides of me. I stopped on Ninth and the simple thing would've been to cross the avenue and then Forty-second and enter the terminal up the block a ways. I didn't want to do that. My body felt grimy under my change of clothes and the bus terminal was the place I could go to wash, but it suddenly felt real creepy to me. I knew that the entrance on Ninth was right near the place where I'd been mugged and I told myself I was being a chickenshit baby about this, a fucking coward. But I knew that wasn't it.

I couldn't figure it out as I stood there on the corner, and finally I just went across Ninth and headed up the hill toward Eighth Avenue, telling myself I wanted to have a little look at the Forty-second Street of the night before. But I can see now that I was just stalling. I was afraid to go into the terminal because that meant I was caught here. It was getting through to me in some way that it hadn't before —I was on the streets to stay. Go wash up in the bus terminal and maybe hang around in there begging for money or looking for something to steal, and just kill time, let the long day run itself out with you walking around and hanging around and keeping away from the cops while deep down you're glad the cops are there to keep things from getting so boring that you'd just as soon go into a john stall and cut your fucking throat and be done with it.

So at Eighth Avenue I looked ahead along Forty-second and the sun was bright and it was hot and there were people on the street, but the life I'd felt the night before wasn't there. It'd be back, I knew, but it couldn't keep me from glancing across to the terminal and thinking I ought to go in there and wash up and take stock of what the hell I was going to do. But I was hungry. I had a little money left and I could get something and that would stall things just a bit more.

I crossed Eighth and turned uptown without thinking and in a few steps I was in front of the pocket grocery store. The Korean guy was standing with a broom at the doorway and he was watching a little Korean kid—his son, I guess, maybe four or five years old—and the kid was wetting the sidewalk in front of the store with a watering can, like he expected something to grow there. I knew I could make my money go farther if I bought from the Korean, but I kept on moving and I glanced away when the man noticed me and I made a wide arc around the kid and the wet spots. The boy looked up at me as I went around him and he squared his face to me and fixed me with a stare, and he seemed like a good kid, there was something sturdy in his face. But I wondered if his old man was turning him into a wimp with the watering-can shit and exposing him to the bullshit pity for this half-breed teenager who needed a break on his tuna sandwich.

I went in a few doors down at a deli and got a bagel from some old Jewish guy and all he looked at was his hands and the bagel and my hands as I gave him the money, and that was fine with me. The bagel was hot in its waxed paper and I carried it out of the deli and I took my first bite as I walked past the Korean. I was walking along the edge of the pavement and I wanted to just ignore him, but I let myself glance over and he was sweeping the wet spots and his boy was right there beside him watching the broom like this was some fucking family tradition or something. I watched the man too long because he looked up and he saw me and for a second he gave me a funny little look, like he was hurt or something, or sad. I couldn't figure it out, but I was surprised to find that it didn't piss me off, which only made me think that I was starting to adjust to all of this, which gave me the guts finally to cross Forty-second and head for the bus terminal.

But I didn't go in right away. I didn't even cross back over Eighth. I walked along the tall cyclone fence of a parking lot that ran for a block opposite the terminal. There were some beat-up overstuffed chairs with black guys sitting in them and talking and waving their arms and then the fence was hung with Hawaiian sport shirts and then with paintings of tigers on velour and then a guy in a Yankees cap was beside me and he said, "Smoke?" and my silence lasted only a moment before he was gone. I crossed Forty-first Street and I turned my head as I did and watched the street run right through the center of the bus terminal, burrowing a little path under the massive bridge of floors that joined the two wings of the building.

I looked down Eighth Avenue and the lights had released the traffic, but I dashed across anyway, one lane at a time, letting the cars rush by, their wind brushing at my back and their windows flashing right in front of me, and it hadn't started out that way, but now it felt like I was using the lanes to block somebody chasing me, I was escaping, and then the last lane opened up and I sidestepped between some parked cabs and jumped over a low yellow fence and I felt safe landing on the clot-red brick of the terminal entranceway. Things were pretty good again.

You might start wondering how this kid could feel okay at a time like this, away from all the American creature comforts that he'd grown up with for ten years. I don't know what to say about that, except that's just the way it was. All the stuff I had in Point Pleasant was pretty nice, but there was no real fun connected to it. It was like I had a roomful of rocks from Mars. You sit there and think, Holy shit, look what I've got here. But what the fuck does it mean to you? You watch the TV or you listen to your stereo or you boot up your computer and all you've got in the center of you is a big hole, like the thing I slept on the edge of at the abandoned highway. And all the sound and the pictures and the colored dots on the monitor just fall into the hole and they never come back up and this hole doesn't stop a few feet down, it burrows its way through the earth and pops out somewhere in an alley on the far side of the world. Does that make any sense? I can feel good sometimes. Like anybody. There were some real good moments in Saigon when I didn't have anything at all. Maybe that was like standing there in front of the bus terminal with nothing at all, a few pieces of clothes that might already be stolen and less than a dollar in my pocket and a pair of sneakers that were about half worn, and for the rest, it was just me. Nothing else but me.

So I just stand there a minute in front of the Port Authority Bus Terminal and I'm feeling pretty good and I'm wondering why I was afraid of this place before. I look behind me, and across the street is some little business school and it's got signs up on its second-floor facade that tell you to build a career by learning business administration or plan a future in bookkeeping and accounting, and maybe that was what I felt was chasing me across the street a moment before, shit like that. And that sends me through the front doors and there's this big foyer and the air is cool, and I stop right where I am and suck in a bunch of this air, like I can store it up and keep it for later or something, like when I'm back on the abandoned highway. I just stand there and think about breathing and there's a sort of background babble, voices, echoes, feet scuffling, and then the word "Vietnam" leaps out at me.

I turn to my left and there's just people going by. Up above the doors three flags are hanging, a blue one and a yellow one that I don't recognize and a real big American flag, and I hear the word again, "Vietnam," and my eyes fall from the flag to some guy sitting right below it, between the two central doors. People are passing between us and I'm trying to look at him—dark hair—he flashes there, a body goes by, he flashes again—dark hair, thin cheeks—a body passes and blocks him off and I step closer.

His shirt looks like an Army shirt—it has a faded name over the pocket, Cipriani—but the green has turned street-grit gray and the guy's face is gray, too, like he's never been in the sunlight. On his chest is a cardboard sign: HELP OUT AN UNEMPLOYED VIETNAM VET. He's shoving an upturned helmet liner at a business suit and he says, "I fought for you in Vietnam," and the business suit swings out wide around him and disappears out the door. I expect this guy to get pissed off at that, but it doesn't even seem to register. The helmet liner just eases back and rests on his knee and his face shows nothing and he turns and looks at me for the first time.

His face is stretched tight, like he's just walked out of the jungle after being cut off from his unit for about two months and he's been living on roots and bugs and he's down to just what's necessary on his body and that's so tough, now, that he's ready to live forever. Only like I said, his skin is gray, though looking at him up close it seems more like camouflage than some kind of weakness. And he's got these black eyes that aren't hard at all, where all the softness from the rest of his face got melted down from the fear he felt in those two months, and the memory of that fear sits there now in his eyes and he's got something else there, too. There's his own kind of street smarts, but something even beyond that. Anyway, he's turned these eyes on me now and he looks like he knows me right away. I think he recognizes my kind of face, and maybe because of that or maybe just because he's connected to Vietnam, I feel like I can talk and before he can speak, I say, "You didn't fight for *me* in Vietnam."

He throws his head back and laughs a laugh as tight and dry as his face and he says, "I can see that."

"What can you see?"

"You're half Vietnamese, aren't you?"

"I'm Vietnamese."

He throws his head back again but he doesn't laugh, which I'm glad about because I think it would have just made me walk away from him. Instead, he lifts his eyes to the ceiling and closes them, like he's contemplating a familiar twinge of pain. Then after a moment he says, "That's right." Then his eyes open and come down from the ceiling and fix me again and he says, "Do you know who your daddy is?"

"What the fuck business is it of yours?" I say, and my legs want to move off, but I decide to stick it out.

He glances off and lifts his helmet liner and shoves it at an old man with a scroll tattoo on his forearm and wearing a heavily starched sport shirt. "Help a Vietnam vet?" And the guy with the tattoo stops and digs in his pants pocket and drops a whole shitload of change into the liner and he's saying, Sure, sure, all the while. After the old man is gone, the vet shoots his black eyes back to me and says, "You wouldn't be in the States if you didn't know who he is, probably. Unless your momma got on a slow boat to Thailand."

"Who the fuck are you?" I say, but I'm still sticking around and that strikes me as a little bit odd.

"Don't get bent out of shape. I'm Joey." He offers me his hand. I look at it for a moment and he says, "Go on, for Christ's sake. Shake the hand. Didn't I know you were Vietnamese?"

While I'm taking a step forward to shake it, his other hand snatches the helmet liner off his lap and swings it out into the path of a middle-aged woman passing on his other side. "Did you have someone in the war, ma'am? Help me out?" She brushes by without a word and as I grasp Joey's right hand to shake it, he calls after her, "I'm a living memorial." Then he looks at me and at our two hands, which are still shaking. "Sit down here next to me."

"You think I'd be good for business, do you?"

He smiles at this. "Smart kid. But I never thought of that, to tell you the truth." He's sitting on an upturned plastic milk crate and he scoots it over a bit to make room for me on the floor. "Sit down for a couple of minutes. You don't have a business meeting or anything, do you?"

So I sit. And once I'm down he ignores me for a little while, using his "I fought for you" line on a couple of businessmen and the "Did you have someone in the war" line on a woman with shopping bags who's maybe sixty and who stops and puts her bags down and takes out a dollar bill and folds it about five times, like she's expecting to stuff it into a tiny slot, before she finally puts it in the helmet liner. And I'm sitting on the floor wondering why I'm there, and all of a sudden something in my head shifts and I wonder why I should be wondering. I liked Joey from the beginning. There was no bullshit about him, it seemed to me, at least in how we started off. And in spite of me trying to say things in a certain way about who I am, I felt good that he at least saw me as half Vietnamese. And he'd been in Vietnam himself, and more than that, he was spending his days pointing that out to anybody who passed by.

So I'm sitting next to him, slouched against the wall, and there's a fat woman approaching with a kid holding her little finger and staying close at her side and Joey lifts his helmet liner but doesn't shove it at her and he says, "Ma'am, can you help out a Vietnam vet and his son who've lost their wife and mother?"

Real fast I sit up straight and if it wasn't so goddam awkward I would leap up too. As it is, I say to the woman, who has stopped and is looking at me like she's ready to offer me the little finger on her other hand, "He's a fucking liar, lady. Save your money for your own kid." And this kid is peeking around his mother's enormous thigh and you can see in his face that he's doomed to be as fat as his mother.

"I'm sorry, ma'am," Joey says. "He's right. I'm a liar."

I look up at him because I hear something in his voice that surprises me. He suddenly sounds like he's speaking from his eyes. The fat woman moves off and Joey watches her go, turning slowly till he's looking back over his shoulder. In my head I'm still hearing that tone in his voice, a sudden and complete abandonment of the wheedler and manipulator and beggar that he's been acting for these people going by. And when he finally looks at me and I can see his eyes directly, I know I'm right about there being something straight in him, something that had come through in his voice. His eyes stutter around at my face and then he exhales a laugh that has no sound in it, only breath. He says, "What have you got against being part American, anyway?"

"I'm not part American," I say, and I know it's a lie, but I realize it's the lie I was going to try to live in Montreal and I feel foolish. I hope he takes it at face value, and if he does, I'm even ready to say my father was Canadian or Australian or something.

But Joey knows what I'm up to. "I get it," he says, and he squares around on his milk crate to face me. "Is that what your mother keeps telling you?"

"I haven't seen my mother since I was six," I say, and something flickers in Joey that makes me think of his closing his eyes to the ceiling a little earlier, and I wonder if he has some kind of wound that acts up now and then. So I ask him. "Do you have a wound from the war?"

His brow furrows for a moment, like I've caught him off guard. I figure he doesn't like to talk about it, but he's been pushing me about my face and my mother, so I go after him. "Did you get shot up in Vietnam?"

Then he seems to relax and he lifts his chin. "I got two Purple Hearts."

"Do they still bother you, the wounds?"

"Sure. I caught shrapnel all over my legs and they had to operate on my knees a couple of times."

"You should wear your Purple Hearts when you're sitting around here."

"Smart kid. But I sold them a long time ago."

"Listen," I say, "will you stop calling me a smart kid? It's like me calling you a crazed killer."

"Maybe that's what I am."

"Then you wouldn't have to be begging."

"Crazed killers don't kill for money. They don't even give a shit about the stuff."

"But you do."

"Goddam right." Joey shifts his helmet liner to somebody passing by, just a shadow to me, and he says, "Keep a crazed-killer Vietnam vet off the street and put his smart half-Vietnamese kid through college."

I shake my head and lean back against the wall and I probably look disgusted, but I feel pumped up, really. I just rest for a moment with my eyes closed, glad to be there, and I can hear Joey trying his lines on people going by. I've heard them all before until he says, "I can't work and I've got two Purple Hearts to prove it. Help me out?" I open my eyes and some young woman with long hair pirouettes to a pause and she bounces some coins in the helmet liner and she's gone. "Social worker type," Joey says. "They need explanations."

Joey tries a few more people and gets a few more coins, and then he turns around to face me again. "What's your name, kid?"

I open my mouth and nothing comes out and my mind kind of shuts down and I'm right back where I started: who the fuck do I say I am? I notice that I can't just say Võ Đình Thanh to this guy and let it be, and I wonder if that's his fault or if it's New York's fault or if it was just a crazy fantasy, part of running away to Montreal and gone now forever. I hate the silence I'm giving off and I start to stammer about it not being easy because I've got two names, but before I can say either of them, Joey stops me with a wave of his hand.

"Listen," he says, and he sounds kind of excited. "I've got a name for you. You're The Deuce."

And so this is the first time I was ever called The Deuce and it was Joey who called me that, not fifteen minutes after meeting him. A few weeks later I would ask him if he'd ever called anybody else The Deuce and he'd say no, and I'd believe him. I still believe him. When he called me that on the first day he just got inspired and he'd been refusing all along to make me into one thing or another—Vietnamese or American—so it makes sense that I'd be the only one he'd ever think to give that name to. And he was excited about it, like he'd done something special right there on the spot. He explained it right away.

"They call Forty-second Street out there the Deuce," he says. "And you're gonna have to watch out for that street. You haven't been in the city long, have you."

"No," I say.

"I didn't think so. You watch out for the motherfuckers out there who want to eat you alive. But that street is still the Mekong, the river that runs right through all of us around here. And something else, and you're going to get pissed off at me again. You can't bullshit me. You're two things. You're Vietnamese and you're American. A deuce."

He's right about me getting pissed off again, though at first I feel like I'm just going through the motions. I say to him, "You don't know a fucking thing about who's Vietnamese. You're just another GI slogging through the jungles and shooting up the trees and then going into Saigon on a pass and fucking these cute little things who aren't even real." By the time I finish this it's not just a pose, I'm really pissed off, mainly because he's made me think of my cute little unreal mother fucking GIs in the dark and me hanging around outside knowing that if I get too close to the door I can hear her moaning and saying do it some more. I'm suddenly aware of the stink on my body and I figure it's time to go wash up.

I'm not even looking at Joey now, haven't really seen him since I got fogged in with anger, and I hassle my arms and legs and back—all of which gripe in pain—so that I can stand up. When I'm finally on my feet, I glance down at Joey and he's in one of those sad little moods again, which still catches me by surprise even though I've already seen it a couple of times. He's kind of staring at his knees, and then when he feels me standing over him, he looks up at me just like he did when I first came near him, with his eyes full of something, and I start thinking like I did before, taking it seriously this time, that it's jungle-fear or some shit like that, it's bombs and wounds and battle. What a dumb ass I was. You'd think at least a kid like me wouldn't be so quick with the Vietnam cliches. But that's all I could think of.

So when I said I had to go wash up, I'd be back in a little while, and he nodded at that, and I went off and washed and came back and found that Joey had disappeared, even with a whole shitload of people with change in their pockets going by, I was real surprised.

NINE

⁙

I climbed the ramp to the highway over Twelfth and even the voices in the dark had split. I found my bag down the hole where I'd put it and nobody had gotten into it, all my stuff was still there. As I was dropping off to sleep that night with the bag under my head, I said to myself that if I had to choose, I'd rather have Joey disappear than the bag. The old man who'd brought me up to the edge of the hole wasn't around tonight either, and I figured I just had to get used to this kind of thing in an American city.

The next day I walked east from Twelfth Avenue again, but when I got to the bus terminal I didn't go in. I crossed Eighth and followed Forty-second, which was bland in the sunlight. There was a booth by the subway entrance selling Lotto tickets—pick the right four numbers and get the hell off the street—and there were stores with the windows barred and guys smoking in the doorways, waiting for the night to happen, I guess. The only places that still hustled a little bit were the sex shops and I'd never been in one of these things and I passed a few by, where the front door led straight in to a guy sitting behind an elevated counter. Then I came up to a big one, and there was a little foyer area with some photos and handwritten signs on the inner wall and I stepped in.

And this is what was on the wall. There were pictures from the peep show films that were ready for viewing inside. I didn't look too close at these, odd pieces of pictures, actually, meant to tease you, I guess. But the signs directed you to various booth numbers and no shit, they said these things: Piercing and Torture, Hot Candle Wax, Ultimate Japanese; Piss Action, Spreading Device Used in Gynecological Tests; Rectal Thermometer in Use, Doctor's Office Hanky-Panky, Enema and Evacuation; Dog-Pig Orgies; Weird Pussy Probing; Girls with Tampons, Sushi Dinner; Soda Bottle Fizzed Up and Rammed Inside a Girl Who Can't Hold It Any Longer. I'm not making this stuff up. How could anybody make up shit like that? I just backed out of the door and went on up the street and I had all these odd images fizzing around in my head, which I knew were off-track but which I couldn't shake. Like imagining what a weird pussy might look like—set in at some funny angle or in the exact shape of Sweden or Vietnam, even. And seeing how they go about getting dogs and pigs interested in each other—shaving the dogs and curling their tails. And trying to see pissing as *action*—maybe using it to push little race cars around a track or something. And I think the "ultimate Japanese" wouldn't be hot candle wax but tampons at a sushi dinner. And did the people running these shops really think that what was going on in the films they showed was "hanky-panky"? That's like me being called Anthony James Hatcher.

And up ahead I saw a triple bill on a marquee and the movies were "Wet Lips" and "The Spy Who Came" and one that struck me like the signs in the store—"Sex Lust"—like there were these other kinds of lust that you shouldn't confuse this one with, and this might even be only one movie in a series, following "Money Lust" and "Political Lust" and "Family Lust," the one where they go from a scene of buying a ranch wagon to a scene of gorging on turkey at a Thanksgiving table with fifty relatives crammed in everywhere to a scene of all the kids lined up kneeling by their beds saying nighttime prayers with the big trees outside the window and endless lists of people and animals to bless and on and on like that, constant action.

So I just walked on a little faster. This was not the time of day to be on Forty-second Street. It was all just a little too crazy in the sunlight. But I felt pretty strong, even though I'd spent my last few cents for a bagel and I didn't know what was next. I went on east, across Seventh and across Broadway, and the leaders of the world were still talking to each other in running lights up above my head, but I looked back at the concrete island between Seventh and Broadway and winter was gone, the two girls with the long hair and the mink coats had stepped and stepped and finally broken free and disappeared.

I went on east and didn't watch the shops or the people now. The bagel must've burned off real fast, because I didn't feel all that good anymore. I was tired and my body felt like a three-day-old bruise, a dull touchiness all over. This made me nervous, what was setting in now. It was this goddam pattern. I'd feel good for a little while and even be able to step back from all the bullshit around me and see it my own way, laugh at it, and then all of a sudden something would happen and all the fucking fizz would disappear and the sun would be too fucking hot and I couldn't draw a deep breath and I'd start to panic just a little goddam bit.

To fight this thing I forced my eyes up, forced myself to look at things, not think, just look. But there was another one of the sex shops, a little place with the windows painted yellow, and I glanced inside as I passed and a sign on a glass cabinet said All New Films, Teenage Boys. And there was no "hanky-panky" in this shop: another sign said Butt-fucking Buddies and I plunged into the street and some cabbie honked and yelled and I told him to go fuck himself and I crossed Sixth Avenue and walked fast along a stone fence and ignored the whispers, Smoke, Nickel bag, Now it's high time. Finally there was a wide set of stone steps and I glanced up and it was the side entrance to the New York Public Library and I took the steps two at a time and I was through a turnstile, and it was cool inside and hard, marble, the floors and columns and steps were marble and I found I could breathe in here.

But there were still people around: a security man and some girl checking the bags of people on the way out the door and a guy standing in front of the elevators talking in a falsetto voice to a baby slung on his chest. So I climbed a marble staircase with rough stone treads on the edge of each step and I came up into some back hallway and there was nobody at all around. I went through an archway and before me were two swinging doors that looked like they were made of leather and the sign said that this was the map division. I wanted a place to just sit and pull into myself a little bit, and so I stepped through the doors.

The room was small, compared to the scale of the staircases and hallways, and there were long wooden tables with brass lamps running down the center. The chairs were enormous and made of dark wood and I realized I hadn't been in a real chair since I'd left New Jersey. There were a couple of people at the far end of one of the tables, but they were hunched over maps and they might as well have been in whatever country they were looking at, because the place felt empty. Even the librarian, who was behind a desk on the wall to my right, just gave me a quick little smile and then ignored me.

So I sat down. The walls were lined with books and the brass lamps had sharp-edged shades on them that kept the light focused on the table, which had a little herringbone design in its wood, like a parquet floor. I ran my hands over the wood and it was very smooth and cool to the touch until I reached the spill of the light, where the wood was warm. I left my hands there like they were lizards sunning on a rock and I sat for a long time like that, just taking in the heat and keeping my eyes lowered to the perfect fitting of the tiles of wood in the tabletop and feeling my own perfect fit in the scooped seat of this chair.

Maybe like the lizards I finally got my body heat back to normal, because I began to feel a calmness about myself that reminded me of the whole point of running away. Sitting in a back-alley room of the New York Public Library I was starting to feel Vietnamese again. Then I heard the rustle of a map at another table and I thought to look at some maps of Vietnam. So I went to the desk and the lady who'd smiled at me when I came in smiled again and she had real tiny teeth that were brown around the edges, which was too bad, since she seemed to be pretty free with the smiles when you'd expect her to be stiff with a kid who was asking her to do things for him.

But I just filled out a form—I made up some address in Hoboken—
and she even thanked me, and five minutes later she had me set up at
the table with a big portfolio.

The first map said in the lower left corner that it was made by the
C.I.A. and the whole country was done in these juiceless tans and
pale greens. Every fucking airfield in the country was on the map but
not much else. My mother's province of Vĩnh Bình only had one city
marked on it. Vĩnh Bình was just full of faint blue lines with low
grass-marks spiking out of them, telling the C.I.A. guys that if they
landed there, they were going to sink up to their asses in marshes, I
guess. The map pissed me off, and I went to the next one, which was
a "Background to the News" map. And there was this big question
across the top: What kind of place is Vietnam and what kind of war
is it? The country was sectioned off with four big Roman numerals
and there were little drawings of jets and soldiers and boats and forts
scattered all over, showing where these things were located, and I
flipped that map over, too, and it made a little tearing noise along one
of the folds. I glanced over at the librarian and she didn't look up,
and then I took a moment and appreciated the noise and I found the
tear and ran my finger between the separated parts and widened the
tear to a couple of inches. This map stuff wasn't doing the right thing
for me, but I looked at the next one anyway.

At least the map was in Vietnamese and I found a date at the
bottom, 1957, when my mother was still a girl in Vĩnh Bình. This
map was full of drawings, too, showing where things were, but there
were fishnets and lobsters and cows and pigs and teacups and water-
falls and water buffalo and rubber trees. Vietnam sure seemed like a
cute little country on this map and it didn't take more than a few
seconds of looking at the cute little fishermen in their sampans off the
coast or the cute little storybook tigers in the highlands for this map
to piss me off, too.

I thought about getting up and walking out, but where the fuck
would I go? I could just push the maps away and sit there and take in
the quiet and relax in a chair. I even sat back and tried that for a
minute. But I was starting to get antsy again and I thought what the
hell, and I lifted the map of The Republic of Cute Vietnam and the

next map sat me up straight and then drew me over it. It was of Saigon and it was in French but you could see all the streets, all the houses even, it seemed, which were these tiny pink squares and rectangles. I couldn't find any familiar streets and then I noticed at the bottom that this was only one of four maps that covered the city.

I lifted the sheet and found section two underneath and I saw the fountain at Lê Lợi and Nguyễn Huệ, near the City Hall. The fountain was three concentric circles in blue and I followed Lê Lợi—the map even showed its median in green—and I reached the big circle at the central market. I could have jumped ahead to where I wanted to go, but I didn't. I made myself follow the streets, like I'd flown back to Saigon and was in a xích-lô now and I was driving along the street, going back to the place where I'd lived but I had to be patient, the driver was old and he didn't have a motor on his rig and he was puffing away. But I didn't care. I'd give him a good tip and I was enjoying just watching the tamarind trees passing overhead and the motorcycles rushing by with these guys on them with wild shocks of hair like mine and some of the cycles with whole families on them, the father driving with the smallest child on his lap and the mother holding on behind him and two children clinging behind her, the last one at the very back edge of the seat over the fender. And most of these people look at me as they pass and they smile and nod with their beautiful teeth flashing at me and you can see that they recognize me. I'm home, after all. I'm in Saigon and heading for a special place, and we go around the circle at the central market and head down Trần Hưng Đạo and I'm looking up ahead now and at last I see the movie marquee where a Chinese kung fu movie is playing, the place where I dashed across the street and gave Kenneth the slip. Then I see the gray facade of the Hotel Metropole facing Trần Hưng Đạo over a little triangular wedge of space, because the street where its front doors open—Nguyễn Cư Trinh—comes in at a sharp angle here, and that's my street, the street of the Texas Girls Bar and the mouth of my alley and the back steps and the apartment where I lived with my mother.

And my fingertip hovers over that building now, a tiny little pink rectangle, but I don't touch it. I look closer and the map even has my alley and all the turns are shown there; it looks like a water dipper with a bent handle, my alley, a straight run from Nguyễn Cư Trinh and then a sharp right turn where there was an old man who talked to himself starting at dusk and his voice muttered in the dark all night till dawn and then he would stop. And I touch that place with my finger and then follow the immediate sharp left and then another right, down to the bottom of the dipper, and a left and another left up to the dead end. The map even shows that place, where my alley stopped and almost connected to another alley that went up to Bùi Viện. Just before Kenneth came along, I had almost figured out a way to get through that space and into the next alley. I'd found a building with a front-to-back hallway that took me to a narrow out-side passageway full of garbage that looked like it was left over from the French, and then there was a crawl space under a strange little building that smelled like the Saigon docks sometimes smelled, a smell I couldn't name till much later, in Jersey, as cordite. I never got a chance to explore the crawl space, but I bet I could've gotten through to the next alley that way. It had a lot more twists in it than mine and I trace them now on the map, the map shows everything, and I find the connection at last, crawling beneath the building with the smell of cordite and I emerge in my alley and I follow it back to my apartment.

It's so clear. The building sat on Nguyễn Cư Trinh and stretched along the alley, and there it is, the tiny pink rectangle sitting just that way, and I move my hand over it and then touch the place and all the questions that I guess I was expecting lift up from the map and fill my head. But she can't still be there, not after this long, not with the problems she'd gotten herself into, not with her body getting old and with nothing else to sell, not with those eyes that had grown a little crazy and that face that had grown haggard, and I close my eyes and try to see her face in the photograph, calm there before the rooftops, and beautiful, and with a little shock I realize that I'd forgotten all about her when I hid my duffel, that she, too, could be stolen out there on the abandoned highway.

So I got up from the table and went out of the map room and out of the library and I walked all the way over to Twelfth Avenue and I went up the ramp and when I got to the hole in the highway, there was no one in sight. I lowered myself into the hole so I could look in the bag without anybody coming up suddenly and seeing me. I crouched in the trash and my hands groped back into the shadows and the bag was there and a knot loosened in the back of my neck. I found the book and then Nghi was staring at me in the dimness of the hole and the face looked all wrong to me now, I wanted her to smile, she should have at least given me a little smile to try to encourage me, but of course it wasn't me she was looking at, it was the invisible GI with the camera. My face and my neck and the backs of my arms were oozing with sweat and I could faintly smell something long dead and I had to get out of the hole. What was I going to do with the picture? It would get crumpled in a pocket and Nghi just stared at me with her hair falling on her shoulders and not even the possibility of a smile, not even a smile that said, When this GI with the camera is long gone I'll still have my child, my son. I put the picture back inside the book and I put the book back inside the duffel bag and shoved the bag deeper into the darkness and I lifted myself out of the hole and got the hell off the highway.

It wasn't even strange to me that I kept walking the same path all the time, though thinking about it now, it seems pretty pathetic to me. Like it was all some little fucking domestic routine. I went right back along Forty-second Street. Still, I guess I didn't have anywhere else to go, and I wasn't exactly in a mood for exploration. This time when I hit the bus terminal I was on the verge of getting hungry again and my money was gone and I remembered Joey. The point was that you could beg money in the terminal, but the first thought of him was more like, What the fuck did you run off for?

But I went down Eighth Avenue to go in the South Wing, just like the day before, and by the time I got to the doors I'd convinced myself that I was down here simply because I already knew it was a good place to get people to give you some money. But as soon as I entered I did look to the spot under the flags and when no one was there I said, "Fuck you," under my breath.

Then I went and stood in the spot myself. The traffic was pretty light at the moment, but that gave me a chance to watch somebody approach and get myself keyed up for them. I guess because of a lingering anger at Joey I just kept it simple, the same thing to everybody: Can you spare some change? I tried this maybe two dozen times over the next twenty minutes or so and at the end I had one quarter in my pocket.

Then a business suit approached and I figured I'd change my line. I said, "I'm having some troubles, can you help me out?" The guy had these real thick glasses and they flashed my way, catching light from somewhere, and his eyes disappeared and he said, "Fuck your troubles, asshole, get a job." I was frozen for a second by my anger and he was out the door before I could get my legs and arms to move. Finally I spun around and maybe I would've gone after him except all of a sudden there's a hand on my shoulder and I spin the other way and Joey is standing there smiling at me with just the left half of his mouth, like I'm an idiot or something, and I'm ready to punch out Joey now. My hands even come up before me.

Joey raises his own hands, showing me his palms. "Calm down now, Deuce. You've gotta learn the first lesson of getting money out of these people. You don't get personally involved in the turndowns. That asshole wasn't talking to you. He doesn't know a goddam thing about you."

So this makes some sense to me. I nod at him and I look at my hands, which are still clenched into fists and hanging between us.

"You don't need those for me," Joey says. "Not for him either. You let these guys get to you and that's just what they want."

I lower my hands but I say, "What the hell happened to you yesterday? I came back and you were gone."

For a second it looks like Joey doesn't know how to answer. His eyes dart away from me but then they return and he says, "Were you coming back? That's news to me, Deuce." And I know he's lying, but twice now he's called me by my new name and it sounds pretty good and I'm not mad at him anymore. Then he says, "You need some money, do you? What've you been telling these people?"

"Telling them?"

"Your line. How do you ask for money?"

Actually I knew right off what he was talking about, but now that

I'm not pissed off at him anymore, I'm embarrassed at how stupidly I've been working these people. Joey's going to think I didn't even notice what he was doing yesterday. So I just shrug and hope he'll drop it.

But he doesn't. "What does that mean?" he says, mimicking my shrug. "Come on, Deuce. Give me your line."

I say, "Don't fucking hassle me, okay? I don't do this for a living."

Joey puts on this big act, getting all wide-eyed and rearing back from me like he's shocked. *"That's* what you tell these people?"

"Look," I say, "you know goddam well I just said that right now to you. That wasn't my fucking line."

Joey rolls his eyes. "Oh, I get it. You don't do this for a living. You're some rich kid from Westchester down here slumming for a few days just for kicks."

I see this whole thing about to blow up, with him disappearing again, and for a second I think, Okay, just let it happen and get it over with. I don't need any more hassles anyway. But then I figure Joey knows some things that may be useful to me, and as soon as I think that, I realize how hard-assed it sounds. And it's not even what I really feel. I don't want it all to blow up, because Joey's okay. That's all. And I find myself wanting to keep the needling back-and-forth going. On an impulse I say, "You're wrong."

"I am?" He cocks his head and his eyebrows arch up and he waits for me to speak, and it's like he knows I'm going to say something smart-assed and he's enjoying it. Then I realize what I'd planned to say: I'm a rich kid from the Jersey Shore. But the words freeze in my head. Not even in smart-ass banter am I ready to say that. Not anymore. I'm no fucking rich kid and I'm no fucking New Jerseyan.

"So how am I wrong?" Joey says.

"Don't push it," I say, and it comes out bad, like I'm just some punk, and I wish I could think of something to soften it.

But Joey simply smiles a little—not the one-side-of-the-mouth smile but something more friendly—and he says, "I got it. Nobody from Westchester could ever be named The Deuce. Right?"

"That's right," I say and my gratitude for him saying this yanks me up straight, I feel like lifting up on my toes.

Then he cuffs me on the shoulder and lowers his voice, like we're getting down to business now. "So what do you say when somebody's walking by and you want some of what they've got?"

"Just bullshit. Nothing that works. I've got a fucking quarter."

"Say it to me."

"Can you spare some change?"

Joey looks me up and down and then glances around the foyer. "You're hungry, aren't you?"

I snip off the bullshit words before they can even get out of my head and into my mouth. I say, "Yes, I'm hungry."

"Let's get something to eat."

"Holy shit," I say. "Did that line work on you?"

Joey laughs at this. "Hell, no. It's so fucking pathetic I just figure you're going to starve to death in this city."

So he flips his head toward the inner doors and he takes off and I follow, about half a step behind, because he doesn't seem to want to talk while we move and he's walking real fast. As soon as we go through the doors, I see the Greyhound ticket windows up ahead and it feels like about six years ago when I was there. But we don't get that far now. Joey takes a sharp right turn and we go down a little corridor and out a door and we're in Forty-first Street under the connecting passageway between the terminal's two wings. A couple of ragged men are slouching around here and we cross the street and go in the North Wing and inside the door is an Arby's. "Wait here," Joey says, and he goes in.

I watch him through the window as he approaches the cashier and then I turn and look around the terminal. The ceiling is real high and it's all an orderly tangle of these metal tubes which must be up there for show or something because I can't imagine any building carrying so much steam or water or piss or whatever that they'd need all these tubes. Hanging from the tubes are big posters with enormous drawings of people and buses and crap like that and you can tell that they've been drawn by kids—the people all have snakey arms and legs with no joints—and the posters have school names on them and for a second I think about how my asshole teachers are marking me absent every morning and wondering how a smart Asian kid like that would just up and stop coming to school, it doesn't make sense.

Then I lower my eyes, and across the floor, near the central steps to the underground bus levels, there's a bagel place and Joey's voice is suddenly in my ear. "If you ever get the urge for a bagel, go to that one and not the one up on the second floor."

I look at Joey and I'm still trying to read the guy; I expect to find signs of him putting me on, but he's staring across the floor with me and then he looks up over our heads and behind us, and I follow his gaze to a second-floor balcony and four faces looking over the edge. All four are boys, probably my age or a little older. Probably older. Three of them are white and one is black and they're all real slender and there's something about them—I don't know what, exactly, but they're not that far away, because Joey and I are right under them and I can see the way they hold themselves, like something's balanced on their heads and they've got to be careful not to let it drop off. Anyway, all this makes them look young when I think they're probably older. They're not Asians, after all, and like me, Asians can look older when they're young and younger when they're old. At least I can. But these four faces finally see Joey and me and one of the white guys gives us a slow smile and then an older face appears beside the one who's smiling.

I don't get a chance to check out the new face. All I see is that it's very round and it surprises me how big it is. Like if you were watching an empty sky and you figure you know the proportions of everything and then all of a sudden the goddam Hindenburg appears. But this is me thinking back about the face. I'm trying to tell this straight. It would be easy for me now, since I've been through all that, to make it seem like I was a lot smarter than I was, that I could see certain things coming. But I'm trying to tell this the way it happened. So like I said, I didn't have a chance to be reminded of goddam Nazi dirigibles when I saw this face, and maybe it didn't even seem at the time to be so very unusual. But as soon as it appears up there, Joey says, "Come on," and he takes off back through the corridor that brought us here and hustles across Forty-first Street like somebody is chasing us and we don't stop till we've cut through the

South Wing as well and gone out a side door on Fortieth and down the street a little ways.

Then finally Joey sits us down on the sidewalk and we lean back against the base of the terminal. Right across the street from us is a storefront with "International Foods Import and Export" on its window and Joey drops a foil-wrapped package into my lap. "It's a beef sandwich," he says. "It's better for you. Stay away from the hamburgers. The frying will give you cancer. Worse than Agent Orange. Which I had some good doses of in Nam. I'm just sitting and waiting for the big C to come knocking on my liver. Eat up."

He tells me to eat up because I guess I'm just sitting there staring at the foil-wrapped package which is the thing that's going to save me from cancer after my desperate escape from the North Wing and the faces on the balcony where I'm not supposed to eat bagels. Things are going just a little too fast. "Okay," I say. "Okay. I'm trying to keep up with you, Joey. I'm going to eat my roast beef sandwich now, but tell me again about the bagels."

Joey stops unwrapping his sandwich and he kind of scoots around to look at me more directly, like this is real important stuff he's about to say. "That's Fairyland up there, Deuce. That's where the Bagelonians hang out, see. At the bagel shop up there and at the juice bar. Fruit juice. You want the juice of some fruit, you go to the juice bar. You want hot buns with a hole in the middle, you get a bagel. A kid like you wanders up there and you get some guys just like you who really think you're special and a nice older guy to make up for what you don't have in the crummy life you've been living and all your bodily openings get stuffed with brotherly and fatherly love and there it is."

I'm busy trying to translate all this and I guess Joey sees me working at it. He leans toward me and he says, "Look, Deuce, you know what a fag is, don't you? A homosexual?"

"Sure."

"That's what's happening up there. Now, I don't care what two grown-up guys want to do in private. I sure as hell ain't no moralist. After the things I did in Nam, I got no place to talk to anybody about anything. Especially if what those two grown-up guys do doesn't hurt anybody. They're better off than a guy like me whose country made him do terrible shit. I'm a veteran of that war over there in your country of birth, Deuce. A real fucking veteran. I've got some shit to really worry about, things I did."

Joey suddenly seems to me to be running off the track and it worries me a little bit. Even as I'm thinking this, he's still going on about Vietnam and how guilty he is, and I interrupt him. "So the Bagelonians up in Fairyland aren't just grown-up guys not hurting anybody?"

He shifts back again like he never left the subject. "The kids who get sucked in up there are fifteen, sixteen, sometimes even younger. And they don't know what the hell they're getting into. Then finally all they know is selling their asses, and you tell me where they're heading . . . Eat your sandwich."

I unwrap the sandwich and all of a sudden I'm not feeling real hungry, but I eat anyway and after I get going at it, the thing tastes pretty good. Joey is snorting and smacking next to me as he eats, like it's been a long time. "Thanks for getting me this," I say.

"It's okay, Deuce. You haven't been in town long, right?"

"Not long," I say, and I realize he's asked me that before. I glance over at him and he's leaning back against the wall, not looking at me, and suddenly he cocks his head.

"I knew that," he says, and I feel a little flush of relief.

"You asked me the same question yesterday," I say.

He slaps himself on the temple with the palm of his hand and the sound of it is loud and his head recoils. "My fucking mind is going. It's the Agent Orange and too many nights walking point when you can't see a foot in front of you in the dark."

"It's just too many fucking roast beef sandwiches," I say. "You need hamburgers. They're good for brain cells."

Joey does a real slow take, turning his head with his eyes forced open wide. It scares me for a second—I think maybe he's serious—and the surprise of this even reminds me of the round-faced man in Fairyland. But then Joey says, "I've taken up with a goddam heretic," and he closes his eyes tight and shakes his head sadly and I know he's kidding. But the image of the man on the balcony remains and I figure later I'll forget to ask, so I say, "Joey, who's the guy that spooked us back there? The older guy on the balcony?"

Joey opens his eyes abruptly, and then he nods like he's been afraid he'd have to get around to that question. "How old are you, Deuce?"

I think about lying. I'd like to try out twenty on him. But I find that I want to talk straight with Joey. I realize I'm hesitating and he says, "You think I'm going to turn you in or something? Tell me your real age."

"Sixteen."

Joey nods as if he knew all the time. "You like girls, right?"

This is not a question I feel comfortable with. I'm sixteen, after all, and it's only recently that I'm thinking I might actually do something about this itchiness I get around them. All that stuff with girls just seems too complicated so far, one more goddam thing that has to do with my face, I guess. But I think I know what Joey means—do I like girls as opposed to boys—and so the answer is simple. I say, "That's right. Girls."

"But you've never had one, right?"

"Shit, Joey, what the fuck's this all about?"

"Listen, Master Deuce, I'm not trying to put you on the spot. Shit, I was a virgin till I got to Vietnam. Hard as that might be for you to believe. I was nineteen before I ever had a woman and she was pure Vietnamese."

This whole thing had taken a very uncomfortable turn. If I was going to start thinking about Joey as one of the GIs who could've passed through my mother's bed, it was best for me to stand up right there and then and walk away.

But then Joey says something a little odd. "Don't get the wrong idea, Deuce. I loved her."

It strikes me as odd because it's just what he had to say to keep me there. That makes me wonder: Did he know what I was thinking, about wanting to get away from him if he was just another GI short-timer? And does that mean he just assumed that my mother was a whore? These are troubling questions, and yet I believe him when he says he loved that Vietnamese girl, whoever she was, and suddenly, walking away from this guy and going off on my own again seems the wrong thing to do. But it's still real tough to figure out how to act, and the easy thing, of course, is to be a smart-ass. So I say to him, "I don't give a shit if you loved her or not. What's all this got to do with the guy on the balcony?"

Joey pauses and it looks like he's retracing his own thoughts. "I'm just making a point," he finally says.

"And what's that?"

"You ask me about Mr. Treen, and what I'm getting around to is this. You take a sixteen-year-old male virgin who runs away from wherever and ends up alone and without any money in New York City and that kid is Mr. Treen's meat. And you might think that he's going to go after the boys who already like boys. But they're easy. They'll find him. Mr. Treen especially likes it if the boy is convinced he goes for girls. And you might think that all the boy has to do is say no. But Mr. Treen is very persistent. He'll back off and wait his time and he'll try again and again, and if all the little tricks don't work, there's always the knife and rape, and from what I hear, that's the way he likes it best anyway."

You know how you can't help getting pictures in your head when you hear things? Look, I know I've got a mouth on me that some people think is pretty foul, but I finally understood what it was that can trouble these people about my saying "fuck," for instance. One time an old woman at school—the home economics teacher—overheard me, and she said, "Don't you understand how you violate my rights when you use that word?" And of course I thought she was just some straitlaced biddy making trouble. But then she said, "I have a right not to be forced to think of that." It didn't make me stop talking the way I'd talked since I learned English in Saigon. It wasn't just a word for me. It was like tones in Vietnamese. The word was part of the rhythm of the language and if you took it out, you couldn't even speak. But at least I understood what the problem was for other people. As soon as this woman heard the word, she actually saw people fucking in her mind. This woman and all the people like her, the ones who have the most trouble with that kind of language, probably are the ones who've got the most stuff like that happening in their imaginations and they can't even control it. It makes you think of them a little different. I even kind of liked her after that, knowing that she had some juice in her, with a sexy imagination that she couldn't stop. Everybody has to do what they can in order to keep their minds where they want them.

Like me. I'm sort of stepping back now and listening to myself. When I heard about this guy Treen from Joey I was scared shitless. I wasn't thinking of any goddam home economics teacher. It's now, going back over all that. I get scared again and so off I go talking about dirty words and old women with hot imaginations and shit like that when I was really sitting there on the sidewalk and there were these pictures in my mind that I just didn't want to deal with and I was like the old lady flashing on the word "fuck," only my pictures had this guy with the enormous head and a knife and he's got some kid in a stairwell.

So I jerk my face away from Joey and I watch the traffic real close, though there isn't a lot of it, and after a cab goes by and I try to read the mileage rates on the side door, I'm desperate for something to go past that I can watch. I look up the street and there's an old truck coming this way and I ignore the odd thing about it and instead I see the old-fashioned design, how the fenders are poufed out from the hood—it's probably a model from the mid-fifties—and the bed of the truck has open-slat sides and it's piled high with stuff—junk is all, things made out of metal that you can't even identify, it's such shit. But as the truck gets nearer, I look back to the odd thing about it. Strapped to the front is this enormous teddy bear and the truck passes now and the teddy bear is beat up as hell but he's lashed to the grin of the grill of this old truck. New York, New York, man. This is my city now. But I tell myself I can give the whole fucking world the slip if I need to. I've always learned my way around and I've done just fine. I even gave Kenneth the slip. Even here, in his own fucking country. I wonder how the old lady back at my school sees that one—"this fucking country"—does she actually have this vision of about a hundred million naked couples going at each other all at once? Is she there, too, over in some corner with the shop teacher banging away at her?

But I'm still trying to wander off. What happened is that Treen scared me and the traffic didn't help and I turned back to Joey and tried to change the subject. I asked him about what I was supposed to say to people if just asking for spare change wasn't good enough. And he was happy to get off onto a different subject, too, it seemed, and he told me some things to say and I heard some of them and some of them I didn't, because there was this trembling inside that came on me like I was freezing to death. I was real aware of the building I was leaning against and I guess it should have occurred to me that I could go somewhere else, though I didn't have a clue as to where. Some other train or bus station, I guess, but it just never entered my mind. Joey had chosen this place and that counted for something, and at least I knew something about it. I knew a couple of spots to avoid and a man to avoid and I was smart enough to realize that wherever I went in this city there would be more corridors to get mugged in or raped in and more Mr. Treens to suck you in. At least I'd already learned some of the dangers at the Port Authority. Anywhere else and I'd have to start over again. And there was something more, I realize now. I guess I was even aware of it when I was sitting on the sidewalk with Joey, but it was a feeling I was ashamed of. There was something familiar already, something knowable, about this bus terminal, and it made me feel good about the place in spite of its dangers. And that's why I was ashamed, because I figured the need for that was part of what I'd run away from. The fucking place was home.

TEN

⬥

But you can't sleep at the bus station, and though Joey and I sat and talked a while longer, he never asked me where I was sleeping. He told me to check the phone for coins every time I went past, and he told me which doors of the terminal I could stand in front of and hail cabs for passengers and try to get tips, but he never said a goddam thing about places where I could sleep. Then pretty soon he got up and he shrugged. "Listen, Deuce, I've got some stuff to do."

"You have a business meeting or something?" I said.

I thought I'd at least get a smile out of him, since I was throwing his own words back in his face in the way we'd been needling each other all along, but he seemed to take it seriously. "It's business. Sure. Begging business. You see what they do to a guy who got shot up for his country?"

Then he walks off and I'm sitting there with this fuck-you attitude in my head and I'm getting tired of that shit. I stay there a while to calm down, and this might even be worse than the feelings of home. Here I am getting bent out of shape because somebody just walks away from me. I can't believe I give a shit about this. I'm the guy who walks away. I don't need all this fucking hand-holding. I don't need a father or a big brother or a friend or anybody else. Hey, man, I'm The Deuce, and I thank Mr. Joey Cipriani for the name, at least, though it strikes me that he didn't really have anything to do with it. The thing is that I *am* The Deuce, and it's like he'd already heard about me, so he just knew to call me by the name. So thanks for the roast beef sandwich. That's all. Have a good day. He's just another passerby who put some coins in my hand, and I get up and I go in the side door of the South Wing and I pass the subway stairs that I went down the night I took the train to Coney Island. Then I'm standing at the edge of the central corridor right next to the Greyhound ticket windows and there are people sitting on bags and waiting in line.

To the right are the doors leading into the foyer with the flags, and I figure Joey is out there doing his business. I head the other way. Joey had given me a good line to use, and for this I thank the crazy son of a bitch one more time. I walk past the main escalators that lead to the suburban concourse and I go up half a dozen steps onto a little brick and tile plaza which is the main ticketing area for all the suburban buses.

I head for a well-dressed woman at the end of one of the longer lines and I say in a voice full of deep struggle, "Excuse me, ma'am, I'm trying to get money to buy a bus ticket home. Could you please help me?" I can say this because I know it's a lie and because it strikes me as pretty funny that a lie like that would help give me the money to stay away from Point Pleasant.

She says, "Sorry, I wish I could help," which obviously is also a lie, because if she really wished she could help, then she goddam would, the woman had a flashy gold watch and real nice clothes.

But I played it cool. You don't take any of the turndowns personally. I just give her a meek, "Yes, ma'am," and I stifle any other words and move on to the next line, which is a little shorter and has a guy at the back who's maybe sixty or so. He's wearing a sport shirt that looks pretty subdued—it's real dark blue—but when you get close you see it's got palm trees and sailboats on it. I use the same line on him and he turns and he says, "If you get home, will you stay?"

I look straight in his eyes and I don't even blink. "Yessir," I say in a low, firm voice. "I'm not going to make the same mistake twice."

He kind of smiles at this and he says, "Promise?"

"I do."

"Why won't your folks come get you?"

I'm thinking pretty fast now. I say, "They're too proud to come and I'm too proud to ask. I've gotta walk in on my own."

This does the trick. The guy doesn't even ask me how much the ticket is. He gives me a five-dollar bill and he shakes my hand. But now I'm in a situation Joey didn't warn me about. One person gives me the whole price of the ticket and he's standing right there where the tickets are sold. I thank him again and I'm looking around trying to figure out what the hell to do. There's maybe fifteen or twenty ticket windows, each for a different bus line or set of destinations, and so I go to the farthest, down by the entrance to the rest rooms. There's only one person in front of me, and I look back over my shoulder.

Across the plaza the guy in the blue sport shirt is looking straight at me. He nods and smiles. I'm starting to figure this out. I nod back and flutter the five-dollar bill at him so he can see it's in my right hand. Then the person in front of me is gone and I belly up to the window. My right side is blocked off from view and I slip the money in my pocket but then immediately, for the sport shirt's benefit, I put a clenched right fist on the sill of the ticket window, like I'm giving the clerk the money. Then I lean on the sill and turn my body a little bit so that the exact transaction is blocked off. I do some time-killing stuff with the clerk—asking about routes and times—and then I ask him for a schedule. He gives me one and it's this that I turn to wave in the air to the sport shirt, who's still watching me, just like I figured.

He's only two customers from the window and I've got to get the hell out of here fast. I wave a final farewell to this guy and I head straight off the plaza without going past him again. But he can still see me, so I head back along the big corridor and I approach the main escalators. I look over my shoulder and the face of this guy is still there in the distance, turned in my direction. I step onto the escalator and I'm gliding up to the suburban concourse and I keep my eyes up the moving steps.

At the top it still seems complicated. He's also buying a ticket that would bring him to this level and I sure as hell don't want to run into him here. I think at this point that I've been a stupid idiot to even try to keep up this bullshit about wanting to go home. I should've just taken the five bucks and turned and walked briskly away and by the time it struck him as funny that I'd leave the ticket plaza without a ticket, I'd be far enough away to duck down some corridor and run like hell. But maybe not. Maybe he would've collared me with the first step I took in the wrong direction. Then I get pissed off with myself over all this indecision. Here I stand, still at the top of the escalator, and this guy could be heading there any second.

I look around. To my right and left are corridors leading to bus gates, including the gate I came in on. I can't stay near any gates. I turn to look behind me and there's a big, square open space with the well of escalators gaping in its center, but all around the square are more doors into stairwells leading to more fucking bus gates. The only direction that seems safe is on the far side of this space where there are glass doors. I head off that way, keeping well back from the balustrade that looks over the escalators, and ahead is another wing of the terminal and it looks brighter than the South Wing and I'm through the final door and there's a smell of shoe leather and I look at a shoe repair shop I'm passing.

I think it's then that I realize where I am, though I don't know what makes it happen. Obviously not the shoe shop, but some deep current in me that suddenly rushes to the top and spills over and it feels like hot water splashing inside my face and in my chest and running in my arms. But my legs keep moving and then the corridor opens up to a bright tan-tiled floor with big square red brick posts and I've never seen it before but I don't even have to glance down the near wall to see the fruit juice bar and the bagel sign because off at an angle, about twenty yards away, I can see a scattering of boys and some of them have their backs to me and are leaning over the balcony looking down onto the main floor of the North Wing and some of them are leaning against a wall and some of them turn their faces in my direction and I stop my legs. I make my legs stop and make them turn me around and they're heavy, like in a bad dream, and I move off as fast as I can back through the glass doors.

Now here's another one of those odd things. You'd think I would just hit the escalators and beat it to the nearest exit as fast as I could. But the only option that seemed open to me in the middle of all that was to deal with Treen and his boys *within* the terminal. I guess my attachment to the place was that strong already. It must've felt like my alleys in Saigon or something, and if I wasn't a master of all the little tricks of the place yet, I figured at least I knew enough to give Treen's pack of boys the slip. I'm not going to be chased away from here by a bunch of butt-fucking buddies, I tell myself.

So when I get to the main corridor at the top of the escalators I glance over my shoulder. I don't see anybody coming through the doors from the other wing and I think about places in the terminal where nobody would look for me. I remember the first few minutes off the bus and I turn to the right and hustle down the hall. I'm still clutched up a little at the thought of what I almost walked into, but I'm beginning to smile at the idea of where I'm going to hide. I figure Fairyland doesn't have a bowling team and I can see the place up ahead now and I can even hear pins falling in the distance.

I glance over my shoulder again, and there are people in the corridor, but they all look like they're coming or going to buses. I even think I see a blue sport shirt in the distance, but there are no slender young men heading this way. Then I'm through the door and inside the bowling alley and the lanes are directly before me. I need to hang around here for a little while, I figure, and it even comes to me that I'm going to have to rent some goddam shoes and bowl. But then I see there's a little gallery of chairs behind the lanes, a place for spectators. I figure you can't just sit there without buying something or the place would be full of bums. But hell, I've got five bucks now and a pretty good thirst and off to my right is kind of a bar. Why wait for the hassle? I step to the bar and order a Coke real polite and I take it over to the seats, making sure to move down the row far enough so that I won't be seen right away if somebody walks in, but not so far that I can't still keep an eye on the door.

This is just fine for a long while. There's only one guy bowling, a guy with a big gut peeking out from under his T-shirt and tiny little feet, though maybe the bowling shoes he rented are just too small for him, because when he runs at the pins he takes these little hopping steps that look like the shoes are hurting him. Anyway, I glance toward the door after every frame and nobody's coming in and the guy behind the bar is reading a newspaper and I'm really starting to relax. The guy with the gut is even finding a groove now, and when he gets two strikes in a row he's starting to beam all over the alleys, which means mostly at me. Then he gutters a ball and starts talking to himself and I look toward the door for about the twentieth time.

Only this time somebody's there. The first sight is a little shock because just for a second it looks like it might be one of Treen's boys. Then in the next second I see it's not a boy at all but a girl, she's got a whole mane of hair but it's twisted up on the top of her head and I didn't see it right away. She's real slender and she's wearing a T-shirt and jeans, all of which gave me that first shock, since I was half looking for one of those guys from Fairyland anyway. But I see her hair swirled up into place and I can see now that the T-shirt is reaching out at the chest, you know how that goes, where your own chest gets a little bit sensitive, like this same part of the girl is reaching out to touch you there and you're suddenly ready for it, your skin's expecting it. Anyway, this girl has a duffel bag over her shoulder and she's looking around the place like she can't believe her fucking eyes, just like I probably looked a couple of days ago. She's got a real nice face, from what I can see from here; it's more round than you'd expect from an American girl this thin and her lips are full and they're not painted up with lipstick and her hair is black.

She looks back over her shoulder, out the door, and then to the bar, where the guy is still reading his newspaper. I think she likes the quiet in here. I can't tell you how, but I can read her mind—first it's, What the fuck is a bowling alley doing here, and then it's, I don't know where the fuck to go out there but in here at least there's no crowd and maybe I can sit down and get my head straight.

So she sort of slides over to the nearest stool at the bar and she perches on the edge of it. The guy lowers his newspaper with heavy arms, like doing this is a real pain in the ass, and I get a little pumped up with anger. I'm watching real careful now to make sure he doesn't give her any trouble. She says something and he turns away and gets a glass and I watch her face and I think she kind of glances at me and then away, like she's shy. Once again I think I can read her thoughts: I'd like to talk to that guy over there; his face intrigues me, it's exotic, but I don't want to look too long at him because he might take me for the wrong kind of girl in this place.

You can see how crazy I was getting in her presence when I can actually start believing that this face of mine is some kind of attraction. But this is Norma I'm looking at, though I don't know it yet. Norma was not your usual girl. And why shouldn't I be able to see that right off? The guy behind the bar gives her a Coke or something and the girl drops her duffel bag at the foot of the stool. But right away the bartender leans toward her and says something. I'm ready to jump up and go after the guy, but the girl simply nods and leans down—the black coil of her hair shimmers and threatens to fall— and she picks up her bag and takes her drink and walks this way. He probably told her that under eighteen she couldn't sit at the bar, and coming into the light of the alleys she looks about my age, sixteen, and after another quick glance at me, she eases into an end seat one row down.

So there I sit as stiff as a fucking bowling pin and I want this girl to roll my way, I'm ready to fall over, but all I can do is sit and look at the stray wisps of her hair, how they touch the back of her neck, and at the swirls of her ear, like you have to have this real intricate thing to say, your ideas twisting and turning just so, in order to find your way into her. And I can't even figure out how to say hello. And now I'm thinking my face isn't so intriguing after all. And then the two of us end up watching the guy with the fat gut doing his little hippity-hop at the pins. The guy even gets a strike and he turns to us and lifts his arms in triumph and for a second I even envy him his being able to look good for the girl. But then I think, She didn't run away to find herself a goddamn bowler.

I guess I'd assumed she was a runaway from the moment I saw her in the doorway, but this was when I first actually thought of her like that. So we watch the guy with the gut and I still feel a little jealous. But this time he rolls a gutter ball and he jumps about three feet in the air and shouts, "Fuck!" and the girl kind of quivers for a moment and then she turns and looks back at me. She's laughing and she's asking me to share the laughter, and I do. Before I realize what I'm doing I'm vaulting over the seats in front of me and sitting next to her.

But she doesn't edge away or even look surprised or anything and I talk real low, like we're sharing a secret. "He said 'fuck' just for you. The other gutter balls he talked to himself. Very quietly."

Looking back I can see that this isn't the best of ways to start a conversation with a girl you've just laid eyes on for the first time. It's not only the word "fuck," though I'll probably always make that mistake with some people. It's talking to her like we've had this conversation going on for a long time, like we already know each other real well and we like to figure out other people together. But this girl is okay. She acts like it's the most natural thing of all to say. She even seems to like it. She smiles and bends toward me a little bit and she lowers her voice, too, and she says, "I'm not impressed. Not even." And with the "not even" she sort of lets her head droop down and her mouth hang open, like she's been instantly lobotomized just by the sight of this guy. I glance over at him and he's up on his toes, his ball tucked on his hip, about to run at the pins again. I flick my head at him and it draws the girl's eyes to the spectacle. The fat guy hippity-hops and the ball goes clunk and then there's that long rolling sound—real long, the guy's ball goes down the alley slower than an old woman with a walker—and finally it clips off the ten pin and that's all.

The girl slaps a hand over her mouth and turns and bends close to me in stifled laughter and I laugh too, glancing just briefly at the fat guy's glare. Then the girl whispers, "If he tried anything with me, I'd puncture that gut of his. I've got a knife. I can handle myself."

I say, "He'd probably whiz around the room like a balloon."

This makes the girl start laughing again and I like it, I don't even care if the guy with the gut can hear it. She's laughing at what I said. I'm doing all right, though I'm starting to worry about my face. What do I look like to her? I realize I'm hoping it's not Vietnamese, and that gives me a little twist of guilt. I look away, down to an empty alley, and the girl is still laughing. I like her laughter and it's starting to make this guilt feel stupid. Her laugh is a soft little sound, not the sound of a girl with a knife, and I think her laughter and her knife are like my face, they make her two things at once, and if I have to be American to get her to like me, then goddamit, that's what I'll be. I turn back to her and her laughter has faded away now and she's looking at me and I say, "Whizzing around," which is so stupid I almost choke on the fucking words as they're coming out. I said that to try to recapture the moment before I'd been idiot enough to turn away from her. She was laughing at something I said and I was worrying about not wanting to be taken for Vietnamese. But even going over that again in order to ridicule myself, some part of me says, Shit yes you should worry about that; otherwise you might as well be sleeping in your bed in New Jersey and playing your stereo and grabbing everything you can from your American life.

"Are you all right?" she says, and I realize that I'm going through this whole debate in my head while sitting there staring at her. I figure I'm on the verge of freaking her out totally.

"Sure," I say. "I was just thinking."

"Well, don't burn all your hair off," she says, and she winks at me.

I don't know what the hell that means, but it sounds great to me and the wink gives me enough courage to say, "What's your name?"

"Norma."

I wait for the last name, but she doesn't give it and her eyes sort of slide away down to the empty alleys behind me, the same spot where I retreated when I was worrying about the American or Vietnamese shit. I figure she doesn't like her name. She's only got one name, but she doesn't like it. I can understand that.

Then suddenly she brings her eyes back to me. They're deep brown eyes, the color of Vietnamese eyes. "And what's your name?" she says.

"They call me The Deuce. That's the same thing they call Forty-second Street."

"I guess you've been here a long time."

"Here?"

"You know." she says. "The city. This area. Since they call you The Deuce."

"Oh, sure. I've been here a long time. I'm on my own."

"You are?" This seems to interest her. She kind of leans closer to me, like I'm going to let her in on some secret. "That's great, to be on your own."

"Sure."

"I'm on my own now."

"That's good," I say, and inside I'm going, I knew it, I knew she was a runaway.

"Goddam right that's good," she says, and she sits back and reaches up and pulls some pins from her hair and it all tumbles down, all this long black hair falls onto her shoulders and I have to work hard to keep from plunging my hands into all that hair.

"Did you just arrive?" I ask.

She looks at me and you can see her trying to hear some hidden motive in the question. Her eyes narrow a little bit. I can't think of anything to say to explain myself, so I just wait it out. Finally she says, "I'm no little kid, you know. I understand how things are."

Then there's another pause and she's looking past me again. It's not clear whether she's going to say any more, so I resort to repeating things. "You're no little kid. I can see that."

"Goddam right. If I want to get angry and show the whole goddam world I'm angry, I can do it."

"Sure," I say, and I wonder who it is she's arguing with now. Her father probably.

"I'm going to get a job," she says, but her voice is a little dreamy and she's still looking off into space.

I just nod. It's a weird feeling, but it seems like she's not really there beside me anymore. She's off somewhere in her head trying to deal with something. I figure this is probably what I looked like to her a couple of minutes ago. I'm about to ask her if she's all right, but suddenly her face snaps back to me and she's there again.

"Where do you live?" she says.

I get this scrabbling in my chest. Instantly I can see that I was right about her just arriving and she's got nowhere to go and now she wants The Deuce to tell her where she can find a safe place to sleep tonight and I'm just a fucking fraud, I've only been on my own for a couple of days and I've been sleeping on an abandoned highway in the middle of whores and bums and junkies and maybe tonight I'll even get my goddam throat cut and she wants me to tell her something that will protect her when she sleeps. Where do I live? I shrug and I say, "Here and there," and that's all I can say and I can see a little flinch of disappointment in her face and I try to explain. "What's okay for me won't be okay for you."

She forces a laugh. "I understand how it is. I'm no goddam little kid, you know."

"Hell, I know that. I could see that right off." I guess I say this to try to convince myself that she'll be all right even if I can't tell her what she wants to know. But it doesn't much work. I'm real nervous now about Norma. And I start pressing too much. "Listen," I say, "whenever you walk past a pay phone, be sure and check out the coin return. You can find some money there sometimes."

She looks at me a little funny and I can hear myself, how the thing about the coins in the phones seemed to come out of nowhere. She just wanted to know where to sleep. She wasn't even asking about how to make money. After all, she said she was going to get a job. It would probably be easier for her to get a job than me. I can't even imagine what to do for myself without drawing a lot of questions that would catch me up. But a girl who looks like Norma can just go into a restaurant and say she's eighteen and right away she's waitressing. Even after going through all this in my head real fast and taking in her funny look—she's staring at me and her mouth has kind of fallen open, like she's trying to figure me out—even after all this, I'm still so anxious to tell her something that can help her that I say, "If you need a few bucks real quick you can always use this. You go to somebody at the back of the ticket line and say you need bus fare to go back home." There's more to tell her about this subject, things I'd even learned on my own this very day, but she kind of squints at me and her tongue slowly moves along the biting edge of her front teeth and I realize I'm fucking this whole thing up.

"I'm gonna do fine," she says in a real firm voice and the bowling pins crash right at the end, like an exclamation point. "I don't need to go back home."

It feels like those bowling pins are falling and spinning in my chest, and I'm frantic to make this thing right, to put things back in order. "I know you don't need to go home," I say. "I wasn't talking about really doing it. You say you're trying to go home to get them to give you money, see."

"I don't need money from home. I don't need anything from that motherfucker and his goddam cunt." She says this real loud and her eyes are ripping away at me.

I don't know how what I said went wrong and I can't stand looking at these eyes and I glance over at the fat guy who's standing in the alley runway. He's watching us now without even trying to hide it. I shout at him, "Hey, mind your own fucking business."

This is the wrong thing to do because Norma looks over at the guy too and she picks up her duffel and says, "I've got to go." The anger at me is gone from her voice but what's there is even worse: What the hell am I talking to this kid for?

"You have to go?" I say, and I can hear how pansy-assed my voice sounds and she doesn't answer the question. She just gets herself up and slings the duffel onto her shoulder and the fat guy is hunched over the ball return even though his ball hasn't arrived yet—he's trying to make it clear he's not looking this way—and I want to jump up and run over there and punch the son of a bitch in the face. But I don't even have guts enough to watch Norma go. Not till she's at the door and then all the pins in my chest silently leap and fall and spin in panic. I jump up and shout after her, "So long."

Norma stops and turns and gives me a little wave before she disappears. I stand there for a second and I'm telling myself, See, she still thinks you're okay, she waved. But it never does much good to talk to myself like that. They're just words in my head, while the rest of me is thrashing around for something to do to make me feel at ease again. Norma's out there with her duffel heading into the streets or wherever and she doesn't know what she's getting into. Not that I'm so smart about New York yet either, but I go up the aisle fast and past the bar and out the door and I can see her down the corridor and she's farther away than I thought she'd be, she's moving fast.

I hesitate again, but when some people in between block her off from view I take off after her. I walk fast, not quite a jog, and I'm weaving back and forth a little to try to get an angle where I can see her up ahead. I catch a glimpse of her hair and the duffel dragging one shoulder down, but she's still moving fast, like she knows where she's going, and then it strikes me that maybe she does, maybe she knows exactly where she's going and I'm about to make an even bigger fool of myself. So I slow down for a second and then I speed up and then I slow down and then I can't see her anymore and I start to jog. Like I'm out of my fucking mind.

When I get to the escalators I've pretty much convinced myself that it's a big mistake to follow Norma. I stand at the top and I can't see her right away, and just as I'm beginning to think that maybe she's still somewhere up here on the suburban level, I see her down on the main floor, passing the bottom of the escalator, like when she'd gotten off she'd headed in the wrong direction. But now she's moving fast again, walking toward Eighth Avenue, which is also the direction of the Greyhound long-haul ticket windows. Suddenly I hope that maybe she's going to get a ticket out of here. Maybe she'll head off to somewhere like Montreal. I think of warning her not to show her money in the ticket line and I grow conscious of the dull pain in my head where I was hit. Then a little shiver runs through me, like I just stepped into a meat locker or something, and I figure I'm afraid for Norma, and one more time I think about going after her. But instantly I feel like a goddam fool and I tell myself there's nothing I can say to her that she'll listen to.

So I back off from the escalators and I decide to just walk away fast and I turn to the left and I catch myself real quick because my first step would run me right into a man standing there facing me. The bulk of him briefly makes me think of the bowler but this man has no fat on him and in a flash my eyes go to his face and it's a round face, a large face, it's Treen, and the eyes in the face widen at me, large black eyes, and over his shoulder are other eyes, the boys from the balcony, four or five of them, and they're arrayed behind

Treen with their eyes set on me and they're like the eyes on a peacock's tail and I'm the goddam hen.

"Hello," Treen says. "Welcome to New York." It's a surprising
voice, real soft and interested, like if you heard it from a long-
distance operator or a store clerk you'd think this is the nicest guy
like that you've ever talked to.

"I've already been welcomed," I say, but right away I know it's the
wrong thing, it sounds like I'm looking for sympathy, and Treen's
eyes roll to my goddam wound and this makes me uncomfortable in a
real complicated way, like there's something shameful about me, like
you're in an elevator with a bunch of pretty girls and some real private part of you is stinking and they smell it and they know where it's
coming from and you've got about fifty floors to go.

"You should let someone clean that up for you," Treen says in that
real sweet voice of his, like he knows everything about me and I'm a
real swell guy and it worries him a lot that a great guy like me has a
bump on the head. I guess there's this one part of your mind that just
listens to voices, maybe because voices are so important in separating
people from the other animals. And the part that listens to voices is
even saying to me, Well, gee, this voice sure doesn't sound like the
voice of a bad guy; maybe there's been a mistake; who is this Joey
character, anyway; this voice you're hearing now is the voice of a
creature way far above the animals, it's the voice of the nicest tele-
phone operator in the world, the gentlest first-grade teacher, the
most loving father.

Fortunately there's another part of me that can see a rat in a rose
garden and that part tells the voice part to shut the hell up and it
makes me take a step backward and makes me think about where to
run if I have to. Treen sort of cocks his head at my step back and he
smiles this smile that is just about as sweet as his voice. It puffs his
cheeks way up under his eyes and the eyes get this squinty kind of
joyful look and it makes me think of Christmas, cotton snow and
mink coats and the good chickies stepping and stepping again. "I'm
Treen," he says. "We're all a family here," he says, and the peacock
feathers rustle behind him, the eyes sway. He says, "You may find
that things get tough, and if you do, you've got friends."

It's like he knows I'm not going to listen to him any longer. He knows I'm about to walk away from him but it's a natural part of the whole thing, like the boys always walk away the first time, like he knows that and expects it and he knows they'll eventually come to him. So when I turn now and I move to the escalator and I rush down the moving steps, pushing past people, hitting the main floor and striding away fast, even my very escape scares the hell out of me.

ELEVEN

❖

That night it rained and by the time it woke me up I was already soaked. Then when the rain stopped and I was about to sleep again, one of the junkies went nuts and he was screaming something about worms and he started climbing the chain-link fence facing the river. He was real near where I was and I stood up and watched him. A cruise ship called Cupid was all lit up on the dock beyond him and this guy went up the fence and he perched on the top and then he leaped over and disappeared. The sound that followed, like one real good hatchet blow into a watermelon, didn't even seem to have anything to do with the guy, though I knew it did. I knew, too, that there'd probably be some police up here to check out where the guy jumped from, so I stashed my duffel and I walked around the streets for a couple of hours and one of the things I thought a lot about was how I just stood there and watched the guy go up and over the top of the fence and watched him fall and listened to him hit and it was like watching a goddam dog piss on a tree or something. It couldn't have meant less to me. I got back to the highway at dawn and I slept some more. I just lay out flat on my back in the grit and the ground glass next to the big hole, and sometimes I'd open my eyes and I was hearing the laughter of a whore and then I'd close my eyes again and the junkie never even made it into my dreams, not even the sound of him hitting Twelfth Avenue.

I didn't get to the bus station until pretty late. Once again I went in the Eighth Avenue doors of the South Wing. Joey was starting to be like the fence post you always grab turning the corner into the schoolyard or the shoe you always put on first. And there he is, sitting under the flag, but he's turned away from me and he's talking to some guy with a bald head and a fringe of blond hair and a City Lights T-shirt. I get real near and lean against the wall next to Joey without him even knowing I'm there and with the bald guy just giving me a brief little glance.

Joey's telling some kind of war story and his right arm is resting on his knee and he has an upturned cap in his hand but the cap is sagging, forgotten, as Joey talks on. He's saying, "So when the smoke finally clears, see, we're standing there in the hut with three dead VC on the floor and they're lying on top of three dead girls who they'd pulled in front of them to shield them from our fire. So you tell me if that's a fucking atrocity or not and if it is who the fuck is to blame. You think the universe gives a fuck about what happens in the jungle?" Joey pauses, like he expects this guy to actually answer the question. The bald guy just sort of waggles his head faintly and glances at me again, but Joey doesn't turn around. He probably isn't even watching the guy he's talking to because after a second he just roars on with his own answer. But the answer surprises me. "Shit yes, the universe cares. The very next day is when I stepped on a punji stick. Goddam near lost my foot. I got a puncture scar on my foot the size of a hockey puck that will tell you the universe gives an authentic fuck about what you do in the jungle. And that even goes if the jungle's in New York, New York."

The bald guy looks at me once more, this time with a steady gaze, and Joey turns and glances over his shoulder and he says, "Hey, Deuce my man. Good to see you." He sounds like he means it, I guess, but it's the same big voice he was using just seconds ago to tell his war stories, like I'm the punch line or something. Then his cap-hand comes alive and rises all the way to the guy's chest. Joey puts the cap right up against the CITY LIGHTS and says to him, "How about helping me out? You're a vet." The guy nods with a last glance at me—one too many; I'm finally getting a little pissed off at him, ready to ask him what the hell he thinks he's looking at—but he puts a buck in Joey's hat and he disappears.

Joey roots around in the cap and I say to him, "That was the longest goddam line I've heard you use yet. You gotta turn over your customers faster than that, don't you?"

Joey doesn't laugh at this like I hoped he would. He's counting the money from his cap and he says without looking at me, "There's more than just going for the sale, Deuce my man. There's a whole fucking life, too."

"Which ones do you decide to tell it to, your life?" I mean this as a sincere question. I figure I need to learn all the tricks. But he shoots me a glance like I'm putting the needle to him or something. He must read all this on my face, because he softens then.

"It's not for them, Deuce. It's for me. Sometimes it's just gotta come out and whoever's there at the moment, they get to hear it." He says this real seriously, sadly. And I suddenly get this funny signal in my head, like he's just a little *too* serious, a little *too* sad, like I'm some guy in a suit passing him while he's on duty sitting under the flag.

I say, "It still sounds to me like you could turn it for a couple of bucks with the right guy to listen to it." I wait to see if Joey is going to keep up with the life's-a-serious-tale shit. For a second I think he is—that tight-stretched face of his stretches even tighter, like he's pulling his ears back.

But then suddenly he smiles. "You've got the right instincts, Deuce. You're gonna do fine around here. But it's not just a matter of telling the right guy. The right kind of women love the stories too."

"A fucking atrocity and who the fuck's to blame?"

He laughs. "I may put it a little different. Less fucking and more tears."

"Is all the stuff you tell them true?" This was a professional question, but Joey flinches like I've just hurt him.

"It's all true, Deuce."

I believe him without even a second thought. Most of what I'd heard—walking point at night, Agent Orange, shrapnel in the legs, all of that—he'd told me directly, and it never occurred to me that any of it was a lie. It's pretty stupid, but I guess I thought there was no reason for him to make something up for a kid with no money.

Joey stuffs the money into his pocket and puts the cap on his head—it's a Yankees cap and it suddenly has a special little glimmer of familiarity about it. And it's not just that I've seen a whole shitload of them being worn in the street, though that's certainly true, especially up and down Forty-second. The drug dealers all seem to be Yankees fans, and when I think about this, the glimmer brightens because I know that it would really fry Kenneth's ass to know how many of his fellow Yankees fans are pushing dope. It was Kenneth in the cap that was familiar. The trip to Yankee Stadium and all that. How about a cap, Tony, let me get you a Yankees cap so you can be a real fan. Back off, Kenneth. I didn't say it to him at the time, though I was cool enough about the whole thing to stop him from getting me the cap. But now I tell him in my head to just back the fuck off.

"Where's your helmet liner?" I say to Joey.

"Some days I give it a rest," Joey says. "See? No sign either." He thumps his chest and it's true, the sign telling the world that he's an unemployed Vietnam vet is gone. Joey says, "You start seeing the same people over and over and so you put a different spin on things. Today I'm the unemployed Vietnam vet who's *also* an unemployed New Yorker, a Yankees fan. That's probably why that guy finally stopped and asked me about Vietnam. On the day when I'm the Yankees fan, people who see me as *both* things suddenly start thinking about the *other* part of me. It's pretty weird shit. I don't know how to explain it."

"It's not so weird to me."

Joey looks at my face real close for a second—he knows what I'm talking about—and then he laughs that sharp, dry little laugh of his, like there isn't a drop of moisture in his whole body. Then he says, "You need something to eat?"

I can feel my shoulders lift. "I've got a few bucks today."

"No shit?"

"Oh, there was definitely some of that involved. *Bull*shit, the bullshit line you gave me about needing money to go back home."

"I'm just trying to do my bit to reunite a runaway with his family. It ain't my fucking fault if you misuse the money people give you."

"I want a hamburger."

"You eat what I tell you to," Joey says, and he gets up and I follow him to Arby's. I go in and buy my own and I don't hassle Joey this time, I buy the goddam roast beef. Going in and going out I stay way back from the edge of the upper-floor balcony, like I'm walking around that hole in the abandoned highway. I'm not about to let Fairyland see me again.

We head back across Forty-first and through the South Wing, but instead of going out the side entrance onto Fortieth, where we ate yesterday, Joey takes us to a bank of three elevators just inside the door from the foyer where he usually works the passersby. I don't ask any questions and we go up to the seventh floor, the top parking garage level, and we step into a narrow corridor with one wall that's just a window over the roof of the sixth-floor level, where these big fans are spinning, and out in the street is the roof of the business school and I'm looking down on the signs telling me about all the opportunities I'm missing in computers and accounting.

I stand at the window a moment and beyond the business school is a clutter of buildings, nothing famous, you can't even see the Empire State Building from here, though this is the right direction, it seems to me, and way off to the left is a tall building with a clock that's about three hours slow. I linger here, I guess, because this is my own first taste of the bus terminal thing about getting up above everybody else and looking down. I can see the parking lot on Eighth between Forty-first and Forty-second and there's all these guys kind of hanging around the fence and one of them breaks off now and then to walk half a block with some other guy who's passing by. Smoke, Nickel bags, It's high time, my man, all the hustling and here I stand with my roast beef sandwich in my hand and I'm way above all that shit.

I turn to see where Joey's gone and he's sitting on the floor with his back against the wall just beyond the elevators. There's a space between him and the elevator that's just big enough for me, and though he's not looking at me, I know he knows I'm here and we're going to have our goddam roast beef sandwiches together. So I look back down in the street and there's a couple of women in real short skirts gliding across Forty-first and one of the guys in one of the Yankees caps picks them up and walks between them and puts his arms around them both, and they're real far away down there. The corridor I'm standing in is making my ears pop with its silence and Joey's waiting for me to sit next to him.

I turn and go to Joey, but I take a step past him and look through some glass doors and outside is the upper parking level, open to the sky. I say, "You don't want to eat outside?"

"You've always got outside to go to."

I look at Joey and I know he's right. I like the silence here. It feels like the chair in the library map room. I sit by him and the two of us eat without talking for a while and I watch the sky through the window. Then a helicopter goes by out there, a pansy little traffic copter painted with red stripes, but we can hear the beat of its engines and I think of home—and by home I mean Saigon, city of alleys and of helicopters, not fucking traffic copters but real ones—and I wonder if Joey is thinking of Vietnam, too; it's obviously something that's often on his mind and I know part of why I like him is because of that. I turn to him and he's pushing a last bit of his sandwich into his mouth and then he looks at his fingertips. I have no idea what's in his head.

I say, "Helicopters make me think of Vietnam."

He looks over at me, his fingertips still poised before his face. "There it is," he says. It may sound like a strange thing to say, but to me it was suddenly familiar. The GIs who floated through my life in Saigon used that phrase a lot. I said it all the time myself when I was learning from my short-timer language teachers. There it is. Like there's something before you or around you or inside you or growing on you and you don't want it there and you don't know how else to react to it but to wait and get fucked over by it or die from it or at best shake your head at it and realize that's the way things are and just wait it out, and there it is, I see it and you see it and there it is.

But I wait, thinking maybe he'll say more, and when he doesn't, I ask him, "Did you ever get to Saigon, Joey?"

He looks away from me, out the window. "I was there."

If you think about it, it seems real strange—at least at first—that I could ask that question. Remember, one of the things that upset me most about Joey was to think that he could've been a customer of my mother's. Not actually *her* customer. The chances of it weren't very great, and even my fear knew that. But it was a big problem for me if he was the *kind* of GI who came and went in the beds of the Saigon bargirls. Listen to that. Bargirls. That's like calling my mother Betty or Mary. Whores. Who came and went in the beds of the Saigon whores, and my mother was a whore, and I just didn't want to be snatched away to the other side of the world by one of those guys and finally get the hell out of his house and then end up hanging around with another one. So why did I ask Joey about Saigon? To give myself an excuse to stop beginning my fucking day with this guy only to end up turning around and finding him gone? No, it wasn't that. I was feeling pretty good with him, sitting there in the quiet of that corridor. Good enough that when I heard the helicopter and thought of my home, I wanted to try to share it with this guy who'd actually been there, for Christ's sake. And the one girl he'd mentioned, he'd said he loved her. Not that the goddam word means anything. I'd heard the word used in our back-alley apartment. Maybe because English was my second language I could hear the word for what it really is. I knew even in Saigon that love is a lizard-tail word; you leave it behind when you're getting the hell away. Still, that same sadness I'd seen before in Joey had come over him again. And all this stuff I'm saying now wasn't really in my head when I was sitting beside him in the corridor. I was just thinking about Saigon and I was liking Joey being there and I wanted to put the two things together.

So I watch Joey and he keeps his eyes out the window and when it looks like he's not going to say any more, I press him. "When were you there?"

He turns his face my way, but I can see in his eyes that he's not really with me. "When?"

"You weren't there long, right? You were out in the jungle with the Agent Orange and the patrols and all that shit. When did you get to the city?"

He looked away and his breath popped out of him and he puckered his lips. Like things were tough to explain. But I wouldn't let him off. "So what's the big deal? You were there in a hospital for the operations on your legs? Or was it R and R? What?"

"Well," he says, "It was for a little longer than R and R. Besides, they were sending us out of the country for that. Sydney. Bangkok. I got to Bangkok for nine days."

"But how about Saigon. That's my city, Joey. Let's talk about Saigon, can we?"

"If you want to talk about Saigon so bad, why are you here?"

"What the fuck is that supposed to mean?"

"I don't know what the fuck it means," Joey says, and he gives me this exaggerated shrug, like he's in a play or something, a farce.

"What's wrong with your talking about Saigon? You talk about the rest of Vietnam at the drop of a hat."

At this, Joey reaches up and gives his cap a little flip and it spins up into the air and falls upside down in front of him. As soon as it hits the floor, he starts talking real fast. "Did I tell you about the time I was walking point in triple-canopy jungle up in I-Corp and the monkeys were screaming their fucking lungs out and the tigers were bellyaching out somewhere in the mountains and we were scared shitless just from all the noise and I tried to hear my feet fall because we were supposed to be keeping patrol silence but I couldn't hear a thing because of all the fucking animals but I was sure I was making a terrible racket and the VC were hearing every step."

"Joey," I say, but he goes on and on and I just say his name every few sentences to try to get his attention and he's telling how suddenly the animals shut up and the platoon is making this godawful sound, crunching the twigs and shit underfoot, and that's when the VC spring their ambush and I'm saying all the time, Joey, Joey, and he says that everybody in the platoon was killed but him. Everybody.

That stops me. "Everybody?" I say.

"Fucking right," he says.

"You were in a fight where everybody was killed but you?"

Joey picks up the cap in front of him and shoves it under my nose. "So how about it? Give a vet a few coins so he can forget all the shit he's been through."

"Did that really happen, Joey?" I don't know whether I believe it or not, but I do know that he went through the telling of it to avoid talking about Saigon. So when he says yes, it really happened, I just put it aside and I press him some more. "But what about Saigon?"

His shoulders heave like I'm this pesky little brat who's never going to shut up, and maybe I am. Then he says, "It's classified, see. You know about the Phoenix Program, don't you? The C.I.A. going around assassinating guys they think are part of the VC shadow governments."

"You can't talk about Saigon because you did something there with the C.I.A.?"

"We had to sign these agreements, Deuce. They'll hunt me down if I say anything. I've seen it happen to others."

After living my first six years in Vietnam, one of the funny things to me about the climate in New Jersey is the way the days get long and then get short and then get long again, and especially how you notice that this is going on. The days get shorter coming into the fall and winter, and it happens gradually, just a few minutes each day. But you notice it all at once. That's what happened with me and Joey, how I knew he was bullshitting me. It had been happening all along, but it struck me all of a sudden. And it pissed me off even worse than if I'd stepped to the window and looked out and then turned to find him gone again.

So I say to him, "Joey, what the fuck's going on here? You're telling me—*me*, not some business suit down there in the foyer, *me* —that you've got two Purple Hearts, shot-up legs, operations, doses of Agent Orange, punji sticks in your feet, atrocities in the huts where you blow away peasant women, you're the sole survivor in an ambush, you love some Vietnamese woman and you were a nineteen-year-old virgin when you fell in love with her, and now you're telling me you worked for the CI-fucking-A in Saigon. Who do you think you're dealing with here, Joey? A goddam imbecile? None of this shit's true."

I can hear my voice quavering by the end of this and I shut up so I can work on not looking like an even bigger idiot with some goddam tears. They'd be tears of anger, though, make no mistake.

Joey never looks at me but once or twice with quick little glances while I'm saying all this. Then when I stop, he keeps his head bowed and he has his fists clenched and sitting in his lap and he seems to be studying them. Finally he says, "They weren't all lies."

"No? Well, how the hell am I ever gonna tell the difference?"

He looks at me and he says in a real quiet voice, "Why the fuck should you care?"

That's a real good question. I know right away that the answer is complicated, but at this point there's no way I'm going to figure it out. So I do the simple thing. Even though I know it's a lie, I say, "I *don't* care," and I get up and I punch the elevator button and I stand there and wait. I concentrate on the extreme edge of my sight and I can make out Joey still sitting, staring at the fists in his lap.

The elevator bell chimes and at the sound a little knot cinches in my chest. The doors open and I step in and turn to face the front. I can't see Joey now and I'm feeling real bad, the knot cinches tighter, and I touch the door-open button. I wait, but there's only silence in the corridor, and then I say, "Are you coming?"

Joey doesn't answer, but I hear a scuffling sound and then he steps into the elevator and stands right beside me. I release the button and the doors close. We go down the seven floors with both of us facing the front like we were two soldiers at parade rest.

When the doors open on the first floor, a Port Authority cop is standing there waiting. All I see is the blue uniform and the shiny buttons and the badge and even before I have time to be afraid, I'm ready to run, to duck and angle out of the elevator and pass under the cop's right arm which would be grabbing at me and I'd run like hell. But instantly Joey puts his arm around my shoulder and pins me against him. Then I can see the cop's face, a black man with a big face and a thin mustache, he's the color of the Thi Nghè River and his neck is spilling over his collar. My limbs are hot with stifled flight and suddenly I worry about whose side Joey is on, especially since I'd just called him a liar and he's got me pinned. All this happens real fast and I hear Joey say, "McGee, my man," and he's walking me off the elevator, edging us past the cop, who doesn't move. I glance at the cop's nameplate to see if he's really named McGee. He is.

"Joey," McGee says. His voice is full of a long understanding of everything I'd said about Joey just a few moments ago, but his eyes are looking only at me. "You still trying to be good?"

"Sure I am," Joey says. "I'm doing great. See who I got with me at last." With this, Joey gives me a little shake and he takes off his Yankees cap and puts it on my head. It's a gesture I understand at once. I know exactly what he's going to say next, and that's the whole point of putting the cap on my head. Like Kenneth at Yankee Stadium, it's the thing a goddam father does. "This is my son," Joey says to the cop.

I'm no fool. I'm not so spooked about all the father-and-son shit that I'm going to say or do anything to make this cop suspicious. It's pretty shrewd of Joey, really. And if Joey's got to be my father to prevent me from being sent back to my real one, then that's just the way it has to be. I even reach up and tug the Yankees cap down lower on my forehead.

"You saying this boy is your son?" McGee's voice is suspicious but only with that sort of background buzz of suspicion that was in it from the first. He's looking me in the eye and I don't flinch and I think maybe Joey and I have a chance at this.

Joey says, "Hey, McGee, you've heard me talk about that girl I left behind."

"You never mentioned a son," McGee says.

"You think that's something I'm going to talk about? How many little McGees are running around the South Bronx that you're not talking about?"

McGee's eyes leave me with a jerk and I'm sure that Joey has stepped in it. But McGee looks at Joey for a second and then he just shakes his head like what the fuck can you say to a guy like this.

Joey says, "Look at him. You can see me and his momma both in his face. Look at him."

McGee's eyes come back to me and once again I'm wanting to run. Fuck all this. I don't need it. I don't need people making a big fucking deal about my face. McGee's looking at me real close and it's just not worth it. But I think of Point Pleasant and I wait it out. McGee keeps his eyes on me but he says, "I don't suppose you've got this boy's papers on you, do you, Joey?"

"You asking me for paperwork?"

McGee shakes his head real faintly, like he's talking to himself in his mind about how hopeless this all is and how much a waste of his time. Then he says to me, "You this man's son?"

"Yessir," I say. "My mother didn't want me anymore and Joey— Dad—has been writing to her for a long time trying to get me. A church group finally brought me out. I came through Switzerland." With each detail I can see McGee's face loosen around the eyes. "I was in Geneva, Switzerland, for about six months living with a Methodist minister." I wait and let the minister soak in. Then I say, "He had a house with flower boxes in all the windows and out back I could see this huge motherfucking mountain."

McGee blinks at the "motherfucking" and he says, "You surely do sound like Cipriani's son."

Joey, whose arm is still around me, shakes me again. "You goddam betcha," he says. "This is one smart little motherfucker." And then Joey wheels me around and he starts to walk me away.

But the cop stops us. "Yo, Joey." We turn, and McGee says, "How'd your son learn to speak English so good?"

Before Joey can answer it, I cut in. "My mother made me learn, and she made me keep practicing. She knew that a smart little Oriental like me would end up in America one day."

"With his loving father," Joey says, and he spins me around again and we walk away.

"Jesus, Joey," I whisper. "That loving-father stuff was too much."

"He'll only think the loving part is bullshit. He bought the father."

"He's just *choosing* to buy it."

"Same difference."

"What year does he think you were over there?"

"Sixty-seven, sixty-eight."

"At least that fits."

We go through the door now and into the foyer and Joey lets go of me. "Don't worry," he says. "McGee's a good guy. He doesn't think like a cop. He's okay."

We slow down and stop in the center of the foyer and I'm wondering what's next. I expect Joey to take off again. But instead, he looks around like somebody might overhear, and then he says, "Where've you been sleeping, Deuce?"

I know I expected this question sooner, but now that it's finally come, I just get pissed off at him again, and as soon as I do, I think about his lies and my anger upstairs, and that just makes it worse. So I say, "What the fuck is it to you?"

He looks at me and the stretch of the skin on his face gets even tighter. "Listen. I don't need this shit. You want to go back to wherever it is you came from? Then I made a big mistake back there with McGee. But I thought you could use a little help."

I don't say anything to this, though I know it's true that he helped me in an important way. I just look at the feet of the people passing us by.

Joey says, "So some of the stuff I've been telling you isn't exactly the truth in every detail."

I look him in the eye at this.

"Okay. Some of it isn't true at all."

I keep staring.

"Okay. You'd be right to call some of it lies. Okay." He's shrugging all the while, even in the silences between our words, and I want to keep my anger going, but it's not easy.

"Okay," he says. "Some of the lies were pretty big. Big lies."

I can hold this hard face for only a few more seconds, but I hang on.

He waves his arms and shouts, "Jesus Christ, Deuce, what do you want? Okay. Some of what I said makes me the biggest fucking liar who ever opened his palm for a handout."

Joey's voice rings throughout the foyer and we both look around at the faces turning to us as they pass. Joey snatches the Yankees cap off my head and puts it back on himself. "You ain't no son of mine, making me expose myself to my potential customers." He says this low and gruff, but you can see he's trying to hold back a smile.

I grab the cap back off his head and put it on. "I'm sleeping on an abandoned highway that's up above Twelfth Avenue."

"Goddam," he says. "That's a shitty place. That's the West Side Highway they never repaired. I don't have to tell you who it is that lives up there."

"You got any better ideas?"

"Yes."

"So why didn't you ask me before?"

Joey puffs out his breath like his lungs are full of smoke. "Okay. I get it. Sure. How many nights you been up there?"

"Who's counting? From the beginning. Okay?"

"I'm sorry, Deuce. I'm real sorry. I don't have a *lot* of ideas about stuff like that. Most of what there is will end you back up in Westchester, or wherever you're from. And I just didn't know you well enough to offer anything else. I didn't know what your hustle might be. That's why I didn't ask you sooner." He stops talking and he looks at me and I don't know what to say. So he puffs out some more air and goes on. "Okay. And maybe most of the time I'm just a self-pitying shit who doesn't even notice what the fuck is happening if it doesn't have anything to do with him." He stops and immediately he shakes his head yes, like I've just said something. "Okay. Not *maybe*. That *is* me, most of the time. You see? I'm trying not to tell some goddam lie now and get myself into trouble with you again."

Suddenly I get that creepy feeling I had on the coaster with Kenneth, like I'm the father and the older guy is the kid. "Look," I say. "You don't have to make any explanations to me. You're just doing what you've got to do to get by."

"I don't have much, Deuce. I live in an abandoned building down on the Lower East Side. But at least there's a roof and we can find you an old mattress or something and it's far away from here."

"You're a goddam commuter," I say, and Joey lifts his face and laughs. The laugh is loud and I look around again and about fifteen feet away I see a guy with a briefcase who had stopped and looked at us when Joey shouted that he was a liar. He's still standing there watching us without even trying to hide it. I take off the Yankees cap and step toward him and say, "Spare some change for an hysterical lying commuter?"

The guy's face jerks like somebody just woke him up from a nap and he walks off fast. I turn back to Joey and I say, "What did I do wrong?"

He comes and stands beside me and squints after the guy with the briefcase. "'A commuting lying hysteric' would've been better."

"I've got a lot to learn."

"You want to stay with me?"

"Sure."

"So go help get us some money and I'll meet you back here at about four. Under the flag. Bring whatever stuff you've got, if it hasn't been ripped off yet."

"Four o'clock." I turn and already I'm thinking about working the ticket lines.

But Joey stops me with a hand on my shoulder. "And Deuce," he says with the hand still there, "It wasn't all lies. A couple of the things were true."

"Okay, Joey. I believe you." And I do. I'm looking at his eyes and for the first time I notice how the part that's supposed to be white is yellow, like a piss stain on snow. But the eyes are real steady and his hand is still there on my shoulder like he doesn't want to let me go until I can make him believe it's all right. So I say it again, "I believe you."

"I really was in love," he says, and of all the things he's told me, I suddenly realize that it's this I've been both hoping and fearing would still be true.

TWELVE

✦

This thing about love. Joey says he loves a girl he hasn't seen in sixteen years. A district attorney in New Jersey is probably calling out the cops and private detectives to track down some kid he thinks he owns. A poster says this girl, who's got to be dead from heroin by now, is loved. Mr. Treen probably uses the word with the boys in the stairwells. And in the pages of some book, I'm keeping a picture of a prostitute who sold her son. You tell me what the fuck this is all about.

And it isn't even an hour after I leave Joey in the foyer that I see Norma again. I don't recognize her right off because when I see this girl standing near the main escalators, the first thing that catches me is her big red flower-bloom of a mouth. When I first saw Norma I'd noticed how those full lips of hers were pale, like they didn't have any lipstick on them at all. Now they're crimson and when I realize it's Norma—the round face, her black hair falling over her shoulders —I see right away that she looks dazed. She doesn't have her bag with her anymore and I think maybe she's been robbed. But my eyes go back to her lips, and it doesn't make sense to me that she'd get mugged and then make herself up.

I go over to her and she looks at me like she's real sleepy, and I tell myself that probably she is, probably she never found a place to sleep last night. "Norma," I say to her.

She looks at me closely and then she says, "I know you," and her voice is sleepy, too.

"Yesterday. At the bowling alley."

"I know you," she says, and I can hear her trying hard to fill her voice with life. "You're The Deuce."

"That's right," I say. "That's me."

She puts her hand on my wrist and it feels like my skin is opening up, like every hair on my body is going to fall out. She says, "Deuce, is there someplace around here to go where everybody's not looking at you?"

"Sure," I say, and we turn and head toward Eighth Avenue and the elevators up to the parking garage. She's walking very close to me and I can smell her perfume, which makes me think of oranges, and under the perfume is another smell, very strong, trying to cut through, and it's a smell something like sweat, but her sweat is different from mine, it's a darker smell, like it's from a deep hole in the ground, and I want to hold her hand, take her arm, something, touch her somewhere, but we just walk to the elevators, and we go up to the seventh floor.

I guide her through the glass doors I'd seen before, out onto the upper parking level, and we're walking under the sky and there's nobody around, not even very many cars. In front of us, beyond the empty concrete and the light standards, you can't even see any buildings, really. There's a few tall apartment buildings up ahead, off to the right, but straight on we can see out to the river and to the Palisades over on the Jersey side, and the bluffs are thick with trees, and there's sky beyond, a lot of sky, and clouds. I think it's all of this that Norma sees when she says, "I like it," and she runs on ahead and I follow and she keeps on going as far as she can, till she's leaning over a little fence by the exit sign whose arrow is pointing at her. I come up beside her and she's looking off to the west, as far as she can see into New Jersey.

I look, too, but it's New Jersey, after all, and so pretty soon I just watch the terminal roadway which curves beneath us, and a bus wheezes out and disappears under a ledge to my left that holds a big silver compressor. I study it close so that I won't say anything stupid to her. It's got Baltimore Aircoil Company written on its side and it's surrounded by a fence with barbed wire rolled along the top of it. I figure the guys who hang around the bus terminal will steal any damn thing. Every once in a while I glance back to Norma, but she's still watching the distant shore, I guess, or maybe she's not watching anything, maybe she's thinking. I just keep telling myself it's okay to stay quiet, it's what she wants.

Finally, she says, "If we were in school together, Deuce, you and me, would I be the kind of girl you'd want to take out? Like to a dance or something?" You'd think this would be a very encouraging thing for me to hear. But the voice is all wrong. In spite of the words and in spite of her being in the fresh air up here and having a view of the bluffs and all—things that she really seemed to like at first—her voice has this little tremor. Like panic maybe, though that doesn't make any sense to me, or like this is a real important question for reasons that have nothing at all to do with me.

When I turn my face to her, she isn't even looking at me, she's still straining out over the fence. I say, "Of course I'd like to take you to a dance, if we were in school together."

She nods faintly at this and she even smiles a little bit. Then she straightens up and turns her back on the river and shakes her hair out, runs her hand through it. "Am I attractive, Deuce?"

This sounds like the same kind of question to me, like it's coming from this one thing that's worrying her. Would you take me to a dance, do you find me attractive. It makes sense that those go together. I know now that I was wrong. It was an easy mistake to make, though I should have heard how her voice had changed. The tremor is gone, and maybe I did hear it but just thought I'd made the tremor go away by assuring her I'd take her to a dance. I say, "You're the most attractive girl I've ever seen," and suddenly I worry that I've overstated this so much that she'll believe I'm a nerd or something.

"I think men find me attractive," she says, and all I can think of is that she's saying this because I'd just proved to her that I'm not a man by saying something stupid.

"Sure they do," I say. "Like me." I mean by this that they're men like me, but I hear how it sounds—men find you attractive just like this boy does.

Softly she says, "Do you think it's true that men sometimes show how much they think something is beautiful by hurting it a little?"

This isn't easy for me, to talk about how stupid I was. But I'm going to tell the truth. When she says this, I suddenly believe that she's talking about me. That somehow what I said hurt her. It's not even worth calling myself an idiot. I was worse. I was a goddam half-breed who wasn't enough of one thing or the other to be much of anything. I was supposed to be part of this rich country full of opportunity but I was begging money and living on a highway and soon to move up to an abandoned building. I was supposed to know the streets but I couldn't even hear the voice of whoever it was that slept with this girl last night and still had his teeth in her. So I apologize for hurting her. "I'm sorry."

She doesn't even hear me. "Love bruises," she says.

"Love bruises?" Now I'm completely baffled.

She turns to me and her hand touches my wrist again and she says, "Am I going to be all right?"

"Yes," I say, and I'm trying to will myself to take her hand in my own. "You're just tired," I say.

"I've got to go now," she says. "I'm not really supposed to be out. I have to be somewhere."

Before I can do anything, she kisses me on the lips as light as a flick of her hair, and she runs off. I watch her black hair flying behind her and she stops at the distant glass doors and she turns and waves to me and disappears. I stand there at the fence easing my tongue over the part of my lips that she kissed, tasting the oily sweetness of her lipstick, and I stay there until the taste is gone.

The kiss took the strangeness and the worry away from the whole encounter with Norma. She kissed me and she wanted to go to a school dance with me and that's all I let myself think about. I went back to the terminal and worked a few more coins out of people with an enthusiasm that left even those who didn't give something to me a little bit amazed.

Then at about three-thirty I went back to the abandoned highway, and one of the whores that lived in the shanties at the dead end saw me from where she crouched pissing in the weeds by the fence and she blew me a kiss. I entered the hole for what I hoped was the last time and I got my duffel bag and at four o'clock sharp I was under the flag in the bus terminal foyer and ready for Joey. I didn't expect him to be on time, but at five o'clock I was starting to worry that I'd have to go back to the highway for the night. Stupidly I'd gone down in the hole with the whore still watching me and my bag wouldn't be safe there anymore.

But a few minutes later Joey arrives. He's got a paper bag cradled in his arm and he says, "You ready?"

I'm not going to complain about anything. It's enough that he's here. "Let's go," I say.

We head out the door and up to Forty-second and Joey turns us east. "We got lucky," he says.

"How's that?"

"I got a bottle," he says, and he lofts the paper bag.

And for me it's like he's saying, Let's go back up on the West Side Highway and party. It's pissing in the weeds that he's got in the paper bag. I think I said before that I've got this thing about booze and drugs, how it really bothers me to give up control of my insides. Shit, things are confusing enough for me as it is. I know how some people run up against real bad stuff in their life and it looks good to them to just sort of blank out. If I was like that, I would've blanked out on stereos and televisions and a big yard and a room of my own with plenty of money behind it and I wouldn't have ended up on the streets of New York. That'd be booze enough for me. But I know, too, that my mother helped me with this. That sounds funny when you think about how she ended up. But she never let me see her drug thing, not so that I'd recognize it, not like all the fucking. I guess she figured that fucking was all right so it was okay for me to hear it, but she was ashamed of the drugs and she didn't want me to know. She must've been ashamed, because she didn't use them till the very end, around the time of Claude. Before that, not only do I feel sure she wasn't on drugs, she clearly hated booze. Couldn't stand it. She never drank, and when one of her men started drinking in the apartment, she'd get real angry and tell him that he had to leave that at the bar. She never liked it and that was always clear to me and I guess it made an impression. It's a little hard to figure her out sometimes. It'd be easier, I guess, if she was just one clear thing.

So I say to Joey, "I don't like to drink," but there's some worries now going through my mind and I think of the yellow in his eyes.

He says, "You're too young anyway. I don't want to corrupt you."

"I just don't like the stuff."

Joey nods gravely, like he's some goddam expert. "I get it. The shit you're running away from probably has to do with that."

"No it doesn't."

"Well, I'm no alcoholic, Deuce. You don't have to get that idea."

"I'm not running away from alcoholics."

"I like to drink. A soldier drinks. Like a goddam bird chirps. But I'm no alcoholic."

"You're no soldier anymore," I say, and I'm getting real uneasy all of a sudden. Not just about the drink stuff. I probably even half believe him when he says he's not an alcoholic. It's what I want to believe. But the thing about being a soldier sounds like the lies starting again.

"I know I'm no goddam soldier anymore. I mean once a soldier, always a soldier, and soldiers drink." Joey stops suddenly and I take another step before I realize it. I come back to him. We're standing just east of a big Live Nudes sign and a guy at the door snaps a leaflet off a stack in his hand and shoves it at a couple of guys going by and he says, "Upstairs, private booths. Check it out, gentlemen," and Joey is saying again, "I'm no goddam alcoholic," and now I just want to drop the whole thing and get on to a place where I can lie down on something other than concrete and sleep without getting rained on.

"Okay, Joey. I believe you."

"But I just want to make sure you're not going to turn into this kid who's always hassling me about what I do. I'm not in this for shit like that. If I get drunk once in a while, that's just the way it fucking is."

"Live nudes," the voice from the door cries. "Live and hot."

I realize that part of what's making me want to get away so bad now is the hope of just lying in a room in the dark and having time to think about Norma, and I'm getting real nervous there on the street near the live nudes and probably weird pussy probing and hot candle wax and shit like that. I say, "I don't give a shit about what you do, Joey. I think you're an okay guy and I'm real grateful that you're letting me get off the highway. If you want to get drunk, why the hell should I care?"

"Good," he says. "Good. I just wanted to get that cleared up." He cuffs me on the shoulder, and I guess he sees my eyes slide from his face to the guy in the doorway who's still going on about the hot nudes. Joey looks over his shoulder and then looks back to me. "Let's get moving," he says. "I hate this goddam street."

It occurs to me to stop him and tell him that if I want a live, hot nude once in a while, that's just the way it fucking is. But even as a smart-ass pose the idea makes me nervous. It's Norma I want to think about, so I don't say anything. I just let Joey lead me and we go down into the subway at Forty-second and Times Square and the token windows there face the turnstiles, but the yellow exit doors are off-center from the windows and we wait for a busy moment and slip on through.

We catch the N train, N for Norma, and we come up out of the ground at Eighth Street in the Village. We turn our backs on all the cute-ass little shops that string along into the West Village and we cross Broadway where there's a block of street peddlers with magazines and used clothes and shit like that all laid out on the sidewalk. And it really was like commuting, because during all the time I spent with Joey we'd always take this same route and see the same things. Joey never would let us change a step of this trip. We might as well have been carrying briefcases and evening newspapers.

And each block was like its own little suburb, changing like Point Pleasant changes to Hoboken. We reach the corner of Lafayette and there's a little jumble of streets coming in from different directions and they're all sorted out by a traffic island with a sculpture on it that's just this big black box up on one point. There's street people always hanging around under it, like they're living there; they've got their things spread out and they're smoking or drinking, and it beats the hell out of me why this black box makes them want to roost. We head on east to Third Avenue and cross it and suddenly we get all these shops in the brownstone first floors and basements selling dresses and jewelry and buttons and beads and posters and they're all so cute they make me want to spit. Flash and Trash; Baubles, Bangles and Thee; French Kisses; Hickey Heaven. Give me a fucking break.

Across Second Avenue the shops suddenly disappear and there are more trees and the brownstone stoops all have these black wrought-iron banisters full of fancy curls and flowers. It feels like people live on this street and if they had lawns they'd be cut and edged real close. Then in the middle of the block, squeezed between the brownstones, there's this narrow gray building with a red door, and the sign on it says Holy Cross Polish Catholic Church but the sign goes on and on saying a bunch of other stuff, only you can't read it because all the other words are in Polish. Whenever I pass this place I give it a special look. I guess I like it because it's run by people who know they're outsiders and who say to the world, We'll tell you what we are here, Polish Catholics, and as for the rest, fuck you, we're just going to talk to ourselves.

On this same block there's another place that stops me and turns me to stare at it, at least that first day on the way to Joey's place. Over the doorway of a brownstone is a child carved in stone the pasty color of a white man's corpse. He's a little boy who's maybe three or four, and draped over him is this thick, loose coil and I follow it over his shoulder and down the side of the doorway and it ends in the head of a snake with its face lifted and its stone eyes fixed on me. I look across the door to the other side and there's another snake, just the same, staring right at the place where I have to take my next step. Joey's stopped and is standing just beyond this space, waiting for me. I follow the body of the second snake up the door and it wraps around the child too, and I look at the boy's face and he's scared, you can see it clearly, his face is tight, his mouth is about to open and cry out from these snakes coiling around him, their tails draped over his shoulder, the body of one of them crossing him at his crotch. I drag my eyes from his face and rush through the gaze of the second snake and I never look at this thing again in all the times Joey and I go by here. I'm no pansy-ass or anything about this, it just makes me uncomfortable, and I have real trouble figuring out why the hell somebody would put something like that on their door.

Across First Avenue the trees disappear and the stoops are suddenly scattered with guys in beat-up clothes and they're sleeping or sitting with their heads in their hands or just watching the street with eyes that may or may not be taking much of anything in. About halfway along the block there are a few trees, like somebody could see what was going wrong around them and wanted to set themselves apart somehow, and at the place of the trees there's a storefront that makes me think of the Polish church. In the window is a blue sign with yellow letters saying Ukrainian Native Faith Inc. I'm starting to wonder how many different kinds of outsiders might be living around here. I even wonder if somewhere there's a storefront with the yellow and red of Vietnam on a sign. The Fuck You I'm Vietnamese Society. But as soon as I play that little fantasy in my head, the thing turns on me. They don't even let me into the goddam society. I'm not Vietnamese, they say. The best they can do is offer me an associate membership for half of me, and I tell them, Fuck you too.

Across Avenue A, we go into Tompkins Square Park, and there are lots of trees now. Joey leads me on a long, curving path to the right, and I think I'm back up on the goddam West Side Highway. A guy is standing in the center of the path looking like he's asleep on his feet, bending slowly at the knees until he's about to fall down, and then he sort of snaps awake and starts the whole thing again. And along the path are benches full of sleepers, men in clothes that may have had color at one time but are grimed into grayness now so that all these guys look like they're in uniform, all part of some badly beaten army. And the women are here, too, some of them pretty young, a real thin blond girl with a dragon tattoo stretching down the length of her arm and another girl under a big bush with some pieces of cardboard set up on end, like she's made a little house there, and she's got her hand up under her T-shirt and her hand is thrashing away under there like she's got a terrible itch that just won't stop.

But there are others in this park. The Ukrainians. Old Russian women walking dogs and I pass them and the women are dumpy in their flower-print dresses and they glance at me like they want to sic their dogs on me. But I have a funny feeling about these women, not a bad feeling, really. I hear them talking to each other in Russian and they move through the park like this is some other planet, and it's not just the druggies and bums they're separate from, it's the whole city and the whole country. They don't even talk the language. They've got these flower-print dresses that they probably sewed themselves because they don't trust the stuff in these alien shops, and they're just exploring here, just living in an outpost in some far reach of the universe. Then Joey and I go around a curve and there's a little section off the main path with stone chess tables and the air is thick with pipe smoke and there's a murmuring of Russian and all the old Russian men who belong to the old Russian women are playing chess, and the American women pissing under the bushes don't mean a goddam thing to them.

We pass a band shell and it's full of bottles and old clothes and mattresses and one old man sweeping up with a ragged broom, and I ask Joey when we're going to be there, and he says it won't be long. I'm tired of looking at all this. We come out of the park on Seventh Street and we cross Avenue B, and the buildings are taller here and the fronts are strung with metal fire escapes and some of the buildings have clothes drying on the railings and flowerpots in windows and thick-armed women leaning out, watching the street, and there's a sign that says "This land is ours, property of the people of the Lower East Side and it is not for sale." And another sign that says Stop Gentrification. And then there are other buildings that have no flowerpots and drying clothes but instead have boards on the windows and some of the boards are broken and torn away and in one of these a red sock is lying on the ledge, and through another one, on a first floor, I can hear a child crying even though the front door of that building is nailed shut and a sign says keep out. And next to this building is an empty lot full of broken stones and bricks and rusted spikes of steel and an old refrigerator and car doors and bald tires and Joey says, "This way," and he leads me across the lot. The building up ahead is tall and boards are on its windows and on its brick side someone has painted a long message saying "They shall rebuild the ancient ruins. The former wasted they shall raise up, and they shall restore the ruined cities, desolate now for generations. Isaiah 61:4." And beneath it, in red paint and a different hand, are the words "Kill Gentrification. Kill the speculators."

At the back of this building is a padlocked metal door, but beside it is a window, only it's a little higher than usual and Joey gets a crate from nearby in the rubble. He says, "Nobody ever comes around to check the place anymore, but we move this away from the window whenever we can. It just draws attention to us." He puts the crate on the ground and is up and through the window and I follow him and drop into deep shadows and a real alley smell, mildew and grease and rotting food and cinders and dust. I pause and close my eyes to the sharp-edged slash of light following me through the window. "Come on," Joey's voice says, and I face into the darkness and I can see his eyes just beyond the length of my arm, like he's swimming under-water. The eyes disappear and I move across a gritty floor and into a corridor and I follow Joey's shape up ahead.

"There's more than just you in here?" I ask.

I hear him snort. "Sure. I wouldn't have this to myself. You think I'm rich?"

We're going up a staircase now and I'm forcing my eyes open as far as I can, but it's still all real dim. Joey's moving fast, easily, and I wonder how he can see. I figure the men who followed him through the jungle when he was walking point must have felt like this. But as soon as I think this I remember it was all a lie, and we come out on a floor and I can see the flicker of candlelight somewhere along the corridor, but we turn back sharply and climb more steps. Joey lied and I'm climbing into darkness with him. I'm not afraid of him or anything like that, it's just that I wonder what all this is going to do for me. Who the hell am I in a place like this? We hit a landing and there are windows here with a crack in the boards and a knife-blade of light cuts us both across the chest and we move on, still climbing, and Joey says, "It's not just guys like us in here either. There's some families."

We come out on another floor and take the turn again and go up and I'm struck by Joey thinking I'm a guy of a certain sort, especially since just seconds before, I was wondering about me and this building. There's a little part of me that's going, Goddam right, guys like us, I'm a guy like him who's a guy like me and we're guys like us. But mostly there's this flopping around inside me, like if I go even a step higher up in this building I'll never find my way down again, I'll come out onto one of these corridors and sit down and I won't be able to get up and I'll stay there until I start coming apart, disintegrating, and I'll end up just so much grit on the floor. All through this, Joey's still talking and I hear him say, "The families with kids come in a different way, down in the basement. I'll show it to you sometime."

I say, "Are we going up much farther?" though I can't shake the feeling that it's too late, I've gone too far already.

"Next floor," he says, and we climb and come out into one of the corridors and we move along it to the far end, and just like it's his apartment, he stops at a door and he fumbles at the handle. "There's a trick to this," he says. "I'll show you later. It's as good as a key."

Then the door opens into more shadow, and on top of the mildew and dry rot there's a smell of piss and a strong smell that I realize is hanging all through the building and that I later learn is the smell of cockroaches. These aren't the big tree roaches I know from Vietnam but little brown fuckers and there's a clenching way up inside my nose at all of this and I want to turn back around and get the hell out. But Joey steps in and I don't know where else to go and I follow him and he closes the door.

And that's quite a sound, as it turns out. The snap of that door shutting is like a switch that flicks off the fears that have been flashing in my head ever since I was on the stairs. That snap of the door puts me in a closed space away from the world outside and there is silence and shadow and already the smells are gone for me and I feel the touch of Norma's lips. But it isn't just Norma, it's the room. There's some real hard shit out the window, but this is a tight little room and my arms and my chest feel a kind of settling, like I want to sleep and I have all the time I need. Like there's a mat on the floor for me and this is one of the nights when my mother is going to sit by the window in the dark and smoke.

That's okay. I don't mind thinking of my mother. There'd been some good times. Why not step into a room full of cockroaches and dry rot and think about the fucking past. She was a beautiful woman and the red spot of her cigarette was like a firefly and they say if you can catch the first firefly of spring in your hand, you will never die. The dark silhouette of a head and torso slides into a jagged square of light before me, across the room. It's Joey. There's one window with most of its wood torn away and he's standing there now. I look around the place and it's just a square room with dim, low shapes— stacks of old magazines, stacks of newspapers, a couple of milk crates, scrounged blankets, piles of clothes, a mattress, empty whiskey and wine and bourbon bottles in a neat row against a wall. Joey, framed darkly in the window, says, "Welcome home, Deuce."

It's funny how two real strong feelings, if they pull in opposite directions, can make you stand there feeling like nothing at all is going on. Your head might be full of real complicated shit, if you let it, but what you're feeling in the gut is nothing much at all. There was enough in me wanting to have a place where I could be still and think, and enough in me wanting to get the hell away from any goddam thing calling itself home, that when Joey says this, all I do is let the duffel bag slide off my shoulder and fall to the floor.

So we stack some blankets for me in the corner and Joey promises a search for a mattress tomorrow. But I lie on the blankets and they feel just fine to me, and I want to stay there and sleep at once. But Joey brings me to an orange crate near the window and he moves it into the exact center of the spill of light. Then he disappears for a moment and returns with two cans of pork and beans and some saltines and we sit down here and we eat and we don't say much of anything. This doesn't seem so odd to me. Joey moves like he's got that same settled feeling in him that I felt when the door closed on this room. His hands lift food to his mouth slowly, and even the stretch of his face is gone in this light, like suddenly his skin fits. And if this is really home, you don't have to say a goddam thing. I just watch out the window as I eat, and the building across the street

is boarded up, too, which disappoints me a little bit. I'd like to watch
the fat-armed women and the curtains blowing out the open windows, but instead I watch pigeons on the fire escape railing and once
in a while one of them leaps off and spirals down, out of sight, into
the street below.

After dinner we sit on cushions against the wall next to the window. I wonder why we're looking into the room, which is growing
more and more dim as the twilight deepens. But Joey answers this by
opening his paper bag and pulling out his bottle. I think once again
of going over to my corner and sleeping, and I could do that now if I
want to. But when Joey uncaps his bottle, all the other distractions of
this day fall away and the lies he told me curl into me like the smell
of his cheap whiskey. I figure maybe he's no alcoholic, but if he's
going to start drinking while facing a dark room, I'd better ask him
right away what I need to ask him.

I say, "Can I get the truth out of you now?"

Joey has the bottle half raised to his lips for his first drink, but his
hand stops. The bottle comes back down slowly. "What about?"

"You know what about. Vietnam. All of that."

Joey's eyes turn to me, and here in the shadows they seem distant,
like when I saw him just after going through the window downstairs.
He looks at me like he's hidden in the forest and I'm out on the path
and a danger to him. But then he lifts the bottle and puts the cap on
it and sets it carefully beside him. "What do you want to know?"

"What did you do in Vietnam?"

"I was a clerk."

"A clerk?" I try to keep the surprise out of my voice, but I can
hear it there in the lift of the tone, like the rising accent in Vietnamese.

Joey hears it too, because he says, "If you're going to give me a
hard time over every lie, to hell with you. I'm not going through that
kind of shit."

"I'm sorry," I say.

"Why don't you pretend you just met me or something."

"Okay. Good. I don't know a goddam thing about you."

Joey puts his head back against the wall and talks into the room. "I was a personnel clerk and I worked at MACV headquarters in Saigon, out at the Tân Sơn Nhứt airport. I lived in a hotel the Army had taken over near there. This was 1967. I left about three weeks before the big Tet offensive of '68. We took a few rockets now and then and I watched a GI get shot to death by a Saigon cowboy outside a bar, but that was about as much action as I saw. Except maybe when the top sergeant's typewriter broke down on him once too often and he threw it across the room and destroyed the water cooler. Everybody in the room got Army Commendation Medals for going through that."

Of course this last bit sounds like a lie to me, a different kind, but still a lie, and Joey must have read the thought. His face turns to me and he says, "No shit, Deuce. It really happened. Top had been having some trouble controlling himself and he was the ranking man there when he went berserk. We were all just privates and spec fours and he made us this offer for our silence. Not that we gave a fuck about the medal."

Joey stops and his hand comes out and grasps the bottle, but it's like a reflex, because a moment later he looks at his hand as if he didn't realize it was there and he lets go. "There's not much more about Joey Cipriani as a Vietnam vet," he says. "They flew me in and I typed the war away and they flew me out."

"You lived up near the airport?"

"Yes."

"The bars you went to. Were they near the airport too?"

"Sure. There were a couple of streets up there with a bunch of bars."

The question about the bars came out of me very naturally, without thought, but I know why this is important to me when I feel the little ooze of relief at his answer. The bars Joey went to were far away from my mother's part of town. And the next question is almost in my mouth before I stop it. I'm not sure whether I want to know more about the woman Joey loved. I can't say why it scares me. It just does. But with Joey's hand fretting now in his lap, waiting to go for the bottle, and with the dark gathering around us in this room we now share, I want to like him. It's just that I get this fluttering in my chest when I try to speak. My scalp prickles and I run my hand through my hair, digging at the roots, and the itch only gets worse. But I feel the wild shock of black there, the thick hair of a Vietnamese, and this is a strange feeling that's come over me. I think of Montreal again and tears even come to my eyes. I could've been Vietnamese. I had a chance to be Vietnamese.

"I met a girl at the bar," Joey says.

I think to stop him. That's enough, I could say. Open your bottle now. But I don't say anything. After all, this is the question I wanted to ask.

"Her name was Mai."

I'm facing the room and I close my eyes and wait for more. But there's a brief silence and then a scrabbling sound. I look and Joey has stood up. He walks into the room and roots around in the far corner and then returns. "Here," he says, drawing me into the light. He has a photo in his hand. It's the size and shape of the photo in my duffel bag and it's not easy making my hand go out and take this thing, even knowing that it would be impossible for her to be anything but a stranger. Her name is Mai, the girl in this picture.

I take it, and the light from our window fills its surface with a reflection of the sky outside and the top floor of the building across the street, and though there is a face hiding in this bright glare, I don't look at it right away. "I loved her very much," Joey says, and I angle the photo just a little and the New York sky disappears and a bargirl with a thin, flat mouth that she's dragged into a smile looks at me from the vinyl seat of a booth in the bar. The smile troubles me. It's clearly forced. Joey's holding the camera and she can't even give him a real smile. Her hair is long and it falls on each shoulder in exactly the same way, like it was arranged there very carefully. I know her type. There were whores like her at Texas Girls. The same night Joey took off forever from Tân Sơn Nhứt, Mai was fucking some other GI and giving the new guy the same smile and he was falling in love with her forever.

"I still love her," Joey says, and he sits now in the light from our window. I hand the picture back to him and retreat into the shadows. Joey stays where he is, staring at the photo, and I'm afraid he's going to do some idiotic thing, like kissing it. But instead, he lifts his face to me and says, "I'm no fool, Deuce. She said she loved me, but I know the word was cheap in Saigon. The thing is that she didn't have to have the same feeling for me that I had for her. I loved her the best way I could, and maybe the world had fucked her over so that she couldn't feel like that, or maybe I was just the wrong guy, maybe somebody could make her feel like that but it wasn't me. That makes me sad, but it doesn't mean what I felt is false. That's why it's love."

These are just words to me. I understand what he's saying, but these are *ideas* about love, and people don't live in their heads. Whatever he's really talking about is left on his skin and on his tongue and in his eyes and I don't know what to say to him.

He says, "I met her in my first week in-country. I was her man for nearly a year. She said she never was steady with a man for that long before, and I believe that. And I told you the truth, too, about her being the first woman I ever slept with. She liked that. And she liked my skinniness. I was always the ninety-eight-pound weakling, Deuce, and the girls in the States don't like that. But Vietnamese girls love skinny men. It's like their own kind. I was this good-looking guy in Vietnam, and Mai was proud of me."

I stop watching Joey. I keep my eyes on the darkness of the room and I'm just going to wait all this out. I'm glad Joey felt good about himself in Vietnam. I still like him for loving a Vietnamese. But at the moment all that doesn't count for much with me because I'm not feeling Vietnamese myself and because I'm getting real mad at the whore in this story he's telling. But I don't know why the hell I should be mad at her. She made Joey feel good for a year. What's so bad about that? I look at him and he's staring out the window and his tears hold the sky like the photo did in my hand. "So what happened?" I ask.

"I wanted to bring her home. But it was this incredible hassle, paperwork that would fill a taxicab." Then Joey turns his face away from the window. He looks into the room. "But that wasn't it, really. I couldn't do anything for her. We were dirt poor from Flatbush. My dad was dead and my mom was sick and my only brother was in jail for grand theft auto. I just turned twenty and if a PFC spends every cent he has on his girl in Saigon, he can be pretty good to her for a year, especially if he doesn't hang on to her too hard and doesn't insist on seeing her every night. You understand?"

"Yes," I say.

"But I don't want you to get the wrong idea. I could hold her in my arms and I could let all that long black hair of hers fall all over me. And Saigon was part of it. I could hear the planes coming in and the traffic in the street and gunfire even, and still I could hold her and when I'd make love to her she'd cry out once in a while in this language I didn't even know, but it meant I was making this woman feel good."

These aren't just words for me. I can see Joey on top of his Mai and I can hear her cry out, "Trời ơi," and I wonder what she really meant.

"Do you understand, Deuce? Do you see why I loved her?"

"Sure," I say. "Sure I do." And then I tell Joey that I'm real tired, that I haven't slept on anything but concrete since I hit New York and I want to sleep now. So I lie down and I close my eyes and I look for Norma's face. I put myself on the roof of the bus terminal. But before she can appear, I guess I fall asleep: there's just the concrete and the light standards and New Jersey in the distance and then there's darkness.

I wake and the room is black. A face slides away in my mind as I lift from sleep, but it's not Norma. It's the face of the thin-mouthed whore. I look across the room and Joey is sitting there in the dark, sitting by the window. I can see the shape of him, and his chin and his cheekbones are lit from below by a streetlight. He's sitting very still and I wonder if it was his dream, not mine, that slid from my mind as I awoke. Then there's movement and he lifts the bottle into the light and he tilts his head and drinks. His head goes far back, so I know he's almost finished, and I wonder what he's thinking. Probably something about Mai, but what exactly? Does the liquor make her better than she was or worse? Is he thinking of the nights he held her in her room in Saigon or the nights when he couldn't afford her and she held someone else?

I close my eyes again, and now I feel Norma's lips touch mine and pull away, I see her hair flying behind her as she runs off. And suddenly I'm puzzled by her words. I'm not really supposed to be out, she said. Out from where? I try to imagine, but it sounds like we're kids and her momma has given her a bath and doesn't want her to get dirty, and it's like the trees of Point Pleasant are all around and Norma's in a frilly dress and she's runing away across a lawn and the lawn darkens as she runs, it's turning black even though the sun is still shining, and I want to run after her, but my legs won't move and now it's one of those little moments when you're two people at once —the guy who's dreaming and in the dream is having this terrible rush of fear, and at the same time you're this other guy who's sitting back in some safe place and knowing it's a dream all the while. The lawn is getting blacker and blacker and Norma is running but never seems to move. She's in the center of the lawn and I recognize the blackness—it's the Thi Nghè River—and then because I know it's the river, Norma is suddenly swallowed there, she sinks instantly without a ripple and it's all my fault and the me that's caught up in the dream begins to flail his arms in anguish and the me that knows that none of this is real looks across the river and the far shore is crowded with shacks and in the window of one of them is the little red spot of a cigarette flaring and then darting off as a woman sits smoking in the dark.

THIRTEEN

⬩
⬩

All of a sudden the days changed. I thought I'd see Norma and I was afraid I'd run into Treen and his boys and I was wary of the Port Authority cops and I was even looking for private eyes that Kenneth might be sending out after his kid, but the next day came and the next and the next and I began to understand the slump of the shoulders in the regulars around the bus terminal and the deadness in their eyes. Real fast, things fell into a routine and there was this who-gives-a-shit-about-anything drag in your limbs and all the stuff I was hoping for or worrying about just seemed like somebody smoking cigarettes across a river in your dreams. A week went by and I didn't see Norma and I kept away from Treen and only twice did I see any of the guys from Fairyland gliding along the main concourse of the South Wing and only once did one of them even look my way. I was real careful about those guys. And the cops never hassled me, though I got a couple of glances from them. Once, a cop appeared over my shoulder in the mirror in the rest room as I lifted my face from a basin of water. The cop was a white guy with about a size eighteen neck and it looked like he was going to say something, but then McGee's face was there beside him and he asked me how my dad was doing and I said fine and he asked me if I was keeping my nose clean and I said I was cleaning it right then in the basin and he laughed and nudged his partner and said I was okay and they left. And this thing about what Kenneth might be doing, it never even occurred to me till I dreamt about it one night there in the room on the Lower East Side. I woke up with my pulse pounding in my throat and there were these two fat guys chasing me all over the bus terminal and I knew they were working for Kenneth and they had these bowling balls that they were throwing at me, throwing them as straight and fast as baseballs, and the balls were just barely missing me and they were crashing into the walls or the posts and smashing out big chunks of tile or brick and I knew the next one was going to hit me in the head. I never shook that dream and I got real suspicious of men in suits looking my way, though I felt pretty confident, really, that I'd covered my tracks out of Point Pleasant. I figured they'd never find the guy from Virginia who gave me the lift to Hoboken.

So that's how things went for a week. Every morning I'd wake up looking at a wall the color of the clothes of the sleepers in Tompkins Square Park. And two or three of those mornings Joey would be lying on the mattress across the room and softly cursing his own head because the day before, he'd gotten a bottle. We'd get up and there was even a trickle of water in this place and I'd wash myself and change clothes. Then Joey and I would walk our same path through the East Village, my eyes avoiding the child wrapped in snakes and seeking out the Polish church, and we'd commute back uptown. And every day on the train I'd be thinking about Norma. I've got to tell the truth about that. And whenever I'd think of her and wonder if today she might turn up, there'd be this sort of fumbling feeling in my crotch, and it even hurt a little bit, like I just sat down too hard. The body can be pretty stupid. You'd think it'd find a special reaction for each emotion. But this one I had thinking about how Norma might show up was the same as I'd have if I'd suddenly seen somebody in the street bleeding from a wound. It would be the same grinding little pain in the crotch that you have to grit your teeth about. That seems pretty stupid to me. So each day I'd try to get my mind off her. I'd remind myself how I looked like a fool the last time I saw her anyway. So by the time Joey and I split up in the Eighth

Avenue foyer of the South Wing, I'd have convinced myself that I was never going to see her again.

But about the seventh day of this routine I turn out to be wrong. Joey and I are walking west on Forty-second and today we're pretty early and we turn the corner at Eighth, and standing there by the fence is Norma. She's there by herself and she's wearing a T-shirt and real tight jeans and black high-heeled shoes and her mouth is bright red, and when I go over to her, she seems real glad to see me. "Hello, Deuce," she says, and her hands come out like she wants to hug me or something, but they seem to run out of energy and they stop and pull back. "I wondered if I'd see you again," she says.

"Me too," I say, and her eyes are real sleepy and I notice their color for the first time—river black, like they're all pupil.

"Deuce?" It's Joey's voice and I turn to him.

"Joey," I say, "this is my friend Norma." It occurs to me now that I don't know Norma's last name. But I don't want to make a big deal of it in front of Joey, so I just say, "Norma, this is Joey Cipriani."

She looks at him sideways, like she's a little embarrassed, and Joey sort of grunts at her. I say to him, "You go on. I'll be a few minutes."

"There it is," he says, and he's gone.

"So how are you?" she says.

"Fine. I'm okay. That was my friend."

"Good. I've got a friend, too." Norma nods past me, and over on the curb, leaning into a taxicab, is a woman with jeans and heels like Norma but a short leather top laced up the back like a shoe. You can see a wide strip of her skin at the waist, the bumps of her spine, and she straightens up from the taxicab window, laughing, and turns.

I've got to know what she is, right? I've had a whole shitload of experience with whores, knowing what they look like, what they smell like, what their goddam singing voices are like, everything. And if Norma's friend is a whore and Norma's hanging around the parking lot fence with a whore and her own mouth is painted red and she's got her high heels on, then I've got to know what's happening with Norma too, right? But for some reason, none of this computes. Maybe I'm so stuck on Norma that it just seems like I know her real well and the only thing she can be is what's in my mind. And maybe on that day she wasn't that deep into it yet. Especially considering what she was about to do. I don't know who was shaping her and what exactly the timetable was. But at least I should have realized that *some* goddam thing was going on. Not that I could've stopped it. What the fuck did I have to offer? We could run away to Montreal and be Vietnamese together?

So even if the woman heading this way registers in me as a whore, I instantly figure she's just Norma's casual friend. Somebody she met at the diner. It doesn't have anything to do with her. Like Joey being my friend doesn't make me an Italian Vietnam vet. Norma says, "Tracy, this is my friend, The Deuce."

"Tracy?" I say. "I know a girl named Tracy."

"There's lots of us," the woman in the leather top says. Her face is pasty white and her eyelids are blue and she's older than you think at first glance, past thirty for sure.

"You want to go someplace for a little while?" Norma says to me, and naturally I think she's talking about going back up on the roof of the South Wing. She liked it up there, when I took her, and her asking me again makes me real springy, like I want to lift up on my toes. But Norma looks at Tracy and the woman's face freezes up and I look at Tracy and her blue eyelids are slashed with little wrinkles and she rolls her lips into a tight, thin line. She obviously disapproves, and that seems to be a big deal for Norma and I'm watching Tracy and thinking, What the fuck business is it of yours?

"Come on, Trace," Norma said. "He's an old friend of mine from school. The Deuce took me to a dance once." I don't know what's going on, but I like the lie she's telling, no matter what the reason. Then after a little pause, she adds some more that's not quite as good. She says, "We were just freshmen, Trace. Kids." I'm watching Norma through the lies and she's concentrating on her friend, not glancing at me even once. Now I follow her gaze over to this woman who seems, mysteriously, to have the final say-so about Norma and me going somewhere. Tracy is looking at me, and her eyes have softened, and I wish like hell I could know what's in her head. She's studying my face, and am I supposed to look like a kid to her, or somebody smart from the streets? Will being Vietnamese let Norma go with me, or American? Or some stupid mixture of the two that doesn't look threatening? I wish I knew so that I can figure out what she sees by what she does, which turns out to be getting a little teary-eyed, if you can believe that. I swear I see tears well up in her eyes and she looks at Norma and gives her this little half smile out of the side of her mouth. Norma says, real soft, "Is something wrong, Trace?"

"Not a thing, honey. Not a goddam thing," she says, and she starts digging in her purse. "It's still early. Why don't you go on back to my place and have a little time with your boy."

"Thanks," Norma says. "I won't be long. There won't be any trouble."

And Tracy keeps digging through her purse—it's black and I can smell the leather from where I'm standing—and she keeps her face down while she's looking, like she's hiding her eyes. "Here," she finally says, and she gives Norma a key. Norma draws near her friend and gives her a quick little hug and a kiss on the cheek and then she takes my arm at the elbow and her grip is firm and she says, "This way."

All this last part, about taking me to Tracy's place, is coming into my head real slow. I'm moving up Eighth Avenue beside Norma and crossing Forty-second and her hand is resting in the bend of my arm before my breath even has sense enough to quicken.

"Where are we going?" I say, and as soon as I say it I know it's a stupid question. I'm supposed to be street smart and cool about things at all times, but shit, this is exactly what I want to know.

"Tracy has a nice little room real close," Norma says, and for Christ's sake, I already knew that. I need more.

But all I can say is, "Good. That's good."

We walk and Norma shuts up and I wonder if that's going to be it, if I'm going to have to ask ever-stupider questions until she's just so fed up with me she'll let go of my arm and run away. But finally she says, "I hope you didn't mind my telling those fibs back there."

"Mind? No. Really. I liked the idea."

"Well, you did say you'd ask me to a dance, if you'd known me in school."

"It wasn't really a fib after all."

"That's the way I look at it. I just wanted us to have a little time together. Like we're going on a date."

I don't pretend to know much more now about what was going on that morning than I did when I was walking up Eighth Avenue with Norma. I run all this over in my head and I hear that phrase that later on I start noticing the whores using to the men they're hitting on. Going on a date. Like the voice from the ramp in the dark at the abandoned highway. But goddamit, it also means just what it says. A little date, like freshmen in high school going to a dance and with fresh sheets and loving parents and a dog with ribbons in its hair to go home to. I just don't know what the fuck it meant to Norma on that morning. And why me? That's what makes me a little nervous when I look back and try to tell myself that no matter what she became later, that morning Norma was just living in some little hole she'd burrowed into the past, like a little rabbit living under the snow. I can't see it in myself when I look in the mirror and see this strange face, but maybe I was somebody who could make that place in the past seem real to her, the closest thing she could find to that part of her she didn't want to give up but knew she had to.

It just makes me feel like punching the fucking wall or something when I go back now to tell this and I hear her say those words. It makes me see her standing in the shadows of some goddam doorway on Forty-second Street and some guy walks by with a leaflet from a Live Nudes in Private Booths place still clutched in his hand and she calls to him, "You want a date?" But I was too ignorant to think all this on the morning she took me to Tracy's place. I walked with her up Eighth Avenue, New York, New York, and her hand was lying lightly in the bend of my arm and I was her date. And it's what she wanted. *She* wanted it. I wanted it too, of course, but I was a child. It was like I was six years old or something. Less. I knew more at six than I did at sixteen. She wanted me to go with her to Tracy's place and if it was a kind of halfway house for her, if it was a way to get used to pleasing whatever son of a bitch had her hooked on dope and hooked on him and who wanted her to show him how much she loved him by doing this kind of thing or wanted her to be even more attractive to him by proving how attractive she was to others, what-ever fucking line he fed her, I was the one she chose. She wanted me to go with her to Tracy's place and I went, and when we got to a doorway between a florist and a sex shop we turned in and went up some stairs and we passed beneath a bare light bulb hanging on a frayed wire and at the end of the hall we went into a room full of the smell of rotting flowers and I saw a sagging bed with the sheets rumpled back and the window shade up enough to light the bed and that's all I saw because as soon as the door closed, Norma stopped and laid her head on the point of my shoulder.

Look, all I know is to put down just how things happen, what they look like and sound like and smell like, and that's how I've tried to talk about all this. But now it gets goddamned tough. Not for the reason you might think. I'm not shy or anything. This is life, and I've had my face rubbed in it since I was old enough to remember, so talking about Norma and me in that room is like talking about any-thing else in my life, as far as that goes. But it's names again. I see and touch and smell that part of Norma that suddenly becomes the center of the room, the center of the world, that draws me into it like it's got its own gravity, stronger than if I fell out the window. And it pulls that part of me that's suddenly my own new center, that stretches my skin outward so tight that I feel it in my scalp and in the soles of my feet. But what are the names of these parts? It's like me calling myself Tony Hatcher or Võ Đình Thanh or even The Deuce. How can I tell you what I'm touching with my fingertips in the light on the sheets? Norma's cunt? No, goddamit. A cunt is a hard, sneer-ing little thing. Her vagina? Only women in Point Pleasant have vaginas. This is Norma, this is a back room in New York City on a weekday morning, this is me, I'm sixteen and this is the girl I've been dreaming about and this is a part of her that's so soft the tips of my fingers feel like they've dissolved. And what is it of mine that slips inside her? A cock? The punks who smoke in the johns at my school have cocks. A cock can't be gentle inside that soft place, can't stop and consider who this is that's so close. And it sure as hell isn't a penis either. Kenneth has a penis, though I'm not so sure, because he made certain I never even accidentally saw it.

Why the fuck do I bring up Kenneth and the women of Point Pleasant when I'm trying to talk about the morning with Norma? It's the fucking names. And there's another name. Fuck. You probably figured out long ago that the word doesn't mean much to me. And for those who do hear anything in it, it's done with cocks and cunts. Intercourse? You can forget that, because it's done with penises and vaginas, and nobody even feels a goddam thing. How about making love? Did Norma and I make love that morning? Maybe so. But I don't like the love part, as you know. It's just another name, only this one can mean any goddam thing you want it to.

Norma and I held each other and I moved inside her and this is a big mystery to me that I'd really like to understand—how something so hard and something so soft, things so opposite, could get along with each other so well. Maybe that's why the parts are so tough to name. All I know is that Norma says to me with her legs hooked over my back and with our sweat between us, "Deuce, Deuce," and then a little later she says, "Hold me," which I already am but I understand her, closer she means, that's what's driving me too, to hold her closer than even this and the smell of the dead flowers is gone and there's only Norma's smell, a smell so strong I can sense it in my mouth, like one of the strong fruit tastes in Saigon, jackfruit or even durian, like I'm a child walking through the market and all the fruits plucked from the trees or the earth are there filling me with their smells and spilling over the stalls and falling on me and suddenly there's a rushing from me and I lift my face at that moment to look at Norma, and her eyes are squeezed shut and so many tears are streaming from her that they're puddling in her ears and I should have known that there'd only be pain from this and I wish I can stop the rushing and I say, "I'm hurting you," and she says, "No. It's nice," and I say, "I'm hurting you," and she says, "No, Deuce. It's nice."

Then we lie still, joined together, for a time. After that, we come apart, slippery and silent, and I want to believe her, I want to believe that it was nice, and I turn my face to her as we lie side by side and her eyes are closed. The tears seem to have stopped, but now her very stillness troubles me. "Are you all right?" I ask.

She turns her head and opens her eyes and she smiles at me and it feels like good-bye. This isn't something that I figure out much later; I feel it at once. And she says, "I'm fine, Deuce. You were lovely." And just like I know she's saying good-bye to me, I also know that she means this. I was lovely. Then she reaches out and touches my face and she runs the soft wetness of her palm along my cheek, and with her fingertips she ruffles my eyebrows, which are as black and wild as my hair, and her fingertips follow the curve off my forehead and onto my nose and she even touches my eyelids, very gently, and then in a voice as soft as her softest part, she says, "What are you, Deuce? Puerto Rican?"

I don't say anything. I just look out the window and all I can see are bricks, the back of some building not much more than arm's length away. I'm confusing Norma now because she says, "It's okay, Deuce. I'm not prejudiced or anything." But frankly, I'm a little confused myself.

FOURTEEN

***

I never did answer Norma's question. We rose from the bed and dressed without much of anything else at all being said. At least there weren't any moments when I thought I was stupid or childish or any of that kind of crap, which had bothered me the other times I was with Norma. But I watched her sitting on the side of the bed and she was dressed now and bending to slip on her high heels, and I watched her feet and they were slim and the toes were long and the nails were pale, perfect ovals, pretty feet, and I almost said to her that I was Vietnamese. Up to that moment my brain had felt like eyes feel when the doctor dilates them—it had gaped open so wide that it couldn't consider a thing without everything getting blurry. But as I watched Norma's feet, the confusion disappeared. Like waking from a dream and suddenly remembering where you are, I decided I was Vietnamese. But even before the words could shape in my mouth, Norma's toes had disappeared and she stood up and I was nowhere and no one again. So we went back down the hallway, under the bare bulb, down the steps and out onto Eighth Avenue and I figured we'd retrace all our steps together right back to Tracy at the fence. But Norma stopped in front of the doorway and she turned me around and gave me a quick kiss on the cheek and I knew I was supposed to go on down the street alone.

I don't know why I didn't take one last look at her face. Maybe it was because she was going to look at my face in return and I figured she'd hear some fucking salsa band playing in the background or something. But I'm real sorry I didn't look at her. There are few enough things to remember in a life, and that sure as shit should be one of them, the face of the girl who took you home from the dance and the two of you found a private place and you held each other as close as you could get. Especially when some raspy little street voice was whispering to you that this girl was as good as dead to you, that very soon she was going so far away so fast that she'd even leave her image behind in the street and you'd see it now and then and all you'd know from it was that she was on some other planet by now.

But I didn't look at Norma. I just turned like I was supposed to do and I walked down Eighth Avenue and I went into the bus station and I began to drift through day after day of this new life of mine and I grew satisfied with the routine. That's part of the slump of the shoulders in all those regulars around the streets, too. It's not just from one goddam day after another, it's from letting go after some great weight has been sloughed off, and the deadness in the eyes is just what these guys want.

It's what I wanted. That way, who the fuck cared what I was. And who the fuck cared if I didn't see Norma the day after we held each other or the next day or the next day or any other fucking day. I didn't expect to see her and if I still hadn't let myself clearly understand the reason I wasn't seeing her, then who the fuck cared about that either. The sun comes up, you go out into the street and find the places where there's a little money and you find a spot in a doorway or on a standpipe or on a bench and there's no hassle, not of any confusing kinds, just putting the coins together to get a little something to eat and staying out of the way of the cops when they get cranky.

I didn't even think about her. I held her, maybe, in my dreams, but those things were gone in seconds when I woke, smudged back into the walls of Joey's place. So in the middle of the night when Joey's voice is very near me in the dark and it's dragging me awake with Norma's name, I think it's a dream. But my eyes are open and Joey's voice is still beside me and I smell his breath full of whiskey and I'm on my elbows and the streetlight is coming through the window and Joey's shadow shifts from my side and blocks off the light before me and his voice says, "Who the fuck is this Norma anyway? Consider that."

He's drunk, I know. His words are a little slow but very precise. "Go to sleep, Joey," I say.

"Consider what a whore is, my young friend."

"Joey, please."

Suddenly the shadow looms very close and Joey shouts, "This girl is a whore, Deuce," and my ears ring with his words and his breath is much more complex now, not just whiskey but bad teeth and a bad stomach as well, and I draw back. "Can't you fucking see that?" he shouts and the ringing vibrates into the center of my head and no, I hadn't fucking seen that, though maybe it wasn't true, exactly, however many days ago it was that I took her last kiss on my cheek, though it's probably true now and I should've seen it coming and I should've understood how that was part of my hearing the good-bye in her voice.

And I drag myself back from him, back against the wall, and I sit up straight and I shout at him in the dark, "Shut the fuck up. You're fucking drunk and you don't know a goddam thing about her."

The shadow rushes at me and my hands fly up in front of my face because I'm sure Joey is going to hit me. But it's only sound, loud sound: "Don't know? Don't goddam know? This Norma is a slut, a fucking whore."

My wrists are clamped hard and ripped down from before me and the pain twists there and I have no strength to fight him and no will because she's a whore now, just since I've held her, and the shadow blocks out any lighter darkness in the rest of the room, there's only the darkness of Joey before me and on my upper lip I can feel the hot slip of his breath. His voice is husky now, almost a whisper, and he says, "You think I don't know a whore when I see one? Did you forget that I'm in love with one? A whorelover always knows a whore and a whorelover always knows another whorelover and a whorelover has taken a pledge of oath to always tell another whore-lover-in-love who it is that he thinks he's loving if that other whore-lover is kidding himself. I've got to do that or they'll fucking kick me out of the fucking club."

Joey has my wrists twisted far down now and the pain is clawing its way up my forearms and I say, "Joey, you're hurting me."

"Hurting you?" he says, loud. "Am I not fucking hurt?"

"Yes, Joey. Let go."

"Yes, Joey," he says, "I am fucking hurt and it is my sworn duty as a whorelover to protect and defend..." Joey stops and his hands loosen on me. "No, wait. Protect and defend, that's the fucking police."

I pull my arms free and the shadow recedes a bit and he says, "A whorelover sure isn't going to get caught protecting and defending, that's for goddam sure."

I pull my legs up to my chest and rub at my wrists, try to rub the pain away, and I wonder if Joey's dangerous. All I've seen before tonight of his drunkenness is silence and sadness at an open window. I try to think how I can defend myself, but my mind won't work at it, nothing occurs to me, there's only a trickle of words, you were lovely, hold me Deuce, and there's a softness on my fingertips and her pretty toes disappearing into black high-heeled shoes, and all of that sucks away any strength I have and if Joey leaps on me now, I know I could do nothing but let him beat me to death.

"Fucking whores!" Joey's voice shrieks from the dark and then there's a crashing sound, a breaking bottle, and it seems to come from the same area as the voice, as if he has smashed the bottle not against a wall but in his hand and I imagine him still holding the neck of the bottle and the jagged edge flares from his fist and who knows what he sees before him in his mind. I slide away, creep along the base-board and then dash to the door, and though I only hear a faint whimpering sound from the middle of the room now, I go out the door and close it behind me and I move through the darkness, down the corridor, feeling my way very slowly as I near the invisible edge of the stairs. I find the brink with my foot and then I hold the banister and go down and there are other voices in the building, distant but you can tell they're angry, they rise and rise and one is a man and one is a woman, and I keep going down until below me is light.

I stop on the stairway and look, and it is only an angled column of light from a streetlamp coming through a broken board in a window, the beam falling against a wall on the landing below. As I look at the light and listen to the faint clash of voices, there are eyes suddenly before me and they have eased into me so silently, so unexpectedly, that I take them for a memory. A child's face is there, a round face pale in white streetlight, and I wonder first if it's me, though I know at once it's not, and then if it's some child I ran with in the alleys of Saigon, but the face is not Vietnamese, the face is of a boy but the hair is curly and these eyes are heavy-lidded and I'm beginning to understand that this child is actually before me there on the stairway landing. The voices in the distance bark and the face lifts slightly toward them and I understand and I say, "I'm on the run, too."

The boy looks in my direction, though I suspect that he has only heard me approach, that he cannot see me in the shadow. I come down the steps slowly and he does not seem afraid, maybe because of what I said. He watches me draw near and then I crouch and his eyes are blacker than the corridor where the voices come from and he says nothing. I slowly lower myself and turn and sit on the landing beside him. Suddenly a great weariness rolls my shoulders forward and folds my hands in my lap and eases my head back to rest against the wall. Just before I sleep I feel a pressure on the side of my arm, just below the shoulder, the boy's head, and my mind is dissolving into sleep so I can't bring myself to say anything, all I can think is that his head is resting gently in just the spot where the bullies in school always knew to cork you with their knuckles so that you'd be sore for a week.

I wake and the light is much brighter. Daylight. I look beside me and I am alone in the stairwell. There is nothing but the dull-scuffed floor beside me, no sign at all that the child even existed, and I put my head back and I sleep again and when I wake once more, Joey is crouching before me. I rub my eyes and twist a kink out of my neck and when I finally confront Joey, his eyes are restless, darting all over my face. "Did I do something to hurt you?" he says.

"You got drunk."

"Did I do something to hurt you?"

I wait to answer this, keeping my eyes real steady, and I know that's mean of me, I know Joey is frantic to have an answer to this and he doesn't remember a goddam thing, but I know what my answer will be and I can't resist giving him at least ten or fifteen seconds of anxiety for making a goddam ass of himself. Finally I say, "No, Joey. You didn't hurt me."

He nods and puffs some air and that's that. We make our little commute as usual that day and when I pass the boy wrapped in snakes, though I don't look at him, he makes me think of the kid on the landing, how his eyes moved from the darkness into the streetlight, and there's a spot on my arm, like my skin has its own memory, and on this spot I remember the weight of his head.

Looking back on all of this, it sometimes seems to me that everything is running together, all the important moments, the things that stick in my mind, the things that seem to add up to how it all turned out. But I know it wasn't that way. Like I said before, there were long hours and days and I guess even weeks of routine. Nothing but the routine. Sometimes that felt okay to me. I didn't have to deal with anything but eating and sleeping and watching the sunlight change in the streets. But other times I got restless. And I think one of those times was that night, the night of the day that I was just talking about, when we commuted, Joey and me, in silence after he'd gotten drunk and broken a bottle and I slept on the stairway next to that little kid and all of that. I never saw a single piece of that broken bottle, by the way. Joey had taken care of it by the time I got back to the place. And I never saw that kid again in the building, if you were sort of waiting for something to come of that. Nothing will. That little spot on my arm has even forgotten now, though once in a while my mind tries to make it remember. You can't bring something like that back by just turning your mind to it. It probably makes things worse, even.

But anyway, sometime along in there I get restless enough that when I meet Joey for our trip back down to the Lower East Side, I tell him I'll come along on my own later. I want to just hang out awhile.

"This is a bad place to hang out," Joey says, and his eyes do that same frantic dance all around my face, like when he wasn't sure what he'd done when he was drunk.

"I know how to take care of myself," I say.

"Goddamit, Deuce, you're around this terminal all day."

"Fuck the terminal," I say, "I want to walk around the streets." And it takes saying this to make me understand what it is I'm looking for. Not Norma, though as soon as I start thinking about the streets, she's in my mind. But it's just the place itself, that flow of energy I felt on the night I came back from Coney Island and walked down Forty-second Street.

"You don't want to do that," Joey says.

"Don't tell me what I want to do."

"Forty-second Street's a sewer. Never go near that place except in the daylight and you're heading somewhere else." Joey says this with his hands out in front of him, like he wants to grab me, and my skin remembers again, this time those hands of his, twisting my wrists in the dark.

"Who the fuck are you anyway?" I say, and I should leave it at that, but I go on. "You think you're my father?"

Joey shushes me and looks around like it's a big secret that I'm not. I guess he's thinking of the cops, like McGee, but it just makes me angrier, and then I say something even worse. "Look, you and Mai didn't work out. She was a whore. She didn't have your kid." Joey's hands fall and his eyes pull away from me for a moment and then he looks back at me with that thing in his eyes that was there the first time I saw him, that softness in the middle of his hard face, that thing that looked like jungle-fear, bombs and wounds and battle, all that Vietnam cliche shit that I was stupid enough to read there before. I know what it is now—the girl in Saigon who no goddam thing in the world will ever root out of him—and I don't know what to say. Except words do come out of me, and it's like I'm just over-hearing a distant conversation. I say, "My mother was some other whore."

Joey blinks real slow and lowers his face and I mumble something about seeing him later and I go out into Eighth Avenue and the traffic is rushing uptown, a horn whines by, I push through the currents of people, jostling shoulders, fuck you–ing any complaints, and I go uptown myself and by the time I get to Forty-second, I've put Joey out of my mind because he's part of the routine, part of the forget-the-world mood and I'm after the rush of things, the hustling and the getting on. I'm suddenly very hungry and I cross twice, Eighth Avenue because I've got the light with me and I can't stand still and then Forty-second, challenging the traffic, tightroping the corridors between the lanes of rushing cars.

And where the fuck should I unthinkingly turn in for food but the little Korean grocery where the son watered the concrete and the dad cut his prices for some guy he thought was a kid but who really was The Deuce. I'm inside the front door and staring at the salad bar before I realize where I am. At the far end of the bar is the father, bending over one of the bowls under glass and shaking green beans into it from a plastic container. He's probably just spent the whole goddam afternoon sitting out front delicately snipping off the ends of these beans. At the register his wife is checking some old lady out who's got a bunch of flowers and a couple of melons on the counter. No one has noticed me yet and I can turn around now and walk out without ever being seen. But I figure what the hell. What's the difference—I play on some guy's sympathies in the terminal to give me money to get home, why not let this Korean guy see whatever it is he wants to see in me so I can get a sandwich cheap?

I step up to the salad bar on the same side with the father and I sort of look at the pots of stuff, the bean salad and the cherry tomatoes and the garbanzo beans and the corn relish and other stuff I can't recognize, stuff mushed together and smelling of curry or dill or sour cream. Nice stuff. Full of old smells, things that take me out of New York altogether but don't quite put me anywhere specific. Nice. I want to eat. I suddenly realize how shitty I've been eating. Too fucking many roast beef sandwiches. Hot dogs off the street vendors.

"Take a container. Help yourself."

I look up at this voice and the owner's square face has come real near me. His eyes are deep in his head, like somebody had to operate on him to free them. He smiles at me in that way he did before, like he recognizes something in me. Suddenly this doesn't seem as easy as I thought. In the terminal it's my lie that gets me what I want. I give them something that's not in me at all. With this guy it's something he's seeing all on his own, and it makes me nervous. It pisses me off that this guy with the square Korean face thinks he sees something in me that I can't even clearly see in myself. The Koreans in Saigon were scary as hell, though they were mostly the soldiers from the Tiger Divisions and had reason to be scary. But they were square in body as well as face and real hard, like stone Buddhas come to life but pissed off at everybody. No more lotus shit, it was time to kick ass.

"You are hungry?" the man says.

"Not really," I say, a lie that I'm real sorry to have to tell. But the Korean doesn't seem to believe me anyway, from the nod he gives me like we'd just gone through one of those bullshit little Asian rituals where you're expected to say the opposite of what you really mean. They do that in Vietnam, I hear they do it in Japan, and they must do it in Korea too.

"I am Chang Ho Sung," the guy says. "I am from Korea."

"I figured," I say.

"Where are you from?"

"I'm The Deuce, and I'm from here."

Sung cocks his head at this. "Deuce? I don't know this name. Is it American name?"

"Sure," I say. "Kind of. It's a New York name."

"You are from New York?"

"Sure."

"You look like you maybe from my part of world."

"Korea?" I'm starting to get fidgety about Sung and his questions and I say this to be snide.

But he just laughs. "No. You are not Korean. That is clear to me."

"Okay. So what am I? You take a guess."

Sung cocks his head again, first one way, then the other, and his eyes go over my face like he's choosing a head of lettuce to put on his salad bar. But I'm real interested now to see what he comes up with. Finally he says, "I think you maybe Vietnamese."

When you consider what I was trying to do when I ran away from Jersey, you'd expect this to please me. I sure expect it as I stand there by the salad bar in those first few seconds after Sung declares me to be Vietnamese. But then it dawns on me as Sung waits for an answer that nothing's happening in me. At least not what I expect. There's no fucking flash of light or ringing bells or any goddam thing that would say, Kid this is you, you've found yourself at fucking last, rest easy now, you really are Vietnamese. I just stand there and my head is going, Wow, look at this shit, this guy from the Far East is telling you you're Vietnamese and he might as well be calling you Polish or Ukrainian or Puerto Rican. Worse than that. If he called me any of those, I know there'd at least be some reaction in me. But Vietnamese does nothing. I'm just standing here thinking and there's nothing else. Am I Vietnamese? Am I Võ Đình Thanh after all? What the fuck good would that do me? A horn blares its way past the door behind me, I can hear the scuffle of footsteps on the pavement, Sung's face is getting squarer and squarer, his eyes are sinking deeper into his skull, his black hair, uncombable, bristles over his head, and he's smiling like he knows he's right, he knows what I am even if I don't.

Sung says, "Vietnamese and something else too. I was in Vietnam. Maybe your grandfather is French. Maybe your father is American. I was there. I know. You eat something now and we talk."

"You don't know who the fuck I am," I say and I can hear my voice rise and I run out of breath. But I squeeze out, "Fuck you, mister," and I turn and I'm in the street and I walk south real fast and cross over and I sit on the Forty-second Street steps of the bus terminal North Wing and I calm myself down. Sitting on concrete before a fumy flow of city traffic I go completely blank, a little trick that comes easy to me after these days in the city, the only little trick that you can depend on, really. I sit there on the steps and I wait for the night and when you're street-blank, time can be two things at once, very long and very short, and so it is tonight; after thinking that the twilight would go on forever I am suddenly on my feet with the feeling that I just sat down, and the sky is black and Forty-second Street is lit up, is alive.

I step onto the sidewalk and move east and there are bodies moving around me, smells, sweat and pot and leather and Old Spice, the bodies jostle and flow, and on the corner with the parking lot and the guys hanging around the fence there's a man with long hair and a black suit with a string tie and he's waving a thick floppy book and he's saying that five sparrows are sold for two farthings and not one of them is forgotten by God and I think of Hàm Nghi Street in Saigon where the animals are for sale and you walk along there and the old women crouch with their cages full of sparrows and their baskets of puppies—I'm moving along as I see these things in my head and the running lights on the marquees and the crowds all slide into the memory, like it's all one big city—and because you're just a little kid when you first see the animals on Hàm Nghi you think the puppies and the sparrows are to hold and cuddle or to listen to their songs at sunrise but your mother leans near and she tells you in a low voice that all the animals you see on this street are to eat, all of them. And this guy whose voice I can still hear over my shoulder says that God knows all about the sparrows, he doesn't miss a one, not even on Forty-second, he says, and I pass a thin old woman at a garbage can and she's got her head cocked and is looking in there and she's wearing a long wool winter coat, like the chickie babies who are probably stepping and stepping up at Times Square, but this old woman is sweating in the heat and her nose is running and I'm moving and I turn my head and in a doorway is a girl, not Norma, but she's got a smooth face and it seems that only her mouth is painted and a guy is going by the other way and he passes near her and she says, Hi, honey, can I go? and she's kind of bouncy when she says it, like she would lick his face, like she really wants to go wherever this guy is going, and they're all for eating, my momma would say, all of them, and the long-haired guy would say that nobody escapes the notice of whoever made all this stuff and I'm walking and a ghetto blaster floats by on the shoulder of some black guy and the drums thump in my teeth and you figure the guy thinks he's in some movie and this is the soundtrack playing as he walks down the street, and everybody's got all this shit to carry, a fucking fifty-pound blaster or a winter coat in the heat or the weight of some guy who passes by who's ready to pay his money and jump on. I move to the curb and I stop and the cars are going by with guys hanging out the windows and the cops' blue-and-whites go by and people on the sidewalk just turn a little bit away and somebody comes close to me and a voice says, You have your fiver today? and the words are so clear that I know they're meant for me and I don't turn and I hear, Nickel bags, and then the voice goes on and I smell fried chicken and I turn and I move along the street, trying to pick up the smell that's gone now and from a dark doorway I hear a woman's voice say, Want a date? and I walk on faster and I pass the yellow lights framing a sex shop window and I see a form inside moving and I'm past it before who it is sinks in.

I stop and step close to a limestone wall in the dark between shops and look back. It's stupid, I guess, because if it's who I think it is he could step out and turn this way and he'd see me. But it's the street. It's out in the open. I'd just walk away. I'm caught now by wanting to know for sure. I want to see if I'm right and just moments later I know I am. Treen steps out of the shop and I press back against the wall and there's this lifting in my chest and I grit my teeth and I know now I'm a goddam fool. But Treen pauses only for a moment and he doesn't even look this way. He turns left and heads west on Forty-second. It only takes me a moment to decide what to do. It feels like me and my friends in Saigon sneaking along somebody's balcony looking for moon cakes to swipe from a windowsill or us roaring off for a ride in a xích-lô while the driver sleeps, but I get this idea to follow Treen. He's some fucking dangerous man maybe, but other than just him being around and looking a little weird I haven't seen for myself what all the fuss is about. I even wonder if it's Joey making things up again, or at least stretching them into something a lot bigger than they really are.

So I let Treen get half a dozen paces along on Forty-second and then I step out and follow him, keeping my distance and ready to duck behind a passerby or into a doorway if he decides to turn around all of a sudden. But following him proves to be a real easy thing. He's walking along like he's going someplace in particular, not looking left or right, just moving along, pretty fast even. We're still on the south side of the street and as we approach Eighth I decide that if he goes back into the terminal I'll just stop following him. I can imagine him simply going straight upstairs to Fairyland and spending the night staring down from the balcony, all pose and bluff, like when I first saw that round face of his. Following him along Forty-second now, I'm seeing Treen as just this guy with a fat head.

Then at the corner by the parking lot, he stops and I stop too and drift to the curb and step off like I'm thinking to cross. But I look back and I catch Treen checking out the street all around him, though he seems already to have looked my way without seeing anything that interests him. He's talking all the time to a tall, thin black guy and suddenly there's a flash in Treen's hand and the size of it is the only thing that stops me from knowing right away what it is. It's a blade. A knife blade as long as a dildo just snaps into life there before him like it was a magic trick—a switchblade, I guess—and the black guy rears back, then takes a step back, away from the blade, even though he says something and Treen says something and the black guy says something else and he's even smiling. There seems to be no bad blood here, but the black guy is real conscious of the blade, which Treen is now using to clean under a fingernail, it looks like, and of course the thing is making some sort of a statement to this man and I'm sure he's in total agreement with Treen about whatever it is he's saying.

So Treen's got a big knife. And sure, I'm thinking that maybe the real bad feelings I had when I was around him are the right ones after all. But the blade disappears and Treen nods a good-bye and I still wonder what a bad guy like Treen does with his nights and I'm ready to follow him some more. He heads north, crossing Forty-second at the intersection, and I'm standing at the curb anyway and the traffic is stopped and I cross where I am, about twenty yards from the corner, ready again to slide off if Treen turns this way. But he doesn't. He keeps going north and disappears at the corner. I jog over and slow down before the turn up Eighth in case he's stopped. I look and I can see his back about half a block up ahead. He's moving fast again and I go after him, moving as quickly as I can, juking around the little clusters of people, and I don't even look into Sung's store as I pass it.

I don't look at anything but the glimpses through the crowd of Treen, and I'm making up the distance and we cross Forty-third and by the time we get to Forty-fourth, I've got to hang back again. He's not going to get away from me and if I had a knife as big as his and I wanted to do something to make the Port Authority stairwells safe again, I could do it. The situation was that much under control, and that felt good, like the C.I.A. guys must feel following the K.G.B. around in Berlin or some such shit. We wait at Forty-fourth with me just a couple of paces behind Treen as a black stretch Cadillac rolls by and then a big Mercedes and I follow them east with my eyes, and the sidewalk just down the way is full of all these guys in tuxedos and chickies in little furs draped over naked shoulders and they're not stepping, they're all just sort of posing under this big theatre marquee, only nobody's taking their pictures except maybe themselves, clicking with their eyes, and the place they're going to go into says it's Majestic and it sure as shit seems so, with another limousine whispering past us while Treen and me and some guy in a Yankees cap and an old woman with an elastic tube on her head that makes her look like a Three-Mile Island power plant and some other guy in a T-shirt and a woman in a black leather miniskirt wait for the cars to go by and the light to change and then we step and we step and we're going up Eighth and we pass a wooden barricade before a building and it's plastered with posters with big cat eyes watching us and one with "42nd Street" bannered on it and a row of all-white girls in dancing shoes kicking high and that sure as fuck ain't the Forty-second Street the six of us know.

We pass a hotel with a bright lobby and a big chandelier and a bus on the curb is loading a whole shitload of Japanese and right now I'm not interested in Oriental faces so I concentrate on Treen up ahead and he and I cross Forty-fifth and the street gets darker and then we hit a hot little yellow stretch of theatres, the first with women blowing kisses off the posters and the next with men in biker's leather and sailors' uniforms and I turn my eyes from this and across the street is a pawnbroker with three gold balls hanging over the front door like it's Fairyland for mutants. I look up ahead and Treen is moving fast and the crowds have thinned out on the sidewalk a bit and there are little clusters of young men and some of them are wearing jumpsuits and some are dressed like preppies with sweaters tied around their necks, though the night is hot, and a lot of them have carrying cases on straps over their shoulders, and one guy wearing penny loafers and a button-down shirt catches me when I get to his face and he slips his tongue out and runs it lightly over his upper lip and I move on fast. I'm just an undercover spy, I'm the C.I.A. following a very dangerous spy and this is a foreign country and I'm from far away, a different place altogether, and this is all alien to me, I'm just doing my job. And then there's a woman on the corner ready to ask for a date and at least this is somebody I recognize a little bit, though she's an American whore, too tall, too broad in the shoulders, long blond hair so stiff and lank it looks phony and it probably is, and as I go by, the whore says, "Do you want good time?" Only the voice is deep and I look again and the tongue flicks out and I know it's a man, and I figure this guy's got a name problem too, bigger even than mine. And frankly, this guy makes me lose my interest in watching the street for a little while and I keep my eyes on Treen and when we cross Forty-seventh, he starts to slow down. There's a bar, a neon sign that says The Haymarket, and he turns in here and enters.

Now, looking back, this whole thing makes me nervous. But as stupid as it might've been to follow this guy, I wasn't totally crazy, certainly not crazy enough to follow Treen into whatever kind of bar would interest him. But I was still crazy enough to keep playing this idiotic kid's game like I'm some fucking spy. Across Eighth Avenue is a little stretch of shops that are closed up, a cleaners and another pawnshop, places like that, and there's about four or five doorways in a row that are empty. So I cross the street and step into the shadow of the doorway with a direct view of the Haymarket. Right away something crunches under my foot and I recoil and I look and it's a hypodermic with the needle kind of twisted and I back out of the doorway and I go down to the next one. It smells bad—piss and worse—but the smell is pretty faint, like it's days ago, and I can see the bar and I stand there and wait. I give myself a half hour or so and after that, fuck this guy, I'll just go back to Forty-second. I still haven't eaten anything. I'll just get some fried chicken or a hamburger or something with the day's beggings and then head on down to Joey's.

So I lean there in the dark and I wait, and only a few bodies pass by and I don't look at any of them, the flitting tongues of the men, the quiet little want-a-dates from the women, I just wait and watch the door of the Haymarket and only men go in and out, jumpsuits and preppies and others too, thick-armed in T-shirts and skinny in clothes that even a homeroom teacher in Point Pleasant would approve of, but all men. I get tired of watching them and I let myself look down the street, and at the corner there's a couple of guys leaning toward each other, talking low, and I look uptown and I see a woman coming this way, though she's walking with her body kind of twisted and it looks like she's having trouble moving her legs.

Then I see why she's walking like that. She's dragging a child behind her, and I don't know it yet, but she's going to be part of one of the stupidest things I've ever done, and all it is is standing there and watching, but I wish I could go back and undo it. She's probably a whore, I see that right away. She's real thin and you just know her arms have got tracks on them and she's got her hair sort of done in a pouf on top and then a long straggle down her back and it's straw blond, like the transvestite's wig, and her face—she flips it up once at me as she struggles along there—her face is drawn and it's got these wide-set eyes and behind her is this little boy, maybe six at the most, and you can see he's her kid because the eyes are just like that, wide-set, clearly his momma's eyes, and I even envy him a little bit for that. But this kid is real upset, though he's not making much of a noise. He's digging his heels in at the pavement and his mother is pulling at him and she's saying, You little brat, you goddam brat, you've got to go with Mommy, and then she tries being softer, saying, Come on, darling, we all love you. That word again. But I hear it and for a second I even hope maybe so; I think, Love the kid, you goddam bitch, but then she starts cursing again and the kid won't move his legs and he kind of falls and this woman is dragging him now till he has to regain his feet to protect himself.

I don't know what to do about this. They're just a few yards away and approaching and I think about stepping out and telling this bitch to lighten up, give the kid a break, but before they reach me, the mother veers into the street and drags the kid across Eighth Avenue and I don't really understand where they're going until she finally gets so pissed off at the far curb she picks the boy up around the waist and she carries him into the Haymarket and the door closes and that's that.

I stand there a little surprised at first. She's a woman, after all. I tell myself maybe she's going in there to buy some drugs or ask some street friend for money and the kid is there to create sympathy, feed my little boy, something like that, but even as I'm thinking this, some other part of my head is starting to fill with a nasty little buzz — what was the kid so scared of — something's crackling there in my head and I smell the old piss in this doorway and the semen and then my mind shuts down altogether. Just before it does, something tells me to walk away right now, but I don't. I guess staying there in the doorway and continuing to watch the place makes me believe that everything is okay. If I walk away now, I'll still think about what might have been going on. But if I stand there and that neon sign doesn't short out or all the glass in the facade doesn't suddenly shatter or the whole place doesn't disappear in a flash of fire because somebody important is watching all the sparrows, I can tell myself that nothing so bad as that could be going on. So I stand there and half an hour goes by, maybe more, and guys go in and guys come out and then the door opens and the woman comes out and she's not cursing now, not speaking at all, and she's got the boy by the hand and he's lagging behind, but he's not resisting anymore. He's walking behind her with his shoulders slumped and his face down and I want to run across the street and grab the woman by the throat and throw her down and beat her fucking face in, but I can't bear to see that child even for a second more and so I move off real fast in the opposite direction, toward Forty-fucking-second.

FIFTEEN

◆

That night Joey is already drunk when I get back to the Lower
East Side; he's curled in a corner in the dark and he gives me a
slurred hello and then he's instantly asleep. And as I stand over him,
even the faint slump of my own shoulders summons the vision of
that boy following the mother who'd sold him—sold him and then
kept him to sell him again, and after all, we all love you—and Joey's
hand twitches in his sleep and the empty bottle falls and in the dark
it makes a kind of scuffling sound and I can hear the boy's shoes
fighting the sidewalk, and watching Joey's stupor I guess I understand what it is that drives people to lose themselves like this. I
crouch beside him and I touch the bottle, lift it, but it's empty, and I
tell myself I don't need it anyway, this was just another fucking day
and it's just like it'd be if I finally saw some Chinese cook in Cholon
put one of us in the soup like we all believed really happened. And
maybe it really did. Any fucking thing can happen. I slid the bottle
into the dark and I went to the corner and pounded my little pile of
blankets to scatter the roaches, like I'd learned to do, and I went to
sleep.

Now, maybe you'd think that would be the end of my curiosity
about walking around the streets in the dark. And time does go by
after that night with me perfectly content to be blank, content to do

the street routine and crawl into my hole at sunset so the night animals can do their hunting. Time went by like that, but I don't know
how much, really. It's like being street-blank on a stoop for an afternoon and time being two things at once. Or it's something like that
book I read in school, by Dickens. It was the longest of times, it was
the shortest of times. Anyway, it didn't last forever. Probably a couple of weeks. But I was sixteen, after all. And though I did get
myself drunk one night to see what it was like, it was just a worse
goddam bore than the routine, and the forgetting it brought on didn't
last, and as I expected, I really did get panicky about losing myself
somewhere, even if I didn't know who it was that would be lost. And
it just so fucking happens that I don't enjoy vomiting all that much.
So one weeknight I tell Joey I'm going to hang around Forty-second
awhile and this time he just gives me a dirty look and walks off.

I figure I know where to stay away from. Fairyland, of course.
And a couple of blocks on Eighth Avenue. But that's no different
from any city. No different from Saigon. Like I said, we wouldn't go
into Cholon. And we knew not to hang around the presidential palace, seeing as how everybody over there was real nervous all the
time, especially since the Americans left town.

Not that things don't catch up with you anyway, even if you
know the worst places and stay clear of them. You see things. I
guess I knew I'd see things, but maybe that was part of being on
the street, why things can get so bad. If you're bored shitless most
of the time, maybe the things you do to break out of it have to be
more extreme. You either do something extreme, or you get to
where you wouldn't mind seeing something extreme. Anyway, I'm
standing on the corner of Forty-second and Eighth and I've just
eaten some fried chicken and I'm picking at my teeth with a tooth-
pick and sucking off the energy from all the people hustling
around and I've got my Yankees cap on and it's pulled down low
over my eyes, like I'm hiding under a rock, and I see red lights
flashing on Forty-first Street, between the two wings of the bus
station. I can't see the police or whoever it is. All I can see is the
red light splashing out of the mouth of the street.

So I cross over and go down to Forty-first and turn the corner, and about fifty yards west there's an ambulance pulling away and a couple of cop cars still sitting by the curb and a little bit of a crowd, mostly bums. It doesn't look like much, but I walk in that direction and there's a funny smell, a burnt smell, and it gets stronger and it smells like somebody has tried to cook some real bad meat. Then it fades into the sour smell of the bums as I go past a few of them who are starting to shuffle away.

I slow and sort of slide off to the side as I near a couple of cops and then I look past them, and the sodium vapor lamps overhead and the flash of the cop car lights make it real easy to see what's on the sidewalk. It's the outline of a man, not the guy himself, just his silhouette in black on the sidewalk, doubled up sort of, his legs drawn almost to his chest and his back bent over, like he's a flattened animal on the highway. The smell is real strong and it fits a smell I've smelled before, a long time ago, and I know it's flesh, and as I figure that out, I look closer and see little sticky spots in the black shape, and about a yard off is a beat-up shoe, a bum's shoe, and I'm ready to back the hell away when a voice says, almost in my ear, "It's a bad business."

I turn and it's McGee and he's not looking at me, though obviously it was me he was talking to. He's got his cap off and his head is a mass of tight little black curls and he runs his hand over his head and puts his cap back on. The Transit Authority still hasn't found him a shirt that will fit his neck and his flesh is lapping over like when I first met him in front of the elevators. He shakes his head. "Bad business," he says.

I figure I always have to act real natural around McGee, like I never have a thing to hide. I just can't shake the feeling that this guy knows Joey and me are lying. So even though I really want to walk away, I figure I've got to talk for a minute so I don't look suspicious. I say, "Are you on nights now, McGee?"

"Nope. I'm just buddies with a guy and I'm covering for him tonight. He does the same for me sometimes."

I nod at this and I wait and McGee just looks at the pavement and shakes his head some more. The timing still isn't right and I'm trying to think of something to talk with him about and McGee suddenly looks at me and says, "You're out and around kind of late, aren't you?"

"Me?" I say. "No, I'm okay. I'm seventeen, you know."

"Where's your dad tonight?"

"He's back at our place. We have a little apartment, like. A room down in the Village."

"I figured Joey didn't flop around here."

"We don't flop at all. We got a little rented room. It's nice."

"Joey rents?" McGee sounds like he doesn't believe this and I get a little nervous. I feel like I'm fucking this thing up, making this guy more suspicious, not less.

I say, "Sure he rents. He gets a nice check from the government every month. He got shot up in Vietnam and he's on disability for life. That pays the rent."

"I didn't know Joey was getting checks for these wounds he talks about." Though the words are skeptical, McGee says this with some warmth, like he almost sounds convinced.

"Sure he does. Ninety-nine percent of that shit he talks about really happened. But why should he tell people he's getting checks? They'd figure he's doing okay and not give him any money."

McGee nods at this. I don't know how much more of this shit to lather on. I say, "But the checks are just enough for the room. The rest we need so we can eat and maybe put some money together to go out west somewhere so he can get a regular job and I can live in a climate that's more like Vietnam. You know how it is."

McGee nods again but doesn't say anything, and behind me some city cop's voice crackles through a bullhorn, "Okay everybody. Break it up. It's all over." And that just makes me think of the black smudge on the sidewalk and McGee is looking at it again, but I'm ready to walk now. I figure I've said enough and I've seen enough.

"Bad business," McGee says to the sidewalk, like the guy who was there still can use some advice. Then he looks back to me and says, "You get on down to your nice little room now and tell your dad to keep you off the streets at night till you're maybe forty or so. The boys who torched that bum may have got themselves a couple of quarters first, but they did it mostly for fun. You hear?"

"I hear you, McGee." And I take off and I don't look back, but I don't return to the East Village either. I go around the corner and I double back into the South Wing of the terminal. Even in the foyer, which has this strong smell of ammonia from some guy slopping a mop around on the floor over by the doors, I still can smell the burnt flesh of the bum. It's faint, like a memory, but it's real, it's in my fucking lungs and I figure it's just going to take time for it to disappear. I draw a little nearer the guy with his mop. I'm even standing in the wet part of the floor, the ammonia water under my feet, but I smell flesh burning and it's some disabled veteran who went up in a column of diesel smoke in the traffic circle at Lê Lợi right in view of Saigon City Hall. There were a few of us kids who were hanging around downtown and we saw the smoke and knew right away what it was and we dashed over and they were putting him out with fire extinguishers when we got there. I have one vision of him: where the black charred patches of his skin had torn away, his body was pure white and slick, like he was this other guy underneath the surface of his skin, a white guy, real white. And I went around for a few weeks looking at my skin and wondering what I was underneath; now that I'd seen just a few patches of this other guy, I wanted desperately to see all of my real body that I knew was hidden there.

And thinking about that body under the skin just makes me restless now and I say, "Fuck this," and it actually comes out even though I'm only talking to myself. The guy with the mop looks at me and I stride through the doors into the terminal and I turn and go downstairs where there will be fewer people. I slow down, I stand and I wait for everything to slow down, and then I walk around for a while, and for me this place is just bright and clean and hard. Then I turn a corner and the wall is yellow brick, and I turn again and I'm facing a little concourse of bus gates and the one right in front of me has a sign hanging by it that says Montreal.

I stop here and it's got to be close to ten o'clock now, but people are lined up, maybe twenty or thirty of them, a whole shitload of people getting away to Montreal in the middle of the night. The brick on the wall is bright orange and the gate door is silver and juts into the corridor like a big bay window, all real neat, and the lights are bright and everybody is in this orderly line and a sign says All Passengers to Montreal Are Required to Have the Proper Documents, and you just know that all these people do. And of course I'm standing there thinking about myself and the ticket that was in my pocket for a few minutes at least. If I'd just hung around in plain sight where nobody'd take a crack at me and if I'd gotten on that bus and gone to Montreal, would I be Vietnamese right now? Could I have done it? Could I have been Vietnamese? I try to see myself. I'm in the dark, on the bus, some old woman is napping on the seat beside me and it's a good thing she's asleep, because something is happening to me that would scare the shit out of her. My skin is starting to tingle, it's starting to fucking peel away and fall off and underneath, instead of being white, it's even darker, and I look at my reflection in the window and you can see the skin falling off my face and the eyelids fall away and underneath, my eyes are purely Asian, like my mother's, and it's true after all, I'm Vietnamese, and by the time we get to the bus station in Montreal the whole world can know me at a glance and so can I.

And of course all this is bullshit. I know it even as I let myself see it in my head. I had a chance not so long ago, I remind myself. And I told Mr. Sung to get fucked. I shake my head sharply, like there's a fly trying to get inside my ear, and it's a reflex of guilt, I guess. I finally found a guy who tells me what I surely ran away to hear, a guy in a real good position to know, and I tell him to get fucked. Of course, he did start talking about the other blood in me, too. It wasn't simple, even with him. You still need the fire, still need to burn away the surface. And the silver doors are sliding open and the line of passengers is stirring, dozens of people who will be in another country before dawn.

I turn around and retrace my steps and I take the next set of stairs going up and I come out beneath the high ceiling of the North Wing main floor and this is not where I want to be. The balcony in Fairyland watches over this place and Treen could be looking at me right now. I just keep my face lowered and I walk fast across the space and out the Eighth Avenue door, and the flash and flare of Forty-second look just fine to me at the moment, thank you very much, and I cross the street and head east on the Deuce.

I don't go half a block before I see her. She's standing at the curb with two other women, though Tracy isn't one of them. I don't even look at the other two. I know what they are. I just concentrate on Norma, and it's real strange because the first glance at her told me who she was, but the longer I look, the less like Norma this woman seems. I search for Norma in her mouth, but it's painted large, far too large, and I search for her in the roundness of her face, surely nothing can be done to coarsen that, and there's a hint of her there, but her face is drawn, her cheeks are rouged so heavily that in the streetlights they seem sunken, and maybe it's not just the shadow and the light, maybe they are sunken, because she looks much thinner, not just her cheeks but her neck, her shoulders, her arms—I don't want to look too closely at her arms—and her flesh shows between a leather halter and a black miniskirt and she's thin there, too, she laughs and I can see her ribs rise and her flesh scares me in its frailty, how easily she can be hurt now, and her flesh draws at me in the parts I cannot name with this feeling of gentle yearning. Then I wonder what the fuck she has to laugh about, doesn't she know what's happened, and I don't want to hate her, I've been around plenty of whores and I don't have to hate her. I knew long ago that she'd gone from me, I accepted that, goddamit, so now I try to figure out what it was when I saw her a few moments ago that told me this was Norma. And I realize it's her hair. Her hair is coiled up on the top of her head and it's like the first time I saw her, in the door of the bowling alley, though her hair's not a casual thing now, it's held up there with a flash of something silver. I concentrate on the coil of hair to try to keep Norma inside me, the Norma I held and kissed. I tell myself that this is not the hair of a whore, curled high on her head like that, but suddenly in my mind I can see a man taking her to a room and putting money on the bed and he asks her to undo her hair and she does and he lies down beneath it and it falls on him. And maybe her hair twisted onto her head is the worst part of her, not the best, worse than the red of her lips and cheeks and worse than her bones rising to the surface of her skin and showing themselves.

Maybe her hair is the thing she's famous for all over Forty-second, maybe the men ride up and down the street all night looking for the whore who will undo her hair for them.

So what do I want to do? Walk away? Yes. I want to turn now and walk away as fast as I can. But this impulse is not in my limbs, it's only in my mind, it's only words. I look at Norma and she's talking with the two women, and the three of them scan the street as they talk, their faces drift to the passing cars and then back again, and I know that I better do something fast because if I simply stand here and watch, I'm going to see a car stop and someone call Norma over and she goes and bends into the window and then she gets into the car and it drives away and there isn't even a hand dragging on her wrist and she doesn't even dig at the sidewalk with her heels and she doesn't even return with her shoulders slumped and full of sadness. And this would be fucking impossible for me to watch.

So I make my legs move. I walk toward Norma and I go kind of slow, waiting, I guess, for her to look over at me and see me and suddenly be transformed into somebody else, her outer skin suddenly peeling away and falling from her like she'd been torched with diesel fuel and from the black smoke the real Norma steps out, restored. And all of this is bullshit. And I get real close to these women, passing into the dense cloud of their three perfumes, and I realize I'm still under my rock, so I take off my Yankees cap and I say, "Norma."

The three faces turn to me and I work hard to focus on Norma. I feel like a kid standing before a three-card-monte dealer and he's asking me to watch the red card, find the red card, and no matter how close you look, you can't tell the three cards apart. But I'm trying; I'm trying; Norma is the one in the middle. The faces just stare at me and Norma's face is very still, like she's looking at a car that's stopped in the street but nobody's rolled down the window yet. The time that actually passes probably isn't as long as it feels. It does give me a chance to think once again of turning and running away, but Norma finally smiles, and it seems like a real smile, and she says, "Deuce." Then she steps from between the two others and takes my arm and she guides me across the pavement and into the shadow of a doorway and the sureness in this, the clarity of her hand on my arm, scares the shit out of me.

But her voice is still her own, and in the shadows I can't see her that well, and frankly, I stop looking. I watch the street instead, and I just make myself feel the nearness of her and let it go at that. She says, "Deuce, how are you?"

"Okay. How are you?"

"I'm doing fine. But listen, Deuce, I'm not Norma anymore."

When she says this, I look at her, and when I do, she smiles. "You look so cute, Deuce," she says.

I don't know what to say about this except maybe Fuck you. It's never been what I wanted to hear and it sounds just as fucking idiotic coming from Norma as it does coming from, say, Kenneth's friends when they think they can see his face in mine. Maybe if she wasn't a whore now, I'd like it, I'd kiss her and she'd turn "cute" into something I want to be. But in the dark of the doorway, I'm just starting to smell the piss.

"Listen," she says, and she's lowered her voice nearly to a whisper. "If you see me on the street again, be sure and call me by my new name."

"New name?"

"Sure," she says. "I'm not a Norma. I never was. My name is Nicole."

"Nicole?"

"That's right."

"You're French?"

"Hey, everybody who's in love is French. Right?"

I wish I could see her face when she says these words. She's still whispering, so I can't tell anything from her voice. Who the fuck does she think she's in love with? The guy who's got her doing this? Or anybody who pays her? What the fuck is she talking about? I wrestle with this in my mind but it doesn't occur to me to speak. Not until Norma looks out to the street and says, "I've got to go now. Stay cool, Deuce."

I almost stop her. I almost grab her by the shoulders and shake her and ask her what the fuck is happening to her. But she kisses me on the cheek and she gives me a little hug which she holds for one second and then another and then another and my eyes fill with tears and I am about to lift my own arms and hold her but just as I think to do that, she's gone.

I don't watch where she goes. I lean back into the shadows and I put my cap on and I pull the brim down low and I lean there in the doorway and there's no way of telling you how long I stayed.

SIXTEEN

◆
◆

The room is fucking bright from moonlight and I can even see Joey clearly as he lies in the corner in a stupor and he's kind of dropped out of the story here for a while because that's the way it was. For a while he was just another smudge on the wall and I don't know why. I don't know what was happening in him. This may not have been any kind of a change, really. Maybe he was always like this, always in some sort of cycle, feisty and alive for a few weeks and then silent and drunk for a few weeks. I hadn't been around him long enough to figure that out. It might even have been my fault. Maybe I pushed him over the edge when I made him admit his lies and got him to thinking about Mai again. I don't know. I just remember walking around in the room not long after running into this new whore Nicole, and the moon was full outside and so bright it made my eyes hurt.

In Vietnam there's a festival in Mid-Autumn that's built around the full moon, the brightest full moon of the year, the one that comes on the fifteenth day of the eighth lunar month. And they tell a story then about the moon. There's this little boy named Cuội who lives with his widowed mother and guards some rich man's water buffaloes in the fields for a miserable few pennies. One day Cuội is in the forest and he finds a little tiger cub and he picks up the cub to take it home and make it a pet. But then the cub's mother comes roaring through the jungle and the boy is so scared he throws the cub down and climbs a tree. The problem is that he throws the cub down too hard and it gets this bad gash on its head and it looks like it's going to die. When the mother tiger arrives on the scene, she sees her lifeless cub and she gets really pissed off. Cuội, meanwhile, is holding his breath up in this tree right above her. Well, the mother tiger looks around and doesn't see anyone, so she moves off a little ways to a certain kind of banyan tree and she gathers some of its leaves and brings them back to her cub. Then the mother tiger chews the leaves and applies them to the cub's wound and right away the baby recovers completely and the two tigers run off into the forest.

Cuội's been watching this and he comes down and checks out this banyan tree. The tree doesn't look so different from any other tree, but he gathers up some of the leaves and takes off for home. On his way he finds a dog drowned in a pond. So he decides to test the tree. He pulls the dog's body out of the water and lays it on the bank and he chews up some leaves and puts them on the dog's head, just like the mother tiger did with her cub. A couple of seconds later the dog jumps up and runs off. Then Cuội thinks, Holy shit, this tree is just what we need. You can even be dead and it's going to make everything all right. So Cuội goes back and he digs up the tree and takes it home with him. (Don't ask me how a little kid does that. Banyan trees are big motherfuckers. But this is the way the story goes.)

When Cuội gets home, he plants the tree in the middle of the yard and his mother is real impressed. Cuội tells her to be very careful about this tree, it's special. And he says whatever she does, she better not piss near the tree. He says, "Piss to the east, piss to the west, but if you piss on this tree, it will fly to the sky." I think that rhymed better in Vietnamese, though I can't remember the words anymore. The kids liked to sing the rhyme a lot during the festival, I guess because piss is a real funny thing to kids and it makes some of their parents uncomfortable. Don't ask me, either, how Cuội knew about the tree being in danger of flying off. It was just something he knew.

Well, his momma fucks up. She has to piss real bad one day and she's out in the yard and so she goes over to the tree and drops her pants and pisses right there. All of a sudden, the tree starts to lift off the ground. The roots all come up and the tree is slowly rising into the air. Cuội returns right at that moment and he runs and leaps and grabs the tree to try to drag it back to earth. But he doesn't weigh very much. He's just a kid. And by the time he realizes what's happening, he's up too high and can't let go.

So what happens is the tree flies off with Cuội hanging on and goes up through the clouds and it heads out into space and it keeps on going until it reaches the moon. Then the banyan lands and plants itself and Cuội sits down under the tree and he's still there today. You can look up at the moon and right in the middle of it you can make out the shape of a banyan tree and a little boy sitting by himself at the foot of it.

My mother must've told me this story. She liked to tell stories about shit like that and she probably even half believed it was true. But I can't remember the exact moment when she told it. I can't put the story and the woman together, and that's too bad because I'd like to hear her voice again and see if she realized that the story was about herself. She was the goddam mother who pissed on the tree. And I guess that makes me the kid who flew off to the moon.

This was the Mid-Autumn tale, and that night in New York when I was walking around the room, I really don't know what month it was by then but it might even have been the fifteenth day of the eighth lunar month, the moon was bright enough for it. And when I finally lay down on my blankets, I could hear singing in my head and it was a child's voice, and you know how when you hear your voice on a tape recorder you don't even recognize yourself. It was like that. I suddenly realize that the child's voice is mine. And I said before that I remember very little Vietnamese, really, but this part of a song came back to me.

Ánh trăng sáng ngời có cây đa to
Có thằng Cuội già ôm một mối mơ.

Look at the clear moon, it says. There is a big banyan tree and there is our old Cuội dreaming forever.

The kids in the alleys liked the songs about the piss better, and I probably did too for the most part, but on the night all this comes back to me, just before I sleep, I finally put my child's voice in a place, and it's beneath the window in our back-alley apartment in Saigon and I'm watching the Mid-Autumn moon and there's a smell of incense in the room and my mother is sleeping nearby, I can hear her breathing, and I can see the banyan tree there on the moon, a gray silhouette, and Cuội is sitting beneath it, dreaming, and I wonder what he's dreaming about. Nghi must be sleeping alone on this night of my memory. She must've just done her prayers and smoked her cigarette. But maybe she skipped the cigarette, because she let me have the place beneath the window on this night so I could watch the moon.

Nghi, Nghi of the Texas Girls, Miss Võ Xuân Nghi, at least you never stopped calling yourself by your real name. A lot of the girls in the bar took on American names or French names, but you were always Nghi. Maybe that was something important to you. You could tell yourself that of all the men who paid to fuck you, not one of them pronounced your name right. Maybe that helped you do it. If they couldn't say your name, it wasn't really you. And at the beginning, when you were ready to turn into a whore but you hadn't done it yet, did you shed tears for the girl you'd been in Vĩnh Bình Province? Just before you began to fuck for money, did you take somebody to bed, someone who made you think of what you were leaving forever? Did you have a Deuce, a Tự Do Thanh, to hold close? And when he held you, did your tears puddle in the hollows of your ears?

On this night in the abandoned building in the East Village of New York, New York, I doze and wake and doze again only very lightly and the song about Cuội dreaming on the moon sings itself in my sleep and I wake for good before dawn. I dress and go out. I walk the same streets I do every day and Forty-second is in a stupor and I go to the curb where I'd found Norma and it's stupid for me to be there, I know. It's not like I really expect to find her. So I just walk on west toward the bus terminal and when I reach the fence, there's a bunch of people in the lot, a couple of dozen or more, near the gate on Eighth Avenue and sort of spilling onto the sidewalk. At first I think somebody's been knifed or torched or some goddam thing, and I come around the fence and head for the parking lot gate where they all are, but then I notice that almost all these people are women, and it's all bare shoulders and arms and lots of hair, leather and tiger spots and fishnet stockings. And the crowd is casual, little clusters swirling together. It's quitting time, is what it is. They're smoking and talking and a couple of them break off and head this way up Eighth, heading for their little rooms over the storefronts and solitary sleep, and one hails a taxi and gets in alone, and I'm looking for a certain round face and I think I see it, between some shifting bodies. Nicole the whore. I catch just a glimpse of a round face and the dark hair is on her shoulders—somebody paid to have it uncoil in the night—and the bodies shift again and I can't see her anymore and I turn away and I head up the street with voices following close behind me, one reedy woman's voice saying that she wishes her fucking hair would turn out blond instead of always fucking pink and the other woman's voice, lower, saying that pink is nice. And I turn at the fence and go back east and I cross Broadway and Seventh and I keep going, past Sixth Avenue, and I end up at the library and I sit on the steps and I wait until it opens.

I want to sit in a chair for a while. A wooden chair. And finally I'm pushing through the fake leather swinging doors and I'm in the map room and I stop. The woman with the bad teeth and the easy smile isn't behind the desk. It's some man with dandruff on his suit-coat. I guess somewhere in my head was the idea of getting the Vietnam maps again, but now that I'm in the room, it seems crazy. The only thing about Vietnam is that it's not Forty-second Street or the East Village, and I know already that if I start roaming the alleys of Saigon with my fingertip, I'll only end up running out into the streets of New York because it's not Vietnam. I've got this problem. But I still want to sit in a wooden chair, and I walk along a row of books and pull one out at random and I sit down and open it before me and it's the whole fucking world in here. And they can't seem to draw a map of just one country, pure and on its own. They're always coupled. Belgium and The Netherlands, Spain and Portugal, France and Northern Algeria, India and Pakistan, Australia and New Zealand, on and on like that, a whole book of these little deuces and it just isn't that fucking easy.

I get up and punch open the swinging doors, but as soon as I step into the hallway I think of Norma out there in the streets and then I think of Nghi, and she's lying somewhere in the dark, and these two are starting to link up like they were countries in that fucking atlas. I'm not ready for the streets this morning, that's clear, and so I turn down this hall full of shadows and the echoes of my footsteps, and when I reach the end I come around a corner and the ceiling suddenly lifts way up and before me are revolving doors, the main entrance on Fifth Avenue. I turn left again and go up a marble staircase and I keep climbing until the walls and the ceilings are full of painted figures. I've climbed as high as I can go, and arched above me is a scene full of naked men grabbing at each other and a muscular guy in the center has fire in his hand. It makes me uneasy, like standing in the bus terminal and looking up at Fairyland, and I lower my eyes to a wall full of a story I know something about.

For a while Kenneth had done what he could to turn me into a good little Christian American. It wasn't quite like Yankee baseball or Coney Island—he tried over a pretty long period of time—but his heart wasn't in it. Still, I know Moses when I see him. He's on the wall here and he's really pissed off. He's in the center of the picture, standing on a ledge, and above him, higher up on the mountain, is the burning bush with flames leaping out. Moses has just smashed one of the stone tablets at his feet and his hair is long and it's lashing out like flames from the bush and he's lifting another tablet in his hands and he's about to throw it down and crush a man and two women below. They're naked, these three, and you know they've been fooling around. The woman on the left has her back to us and one hand is raised toward Moses, pleading with him not to do it. Her other wrist is being held by the man, who's turned away from Moses, and he's bent over and he's covering his eyes with his arm. Beside him is the second woman and her hand is over her mouth and her wide eyes are cast up in fear over her shoulder, toward this old man who's about to crush her.

A couple of whores and their john, and here's the wrath of God about to fix it up. Somebody really loves one of these women but she decided to fuck around instead. And some little boy is the child of the other woman and he's got to listen to her in the night. Right? I keep looking and this is how part of me sees it, but when my eyes go back to Moses, things get complicated. His eyes are terrible, this guy from God. He's got this wild silver beard and hair like the flame leaping from a torched bum and he's got these enormous, raging, pitiless eyes and I look back to the three naked people and they're frail and they're scared shitless and behind them is the thing that caused all the fuss, the golden calf, and it's kind of cute, it's got a green wreath around its neck and it's got this real gentle cow face and its ears are lying down like a rabbit's and suddenly I think that these three naked people are just kids themselves playing with a toy. The cow is like a teddy bear and it's just kids going, Oh Teddy, I love you more than anything, and then they hold each other and say, I love you more than anything, too. And what the fuck's this old man so pissed off about? Is that rage of his any better than their getting naked and rolling around together? Not that these three aren't fucked up, but I look real close at the naked guy's hand on the wrist of the woman next to him. Then I look at his face. He's in deep shit and he knows it and he's so scared all he can do is cover his eyes, but this hand of his is still trying to comfort the woman, he's telling her don't worry, I'm here with you. And I look up at the old man on the ridge and I say out loud to him, "Fuck you." And after that, I go downstairs and out onto Forty-second Street and I head back west to find Joey and put in a day of lying and begging and hanging around and letting the time pass, and nothing is simple. I don't go half a block before I wonder where that naked woman's child is and I whisper a little fuck-you to her as well.

Then I walk on faster because telling enough carefully worded lies to eat each day is pretty simple compared to other things, and I begin to wonder if Joey's going to be pissed off when I find him, since I disappeared from the room before he even woke up. As usual I turn on Eighth and head toward the South Wing, but as I cross Forty-first I catch some fast movement out of the corner of my eye. I look and

it's Joey charging across the street, heading for the door into the
North Wing. I stop and turn to watch him, a little afraid to call out
to him and thinking that he'll notice me in a moment anyway. But he
doesn't. He's moving fast in a jerky, driving sort of way, and it's like
he's scared about something and I think, Oh shit, it's about me. He
disappears into the North Wing and I stand there like an idiot wondering what to do. I try to tell myself that he wouldn't get that
nervous about finding me. Then when I realize that maybe he
would, shit starts to run through my head like, I can take care of
myself, he's not my father. And all this time I'm letting him get
deeper inside the North Wing. If I wasn't so goddam stupid, if I
wasn't so goddam wrapped up in my own fucking problems, I
could've caught him right away and taken him out of there, and
nothing bad would've happened. Let that son of a bitch Moses throw
his tablet down on me if he wants to crush somebody. I stand there
doing the same old mixed-up routine: nobody bosses me around because I'm the street-smart Deuce so leave me alone because I'm just
this poor confused half-breed. And that's goddam pathetic.

Finally I decide I better go in and find Joey. And still I don't move
fast enough. I creep toward the door and by the time I step inside and
can smell the roast beef I know where he is. But I fight it off. I don't let
this thing run through me and suck away my strength, because that's
what would happen. I put it out of my mind and instead I try to think
he was real hungry and was hurrying for a sandwich and I go and look
in Arby's window and of course he's not there and then I actually take a
few steps toward the big open space like I think he was rushing to look
at the banners made by the fucking schoolkids and hanging from the
ceiling. Then I hear sharp voices up a stairway off to my left. I know it's
Joey and I know where it's coming from and I've got no choice now, and
to stop the flutter of fear inside me I tell myself I've got to do something
because it's Joey up there, and with all the stuff this morning about
Norma and Nghi, I feel close to him, he knows about whores, he's lived
with all that too. Joey and The Deuce, fucking Belgium and The
Netherlands, and I move my legs, force them to the stairs, and I climb
into Fairyland.

I'm halfway up and the voices turn into words. I hear Joey say, "If you even so much as look at him funny—"

And Treen's voice, smooth and calm, cuts him off. "He's nowhere around here, as you can see."

"You think that fucking proves anything?" Joey yells, and their heads come into sight now, profile and profile, and Joey is shorter than Treen and he's got his face pushed up at the bigger man and he's less than an arm's length away.

Treen leans slowly down, drawing nearer to Joey, and as I hit the top step, Treen says, "If you interfere with me I'm going to kill you. Nobody even notices a bum who's been butt-fucked by a knife." It takes a second for these words to sink in, and once they do, I instantly doubt that I've heard them because the voice is still this sweet may-I-help-you voice, but I remember the flash of Treen's blade out on Forty-second and I see Joey blink and recoil and then I get this rush of energy and I stride forward and there's a gallery of eyes around, Treen's boys, and there's Treen's face turning to me and looking as big as a fat man's ass and he smiles and Joey's face comes around and you can see the sag of relief and then a blink and his ears shoot backward and his skin stretches tight in anger.

"Where the fuck have you been?" Joey says to me.

"Not with this asshole," I say, flipping my chin at Treen. It's like I spit in Treen's face, because he sniffs in hard and he rears back.

Joey barks a laugh and turns to Treen and he says, "Stick that up your well-oiled butt."

I'm real keyed up now and bouncing on my toes and when Joey says this, I laugh real hard, but the laugh catches in my throat when I see the slow, smooth look that Treen gives Joey. Joey doesn't see it because he's come over with me now and is still laughing and I say to him, "Let's get out of here."

He starts to turn around to face Treen again, but I grab Joey's arm and drag him to the steps and he starts talking under his breath to Treen, calling him names, but he lets me move him and he actually picks up the pace, he's no fool, and by the time we hit Forty-first we're running hard. But Joey veers away from the South Wing. He cuts east on Forty-first and I figure he's afraid Treen will try to find us in the terminal.

We go straight across Eighth and run along the south edge of the parking lot and then we slow to a fast walk beneath the enormous brick back wall of a Forty-second Street theatre, and there are a bunch of guys sleeping here in the doorways and around the foot of a Dumpster and beneath the black snake of the fire escape and we're coming up to an empty stretch of wall and Joey slows us down and he says, "Let's sit here for a minute."

I figure he just needs to rest, so we stop and sit and stretch our legs out and the smell is pretty bad, like we've just crawled inside a bum's coat, and across the street a little bottle gang is leaning against a wall and the bottle, wrapped in a brown paper bag, is passing on from a guy who looks like he's about to double over and fall to the sidewalk. The guy who takes the bag shoots Joey and me a glance before he lifts it to his lips, like he's afraid we're going to run across and mug him for the bottle.

"Where the hell were you this morning?" Joey says, though there's no anger or fear or anything like that in his voice, not even any straighten-up-because-I'm-responsible-for-you. He just sounds tired.

"I went out early. I couldn't sleep."

"You got me in big trouble," he says.

This doesn't really come through as an accusation; his voice is soft and there's something odd in it, a little bit like that thing in his eyes when he's thinking about Mai. But I go through the motions of bristling at this. "I didn't ask you to go charging up to fucking Fairyland."

Joey looks at me, but his voice stays weary. "He wants to get his hands on you. That word's going around. I got scared, that's all. It was a mistake."

"*Your* mistake. Don't blame me."

"I don't."

"You said I got you in trouble."

"I didn't mean it that way. It wasn't your fault."

"All right," I say, and I don't feel any pleasure at all in winning this little fucking argument. "Let's just get that straight."

"Treen's not the only one," Joey says.

"Only one what?"

"Who's after you."

"What're you talking about," I say, though I probably already know.

Joey digs into a pocket and pulls out a stiffly folded piece of heavy paper. He hands it to me and says, "Look what I ripped off the window of the police office up on the second floor."

I unfold the paper and there's my face staring at me. Just like it's stared at me ever since I happened to see it in that tailor shop mirror on Lê Lợi after Kenneth showed up for the first time. The picture on this poster is one of those department store package portraits with a backdrop of painted trees and clouds and even a fucking picket fence in the distance. Kenneth dragged me to this because I'd always ducked out when the school pictures were being taken and he wanted something for the wall of his office and for his wallet and you can see from the hard set of my thin New Jersey mouth that I don't like what's going on. And my eyes still amaze me, how they can hover between these two worlds, how they can look for a second like the eyes of any of the all-American types in school and then in the next second you realize that there's this vague appearance of an incision about them, across the top, like they've been cut very cleverly out of my face, the look of the gook coming through, but not quite that either, you study me closer and there's a definite eyelid. It's definite, then it's not; these are the eyes of an American, then they're the eyes of a Vietnamese. So I leave the eyes and I follow this long nose, stretched and thinned by Kenneth's genes, down to that mouth that looks like it's about to spit. Come on and smile, the asshole at the camera says, and I half expect him to pick up a squeeze toy and squeak it at me to get me to laugh. And Kenneth is over his shoulder and he's watching me and he says to the guy, "Just go ahead and take the picture," and I can hear the resignation in his voice. No anger. Just another little failure with this kid he's trying so hard to make his own. I look away from this face on the poster in my hands.

Joey says, "Somebody's getting close."

I look back at the poster, but not the face this time, the words.

Across the top in big letters it says: MISSING. And underneath that is the name Anthony James Hatcher and already I feel uncomfortable. I skip through the description, height and weight and all that shit. HALF AMERICAN, HALF VIETNAMESE. Big fucking deal. LAST SEEN IN BLAH BLAH WEARING BLAH BLAH. Why am I doing this? MIGHT BE CALLING HIMSELF Võ Ðình Thanh. This surprises me, but Kenneth sometimes does. He's a smart man, in some ways. I'm just getting tired of reading his wanted poster. I start to fold it up, but down at the bottom is a little box with a couple of lines of red type and I look at them and they say, TONY: PLEASE GIVE ME ANOTHER CHANCE. IF I'VE BEEN CLUMSY IN ALL OF THIS, I'M SORRY. PLEASE COME HOME. WE LOVE YOU. KENNETH. When he's apologizing, I feel something for this guy. He sounds like he means it, and I feel bad for him having to go through all this. But then there's this part about home, like he knows what my home is. Then he uses that word "love," and things are kind of getting out of hand. And then I go back to the start of that love sentence and I notice that it says *we*. Kenneth and Point Pleasant Tracy, I guess. I must've missed the wedding. What a fucking shame. And it's not doing any good, going over this. But there's one more line on the poster, and some part of me must've noticed it before this. The letters are pretty big and it's right under the picture. I guess I knew what was there and I just didn't want to deal with it. The line says that there's a ten-thousand-dollar reward for information leading to my return. I'm for sale again, and I'm ready to rip this fucker up. I look at Joey and I wonder if he noticed the reward. I glance over at him and he's watching me.

He says, "If I wanted the money, I wouldn't have shown you the poster."

Joey wouldn't sell me. I should've known that right off. I say to him, "That's why you're such a goddam good beggar."

"Why's that?"

"You read minds."

Joey taps his temple. "It's knowing the psychology," he says, and he keeps tapping and the sound is like his head is made of bird bones, hollow, a sound that makes me real edgy. It tells me how fragile he is. And me too.

"So what do we do about this?" I wave the poster at him.

"You lay low. I got the public poster down, but there's others in the police office."

"If McGee sees it, he'll know right away."

"The next day or two will tell. I think it's okay for me to hang around a little. Test the water."

"Okay. Okay." Then I lean my head back against the wall and I do this because I've got no choice, I can't hold my head up anyway. All of a sudden something's running in my veins other than blood. It's hot and it's heavy and I think about one of my lies to somebody. I look at Joey and I say, "What about us two getting the hell out? Maybe we can hitch out west or something. Get some jobs. Get the fuck off the streets."

I shouldn't have sprung this thing on Joey just like that. It had only that moment come to me and I should've held my tongue till I thought over how to bring it up. As it is, he looks at me and his eyes are darting all over my face like they sometimes do, and he says to me, "Christ, Deuce, are you fucking crazy?" His face jerks away from me and he looks across at the bottle gang and then he thumps his head back against the wall, hard, and then he does it again. He says, "I've been shot up and patched up and there's nothing but spit and city grit holding me together. You've got to be fucking crazy to think I'm going anywhere."

I start nodding at this and he doesn't even look at me and I nod some more and I just keep nodding, like I'm crazy or something, and why the fuck should I care if Joey wants to start the whole bullshit shot-up-in-Vietnam thing again and live his whole, brief, bullshit life on this street. Finally I stop my head and then I concentrate on holding it real still and then I lean back against the wall and close my eyes, and when I open them I don't even know how much time has passed. All I know is that Joey is gone.

SEVENTEEN

∴

After Joey disappears and I find the runaway poster still clutched in my hand, I figure there's nothing keeping me in New York. Joey and Norma are doing what they want to do. Kenneth is closing in. I don't need Joey with me to hitchhike the hell away from here. I can go anywhere I want to. But it doesn't take much thought to realize that's nowhere. I can't think of a single goddam place. I don't even move from where I'm sitting. I just sit there and watch the bottle gang fidget and drink and then finally break up and stagger away and I watch the daylight fade and the shadows deepen and the only time I get up is to go piss against a wall. Finally there's lights coming on down along the street and it's dark enough that I can't see the bums under the Dumpster anymore, and this wasn't so hard, really; the day has passed and I didn't string even two sentences together in my head the whole time.

But I'm hungry and I do have a buck or two in my pocket and I have to go back to the Lower East Side once at least, if for nothing more than to get my stuff. So I get up and my body creaks and twinges like I'm about ninety years old and I head off for the subway, stopping only twice. Once to tear the poster into about a hundred little pieces and then scatter bits of it into three different trash cans along the street and once to eat a hot dog from a vendor who gives me a glance while he's squeezing on the mustard that makes me think he's seen the poster and is about to call the cops and collect his ten grand. But he keeps his mouth shut and I've bought from this guy often before and I tell myself he's always looked like that at me.

So I just saunter away from him like everything's okay, and when I get to the subway I buy a token, even though I had a clear chance to sneak through. No risks for now. And I make that long walk east on Eighth Street and around Tompkins Square Park and when I cross Avenue B, the block of Joey's building, I get a little uneasy. Is he going to resent me so much now that there's going to be a bad scene? If so, I'll just get my stuff and head back to my place on the abandoned West Side Highway. Or are we just going to pretend I never said anything about getting out of the city and getting jobs, all that shit that he found so outrageous. If it goes like that, maybe I can hang around with him a little longer, till I figure out where to go.

I'm thinking all this out as I walk, and when I get to the field full of rubble next to the building, it's night and it's dark and there's people hanging around the stoops of the buildings and there's salsa music playing and somewhere else funky drums and there are people shouting and some kid crying, all of this not anyplace in particular, just in the air. And I figure that things will be okay with Joey. He knows me, he ripped down the poster and gave it to me, he can let this thing go. And it's just these thoughts and the sounds in the night and the smell of dust and an open wood fire somewhere that are in me when I see what looks like a pile of clothes up ahead and then a body for sure and then I can see it's Joey and I think of Treen and I lunge to Joey's side and all the smells of the East Side dissolve in the smell of whiskey.

Even smelling this, I'm looking frantically for the blood and there is none and Joey is face down with his head turned away from me, and I hop over to his other side and bring my face close to his and my eyes water from the fumes of the liquor and I can hear the faint rattle of his breath. I push at his shoulder and the breath snags and turns into a snore and he's drunk. Simply drunk. And I sit back and I look around and the lot is empty. There's nobody around, but Joey can't spend the night in the open like this. I can see that silhouette on the pavement on Forty-first. There's guys down here who'd get a kick out of that, too.

I start shaking Joey and I get close to his ear and start calling him names, telling the stupid son of a bitch to wake up. But he's gone. He's not even twitching when I push at him now, his snoring isn't even changing pitch. I'm still bent near him and before I pull away I say, "What the fuck's wrong with you?" And I really want an answer to this, though he sure as hell won't have any thoughts on the subject for quite a few hours. So there's nothing I can do but sit there by him all the goddam night and hope if things get too boring for some of the guys in the neighborhood, fucking with this bum in the field won't be worth any hassle to them, even from a sixteen-year-old kid they could get rid of real easy. I gather a pile of stones that I could throw, and I sit down to wait for the morning.

I fight to stay awake. It's like there doesn't even have to be a gang to do this thing, Joey's ready to go up in flames any second, a car goes by in the street with a dragging tailpipe and one spark can jump across the field and Joey would go up like a handful of straw in an alley, and he wouldn't even leave his outline behind in the dust of this field. So I get up and move to the street side of him. I want Joey to live through this night. That's the only important thing in the world. If he wants to drink himself to death, there's nothing I can do. But he's going to live through this night. And I think of Treen and his knife and how he could suddenly appear there on the street and creep this way and if I'm here, he'd think it's even better for him. They say he gets off on using that knife. He prefers the boys who don't want him because that gives him the excuse to stick them and that's the biggest kick of all. That's what they say about him. But even if Treen showed up I'd stand and I'd have a rock in my hand behind my back and I'd let him get closer and closer and he'd be smiling and he'd have a hard-on thinking about sticking that knife in me and when he got real close, I'd lift my hand and I'd throw the rock and it would hit him on the temple and he'd fall and die, and it would all be so sudden he'd still have that smile on his face and the coroner would have a good laugh at him when they took Treen's pants off because this corpse would still have the hard-on that finally got him into more trouble than he could handle. And Joey would live through the night. He's my friend. He understands some real important things about me and about the way things are in the world and by God, he's going to live through this night. Moses himself could appear on the fire escape of the building that rises over us and his beard is thrashing like a flame and he's got his stone tablet saying how you can't get drunk and you can't tell lies and you can't just get by from begging and hanging out in abandoned buildings and you can't love a whore and get away with it, and I'd pick up a rock and I'd look straight into those raging, pitiless eyes of his and I'd throw the rock and catch the motherfucker right in the center of his forehead and he'd fall, and Joey Cipriani would live through this night.

And as it turns out, he does live, but no thanks to me, because I wake with a start and I'm slumped over on the ground like a drunk and the sun is already up and the air feels wet, though I turn my head and the sky bites at my eyes with its brightness. I sit up and some old woman is pushing a shopping cart by on the sidewalk and I look at Joey and he's on his back and sleeping with his mouth open. I stand up and I feel like shit for maybe five minutes, till I walk around the lot to stretch out my limbs. When I get back to Joey, he's just like I left him but he's smacking his lips. I wonder if he's dreaming, but then he opens his eyes and he's looking straight at me and he's still smacking his lips.

I say, "If you tell me you want a drink, I'm going to kick the shit out of you."

He rises up onto his elbows at this, and he flinches from the pain in his head. "Only water," he says. "You wouldn't kick the shit out of me if I want some water, would you?"

"I might."

"Give me a break, Deuce."

He says my name and his saying it sounds so good I crouch down by him, like it's the first time he called me that or something. And there's all this floating stuff going on inside me, it's not my blood again but something light now, like I'm being carried off down a stream and I don't have to do a thing to keep from sinking, it's all real natural to me. And it's because Joey called me Deuce and because he lived through the night.

"What is it?" he says.

I can't say any of this shit. I'm not even very conscious of it at the time. So instead I say, "Are you up to climbing through a window?"

"You mean you're not going to run up and get the water for me?"

"Hell no."

"Okay," he says. "This doesn't surprise me." And he struggles to his feet and he goes off a ways and pisses and throws up and then we go through the window and up the stairs and while Joey is off in the kitchen with his face under the trickle of water in the sink, I stand staring at my duffel bag and my clothes scattered around and I feel the urge to blank out again.

So I lie down on the floor beneath the window and I can see the gray stone parapets on the roof of the building across the street, and beyond I can see the sky, and pretty soon Joey is lying beside me and we're both watching out the window, like a couple of kids lying in the field trying to find animal shapes in the clouds, only these clouds are just clouds and after a while Joey says, "I'm sorry about coming down hard on you yesterday."

"It's okay," I say.

"You understand what my problems are," he says.

This would be the time to ask him the question I asked him when he was drunk outside, because I really don't know what's wrong with him. But something scares me in his words. He's got his mind back to the blow-up the day before, and he said then that he was shot up and put back together. This thing now about his problems may mean he wants to start all that disabled-veteran crap again. But I'm a goddam coward and I say, "Sure. I understand."

And he won't let it pass. "Do you really understand?" he says, still watching the sky.

"I don't know. What do you want out of me?"

"The truth."

"Then no. I don't know what the fuck's wrong with you."

Joey looks over at me for a second and then back to the sky. "Well, I don't either."

This isn't as bad as I expect it to be, but it pisses me off anyway. "Great," I say. "I'm glad we got the truth out here."

"But I know what's *not* wrong with me." He says this and then he pauses and I look over to him and it seems like he's studying the clouds, trying to find a shape there.

I'm getting a little impatient with this, expecting more bullshit eventually. I say, "So?"

"It's not Vietnam," he says, real softly. "I know that much. It's just me. All Vietnam did was give me the only beautiful thing I ever had."

His eyes are fixed on the sky and I look too, and there are no clouds at all, just a blue that makes me think of bird eggs on Ham Nghi Street. And we lie there like that for a long time, but I'm not street-blank, even though there's not much in my head, and Joey isn't street-blank either because finally he says, "Maybe we can do it."

"What's that?" I say.

"Maybe you and me can head west. Maybe we can live in a hot climate and get some jobs and think about Vietnam now and then."

"Sure," I say, and I look at Joey and he's looking at me. "Sure. When do you want to do that?"

"Before the end of the week."

"Don't fuck with me," I say, but I make sure my voice has a soft edge. "Do you really want to do this?"

"I'm not fucking with you. I've got to see some people first who owe me a few bucks. It'd be nice when we hit the road if we didn't have to worry about hustling for money for a couple of days. But either way, we're out of here."

"And the goddam bottle?"

"You sat with me all night, didn't you."

"Yes."

"Don't worry about that," he says. "I'm an alcoholic."

I know he's not just being a smart-ass, and I know, too, that the biggest danger of all would be for him to bullshit me and bullshit himself. So okay, if he's telling me he's an alcoholic, I figure maybe I can stop worrying about that. Then we talk about our plans for what to do in the next day or two. Joey says that he's going out right away to start trying to put a little money together and he tells me to hole up in this room till we hit the road. I don't like the idea, but I agree, and by the time he comes home that night, I'm talking to the cockroaches. I tell him tomorrow's got to be different. He doesn't like this. He's worried about me, he says, and I believe him. He says he may only need one more day and we can take off. But if tomorrow is my last day in New York, I'm sure as hell not going to spend it in this room.

"What's so goddam important about New York?" he asks, and it's dark in the room and he didn't bring a bottle back with him tonight.

"I'm The Deuce, so it's important to me."

"I don't suppose there's any way I can at least keep you down in the Village."

I haven't thought at all about what I'd want to do on a last day in the city, but I know I can't leave without going to the center of things. "I'm The Deuce, I tell you. I'm not hanging around the goddam Village."

"Then can I get you to wait till the nighttime? When you won't be so visible."

Only now do I really understand what I want. After dark will be just fine. He talks on, explaining how one of the people he has to see is a bartender, an old buddy, who doesn't come to work till early evening. I'm not really listening, though. I'm thinking about Norma. Nothing in particular. Just little glimpses of her face, her face as a whore, but it's from a distance, with other bodies between us, shifting and showing her, shifting again and covering her up. I'm thinking about her and the thing is that even if I don't see her again, I can't leave this goddam city without going to a couple of the places where we'd been.

"Deuce," Joey says, sharply, like he's been trying to get my attention for a while, and maybe he has.

"What is it, Joey."

"So are we gonna meet somewhere tomorrow night and come back down here together?"

"For the last time?"

"Goddam right."

"Let's meet on the corner of Forty-second and Eighth Avenue."

"There it is," he says, and we sit in the darkness for a little while and we don't say any more. Finally Joey stirs. "Well," he says, "since I'm a goddam alcoholic who had enough goddam sense not to bring home a goddam bottle, there's nothing left to do now but go to goddam sleep."

And we crawl to our separate corners of the room and I lie down on my blankets and I won't say exactly that I'm full of all the American Dream shit, heading west and working your way to the fucking top and shit like that, but I'm okay. Things are okay. I feel real easy inside me and then I think of one last detail. "When?" I say.

"When what?"

"When do we meet?"

Joey starts thinking out loud. "My bartender buddy's just part-time. He gets on at about eight." His voice is sounding sleepy.

Then there's only silence and I try to keep his train of thought going. I ask, "How long is it going to take with him?"

"I don't know. Maybe half an hour. I gotta talk him around a little."

I expect this to bring on an answer about the time, but there's only more silence and I sit up on my elbows and stare into Joey's corner of the darkness. I can feel him over there wanting to drink and maybe even convincing himself that his brain doesn't work right without a drink. He worries me. He goddam worries me. "So where's your buddy's bar?" I ask.

"At the Port Authority," Joey says. "Up by the bowling alley."

"Then let's say around nine to meet. Right?"

"Sure," he says, but only after another pause and I tell myself it's just that he's figuring out the times.

"Are you okay?" I ask him.

"Sure, Deuce. Nothing stays the same."

The next evening, on the curb of Forty-second Street a few strides from the doorway where I last touched Norma, I think of Joey's words. No one is here and nothing stays the same. One night this spot on the pavement is where you find Nicole with the long hair ready to fall, and another night the spot is empty, though maybe that's because I can look off to the west from here and see all the way down to the river and to the sky beyond and there's still a little blush of sunlight there and the whores want the sky to be black and the neon of Forty-second to be the only sun before they come out. Of course I've seen whores trying to work in the daylight, but they always look awkward then, like they realize their faces aren't right. The only face they know to put on fits this blare of light and they can't be two things at once, they can't look beautiful on Forty-second at night and come out in the daylight and have the shadow and the blush and the cry of color in their faces be anything but phony. In the sunlight you know for sure there's another face underneath.

So maybe it's just too early. I step into the doorway again, and this isn't a good place for me. Who the fuck is she in love with that she should think she's French? Plenty of whores in Saigon were half French and they were named Thủy or Noi or Nhung and being French didn't have a goddam thing to do with being in love. I step back out of the doorway and lean against the wall and I wait and it's finally dark enough and a couple of whores stroll by, but this is stupid. She's working somewhere. She's the most beautiful goddam whore in the city and she's working all night, sweet Nicole, the fastest pussy west of the Texas Girls, and I'm never going to find her. But I go walk around a little bit, up and down Forty-second, and I don't notice the fucking lights anymore or the people hustling around, I'm looking in the doorways because I'm lying to myself if I say I can just walk away from all this and leave her. And I head up Broadway and cut over Forty-third and up Eighth and head over Forty-fourth and the whole city is just a string of doorways in dark shadow and sometimes a voice comes out of one and it's never her voice and the city has street corners and women going up and down like they're waiting outside a locked toilet door and they have to piss real bad. And all of this is making me just about as edgy as they seem to be, and it's nine o'clock finally and I head back toward the corner of Forty-second and Eighth and I don't see a goddam thing on this street anymore. Okay, I think, I'm ready to leave this town.

I get to the corner and I even half expect to see Joey waiting for me, and we can get the hell out of New York. I'm going to tell him we should hit the road tonight, we should go back to our place and grab just what we need and we should hit the road tonight. But Joey isn't here. I figure he's still putting the hustle on his bartender friend. So I wait. And the time drags on. And for a while I'm not unhappy to wait because the whores all go by this corner and I still want to see her again, though I'm not sure what I'll say to her if I do. Come with me, maybe. I'm heading west and I want you to come with me.

And I fidget around and people stay away from me because I must look like I'm really whacked out on drugs or something and it looks like I'm about to freak any second and who knows what I'd do then. And the time keeps going by and I'm pacing around and looking up and down and once in a while I kick at the chain-link fence and say, Fuck this, I don't fucking need this, and I even say it to some guy in a goddam Mets cap who gives me a stare as he's going past and I don't know what he's doing around here in a pansy-ass blue and orange Mets cap anyway. And as the time goes on, all this energy I've got keeps perking away in me, keeps me doing all this stay-the-hell-away-from-me stuff, but the thing that's behind it all starts to change. It goes from the idea that Norma's about to walk by any second to the idea that Joey's late because he's up in that bar drinking himself into a goddam stupor and our plan to head west together is just a bunch of crap. But I'm good now at letting time pass. I keep looking for Norma and I keep looking for Joey, but for a lot of the time I just keep going through the motions of waiting and looking while inside me there just isn't much of anything. It's like sitting on a stoop. This is another kind of street-blank, where you just stay in motion and pretty soon nothing and nobody in the world can figure out exactly where you're going to be in the next second and so they can't get inside you.

Except finally I can't keep Joey out of me. It's real late now and something's gone wrong. I walk down Eighth and cut over to the west side of the street at Forty-first and I'm heading for the door into the South Wing and I guess it's in my mind to go into the terminal and find him. But that would really piss me off, if I go in and get grabbed by some Port Authority cop and sent back to Jersey while Joey's got all the money we need and he's only had a couple too many drinks, and while I'm getting collared, he's out on the street ready to say he's sorry for being late but it's okay because now he's got the money and we're ready to take off. This isn't impossible, and I just walk on past the door and turn west on Fortieth and it's dark over here and I pass the place on the curb where I ate my first goddam roast beef sandwich and Joey told me about Treen and it's fucking nostalgia time and I keep on walking and I look up at the dark rise of the terminal and I can see the open sides of the upper-level garage floors and there's a spot I'd like to go back to before I go, though it's impossible, the place where I took Norma and she asked me if I'd take her to a dance, and we did go to a dance, after all, we danced together beside an open window looking out at a brick wall and it was okay, I was lovely. And now I'm getting near Ninth Avenue and I see two women on the other side of the street, on the corner, watching the traffic rush downtown, and as I get nearer, the light changes and the cars stop and one of the women is real tall and thin with blond hair and the other woman is sort of blocked off for a second and I'm almost at the corner and the other woman is visible now and I'm close enough that I can even see the rouged shadows of her cheeks that make her face seem not as round as I know it is. It's Norma, and her hair is coiled up for the fourth or fifth goddam time tonight, and she and the other whore are strolling up the line of cars now. Half a block south is an entrance to the Lincoln Tunnel and that's why there are so many cars lined up in that lane, they're waiting to make the turn to head for the tunnel. And what kind of whores are the ones who work the guys heading back to New Jersey?

The tall one suddenly bends down to one of the cars and she's talking through the passenger side to the man who's driving. Norma keeps walking up the line and another car has a solitary male driver and she bends down out of sight on the far side of the car and all I can see is the man behind the wheel with his head turned and any second he can lean over and open the far door and Norma will disappear. So I wanted to find her, so now I have, so what the fuck am I going to do about it? The man is still turned and listening to whatever shit she's saying to him and I have this racing inside me and I don't know what to do with it, but I'm fixed on the driver and I can see his jaw working, he's speaking, making a goddam offer, and I think about dashing across right now before he gets Norma into the car, and I can open his door and drag him halfway out and then slam the door across his chest as he falls, and all of this is bullshit and if I'm going to do something it's got to be now and I realize I'm just fidgeting around on the sidewalk and I don't know what to say to her but I've got to get to Norma before it's too late and I stride off the curb.

Then the light changes and I take one step, two, thinking to run, thinking to beat the cars before they can start, but it's too late and the cars are moving and a horn blares from my right and I look and it's a fucking cab rushing at me and I jump back and if I could reach in and punch the taxi driver going by, I would, but I just back up some more till I'm on the sidewalk and I look and Norma's there, she's still there, standing next to the tall whore and they're watching the traffic again and a horn honks coming up and a car slows and both Norma and the other whore bend to this one when it stops and I can't watch this. I turn my face uptown and wait for a chance to run across the street and the first clot of cars has almost passed and I look back and the car that had stopped is pulling away and Norma's still there on the sidewalk and the other whore is too and she yells after the car, "Don't leave for home without me," and Norma laughs so loud I can hear her over the traffic, she thinks this is about the funniest goddam thing she's ever heard in her whole fucking life.

And then the street is clear and I run across and the faces of these two whores turn to me and they're both wide-eyed like I'm going to fucking kill them or something, and I pull up and I say, "Norma," and it's still like she doesn't know me and I say, "It's The Deuce, goddamit." The tall whore looks at Norma like she wants to know what to do about this, like maybe she's got a gun in her purse and she's looking for a little nod to use it. But Norma rolls her eyes now and shakes her head no, like I'm some stupid child, and I take a step toward her and she's just out of my reach and I'd get nearer but the tall one edges in between us. So I step back and move to the side so I can see Norma and I say, "What are you doing to yourself?"

"Listen," she says, and she sounds like she's been eating the grit off the West Side Highway, "I've told you my name is Nicole."

"Your goddam name is Norma." And I can hear my voice ring off the bus terminal.

"Get away from me now," Norma says, and her voice surprises me because it's soft and full of tears. "Don't mess up what we had."

"Me?" I'm still yelling and I don't want to be, this is the last thing I want, I want to move to her now and hold her in my arms, but I can't, I feel suddenly very weak, I can't let her have what she wants of me, a memory or some goddam thing, because there she stands and fuck all our memories, and then I think yes, fuck the memories, there's just right now and I want her to live through the night without a stranger in her body. That's why I looked for her, that's why I crossed this street, I want her to live through the night. Only this is too goddam tough. It's not just sitting in a field and making sure the dogs don't come and eat your friend the drunk. This is a woman, and she thinks she's got to do certain things to live, and I'm tired of all this, I can't do anything, not me, whoever the fuck I am. There's never been anything I could do. And I try not to yell, but I say, "Me mess it up? You're the one who became a fucking whore."

And Norma doesn't yell, though I would like it better than the deep breath she takes and the blank that comes over her face and the low rasp of her voice that says, "Get away now. My friend has a gun." I look and the tall whore has her hand resting inside her purse, and Norma says, "Besides, I don't fuck spics."

And this finally strikes me as funny. I start to laugh and the laughter bounces off the bus terminal and all over the street and I'm probably making the tall whore real nervous but I can't stop laughing at this and finally Norma turns away and walks off and the tall whore follows and I call after Norma, "They've got better whores than you in San Juan. I go home there now and forget all about you." I don't know if she hears this but when the words come out, my laughter stops and I feel like shit and I can't let it end this way. I start to run after them and I cry, "Wait, Norma," and the tall one, who's trailing, pauses and she turns and she squares around and she's raising her arm and I can see a pistol in her hand, rising, and all I can do is stop my feet but they don't right away, they take one step more and the pistol is sweeping upward, and one more step and finally my feet stop and so does my breath, and the pistol is rising and it stops too and I can hear my heart very clearly, beating in my ears, slowing, the gun is pointing at me now and it is very steady and I hear one thump in my ears, another, and I can only wait, and to tell you the truth, I don't give a fuck right then, I figure maybe this is the simple way out of all the shit. "No." It's Norma's voice. "Tracy, no." Still another fucking Tracy. And her hand comes down just a little bit and I have sense enough to turn around. I put my back to the gun and I take one step and another and I just keep walking and I don't look back, not even when I reach the corner.

I stand there and I'm gasping for breath now and I think about maybe just sinking down and sitting on the curb for a few minutes, but I don't. I want to stay on my feet. If I sit now, it might be the morning before the blank would end. I keep my feet and I watch the cars streaming past, rushing across Fortieth and then slowing and taking the turn into the tunnel. Not that I'm looking inside the cars or anything. I don't give a shit who's inside. It's just motion and lights and a rush of air against me, and finally my breathing is okay and I can move my legs and I cross Ninth Avenue and go back to Eighth and then I turn uptown and I head to the corner at Forty-second thinking he might be there. He's waiting and ready to say he's sorry. But when I get to the corner, it's just junkies and a passing whore and a bunch of people hustling around, and it feels like I've just landed on Mars. I know something is wrong with Joey and there's nothing for me to do now but find him.

So I turn around and I go down to the South Wing and I look through the door into the foyer and there's no cops and I go in. The first thing I do is glance over underneath the flags and I'm getting a little desperate, I guess, because I even think he might be there, sitting where I first found him and telling the passersby that they should help him out, he's a Vietnam vet and he and his son from The Nam are trying to get some money together to go home. But of course he's not there and I go to the doors into the concourse and I look through, and there's a cop over by the patron assistance booth, but he's talking to a man and woman with baggage at their feet and I slip in and walk as fast as I can without drawing any attention to myself and I keep my face down till I'm at the escalators to the suburban concourse. I've got to look up now because there could be a policeman at the top.

Again I'm okay. A couple of black kids are up there leaning over the balcony, staring down, doing a power thing, and I know where their heads are and they're fucking pathetic. But I got no room to talk and I just lower my face again and I'm going up and I look away from all that security stuff in the center, the TV monitors and all that, and when I hit the top of the escalator I do a quick full turn and check out who's up here. Nobody much, these two kids who don't even give me a look, a guy with a mop and bucket over near the doors to Fairyland, and some stragglers here and there. But no cops, and no Mr. Treen either. He's probably up on Eighth Avenue. I move on down the hallway, past the gate that dumps people in from Hoboken, and I can see the bar up ahead. There's lights and I can see bodies hunched inside and I go straight to the door and that's a mistake. I stop there and I'm looking closer at the guys with their backs to me along the bar. One's too old, there's two guys together and both are too muscular, but there's another with his head buried in his arms who might be Joey, might be, and then there's a hand on my shoulder and I spin around and it's McGee.

"Goddamit," I say, and my chest is still clenched at being startled, but the words are for Point Pleasant and the big goddam reunion and all that shit, which is what I'm reading in McGee because his face is easing toward me and it's full of that real concentrated I've-been-after-you look.

"Sorry," he says. "I didn't mean to scare you."

He takes his hand off me and I'm thinking about that hallway heading the way I just came. How fast can this guy run? He's too big. I can handle this. But then his hand comes back down on my shoulder. I expect it to tighten and drag me off, but for now it just sits on me. "What are you doing here?" he asks, and there's something a little shaky in his voice.

All I can think of is to keep up the lie. "I'm looking for my dad. He's a fucking drunk and I thought he might be up here."

McGee blinks slow and kind of lowers his eyes at this, and he says, "I was afraid of that."

"What are you talking about?" I say, and all that's really in my head is that maybe McGee hasn't seen the poster yet.

He raises his eyes again and starts to speak, but then he stops. "I don't even know your name," he says.

This cinches it, and I jangle my arms a little. I'm okay. "Who the fuck cares, McGee? They call me The Deuce." I say this and I'm distracted by being let off the hook and I'm looking at this man who is trying hard to do something that's tough for him, and I'm too stupid to put it together.

"It's your father," he says in this real low voice, and he looks down again. "We found him dead tonight."

For some reason, maybe because my mind's on New Jersey, I get this idea that he's talking about Kenneth. This gives me a real weird moment, thinking, Oh shit, McGee knows about me after all, but then thinking, What's it really matter if Kenneth's dead anyway, and then thinking, You shit-head, how can you find out Kenneth's dead and just have fucking selfish thoughts like these.

All of that comes to an end when McGee says, "We found him in a stairwell. He'd been knifed to death."

"Joey," I say and I get real weak real fast and McGee's hands grab me and hold me up and he takes me away from the bar, into an alcove, and he leans me against a wall.

"Just rest for a bit," he says. "Then we can go to the office."

"No," I say. This would for sure lead straight to New Jersey, and I know it right away, in spite of the fact that I'm only getting this buzzing noise in my head and I still don't feel too good, which I figure for a second must be from not enough food today and the late hour, and then I think of Joey lying dead in a stairwell and it's like I'd forgotten that for a second and I almost fall down again.

"Look," McGee says, "we've got to go and sit and work this out. There's a detective who needs to ask you a few questions."

"I'm okay now," I say, and I brush at McGee's hands and they go.

But he's still looming in front of me and I've got to get him off guard. Joey's dead. He's fucking dead and all I want to do is get the hell out of here. "I'll go with you in just a second. Okay?"

"Sure," McGee says, and he seems to decide I need some space, some air, and he backs off a couple of steps.

I say, "I just need to walk this off a little."

He nods at me and the guy even turns his head a bit, looks away to give me some privacy, and McGee is okay, he's an okay guy, and I hope I won't get him in any trouble. I walk around in little circles for a few seconds and I slide off farther away, to the corner of the wall that turns into the concourse, and I glance back to McGee. He's watching me without really turning his eyes directly on me and I figure I better put on a little show for him for a few seconds, wag my head in despair or some such shit, and then I do it. I lower my face and I slowly shake my head no, and goddamit, it's no fucking show because tears fill my eyes and start rolling down my face and it's like I'm both crying these tears and standing back watching, like I'm two different people inside here, and I wonder who's who, probably the American is crying for Joey Cipriani and the Vietnamese is watching and saying, Head for the alleys, get the fuck out of here or you'll be back where all they can do is kill your luck. And that's when I start to walk around in a circle again, still shaking my head, but the arc of the circle goes beyond the turning of the corner, and as soon as I'm out of McGee's sight I take off running and I go down the escalators and along the concourse and out into Eighth Avenue, dodging the blare of horns, and I run past the junkies along the fence and I take the corner and head east and Forty-second just turns into a blur of light and bodies and curses and the Vietnamese may be pumping my legs but the American can't keep from strewing his goddam tears all along this street.

EIGHTEEN

◆

I knew it wouldn't be easy, but there was no choice except to go back to Joey's place. My stuff was there and I was goddam sick of the streets. The darkest corner of an upper-floor room in a boarded-up building sounded just right to me. Even if Joey's ghost was there. I knew there'd be Joey's ghost. The second I step into that empty lot next to the building I know Joey's around. Ghosts are a big deal in Vietnam. That shrine in our apartment where my mother prayed was there because of the ghosts. She believed that all her dead family was hanging around in the room with us. I used to wonder what they thought of the sounds Nghi made with her men in the night. My mother fucked for a whole goddam crowd and they were all blood kin and I'm not sure the incense she burned made them any happier about what was going on. But I step into the empty lot and my legs are getting heavier and heavier as I walk and finally I drag myself over to the spot where I'd sat by Joey's sleeping body just the night before last, and a lot of fucking good I did him. I stop there for a moment and I think about maybe just forgetting about my stuff. I can turn around and walk away from all this. But the streets are worse. I want the darkness, and I could always find an empty room of my own in that building. I don't have to stay in Joey's place.

I start to drag myself on, but I look down a last time at the spot where Joey had been. A little patch of dirt with a couple of tufts of weeds that are black in the moonlight, but the air is thicker there and it's more than memory, my mother would tell me it's a ghost, and I step into the center of that space and it's like I've just waded into shallow water, a faint resistance up to my knees, and as soon as I feel this, I realize something that I must've known from the first moment I'd heard about the killing but I just wasn't ready to deal with. It was Treen. He'd had hard words with Joey and he'd even threatened to kill him. And Joey was found stabbed in the stairwell. Treen's favorite weapon and his favorite place. Something more happened between them tonight and Joey pushed too hard and that was that.

And I must look like I've really gone crazy because I start jumping around and cursing and I start throwing the stones I'd piled up last night and they go off in all directions, crunching against the side of the building and ricocheting off other stones in the lot and clattering out into the street and I don't give a shit what I look like, even to that Vietnamese guy inside me who's stepped back a little ways, and finally I'm real tired, not even the tiniest bit less enraged but just too goddam tired to keep carrying on like this. And I stagger away toward the back of the abandoned building and I'm running little scenes in my head where I sneak up on Treen and he's hanging over the balcony at Fairyland and all I do is bend down and grab him around the shins and I lift and he falls and his screams cut off just a split second before he hits so I can hear his head crunch open or I sneak up on him and pull his knife real fast and the blade flashes and it's up his ass before he can turn around and his scream fills my head.

But dropping now into the dusty darkness of the building, I suddenly feel like a goddam fool. I'm a child, all I could do was sit by Joey in the field and the only reason the night went okay was because all the bad guys had better things to do. I've got no power at all except maybe to run and hide. Like I've always done. It's been my only talent, the only thing I can really do, knowing where the narrow corridors are, the empty balconies, the unlocked doors, the turns in the alleys, where to hide my face when the people with the choices do their thing out in the street or across the room in the dark. I'm just a goddam child, and I climb the steps that I can't see but I know by heart, and I go down the corridor and I step into our room and I wait to figure out where his ghost is.

Over in his corner. I can feel the air he's displaced pressing against the side of my face, touching my eyes. This is where he was alive until tonight. I fear this room but I'm drawn to it, too, like there's some explanation here of what it's like to die, like there's something left behind, a scent maybe that you can sniff in and know what he knows right this second, or a thin film of something on all his things, his old field jacket, his blanket, the tin cup he carries into the kitchen each morning for a little water, and if you touch these things, your fingertips can figure out exactly what he knows right this second as he wanders through the Kingdom of the Dead. All those relatives crowding around my mother's altar were there to tell her what it was like. But standing now in the doorway of Joey's place I decide I really don't want to know. All I want is just to live through this night.

I creep into my own corner and I lie down and I sleep and I groan awake and the room is light and I try to go directly to street-blank. I focus on a dim water stain on the wall near my face and I wait for the deadness to come over me and I guess it does, but it feels now like a special kind of pain, like every pore in your body has a hair-thin pin driven into it, but because it's every pore, you've got nothing to compare this feeling to and it tells you it's natural, and because you put the pins in yourself, you even think you like it. And I know it's always been like that, the street-blank, but I've just never recognized it.

I force my face away from the wall and I sit up and I look around for Joey's ghost. Can that dark stripe of a shadow holding very still on the wall behind his mattress really be caused by the way the morning light comes in the window? Or is that what the shadow would want me to think? And if it is Joey over there and if he had a voice, what would he say to me? It was Treen, he'd say. If you're my friend, you've got to make Treen pay for this. So I rise up from the bed and I go to the wall, and it's not a shadow but another water stain and I look around me and there's nothing mystical here, it's just a crumpled blanket, it's just a field jacket sprawled against the wall, it's just a tin cup with a little water still in it sitting on the floor. It's just a grimy business envelope tucked under the corner of the mattress. I bend to this envelope and pick it up and inside is the photo of Mai and I pull it out and she has that phony smile and I take her face in my two hands and I tear it down the middle. If Joey's ghost is in this room, he's probably pissed off at me for this. But maybe not. Maybe you get a little smarter about things like that in the Kingdom of the Dead. I wonder if she's already over there herself and he's slapping her around for fucking his life up. Or maybe they're kissing and saying how good to see you. Who the fuck knows. I just wish I could think Joey's okay. But I can't.

I drop the two halves of this whore and I turn and I go to the window and I lie down there, like Joey and I did when he said he'd go with me, and the sky has no shapes in it but it has no blue either, it's just a pale gray, and I look at it and I get the same feeling that I would looking at a white cloud and seeing a tiger or a house or something. A big arc of gray over the whole fucking world—hey, Joey, look at that, I know what that is. It's smoke. It's a whole shitload of smoke from this big motherfucking fire that's way out of sight but is burning like a son of a bitch. There's these big flames lashing up somewhere and I know what they're all about. The problem is I only know how to spit at them. I've got to get Treen, is what it is, but I know all that stuff I've been thinking about, going up to Fairyland and killing him, is just a child's fantasies. It's kung fu movies on Saturdays at the theatre down the block from the Texas Girls. It's going out in the street afterward and waving your rigid hands and kicking your leg in the air and you're just a fucking kid with no power at all in the real world. Treen has power, he's got all those other guys around him, and he's done this kind of thing before. If I took him on by myself, I'd just end up in the stairwell like all the others. I know that much about who I am at least.

Then I start thinking that I can simply pack my duffel bag and hit the road and let the cops figure it out. McGee said there was a detective. So the detective can solve the case and Treen'll end up in Attica for the rest of his fucking life or something. That's a good thing for him to do. You kill him and at best he goes straight to the eternity out there in the Kingdom of the Dead, and he's going to come to that eventually anyway. Keep him alive in this world and make him goddam uncomfortable for as long as possible. That's what I should want. No little kids in the john of the Haymarket, no boys to hang around Fairyland with, just the goddam cell and some big mother-fucker of a murderer who doesn't like the way this fat-faced guy is looking at him.

But who am I kidding? Who's going to rat on him at the terminal? Some junkie who just happened to be up on the next landing when it was going on? His boys? I sit up and I bend way forward until the top of my head feels like it weighs about fifty pounds from all the blood there. I don't like how this is going. I can't run off and let Treen get away with this, but I know goddam good and well I won't be able to kill the fucker. And I know just as well that he's covered his tracks at the Port Authority. Nobody around there gives a shit about Joey Cipriani except me, and for sure nobody's going to put their own balls on the line to tell the cops anything about Treen. So all that's left is for me to do it. I can go and tell them what I know. I can tell them about the scene with Joey and about Treen's knife and about how he uses the stairwells, and then they've got something. I'll fucking testify. I'll go to court and I'll stand up in the box and I'll say, Yes, that's the butt-fucking buddy over there who killed Joey Cipriani. And they'll make him real uncomfortable for the rest of his life.

And I sit up straight and the top of my head lightens and I know what all of this means. As soon as I walk in and start talking to the cops, somebody's going to know that a New Jersey district attorney has a claim on this kid, and that will be that. So I go back to the first plan. Just pack my bag and hit the road. It's still early in the day. I can take a PATH train into New Jersey—I can catch that down a subway entrance, no risk at all—and I'd be hitchhiking west before this day is done. Not bad. And it's what Joey would want for me, after all. He wouldn't want me back in Point Pleasant. Take off, he'd say. There's nothing you can do here. I can hear his voice real clear. I know it's in my head, but it's so clear that I turn and look around the room like I expect to see some quick shadow of a movement that you only catch out of the corner of your eye. And Joey says, Run away. We're friends, Joey says. I want what's best for you, Deuce.

And as soon as he says that name, I jump up. "Wait a goddam minute," I say to him. "You're right we're friends, and so I can't let Treen murder you and then just walk away from it. Even if it means I go back to fucking Point Pleasant for a while. I can always run away again." And I realize I'm talking to an empty room. But what I'm saying is still right. Even if you die in Vietnam, there's some other guy as fucked up as you who gives a shit about it, and they keep on shooting at the guys who killed you.

So that's settled. I look around the room a last time and I don't feel him here anymore. I figure he's done what he needed to do. I see my stuff scattered in my corner and I wonder if I should pack it all up and take it with me. So this big debate starts in my head. If they figure out who I am and collar me, I don't want to have to lead them back down here to get my stuff. But why should these ratty clothes be so important? Because they feel like mine, for one thing. If I go back, these are the things I want to wear. And I want that duffel bag because I'm going to use it again. Besides, if they don't figure me out, I'm packed and ready to head west. I think for a second about them maybe never catching on to me. But they've got to. The poster on me is too recent. So I'll pack. But what if I can run? What if I tell them everything I know and only toward the end do they figure me out and since I've already fingered Treen, I can run. That's the reason not to pack. But there'd be a trial. If I'm the only guy who's going to speak up, I've got to be around for the trial.

"Shit." I say it aloud and I'm glad Joey's ghost took off so he doesn't realize how much I hate this and start feeling guilty about making me do it. So I pack the duffel and I get out of the room without looking back, and you understand I don't really believe in ghosts. That's something Nghi would believe in and probably all the other whores in Saigon, and I guess all the Buddhists in Vietnam, for that matter, with their little shrines to their ancestors. But a bunch of the Christians in America do, too. The Catholics think they can talk to the saints, and those are just ghosts hanging around, if you look at them close. But anyway, for me it's just a way of talking. It's just memory and little mind-games so you can talk to yourself without thinking you're crazy or something.

This is probably where you'd expect me to go off the track again, telling this story, like when I was trying to explain how I left Saigon. But I'm not going to get off on Vietnamese ghost stories and shit like that, little tales my mother told me or whatever, so I don't have to face all the things that happened next. I'm going to tell this straight. I sling my duffel over my shoulder and for the last time I walk that path through Tompkins Square Park and west on St. Marks Place till it changes names to Eighth Street and I go into the subway and right through the yellow exit doors and I ignore the shout behind me because if they grab me now, it's just a quicker way to the police station. But they don't grab me. A train is pulling in and I step right on it and then I'm coming up out of the ground and it's Forty-second Street. I stand there on the corner for a long moment and I can't move my legs. For a second I think it's facing the police that's the problem. But then I realize it's just Forty-second Street. I'm fucking fed up with the place. So I turn around and go one block south and head west on Forty-first, and it's this real dull street, except I have to go past that place where Joey gave me my runaway poster. But there's a bum sprawled there asleep, right in the same spot, and the place is his now, he can have it, they can have all this shit. Next time I run away, I'll head in a different direction.

So I know right where to go, and to get there I even go down the stairs and across the south roadway and along the corridor where I'd been mugged, and some old woman is sitting on the floor there cracking her knuckles, and then I go up the escalator, like I did that first night. The venetian blinds are closed on the police station and I step to the window and I take a quick glance at the posters. I'm not here, but there's a blank spot where Joey probably found me. And I scan the other grainy faces, kids, some real young, a lot younger than me, and I wonder who's worse off right now, these kids on the posters or the boy who actually has a goddam mother and a bed to sleep in but gets dragged off to the Haymarket when Momma needs some money. But I don't look too close at these faces. I've got enough on my mind. I do check out the names real quick, though, and Debbie Ann isn't here anymore and I wonder where she is. Home at last with the parents who drove her away? Selling herself to men in cars heading for the Lincoln Tunnel? Lying in a drawer in the morgue with a tag tied around her toe? Thinking like this just makes me more pissed off at Treen, and that's good, because I need the guts right now to go ahead and do this thing. And I do. I charge around the corner and into the station. Right in front of me is a woman in a uniform behind a high booking desk, and over to my left is a man behind a regular business desk. I glance that way and he's wearing a white shirt with the collar open and his tie is twisted to the side and he's sitting there flipping through some papers with his feet up on the desktop. I decide to go to the uniform first.

I step forward and the woman is young and her blond hair is pulled back in a knot and she's squared around to deal with me as soon as I get there. The top of this long desk is about at my chin and she's looking down at me and it strikes me that if she undid that hair and put on a bunch of makeup and a halter top, this cop would make a pretty good-looking whore. You see, I'm getting real nervous about this, and I don't like these people already. But I like Treen a whole lot less. So I say to her, "I know something about the murder of Joey Cipriani."

Her face sort of pinches a little, but I'm not sure she understands. I do hear a clunk behind me and I figure I made the guy in the white shirt put his feet down. The woman says, "Who's this again?"

"Joey Cipriani. The guy who was knifed in the stairwell last night." And I figure, what the hell. I add, "He's my father."

The woman's eyes shift just a split second before a man's voice comes from over my shoulder. "Maybe I can help you," he says.

I turn to this guy and he's standing behind the desk, but he's not smiling or offering to shake hands or anything. He's got a long, skinny face and bad skin, cratered from what must've been a pretty miserable childhood with skin that bad. I say to him, "No, it's *me* who can help *you*." I don't like the smart-ass things trying to get out of my head. They're just going to make these people have less trust in what I've got to tell. So I step across to this guy's desk and I put this throb in my voice and I say, "I really want to help. My father got murdered here last night," and it happens again, I try to put on a pose of sadness for a cop and it really starts to happen inside me. Joey's fucking dead, and my eyes fill with tears and this feels stupid, me always starting to cry around the goddam cops, and this guy's hands sort of come out toward me and hang over his desk because the tears are streaming down my face now and I'm trying to make it silent, I'll be damned if I'm going to make any sounds here.

I lower my face and the guy says, "Sit down. Please."

So I put my duffel on the floor and I sit and there's a stuttering in my chest and at least he's not asking me anything. I just wait for all this to pass, but I keep thinking, Poor Joey, poor fucking Joey, and in my head I'm getting one flash of his face after another, like I'm thumbing through some goddam family photo album or something: Joey looking up from his upturned milk crate under the flags and he's got that sad look in his eyes, Joey sitting in the dark by the window and lifting that bottle to try to forget all the shit, Joey looking at that photo of Mai and his face is full of yearning. And we almost made it out of here. Almost.

Anyway, I go on like that for a while, and then I finally sort of dry up, and when I lift my face, the guy in the white shirt has his elbows on the desktop and his chin resting on his clasped hands and his eyes are dead, it seems to me, and I feel another set of eyes. I glance over to my right and the woman in the uniform has slid down to this far end of the high desk and she's looking at me real close, studying me, and that makes the wetness on my cheeks turn cold.

I figure I better do this quick, but I'm still not sure these people here even know what the fuck is going on. I say, "Do you know who I'm talking about? Joey Cipriani."

The man says, "Yes, I know. I'm Detective Koppelman." Now he offers me a hand to shake and I shake it. "I'm working on the case."

"Okay," I say. "Good. I know who killed Joey and I want to help you get the son of a bitch."

"Good," he says. "But let me get some information about you first."

"Me? Listen, this guy who killed my father is probably hanging around the terminal right now. Shouldn't we get this thing rolling?"

"If he's here now, he won't escape in the three minutes I need to find out who I'm talking to." Koppelman shoots me a little smile at this, his first, and it feels like somebody's taken a trowel and scooped out the center of my fucking chest. This was all a big mistake. Koppelman has this form in front of him now and he says, "Your name?"

This is not the question I want to hear. This is how all the shit began. So I try something I know isn't going to work. "They call me The Deuce."

I'm surprised to see that he writes this down. But then he says, "And what's your given name?"

"Given by who?"

Koppelman sits back in his chair like he's starting to get a little pissed off. "By your parents."

It's all such bullshit that it occurs to me to treat it like that, like this is a line I'm using on somebody to get some money. "Well, see, that's not as easy to answer as you might think. Joey was my dad, but you can tell by looking at me that I've got some other blood in me. My mom is Vietnamese, though she's still back in Vietnam. Her name is . . . Mai." I say this so if Joey's ghost is watching all this bullshit, he'll get a nice little smile. A nice little coulda-been.

"So where does that leave us in the name department?" Koppelman says.

I start to say Võ Đình Thanh, but then I remember how clever Kenneth has been and so I say, "My Vietnamese name is Phan Thanh Giản," which in fact is the name of some Vietnamese patriot they named a big street after in Saigon.

Koppelman asks me to spell the name and as I'm doing it I remember that Giản's big patriotic gesture was to poison himself to protest the French taking over the country. I don't know why he should be the guy I remember. I wish it had been some general who knew how to kick ass. But I'm stuck with this.

After Koppelman finishes checking the spelling, he says, "And you say that Joseph Cipriani was your father?"

I kind of flinch at the Joseph stuff, like dead men can't have friendly names anymore. And thinking of Joey, I suddenly worry about something that sounds crazy, but all this has put me in that kind of mood. I worry that using Mai's name won't make Joey smile, if he's a ghost hanging around here, it will just make him sad again, thinking about how he got fucked up.

"Yes, he was my father," I say.

"And do you have an American name?"

"Yes, I've got an American name." And I can hear the smart-ass coming back into my voice and I'm getting real fidgety.

"Can I please have that name too?" Koppelman says.

"Sure," I say. "Mario Luigi Cipriani."

And the stupid son of a bitch writes it down. If he believes my name is Mario Luigi Cipriani, why shouldn't he believe any goddam thing that Mr. Treen tells him? My only hope is that if lies sound true, the truth will be even better. I say, "Joey's killer is this guy named Treen."

But Koppelman raises his hand and stops me. "One more thing first," he says. "What's your address?"

"My address? We didn't have an address. We lived in an abandoned building on the Lower East Side."

Koppelman nods like he already knows this and he writes something below my name. Then he writes something else in a space farther down on the form.

"Look," I say, "how much more of this bullshit do we have to go through? I've got some important stuff to tell you."

Koppelman looks up real slow from his form and this is supposed to scare me, I'm sure. He talks slow too, saying, "I know this is a difficult time for you. But I assure you, Mario, that we're going to do everything we can."

He tries to look mean, but then he talks that phony I'm-a-reasonable-man bullshit. I know the fucking type and if this weren't real important, I'd get the hell out of here right now. But I try to keep it together. I say, "Call me Giản, okay?"

"Gian?"

"Phan Thanh Giản. Remember?"

Koppelman squints in displeasure at this. Fuck him. "All right, Gian," he says, and he butchers the pronunciation. "We can get a few more details later. What is it you have to tell me about the death of Mr. Cipriani."

It's Mr. Cipriani now and I want to play dumb, act like I don't know who Koppelman's talking about. But he's finally ready to listen to me, and that's more important. So I tell him everything I know. Every detail of Joey's confrontation with Treen, the exact threat on Joey's life, everything, and all the stuff about Treen's knife and about his fondness for the stairwell to do the things he wanted to do out of sight. I make it all real clear. After I say all of this, nobody can have a doubt about who the killer is. So I sit back in my chair and I figure whatever happens about me now is okay because I've taken care of Joey, I'm making Treen pay.

Now remember, I'm this smart Asian kid. More than that, I've lived on my own in the streets of two pretty scary cities on two different continents. And yet sometimes I'm just about the stupidest guy in the world. It even surprises me that Koppelman doesn't jump up and tell the blond woman to call out the patrolmen and head for the second floor of the North Wing, we've got our killer. In fact what Koppelman does is sit back in his chair and tent his fingers in front of him and say, "And where were you exactly when the crime was being perpetrated? That is, when Joseph Cipriani was being killed."

I know what "perpetrated" means. My goddam father's a D.A. Koppelman's starting to piss me off with the way he talks, and I don't like the answer I've got to give for this question, either. He's waiting and I can't see how to bullshit this one. "I don't know where I was, exactly. Somewhere out on the streets."

"So you didn't witness the actual event?"

"No."

"And did you see this Mr. Treen at any time on the night of the event?"

The answer to this is also no, and I'm starting to understand what's happening. I say, "The event? What event is that? We're talking about a knifing in a stairwell, not the fucking Icecapades at Madison Square Garden. Right?"

Koppelman leans forward in that slow way of his and he says, "I don't like the way you're talking, Mario."

"Giản."

He flinches and you can see that he's really pissed off now. "Gian. I can appreciate that the death of your father is a traumatic thing for you. But you are going to stay calm with me or I'll have you put in detention right away. How old are you anyway?"

I don't get a chance to answer this one because the bitch with the blond bun is suddenly beside him and leaning down and spreading my runaway poster in front of him. Before I can even think to do anything, she's come around the desk and is standing beside me, and I know I'm fucked.

They ask me some questions, but I just shut up, and they sit me in an interrogation room with a bare table in the center and they close the door and that's where I stay for a long time, street-blank again, though I guess now I'm doing what they do up there in Attica or wherever, this is jail-blank, and there's not much to think about now anyway.

Finally the door opens and it's Kenneth and he nods over his shoulder to the cop to tell him to go away. Then he steps in and closes the door. He's wearing a Rutgers T-shirt and jeans, which later I realize he must've changed into because it's a weekday and he had to come from work. He didn't want to meet me in his three-piece suit, which shows you how clever he can be. I stand up as soon as he comes in because if he sits down, he's going to want to talk, and that's the last thing I want to do. I think to say to him, Hey, how you hanging, GI, fuck you and the horse you rode in on. But I look at his face and he looks pretty bad, to tell you the truth, drawn and real tired. Give him a couple days' growth of beard and a beat-up Yankees cap and he could make a pretty good street beggar. And I figure if I play the smart-ass with him, it'll just lead to talk, so I don't say anything until he says, "Hello, Tony."

That smart-ass voice in my head wants me to tell him to call me Mario, but I just say, "Hello, Kenneth."

"They say you walked in."

"A friend of mine got knifed to death last night. I thought I could do something about it."

"I'm sorry about your friend," Kenneth says, and he looks down at the floor, like he really means it.

"Yeah, well, maybe the detectives will do their fucking jobs."

"I hope so."

I feel him working up to some long explanation which then would lead to a bunch of questions I don't want to answer, so I figure I better get us to the point as fast as I can. I say, "You want to take me to Jersey now."

He looks at me closely, obviously trying to figure out my mood.

"Yes," he says.

"Then let's get it over with."

He nods once and he opens the door and I go out first and head for the outer office. Kenneth stops for a minute and has some final words with the detective, but I go straight to the door to wait. I can see my face very dimly in the glass. I see the stretch of it from my brow to my chin, just like the face that appeared in the interrogation room door. I look about as tired as him, too. I am tired. Shadows flicker by, somebody passing, heading for the main floor concourse, and I think of Treen upstairs. Even if I wasn't a goddam witness to the killing, at least I gave the detective a good lead to follow. At least that.

Then Kenneth is by my side and he's got my duffel bag over his shoulder and I reach for it and he says it's okay and I say I want it, and he gives it to me. So I follow him out the door and we walk straight down the concourse and I just keep my face down and when we reach the big escalators, I even turn away, I just don't want to look, and we pass the Greyhound ticket windows and we go through the foyer and I look away again when I near the place beneath the flags. It's bad enough crying for cops, I sure as hell don't want to cry for Kenneth.

We go out the Eighth Avenue door and Kenneth leads me south and around the corner onto Fortieth and there's Kenneth's car—a steel gray Thunderbird—parked at the curb, and as we approach it, I can see a parking ticket flapping on the windshield. I stand by the passenger door and Kenneth circles the car and he grabs the ticket off the window and stuffs it in his pocket. I have this little pop of feeling for him. Straight old Kenneth would actually do something illegal to go get this kid of his. But when he disappears into the car and I stand and wait for the door to unlock, I decide that it's just because he can get any ticket fixed, being that he's a fucking D.A. and all. I look up the street and think about walking away. But I wouldn't get far. And I'm feeling real tired right now anyway.

So the door clicks and then it opens a crack and I know we're heading for the Lincoln Tunnel and this is all getting weirder by the second, but I open the door and throw the duffel into the back seat and I get in and Kenneth tells me to buckle my seat belt and I just sit there and I smell the leather seats and I'm being reminded to buckle up for safety and I wonder how I'm going to get through this. But I buckle the goddam belt, and we pull away from the curb and at the next corner we hit a red light, and it's the corner where Norma was waiting for Thunderbird doors to click open and men to take her to New Jersey and I wonder if they made sure she buckled up. She's not on the corner now, though. There's no whore at all, and I'm glad for that.

"Tony?"

For a second I honestly don't know who Kenneth is talking about. I look at him, and he's watching the light.

He says, "Do you want to talk?"

"No," I say, and the light changes and Kenneth doesn't speak another word all the way back to Point Pleasant. And the silence holds when we get to the house. I get my duffel bag from the back seat and I go in and the house smells of furniture polish and pine-scent air freshener and I expect to find Point Pleasant Tracy waiting for me, but she's nowhere in sight. I hear Kenneth's footsteps on the porch and I go up the stairs without looking back. Kenneth is following but I know where my goddam room is and he says something about clean towels and I just go into the room and close the door.

I put my bag down in the middle of the floor and it's all exactly the way I left it, computer, TV, stereo, rag rug, my bed by the stippled wall. Christ, Joey, look at me now. You'd know that all this is no better than our room in the dark, wouldn't you? Can you find me here, Joey? Or is the Kingdom of the Dead just like anyplace else, with certain streets for people like you and Norma and all the other hustlers, and different streets for the D.A.'s and the lawyers and the gynecologists? I wish now I'd told you more about all this. I never talked about it, really. I never said the name Point Pleasant to you, so you don't even know where to look.

I lie down on the bed and it feels strange, too goddam soft. It's always been too soft. I doze, I think, and I just let time pass, and late in the day Kenneth knocks and when I don't answer, he says he's leaving a tray of food for me. He's trying real hard, I guess. And eventually I eat the food and I put the empty tray back in the hall and I close and lock my door. And when it gets dark and I'm ready to sleep again, I pull the blankets down from the top of my closet and I put them on the floor and that's where I sleep. The moon is very bright outside and it's still almost full, but I don't even know what to wish for tonight and Cuội and I are worlds apart.

NINETEEN

◆
◆

When I think back on the time in Kenneth's house just after
Joey's death, there are days lost to me like many of the weeks in
New York are lost, time that left no smell, no sight, no sound that I
can use to claim it again and make it part of this story. Much of the
time in Point Pleasant passed like I was a cicada burrowed by the
root of a tree, waiting his long wait to emerge one night and finally
play out his life. But it wasn't as simple as that, either. There were
interruptions. To grieve, for one thing. The first day or so I would
be lying on the floor and for a long time the sky would just hold me
in the suspension that I guess I wanted, but then for no reason at all
I'd think of Joey, like it struck me that he'd lost this sky, it wasn't his
anymore, and I'm sorry to admit this, but at moments like that I'd
try to talk myself out of any more tears, I'd say I only knew this guy
for a couple of months and it was too bad and all, but he was doomed
from the start, he came up out of the ground and crawled onto the
tree and he began to sing and that was the end, like it was always
going to be. But that never worked for long, and when it didn't, I
was glad it didn't. So I'd go ahead and put my time in crying, but
pretty soon that stopped. And then something funny happened
about these hours of suspension. I don't know how I understood this,
but I'm sure the lost hours themselves became a kind of weeping. It

was no longer street-blank. In my blankness I think I was trying to share Joey's death with him. But maybe that was always part of the street-blank, too. The bums were all in this state of mourning. They were all sharing somebody's death, even if it was their own.

And through all this Kenneth keeps his distance and his silence, and the longer he does this, the more I find, when he softly knocks at the door to tell me there's food, that I'm tempted to open the door and at least look him in the face. And on the second or third day I finally do this. He knocks around noon and he doesn't even wait for my silence. He says, "Tony, I'm leaving the food."

Without planning it out or anything, I jump up from the pile of blankets under the window and I go to the door and I open it. Kenneth is still holding the tray and he rears back a little, and I realize that I've opened the door with a yank. He's expecting anger from me. And I just stand there and I really don't know what to expect from me either. I just wait and he collects himself and he says, "Hi."

I realize that he's in a sport shirt and jeans and here it is the middle of what I'm pretty sure is a weekday. I say, "You on vacation?"

"Yes. I've taken some time off."

So he's just been hanging around the house waiting to see what I need. I feel like I owe him a couple of minutes, maybe. I say, "I don't want to do a lot of talking."

"Whatever you want."

So I pull back to show him he can come in. He leans forward a little, like he wants to make a move but he's not sure. I've got to give him a fucking invitation now, and that starts to piss me off. But I fight that and I say, "You want to come in for a mintue or two, it's okay."

"Thanks," he says, and you can tell he's trying to keep the eagerness out of his voice. So he steps in and he glances at the place on the floor where I've been sleeping but his face stays blank about that—another effort, I know—and he puts the tray on my desk. "Can I sit?" he says.

"Sure," I say, and he does, at the desk, and I sit on the edge of my bed.

I wait and naturally I'm thinking this is a big mistake. I don't know what to say and neither does he. Finally he puts the burden on me. "Do you want to tell me anything?"

"If I did, I'd know where to find you." This comes out sounding more irritated than I really mean it.

"Okay," he says, and he doesn't seem angry. "Is there anything I can answer for you?"

This strikes me as odd, at first, but then I catch on. So I ask him. "Did you marry Tracy?"

"Yes."

I think to ask him which one, but he wouldn't get it and I sure as hell don't want to explain. I simply shrug.

He says, "She's off visiting her mother in Oregon for a week."

This strikes me as real smart of them. Discreet. I try to work up a little irritation about all this, but I can't. I guess I don't really have anything against her. At least Kenneth has found somebody who's going to stick around. The whole thing just doesn't seem to have much to do with me anymore.

"Tony," Kenneth says, and he looks away, out the window, and I hope he's not going to rush this talking stuff. He's obviously wanting to say something he thinks is important. You can feel him holding his breath while he decides how to start. Then he suddenly puffs out all the air he's been holding and he turns back to me. "Tony," he says, "I'm trying hard to do the right things this time. I don't want to press you, but can I ask a question?"

I'm not intending to answer right away no matter what, but as it is, he can only stand a few seconds of my silence before he says, "This is tough, because I really want to say that I care for you. But I know now how that sounds to you, how it's always sounded."

"So you won't say it."

"No."

I want to laugh at this, but I tighten my face to hold back even the tiniest smile. I don't want to give him any wrong impressions, especially the impression he should go ahead and say a whole lot more. But it strikes me as funny, him using this courtroom trick on me. He tells me exactly what he knows he's not supposed to say, just so the jury can hear the inadmissible evidence anyway. Well, the judge says to disregard it, and that's what I'm going to do.

Kenneth's out the window again and right away I figure the question has to do with sex. He's puffing and fidgeting, but at least he doesn't have his thumbs tucked into a goddam vest. What he's doing is bad enough, but if he was handling this real smooth, in his best D.A. style, I don't think I'd ever be able to talk with him. Finally he looks at me and says, "Tony, I know that a life on the streets of New York is real tough." Now his eyes slide away from me again and out to the trees or whatever. "And I know you can form all kinds of . . . friendships."

"You want to know if I got fucked up the butt by some Forty-second Street buddy."

This just comes out. A reflex. I'm glad he isn't playing the district attorney but I'm still getting a little pissed off, I guess. As soon as I say this, though, I expect one of only three possible reactions. He gets pissed at me. He gets talky and bullshit psychological with me. He maybe gets quiet again, taking this as the end of the conversation. But I don't expect what actually happens. He doesn't flinch. He just turns his face to me and he looks sad. Why does this look in other people always surprise me? And he says, real gently, "I'm a fool talking to you the way I do. From the day I found you in Saigon, you've never been a child. And until about forty-eight hours ago, I've never imagined you as anything else. I'm sorry for that, Tony. It's my own fault. I came back too late to get you. I pissed away your childhood and I've never really accepted that."

I don't expect my reaction either. First I think he's a fucking liar. Somewhere along there I was still a child. And then I think he's right, and I've been fucking robbed. I want my goddam childhood back. Before I start showing any of this, I say, "That's enough talk now."

Kenneth's voice is still gentle, and he says, "Okay." Then he stands, and I know he wants to pat me on the shoulder or something as he goes by, but I make it hard for him. I kind of lean back on the bed and he passes by without even a look. And me leaning on the bed and him not looking makes me hear another assumption running under his words about my never being a child. I jump up and step into the hall and I call after him, pretty sharply, "Hey."

He stops and turns around and he still has that sad look and I try to keep my voice calm. I say, "Nobody touched me in New York."

He gives me a little smile at this. Like he believes me right away, and like he's glad I told him, and like he's still working on the jury to convince them that he cares for me. This makes me sad. I get a flash in my head of McGee saying my father was dead and when I thought he was talking about this guy standing here before me now, I really didn't give a shit. Kenneth, the problem isn't whether you care about me, it's that I don't care about you. No matter how hard you try or how much I try to see what's good in you. But I can't say any of this to him. Not even when I'm pissed. So I turn around and close my door.

But when the light has faded and his knock comes again, to tell me my supper is there, I open the door and I've thought of a question for him. Not exactly in the shape of a question, more a statement to see what he does with it. "Sit down," I tell him and he does, in the same chair. I go to the bed, but this time I put my back up against the wall. "So I never was a child. So you can't be a child without a mother." That's it. That's all I've got. I wait to see what he makes of it.

Kenneth is waiting too, apparently to see if I have more to say. Then after a few moments he nods his head and he says, "I've never made that right."

"It doesn't mean finding some American woman to marry."

"I know that. That's not what I mean."

"You're going to tell me she was strung out on drugs when you found her."

"That was a hard thing for me."

"For you?"

"I know it was worse for her. But aren't you asking about *me*, about why I did certain things the way I did? I was very worried about her."

I leave the wall and bounce to the edge of the bed again. "You tried real hard to get her off the stuff, right?"

Kenneth looks away, like he's fucking wounded. "She made it very clear she didn't want to change anything."

"What? She didn't want to exchange that goddam back-alley apartment for a big house in Point Pleasant, New Jersey? You telling me that?"

Kenneth's face snaps back to me and he says, "*You've* never found the exchange to be very good, have you? Maybe she already knew how hopeless this was."

I want to crawl back away from this one. He's right, I guess. Maybe she was just too smart to think this could work for her. But not smart enough to think it'd be the same for me. And I look around the room and then I go to the wall again and draw my legs up to my chest.

Kenneth gets up and takes my spot on the corner of the bed. I don't like him this close right now, but I just tuck my face between my knees and I remember Nghi in the photo on the balcony. Saigon surrounds her and her face is placid; the eyes, the mouth are so clearly what they are, she's Nghi and she's Vietnamese and this is her city and if she's doing things that are bad for her body, too many drugs and too many men, at least she has her city.

"Did you really try to convince her?" I say.

"I won't lie to you," Kenneth says. "Not very hard. I loved her once. But she changed. There was nothing I could do about that."

I lift my face now and look at him. A question comes to my lips without sounding itself in my head first. I listen, too, as I ask, "If you'd held on to her the first time, couldn't it have been different? If you hadn't treated her like your whore, if you'd taken her to a dance or something, couldn't she have been different?"

The question comes out sounding a little stupid. But it tells me why I'm asking. And so I know what a coward I am when Kenneth says, "No, it couldn't have been different," and I feel relieved.

We both fall into a silence and Kenneth has sense enough after a while to simply get up and move to the door. He doesn't say good-bye, but this time he stops by the bed and he reaches over and pats my shoulder and I let him do that.

It's not like I've just written Norma off. But I think somewhere deep inside my silence of the past two days I've been churning about how little I did for her, and the churning stops now. I lie down to sleep that night and it's like you've had a dull pain for a long time and you get so used to it that you don't really know it's there until it's gone. That's how it was about me and Norma. Not that suddenly I get a good night's sleep or anything. In fact, when I figure I understand about her, something else that's been going on inside me just takes on all the energy that was going to Norma. And so I pass a night of shallow sleep and thrashing and cursing, and before me all the time are Treen and Joey, the round face and the thin, the fleshy hands and the bony hands, the man with the knife and the man angling a photo of a Vietnamese whore into the light and saying he's still in love and maybe he's the only person I've ever known who used the word and I can look back and believe it. And here I lie in this soft, safe room and Joey's dead and Treen's leaning over his balcony like always with the peacock-tail eyes quivering behind him and Kenneth's down the hall and he's a goddam district attorney and he's sleeping safe too and I get mad at Kenneth every hour or so, in between the dreams of my arms and legs being so heavy that I can't move them even though it's not quite too late, I can still save Joey except that this goddam body of mine won't move. The dream drags through my sleep and then I thrash awake and I sit up fast and my heart is thrashing too, and after I pound my fists on my thighs a few times and call myself a goddam pathetic child, there are always a few moments of anger at the room I'm in, the quiet of the backyard, and then it's Kenneth, goddam him, who seems so petty in his concerns over his half-breed child when there are people in the world who are getting away with fucking murder.

So when the knock comes the next morning, I go to the door ready to talk about Joey. I'm going to explain it all and I'll just wait for the D.A. to stick one thumb in his vest and one up his ass and say that nothing can be done for the death of a person like that. I open the door and Kenneth doesn't have a tray in his hands. He says, "I can bring you a tray if you want, but I thought you might like to eat at a table this morning."

I'm already worked up to be angry with him and this takes me by surprise and just sharpens the anger. But the surprise keeps me from speaking right away and Kenneth adds, "I don't have to hang around while you eat, if you don't want."

I'm finally thinking clearly, and if I'm going to deal with Kenneth the way I feel I want to, it's not going to be over some goddam trivial thing like where I eat my fucking breakfast. So I keep cool. I say, "I'll figure that out a little later. I want to talk first."

Kenneth must hear something in my voice because he comes in but he looks nervous, and he even glances again at the blankets beneath the window and this time he flinches just a little bit. So we go to our places, him on the chair at my desk and me on the corner of the bed.

And I try to make myself calm. It's Joey I'm talking about, after all, and though I expect Kenneth to piss me off somehow, I want to do right by Joey. And I tell Kenneth everything. Joey the beggar, Joey the lover of a Vietnamese whore, faithful to her even all these years later, Joey the provider, giving me a place to sleep and a way to keep eating, Joey the Vietnam vet, though I don't talk too much about the lies, Joey of the sad eyes and Joey the alcoholic who was quiet, simply quiet, when the bottle was empty, and Joey of the night of our plans and how there was no bottle at all when he decided to go with me. And Joey the protector, going up to Treen's kingdom and challenging him to keep away from me. And I tell Kenneth about Treen. About the Haymarket and about the threats and about the knife and about the stairwell. And when I'm finished telling all this, I've forgotten how Kenneth is supposed to act, I'm just trying to squeeze back the quaver in my voice and the tears in my eyes, and I stop talking.

But I can feel Kenneth about to make a move, to comfort me, and I sure as hell don't want to let him mask his contempt for Joey by doing the concerned-father act. So I straighten up and I look him in the eye and I say one more thing: "Joey told me something not long before he died. He said he knew Vietnam wasn't the problem with the way his life had gone for him. He said Vietnam gave him the only beautiful thing he'd ever had."

So now I scoot across the bed to the wall and put my back against it and I wait for Kenneth to react to all this, and right away he confuses me. I tell myself he's a D.A., he's used to masking his real feelings, his purpose, but Kenneth simply lowers his face and then he slowly looks around the room, like he's not quite sure what all this is and he's trying to understand the place. I can't even imagine what's in his head, and what I really want is for him to say something, any goddam thing.

Finally he looks at me, and for a second his eyes are the way they've been while he's been checking out the room. I'm like the furniture and the rug and the TV and all that, something he sort of recognizes but can't quite place. I even wonder for a second if he's on drugs. But then he says, "I'm really sorry about your friend."

I can't make out what's going on inside him, so I just sort of put myself on automatic pilot. I say, "A lot of fucking good that does him."

Kenneth ignores this. He says, "I've known men like him."

"Like him? What kind of guy is that? You've seen some bums in a bus station?"

Kenneth blinks at me, like he's coming out of a daydream. Then he frowns. "I'm not talking about bums. You're not going to get me to put your friend Joey down, because that's not what I think about him."

"Oh no? Who the fuck is he, then, that you think you've known people like him?"

"One of the best lawyers in New Jersey is like your friend. Other guys too. People I know. People I've prosecuted. A bunch of guys. Some of them aren't as smart as your friend Joey. Most of them aren't. They figure that Vietnam screwed them up. And it did, in a way. But they think it was because it was so bad there, so much horror, fear, that kind of thing. But what Vietnam really was for them was the only time in their lives when you'd get up in the morning and see the sky really clearly or really appreciate a shower or a dry pair of socks. And not just little things. It was the only time in their lives when every day you knew for sure that there's something very important at stake on the planet Earth, that the issues of life and death and love and even eternity, heaven and hell, are all real, these things exist. You knew that, and you never forgot it for a second, and then you came home and all of that faded away. We've got all this stuff." And at this Kenneth waves his arm around the room. "We've got a quiet street and neighbors who talk about the weather and about the Yankees and we've got food and money and clothes and daily work that absorbs us, but because we've been to Vietnam, all of this just doesn't measure up. It's not important enough."

So Kenneth surprises me again. I understand what he's saying and it makes sense to me and all I can do is think that he uses too many words. And so I end up getting pissed off at myself. In my head I'm thinking Kenneth is okay, but I just don't have a goddam feeling for him. I say, "Is what you're saying true for you as well?"

"Yes," he says, and the guy looks me in the eye and I know he's telling me the truth and all I can do is draw my legs up and look away from him. "Maybe I'll take the tray," I say.

It's not because I'm angry with him that I eat alone this time. I'm even glad that he thinks Vietnam was something good in his life. Things are just too complicated right now. But when I finish breakfast, I carry the tray down the hallway and down the steps, expecting to find Kenneth any second and I'll be civil with him. I realize I'm even a little eager to just sort of run into him and have a chance to say something offhand. I stop in the foyer and look one way into the living room and I don't see him and the other way into the dining room and I don't see him, and the house is real quiet. I hear a clock ticking from a mantel in the living room and that's about it. That and the trees rustling outside. The front door is open and a breeze is coming through the screen.

I turn around and follow the hallway to the kitchen, and the back door is open, too. The table has two places set very neatly, the silver and the folded linen napkins arranged just right. I put my tray on the counter by the sink and I look through the window. The yard slopes gently to a distant redwood fence, and the wind seems to be coming from a few directions all at once, because the air is moving—I can feel it rushing through the house—but the trees aren't bending one way or another, they're upright and quaking like they've had a bad scare and don't know where to run.

I step outside and the sun feels good and the air is swirling around

and the stillness of the neighborhood nags at me, makes me think of
Joey and all that, and I start to quake, too, like the trees. I move into
the yard and into the shade of a big sugar maple, and I just stand
there for a while and look up into the web of limbs and watch all the
frantic leaves and I feel Kenneth behind me even before he says
anything. I turn around and he's a few paces away and he's standing
very still, not wanting to butt in, and I say, "Hi."

He says, "Hi," and right away I know something's wrong. His
face is drawn down and his mouth is set hard. It's the face I'd expected to see after I got snatched back home, but when I see it now, I
know instantly and for sure that it's not me he's upset about. But he
is upset, and it's real. It's not something he's putting on, so he surprises me once more when I find out what it is. "I've made some
calls," he says. "There are no witnesses coming forward. Not even to
place your Mr. Treen near that part of the terminal on the night of
the crime."

"What do you mean?"

"I called Koppelman to see how things are going. He's got nothing."

"They just don't give a shit about a dead beggar." I spit this out.
Then I say, "I told him all about Treen."

"Exactly what you told me?"

"Yes."

"And that's everything you know?"

"Everything."

Kenneth looks up into the trees and for a second I think there's
some animal up there he's trying to scare away because he makes this
guttural sound, but then he says, "I'm in the wrong fucking business."

I don't think I've ever heard him use the word "fuck." Even with
the first Mrs. Kenneth, and things got pretty heated with her. I say,
"What fucking business?"

Kenneth brings his face back down to me. "I know too goddam
much about how all this works. I sure as hell don't want to be the
one to tell you how hopeless this is. But please understand that I
knew we'd get to this moment when I walked out here. It's just that

I'm determined to treat you like the adult you are. I got the news and now I've got to give it to you straight."

"How hopeless?" I ask.

"With things as they are in this case, without a witness of some sort, it's finished. It's done."

"Treen's going to get away with this."

I'm already starting to get frantic inside and I sure as fuck don't want to hear any words right now that sound reasonable. But Kenneth's eyes rivet me and they shock me how hard they are, and for a second there's nothing in me but these eyes and the fist of his voice. He says, "My job is to try to make people like Treen pay for what they do. I've lost a wife and a son to that goddam job, and I've lost any of the bullshit idealism about people not being able to get away with murder. They can, and in fact in some very common situations they usually do. I wish I could tell you the world is different, but it's not."

The frantic feeling is gone from me. Kenneth's hard, clear eyes are like holding a baby tight when he cries. I'm real calm all of a sudden. It's okay, too, when Kenneth steps closer and he puts his hand on my shoulder. That helps some more. I'd probably even stand here like this with him for a while longer if I didn't hear the maple above me quivering in the wind. It pisses me off a little bit, that quaking tree, and I say, "I think I'll go upstairs now."

Kenneth gives my shoulder a little squeeze and he steps out of my way and I move past. But when I get to the back porch steps, I turn and he's watching me from the spot where I left him. I say, "Thanks for finding out."

He nods and his face is still hard and he even turns before I do and drifts off toward the back of the yard, his hands stuffed into his pockets, and you can see that all this troubles him.

I head into the house and go straight for the same book in his study where I'd found money the last time, and sometimes Kenneth can be pretty dumb for a guy who spends his life around criminals. There's money here again. Then I go upstairs and look out my window and Kenneth is sitting on a picnic table down the slope, his back to the house, his shoulders slumped forward. I have one twist of regret now at having to worry the shit out of him again. I cross the room, set the lock, step out into the hallway, and close the door. Then I walk down the hall, down the stairs, and out into the quiet Point Pleasant morning. I don't know how the fuck I'm going to do it, but I figure I've got to make Treen pay.

TWENTY

⧩

By the time I see New York again, the day is just about gone. I'm on the Hoboken bus and we go up the viaduct leading to the tunnel and the city is ripped against the sky and the little spots of red or white are real clear now at the tops of the big buildings and you can feel the rest of the lights just waiting for the juice. The sky beyond is starting to bruise and whatever I'm going to do about Treen will have to be done at night. But that's okay. It's his time of day, I figure. He's going to think he can't be hurt at night. And maybe he can't. Till I stepped onto this bus I thought only about Kenneth finding out right away what the silence in my room means and coming after me. But now I can't avoid making plans for Treen and I suddenly feel real cold. The fucking air-conditioning on the bus is too high or something and I raise my hands from my lap to rub them and warm them and they're trembling. I know it's not the cold. I recognize these hands, and it surprises me. It feels like somebody else's fear, not mine. But here I sit, alone, riding a bus into the city and the night, and I want to destroy this man, see, this killer who rules a dark little kingdom and who has all these lost children surrounding him and they're under his spell and they want warmth and they want buddies but they've been captured by this evil king and turned into killers, too, and what do I have to put against them all?

This scary little game that I find myself doing now, turning all this into some goddam folk tale that my mother would tell? The lost Vietnamese prince from Black Elephant Mountain come to throw the wicked Chinese out. But the prince had a magic ring or his warrior father's sword or some goddam thing. I didn't even have brains enough to grab a kitchen knife to bring with me.

The bus plunges into the yellow light of the tunnel and I clench my fists to stop my hands from shaking and it really is too cold in here, that's part of the problem, and my head is full of this yellow blur and not much else. One thing I know is how to lure Treen away. He wants me, and the nighttime is when he'll be really open to that, the time when I can draw him out alone. And then what? What the fuck do I do then? I lean my cheek against the window and the glass is so cold it feels like a lick of flame and I pull back and I feel myself running in the alleys with flames spraying from the burning straw in my hand and the other kids are running behind me and it's the heavy, food-rotted dark of Saigon, the dark of rocket rounds and weeping whores and these hulking GIs staggering down the back stairways, and I run in the dark, run and run and the footsteps are clattering behind me but I can run away from all that if I want to, I know the alleys, the turns and the passageways and the balconies and I can go this way or that way and I think of running from Kenneth, running and hiding, and if I wanted him to follow me anywhere, even into the river, I could do it and I could always stay ahead of him.

The bus rises and rushes from the tunnel and into the twilight and we start to turn and climb into the terminal and I know that there is nothing I can plan in all of this. I just have to light the straw and run and see where I go. And if Treen catches me and this final thing happens and he sticks me with one thing or another, then my life ends either way. But goddamit, the life would've ended anyway, sunk deep in the bed in Point Pleasant, alone, and I would've let them all down, all goddam four of them, Nghi and Kenneth and Norma and Joey. But this way at least I tried. I went out into the alley and I ran and if that's all I've ever known how to do, at least this time it was for Joey.

Then the bus stops and I go down the steps and into the lights of the concourse and I think about the timing. I want it to be dark out. I've been watching the moon and it won't rise till later and there will be a deep dark for a couple of hours after sunset. So I slip into the little alcove where McGee leaned me against a wall at the news of Joey's death, and I go to a corner and I sit and I wait, and the blankness now feels like sleep and my hands sit on my knees and are very still and then finally I know it's time.

I get up and step out into the concourse. Behind me I hear the faint crash of bowling pins and ahead of me a few business suits are still hustling along and there's one last little resistance, my legs get real heavy and I'm suddenly having trouble drawing a deep breath. But it only lasts a few moments and then I'm moving fast along the concourse and I see the escalators up ahead and some black kids hanging around and I take the corner and the kids look at me for a second like they can sense something real heavy going on. I stride toward the glass doors that lead into the North Wing and a guy in a suit is coming at me and he's got his head down as he moves, only thinking about his goddam bus to his suburban home, and I don't change my course an inch and we hit shoulders and he glances off, falls away, and I haven't missed a step and I just push through the glass doors. I slow up now before I get to the corner that opens into Fairyland. Something's working in me, words are shaping, I know what I've got to do up here, and I wish the rest of it was this clear.

I come to a stop and I take a quick look around the corner. The floor is bright and mostly empty and between a couple of the big, square red brick posts in the center I can see the far balcony real clear. He's there. He's got his back to me. He's leaning over and watching the world below, and to his right are two young men, also leaning and looking, and to his left, a little farther away, is another of his boys, a tall, thin guy in a pale blue jumpsuit who's propped against the balcony but facing this way. This guy doesn't see me. He's watching something opposite him, that I can't see. I lean farther forward and I look along the row of shops and I see the bagel place and a little cluster of Bagelonians down there, three or four more boys, a couple of them in black leather. I've got to remember they're behind me when I confront Treen. It also means I've got to get closer to Treen than I want, to keep them from hearing me right away. If they get alerted too early, I could be surrounded instantly and that would be the end of it.

The way all these guys are arranged at this moment seems about as good as it's going to get, so I step out and I cross the floor, moving over the bright tan tiles, past one red pillar, and Treen and the two boys are motionless leaning over the balcony but the one in the jumpsuit is turning his head this way and I move and this seems like a real big space I'm covering, much bigger than I realized just looking at it, and this is a long time crossing to the balcony and a long way to run back when I'm done, and the next pillar passes and Treen is straightening up and the jumpsuit is looking at me and I'm maybe ten feet from Joey's killer now and I stop. "Treen," I say and he's turning and the two guys to his right are straightening up and I keep my focus on Treen and the great round face appears and his eyes widen and I glance over my right shoulder and the Bagelonians are still in front of the shop and not looking this way.

I glance back quick to Treen and he's upright now, a tall man, and his hands come off the balcony and they're much whiter than his face, very white, white like he's just taken them from a fire and the outer skin is all burned off, but the man underneath is the same, these hands want the same thing down to the bones. I say to him, "I know what you did and why you did it." His eyes narrow and I glance at the three other faces that are pulling in closer to him. It feels like I'm panting now, though I don't think I'm making any noise. I smile at him and I know what the words need to be, but it's hard, it's real hard, and I stretch the smile wider and he cocks his head and I say, "You must want a date with me real bad." I glance over my shoulder and the Bagelonians are all staring this way, though they haven't moved. I look to Treen and he's taken one step toward me and I pull back one step. "It's okay," I say. "I have to say I'm flattered." I know my time is running out here, but I've got to make it sound right. I say, "You want a date? You like the risky, the unusual. Meet me in the dark. The corner of Eighth and Forty-fifth in fifteen minutes. Check me out from across the block. I'll be all alone.

I'm intrigued. Blood's just like flowers and candy. Right?"

Treen's eyes are fixed on me now and they're sparkling, fucking sparkling, like somebody's shining a light in them. I figure I've got him and I turn around and there's four guys making a wall right behind me, blocking the way I came. But I remember the day Joey was up here and I feel an opening and I cut straight to my left and I stride, stride, and I hit the steps down to Arby's and I take them fast and I don't hear anyone behind me and at the bottom I glance back up and there's nobody at all, and I slow down. I know Treen stopped the others from following. I even go to the left now and walk out from under the balcony and I stop and turn and there's Treen's big moon of a face looking down on me just like I expected, and you look for the banyan and old Cuội on this moon and you can almost see them and this Cuội's dreaming only of me and as bad as I want to get this guy, my knees almost buckle at that thought and I take a step back and another, and Treen's smile is as smooth as that voice of his, and I take another step and I'm still looking at him, and then his lips pucker and he throws me a delicate little kiss. I force my face to smile, my head to nod, my hand to rise and wave at him, and I turn and I walk how I know I'm supposed to walk, slow, rolling a little bit, and Christ this is the hardest thing I've ever done, except I know it's going to get even harder and finally I'm out the door and into the rush of Eighth Avenue.

I've chosen Forty-fifth to get away from all the crowds of Forty-second and make Treen bolder, make him extend himself somehow, but anything else that might be shaping in my head is still vague. That's okay. I'm ready to trust my instincts now. I'm waiting to cross Forty-second on my way to the meeting place and a few yards west is a little circle of cops and I think to use them somehow. But if the detectives don't give a shit about Treen and what he's done, how can I expect the beat cops to care? Besides, what am I going to get Treen for? Following me around? At worst, carrying a nasty knife. Big deal. Am I going to let him rape me and then get him for that? I shiver at this, an immediate real shiver that has its center in my stomach, like I just drank down a glass of water and suddenly realized it was rat piss. But I know that Joey's going to get fucked over one more time if I don't make sure Treen is put away, and I'm going to trust my instincts about all of this. Even still, they scare me, my instincts. They scare me but they also make me feel like I'm okay, because they're going to put Joey first. I wait at the light and there's a lot of traffic and I watch the cops and they're laughing, goofing around and doing imitations of guys on the street, just playing grab-ass, and they're waiting for something to happen. Until somebody gets knifed or set on fire or raped, they're worthless.

Finally the light changes and I cross and head uptown and I realize I've got to stop thinking about all this. Too many words in my head. That's dangerous. I keep moving, but I concentrate on not jittering around, not running. If I act out the panic, I'm going to start feeling it. I slow myself down. Treen is probably looking at his watch about now and getting a goddam hard-on and he fingers his knife and that's what I've got over him. He wants to do this his way and it'll just be the two of us. And what I can do is run. The thing is, I have to run to the places I know. I cross Forty-fourth and I'm not so sure now, about these blocks. But I couldn't lead him around the terminal. He knows the goddam place better than I do, probably. It's dark along here and I glance at a woman in a doorway as I go by and she lifts her head and I can see the craters in her face, the slack skin of her throat, and she's too old and too tired to even speak and her eyes are even too tired to hold still on me. They slide off to look behind me, down the street. Maybe she's waiting for somebody. I hope she is.

And the corner is up ahead and I'm getting this fluttering in my chest and I'm finally there and I stop and start to turn around, rotating to my left, and a newsstand is here on the corner but it's closed up, folded tight, and down Forty-fifth are lights, a crowd under a theatre marquee, and I'm still turning and there's a shape I see in the corner of my eye and I come around and Treen is standing so close to me I can smell his flowery cologne and I leap back a step, my insides all squeezed up into my throat. Treen moves forward and he puts his hand on my shoulder and it lands softly there and I pull back again and he lets the hand fall beside him.

I say, "That's not the way you want to do it."

I'm watching him real close for his next movement, but he keeps his place for the time being. He says in that fleshy friendly voice of his, "You seem to know a lot about me."

"I do."

"You were a friend of Joey Cipriani?"

The lies I have to say are bunching up in my throat like my insides were in that moment of fright, and I have to make myself go slow to get the words. "Not exactly a friend."

Treen smiles. "Didn't he treat you right?"

"He was just a drunk. Somebody who had a place where I could crash."

"Did he fuck you, Deuce?"

Maybe I know now what the little old ladies who hate that word go through. I'm real uncomfortable with the image in my head. But even worse is his using my name. I'd simply stammer now if I let myself, and the only alternative for a few moments is silence. Then Treen says, "Did he?"

"No. Never touched me. This is all new for me, Mr. Treen. Is it good?"

Treen's chest rises real slow and falls, like he's calming himself, and he says, "Oh my child, you can't imagine how good it is. The best father in the world, gentle and tough both, and the most loving son, one flesh."

This can't go on much longer and I say, "I like the chase, Mr. Treen. Into the dark. Do you like that?"

Treen smiles and he starts to move toward me and I back off exactly the step he takes and as soon as I do, I know my direction. I turn us west on Forty-fifth. He steps, I step, and I'm ready to spin and start running as soon as he tries to rush me. But first he stops and his smile flattens and he says, "This is just fine, this game, but you understand that it means tough love when the boy is caught. Some boys need tough love."

I say, "You have to catch me first, Mr. Treen." And I turn and start walking fast and I glance over my shoulder and Treen likes this, his chest is going up and down and he starts off after me, walking only just as fast as me. I lead him into the lights of the theatre and I weave through the tuxedos and the tiaras and the perfumes and I juke and dodge and I get these snooty little one-syllable rebukes, like "Now" and "Say." When I get beyond them I sprint past the stage door flanked by columns and then something that I don't like flashes by, a brownstone stairway with more concrete snakes, and I go about fifty yards farther and stop just east of the mouth of a little parking lot with the BMWs and Volvos rolling in. I see Treen coming out of the theatre crowd and he looks a little dazed already and I yell to him, "Treen!" He freezes at the sound of his name and I wave to him and he moves this way, not very fast, and he moves without his upper body bouncing at all, a smooth glide, and he passes the snakes on the stairway and they probably hiss hello and I can see his face real clear now in a spill of light and the smile is gone and the eyes are very bright.

I turn and move on at his rate and I look over my shoulder and he's only three steps behind and closing fast and I leap forward and I run hard toward Ninth Avenue and I stride and stride and I'm nearing the end of the block. I look back and he's running too, though he's fifty yards back now, and I hit an uneven place, hard, metal, and my right ankle twists and I stumble and a pain shoots up the inside of my leg and there's a rushing of hot air, it's an iron grating underfoot, and I can't let myself stop, I run toward the corner, and the avenues are going to be a big problem because the cars are racing past and I think of turning uptown. But when I clear the corner shop I see a big gap in the cars and I ease up just a little and the pain has dissolved inside my calf and my ankle is tender but okay and then the gap comes and I dash into the street and when I hit the center, a taxi racing downtown blares and I pull up, let him pass, and then I run to the far curb and I glance over my shoulder. I stop again. Treen still isn't crossing.

My chest is heaving and I bend and rest my hands on my knees and I know it's as much from the scare of Treen's little burst back there as it is from the sprint I just made. Treen's waiting patiently for the light and he sees me waiting and he puckers his lips and throws me another kiss. I look away from him. I'm standing under a neon smiley face wearing a baker's hat. Treen has stepped off the curb and he's looking uptown, watching the traffic, and the light is amber now and I lift my right leg and rub the ankle for a second and then I turn and start to walk.

I look up ahead and far off I can see a strange, thin line of lights rising against the black. The river is there. The West Side Highway, my first New York home. And this must be one of the ships. I look back and Treen has crossed Ninth and he's walking at my speed for the moment. This is getting awkward now. I've got to keep my eye on him all the time or he can put on a burst of speed and grab me before I have a chance to get away. The street along here is pretty dark and there's nobody around at all, apartment buildings with canopies and glass doors and bright foyers and where the fuck are all the doormen? Up ahead is an empty stretch of sidewalk and so I turn around and walk backward for a while and Treen even slows a little to keep our interval, which is about twenty yards.

I say, "Too fast for you, old man?"

"You're the one who's been having trouble keeping his footing."

This makes me real uneasy for some reason, his noticing my stumble. But even as I'm recognizing this unease, words come to my lips. I say, "Do you like to be the first to fuck a boy?"

"Oh yes," Treen says. "It's almost as good as being the last."

At this I want to turn around and sprint again, but something is whispering in my head and it's saying this is the only way. If you want to help Joey, this is the only way. Work him up. I glance over my shoulder to make sure I've still got a clear path and then back to Treen and when I look at him, he's still walking at my speed, but it seems like he's maybe a step or two closer now, like he hurried up in those few seconds I was checking behind me. I hope that the little whisper in my head is really me and not somebody out to get me. But I go on. I say, "And when you're the first and the last both, that's best of all."

"That's right."

"Especially when the boy knows you're a killer."

"All my boys know that."

"Did you knife him up the butt like you said you would?"

"You mean Joey?"

"Yes."

Treen smiles and he stops altogether. "Watch out," he says and I look behind me and I'm about to back into a row of trash cans set before an iron fence. I stop and then I yank my head back to Treen. But he hasn't moved. "I'm afraid that threat was just rhetoric," Treen says.

He doesn't say any more and I get this queasiness in my face and throat and I wonder if I'm hearing him right. "Rhetoric? You mean you didn't kill him?"

Treen laughs. "Of course I killed him," he says. "I just did it much more conventionally. Through the liver, through the stomach, through the groin was sort of a special little moment, but not up the ass."

I fall back against the cans and they make a big racket and Treen laughs again and I scramble away and I turn and I start to walk, though I keep my face twisted over my shoulder to watch him, and he's coming after me. But he pauses and kicks one of the trash cans back against the fence and he calls out to me, "You better watch your footing from now on. The next time we speak will be a much more intimate conversation."

I put my face forward and lower my head and I sprint away, run hard for maybe fifty yards, and I could keep on going, I know, and I want to do that, I want to just run away now, turn the next corner and escape. But I can't. The more I hate this guy Treen the more impossible it is to forget what Joey needs. Joey was my friend and this man behind me has to pay and I know the whole thing is getting more serious now, and if I've got to lose something, then that's the way it's got to be.

I slow down, slow from a sprint to a jog, and I look over my shoulder and Treen's maybe fifty yards back, a lot closer than I expect, and he's running pretty hard and his head is down. I look to Tenth Avenue coming up and the light is green heading west and I see cars four lanes wide ready to rush uptown and I've got maybe fifty yards to run yet before I can cross, and I start to sprint again and I take only a few steps before the green is yellow. I can't get stopped here, so I press hard, I run and run and the yellow holds and the corner is coming up and I race past two bums in a doorway sleeping in an embrace and I lunge off the curb as the red is turning and I pass one lane, another, and then the cars are rolling and I'm in the middle. The channels of steel and glass flow fast at my feet and at my back and there are no horns this time, I'm invisible here, and I turn my head slowly and he's on the curb, just those two lanes away, and this time instead of blowing me a kiss he lifts his knife and he shows it to me and he smiles and the knife disappears.

I look downtown and in the two lanes that separate Treen and me there's a big gap coming, half a block off. In the other two lanes, blocking my path, there's no space approaching that goes all the way to the curb, but there is a little one in the third lane at about the same place as Treen's and then a rushing line of cars in the fourth, and I think if Treen gets to me, he can knife me in the middle of Tenth Avenue and leave me to fall while he races back east. The gaps are coming and I try to tell myself that he wants sex first, but maybe the knife is all the sex he wants tonight and here comes the space and I slip across the third lane and in the final lane the cars are too fast, raging at me with their horns now, and I look over my shoulder and he's there, in the center of the street, one car-width away now, and a gap is coming for him, in a few seconds, and for me there's no hope, a taxi passes me this moment and I have maybe two beats before a slope-nosed VW and I lunge in front, leaping across, brakes scream and a pansy-ass horn and the faintest brush of metal on my flying left heel, and I stumble up onto the sidewalk and then I'm running again, thank God running, past a big, bright Hess station stretching from the corner, and I flash by the odd, yellow flower of a fallout shelter sign on a building facade and then the block is full of the orange brightness of sodium vapor lamps and I'm not looking back, I'm just running hard, and my chest is getting tighter and tighter and my legs are starting to knot, but I push and push and he's got to be feeling worse than me, though every second I'm waiting for the touch of his hand or the thrust of his knife and I run hard and up ahead the thin string of lights is clear to me. It's the aircraft carrier by the West Side Highway. And the highway is home. I know the highway. And I know this is where I'm leading him.

But that's all I can think before my mind blurs and heaves and I

don't know if it's fatigue from the run or if it's seeing the highway
and knowing how much is going to be on the line, but the panting
has broken from my chest and is filling my body and it's in my head
and I push at my legs and I watch the strings of yellow lights racing
down from the top of the aircraft carrier and they're cut off by
stripes of darkness and that's the highway and I'm crunching through
broken glass and I look down and leap over a jagged curl of a bottle
and I'm passing a building facade with spray paint: FUCK ME. Fuck
me, not you, and this makes me real nervous and Eleventh Avenue is
up ahead and I've got the light and I'm running, I'm moving fast, but
it feels like I'm dragging my legs, and I keep running and before I get
to the corner, I look behind me and no one is there.

I clomp to a stop and I turn. This street is brighter than the others,
with its run of sodium lamps, but in the orange haze before me is
only an empty sidewalk and this has all been for goddam nothing.
The fucker just didn't have it in him. Or I was the stupid one. I ran
away from him. That would be the worst of all. Even when I think
I'm finally doing something for somebody else, when I think I'm
ready to actually give something up that hasn't already been taken
from me, it turns out to be just running away after all.

My mind fights this. Maybe Treen is panting against some wall
down the street, beyond the sodium light, and he's kicking himself
for not being in better shape and he's hoping I'll come back and get it
started again. So I walk back east. I pass a big U-Park lot full of
moving vans and old cars and from across the street comes the smell
of fresh-cut wood, a lumber company, and on its sign is a big yellow
smiley face. There's a whole shitload of Good Days in this part of
town. And a FUCK ME in red. And a bed of broken glass. And
sirens in the distance. And up ahead I look way past a string of
warehouse fronts and there's no one on the street but me. Maybe
beyond the orange light, down by the Hess station. Maybe he's hiding in the fallout shelter, hit by a sudden fear of the Bomb. I'm
moving along the front of a dark warehouse building and the idea of
hiding that came into my head in a joke makes me see the recessed
doorway I'm approaching and makes me hear something and this
idea is maybe coming a little late because I'm only a step from the

doorway and my body is still moving but I hear his breathing, that's what makes me hold back that last step, his panting, and he knows it, Treen is suddenly before me and his hand is sweeping around and there's a flash and I pull back, my left arm rising, and like the car at my heel, the blade just whispers against my flesh but I feel a sudden chill there and I think I'm cut and I'm turning and running again and I can hear his steps behind me and I'm running hard and I glance at my arm and there's just a faint line, not quite a cut, like one of the little kisses he was blowing to me, and I look to Eleventh Avenue.

The light changes against me but after a small clot of waiting cars flows away, there's only a flash or two more heading downtown, and I'm running along the U-Park fence and into Eleventh and I lunge before a honking car and I'm on a dark, dark street and it's full of women, the whores, and they're nearly naked here in the shadows, I run past a glow of flesh with a black V rising from the crotch and a woman's voice says what's your hurry and the cars along the curb are full of sounds, passing in fragments, a deep breath, a moan, a laugh, a car quivering, two women in a doorway with breasts bared, and I can see the flank of the West Side Highway ripping across the lights of the ships, and the whores are gone and the buildings are gone and Twelfth Avenue is coming up and I glance back and he's there and he's running hard and he's only twenty yards behind me, he's fast, and he still has the knife drawn and as he runs, it catches every little spark of street light and its efficiency chills me and I look ahead again and Twelfth is here and it's empty and I'm across it and into the shadows of the highway and I veer right and the ramp is before me and I'm running in glass and grit and the ramp is a great black tongue and I can see nothing but a faint glow at the top and I start to run up the ramp and I think of that soft thing I stumbled on my first night here and it could be me tonight, that shape, and a woman's voice slithers from the shadows and it says what's your hurry and I come up and off the ramp and I'm running on the highway and the cruise liners are lighting my way and I wonder if the Cupid is in port tonight.

And for a second I figure I'm fucking crazy making this little joke to myself when I'm about to get knifed to death, but then I realize that there's something stirring in me and I remember the nights I spent sleeping up here and I know where I want Treen and I'm running hard and I know this space and I'm getting close to where I want to be and I can see up on the left where the whores' shacks are and I want to make sure Treen is ready for this. I look back and he's dim behind me but I can see he's dropped back to about fifty yards and I'm tight in the chest and he must be too. I stop and turn to face him and he's still coming and I even take a couple of steps in his direction. He slows and you can hear his feet dragging and he's getting closer and when he's about twenty yards away he comes into the back-glow from a streetlight on Twelfth and I say, "Far enough."

He takes another step and I say, "I'll run."

He seems to want a rest so he does what I say. He stops.

I'm still trying to catch my breath. I need my strength now. I say, "Back into the light. I want to see you."

He hesitates, but then he backs up. "Daddy's real angry," he says. "Where's Daddy's knife?"

Treen raises the blade and I can see it clearly and that's good. I want it in his hand. I wait, catching my breath, coiling inside. We both stand there for a time, panting at each other, and then I'm ready. I say, "You rested now?"

"Enough to catch you."

"There's a down-ramp just a few blocks north. If you don't catch me by then, I'm going to run away from you forever."

"I've been pacing myself," Treen says. "You've made a big mistake. You don't know how good I am at this."

I say, "Put that knife away, you motherfucker. You're never going to get a chance to use it."

At this, Treen lifts the knife and points it at me and then he charges and this burst freezes me and he strides and strides and I can see his eyes even in the dark and something in my head goes oh shit and I turn and I lunge forward and I'm running hard and I can hear him right behind me, right behind, I can hear his breath like he's fucking me already and I can see the median in the dark now and I have to get the steps right and I stride and I stride and I'm at the median and I stride and I can't even see what I know is there but I stride and leap and the air that I fly in is hot as Treen's breath and it slows me and there's nothing beneath me and I think to pump my legs but they are simply spread wide and I remember the iron rods thrusting from the edge of the broken concrete and this is what waits for me if I've done this wrong and I feel the chasm beneath me and then I sprawl, hitting my knees with great scrapes of fire and my elbows and my chin and I slide in the grit and yet I can hear the sound of Treen, his gasp and then the sound of the steel rods gouging like they're crying "Flesh!" and he cries in answer a deep liquid bray that fades and ends in a heavy sound, deep in the highway, his body landing, first his ass, a thump, and then the broader whomp of his body, and then the clear cracking bone sound of his head, and then silence.

And I put my cheek against the concrete and I lie there until the quaking in my body finally stops. Then I drag myself to my knees and I go and I sit beside that chasm and I listen for more sounds. And there is nothing. Not a moan, not a whimper, not a breath. I can't say how long I sit there in the dark, but it is a very long time. I sit there and listen to the silence that speaks of the death of Mr. Treen.

TWENTY-ONE

❖

So am I happy that I killed a man? I'm glad I stopped along the way and it came out that he really did knife Joey. And I'm glad he had his knife out in those last few seconds. You know if he'd caught me I never would've lived. And I'm glad that it happened the way it did and I didn't have to put my hand to him. But I'm not particularly happy. It would've been a lot better if I'd figured out what to do for Joey when he was alive instead of dead. I should've done something earlier. And I'm this smart kid, see. I know what I'm saying here. I made the same mistake Kenneth did. He's smart, too. He's a district attorney in the state of New Jersey in the United States of America. And we both fucked up.

It's funny about that last night in New York. As instinctively as I knew what to do about Treen, I finally just got up without thinking and limped on back to the Port Authority in time to catch a bus to Point Pleasant. And Kenneth patted some goddam burning stuff on my scrapes and he let me go to bed without saying anything. But the next morning I came downstairs real early and I was sitting at the kitchen table when he walked in rubbing his eyes awake, and he didn't even make his morning coffee. He sat down with me right away and he waited to see what I had to say, and I told him just what I'd done. And when I finished, my hands happened to end up on the tabletop, and he reached out and put both his hands over mine for just a second and he gave them a little squeeze, and then he sat back and waited to see if I wanted to say anything more. I realized that I did. I said, "Do you ever miss her?"

And he said, "Yes."

Even now it's not easy feeling anything strong about my father. But sometimes it's right to follow your feelings and other times you have to be smart and figure out what's right, and then you tell your feelings to get fucked and you do the right thing. In America kids don't hang around their parents for the rest of their lives anyway. But Kenneth deserves something and so do I.

And maybe what I really wanted most is already mine. It was early this summer, months after I came back home, that I woke up in the dark and I heard a voice in the tree outside my window. It was the reedy voice of the first cicada, and he'd been sleeping for as long as I've been alive, all his seventeen years, right next to this house. He woke me with his bargirl's voice and I could hear my mother sitting with her friends at the back of the bar and she'd finished her prayers with the others at their little shrine and they were laughing together and she suddenly began to sing. I was perched on a stool up at the front and I turned from watching the motorcycles going by in the street and I don't remember now what she sang. Some song about true love, probably, because even as I lay in my bed in Point Pleasant I could remember her smiling.

My father does miss her still. And that's a big help to me. I don't have to do it all myself. I can even turn my face to the window and listen to the cicada and I can feel my mother's blood in me, and I don't get angry anymore and I don't get any more sorrowful than the song of this sorrowful insect. And I'm going to figure out when Wandering Souls' Day is and I'll say some kind of prayer for her, just in case she's dead and just in case the Buddhists are right about all that. She believed in it, even if I don't, so it's the least I can do for her.

And I lay awake that night early this summer and I listened to the cicada singing and I remembered crying on this bed years before with Mrs. Kenneth standing beside me, my Saigon sandal in her hand and my luck dead on the lampshade. And I remembered how the crack grew along my own spine as I lay there and I yearned to climb out and sing in my own voice. And now I know what voice I have, and who it is I am. A guy on a beach in Vũng Tàu tells me I'm Vietnamese. A civics teacher in Point Pleasant tells me I'm American. Kenneth James Hatcher tells me I'm his son, and I'm the son of a woman named Võ Xuân Nghi who's lost somewhere half a world away. I'm a lot of things but I'm one thing, and I have no doubt about that. I'm The Deuce.

ABOUT THE AUTHOR

ROBERT OLEN BUTLER is the author of seven critically acclaimed novels—*The Alleys of Eden*, *Sun Dogs*, *Countrymen of Bones*, *On Distant Ground*, *Wabash*, *The Deuce*, and *They Whisper*—and a collection of short stories, *A Good Scent from a Strange Mountain*, winner of the 1993 Richard and Hinda Rosenthal Foundation Award from the American Academy of Arts and Letters as well as the 1993 Pulitzer Prize for Fiction. He lives in Lake Charles, Louisiana, where he teaches creative writing at McNeese State University.